Hope for Tomorrow

CHARLOTTE EVERHART

NEVINLY PUBLISHING

This is a work of fiction. The characters, incidents, and dialogues are products of the author's imagination and are not to be construed as real. Any resemblance to actual persons, living or dead, is entirely coincidental.

FIRST EDITION

Cover design by Tugboat Design.

ISBN: 9781737988632 (print)

ISBN: 9781737988625 (ebook)

Library of Congress Control number: 2021923558

1. Women's Fiction 2. Family Fiction 3. Small Town/Rural Fiction 4. Contemporary Romance

This book is dedicated to Becky.
You made it happen with nine little words.
"So, when are you going to write this book? "
Thanks for the kick in the pants, girlfriend!

Contents

Chapter 1

Olivia was running late. As a result, she was driving a stretch of road she had avoided for the last year. Today, however, it was the most direct route to her unfortunate destination.

This stretch of Harlow Road was known as the Outcrop by locals, named for the outcropping of granitic rock that bordered the road on the south side. The eighty feet of impressive rock, coupled with the high winds off Lake Superior on the north side, created a wind tunnel in snowstorms that reduced visibility to zero in this spot. Residents of Nicolet were smart and knew to stay away during winter storms, but every year at least one fatal accident occurred there. Olivia had learned the hard way that it could be just as treacherous in rainy conditions. An investigation had revealed that this portion of the road lacked sufficient cross-slope, causing water to pool there during heavy rain.

It didn't appear to be at the top of the city's priority list, and it still hadn't been fixed. On this beautiful, sunny October morning, though, it was hard to believe this spot had claimed so many lives.

Olivia tensed, bracing herself.

There it stood, some forty yards ahead, staked in the grassy area between the roadway and the bike path. She'd have thought after a full year it wouldn't hurt so much to see that white cross on the side of the road. But it did. Blinking back the sudden sting in her eyes, Olivia eased the death grip she had on the steering wheel and forced herself to take a deep breath. She shuddered slightly as she exhaled.

Someone, she assumed it was Nate's mother, had placed mums of vibrant oranges, yellows, and reds at the base of the three-foot cross. Olivia was told seasonal flowers adorned this roadside memorial all year long, even with faux poinsettias in the winter. This season's display, which mirrored the colors of the changing leaves all around it, was beautiful, and the care given to it was obvious.

Nate had always loved the fall, especially here in Michigan's Upper Peninsula. The U.P. was at its color peak right now, and the little town of Nicolet was hopping with happy tourists visiting for their annual color tour. What a contrast she made to them.

A few moments ago, she'd driven through the downtown and past Nicolet Harbor. Although it was Sunday, the entire area was bustling with smiling visitors who drank their coffee in the sidewalk cafés and shopped for their souvenirs in the quaint, locally owned shops. She didn't begrudge them their happiness, but she couldn't help but wish she could find some of her own today.

Autumn had always been Olivia's favorite season too—especially once she'd moved with Nate to his hometown of Nicolet three years ago. She'd lived in a few different places, all pretty in their own special ways, but there was nothing quite like this part of the U.P. with its vast forests and endless Lake Superior shoreline.

Nicolet was an interesting combination of wholesome wilderness landscape and beachy college town. Somehow, it pulled it off. The miles and miles of hiking and biking trails and pristine beaches were absolute perfection, and Olivia couldn't imagine ever living anywhere else. She hoped her daughter, Nora, asleep in her car seat behind her, would stay here forever too. With a state university right in town, there would be no reason to leave unless she wanted to.

Olivia sighed. *Nora.* She would grow up never knowing her father. Last October, Olivia had been three months pregnant when she'd gotten the devastating news that had wiped out the vibrance of both autumn and of Olivia herself.

Morning sickness didn't just happen in the morning, Olivia had quickly come to learn, and she'd been hovering over the toilet that night when the knock came at the door. With a tear-streaked face and hands clenching her stomach, she stood up with a start. The pounding came again. It was both urgent and authoritative, and even before she opened the door, she knew. Somehow, she just knew.

"Good evening, ma'am," one of the two officers greeted somberly, addressing her with his hat in his hands. "Are you Mrs. Olivia Reeves?"

She nodded, taking in the flashing blue and red lights of the patrol car in her driveway. She'd been unable to look away from the mesmerizing pattern of those bright lights, becoming almost transfixed by them. It allowed her to tune out most of the words spoken by the officer, but not all. Not the important ones. Not the ones that changed her life forever.

"Husband . . . accident . . . dead on the scene . . . so sorry . . ."

Checking her mirrors to make sure nobody was behind her, Olivia pressed down on the brake. There was no place to turn off here, but she wanted a little more time to gaze at her late husband's memorial. She rolled down the passenger window and continued to stare.

"I'm sorry," she whispered to his cross.

Only a few people knew how it had really been between them at the end. She wished she could forget and only remember the good times. The stinging behind her eyes intensified, and Olivia swallowed hard at the lump that had formed in her throat. But she would not cry. She would not let herself cry for Nate ever again.

Olivia shifted her focus away from the cross and took in the view of the lake, which served as the memorial's backdrop. Superior had moods. This morning, it was tranquil and amiable, but it could also rage and churn with enough power to take down 13,000-ton freighters.

Like the ocean, it could appear grey and intimidating or a deep, welcoming blue. Occasionally, it even mimicked the tropical turquoise she'd seen on Hawaiian postcards. But no matter its color or its mood, this lake was always crystal clear, vast, and majestic, and it was a fitting place for a memorial to Nate. He'd always said that Lake Superior water might as well run through his veins.

Olivia thought back to those early days of their marriage when they'd lived in lower Michigan. They'd been so happy. She'd finished up her master's degree in guidance counseling and Nate had loved his position as assistant coach to Michigan State's hockey team. They had fulfilling careers, a busy social life, and a fresh and exciting marriage.

Despite that, Lansing didn't really feel like a forever home to either of them, so when the call came offering Nate the head coaching position for Nicolet State University, they'd jumped at the opportunity, and in a stroke of luck, Olivia had found work right away herself. A counseling position at Nicolet High opened up at exactly the right time, and a week after Nate turned in his resignation, she had a job offer in Nicolet as well.

When they went out to their favorite restaurant to celebrate, Nate had clinked his glass against hers and said, "We've got the Midas touch, babe. Both of us." And it really had felt that way. But nothing lasts forever.

Seeing a car slowly approaching behind her, Olivia reluctantly brought her van back up to speed. On to the next memorial to Nate.

Nicolet's residents had grieved the loss of their golden boy intensely. He was a legend in this hockey town. They'd long since forgiven him for defecting to Michigan State, choosing to remember him instead as the amazingly talented local boy who would have gone to the NHL if that awful concussion hadn't permanently sidelined him in his last college hockey game. When he'd come back as head coach, the people of Nicolet received him with open arms.

Janet and Karl, Nate's parents, went to the cemetery every Saturday to visit their son, so Olivia had chosen Sundays for herself. Relations with her in-laws had been strained in the best of times for reasons Olivia had never quite understood, and now that Nate was gone, well, it seemed prudent to give them their space.

Olivia wasn't unaware that her trips to see Nate had become less frequent as time passed. But she found there was nothing more for her to say that she hadn't already said, and she wasn't one of those people who found much comfort talking to a headstone. Still, each visit, she told Nate she loved him, which remained true. She would always love him, despite what he'd done. She told him about Nora—about how much she looked like her daddy and how big she was getting. At six months, she was nearly crawling now. But even this vein of conversation was growing tedious. It was one sided, after all. And Olivia had to admit, there was less and less to say to Nate, and so her visits were getting shorter and shorter and fewer and further between. It was one more thing to feel guilty about.

But if Olivia were honest with herself, sorrow and guilt weren't the only things she felt. A bitter resentment that had begun that night was now her ever-present companion. Oh, she fought against it. She didn't want to feel it, but it lurked in the shadows all the same. Nate had given her Nora, and she would always be grateful to him for that. But he'd taken so much too. She feared he'd destroyed her ability to trust—both other people and herself. Even the joy that autumn had always brought to her was now gone. She wondered if she'd ever be able to love it fully ever again.

There'd been no baking of apple pie this year or last, no drinking of pumpkin spice lattes. And the simple pleasure she'd always found in pulling out all her cozy fall sweaters once the cool, crisp air set in . . . Forget it. Instead, Olivia felt gloom wrapped around her like a tight, heavy shawl. She wasn't even bothering to rake the leaves out of the yard this year, something she'd always enjoyed doing. This year she'd simplified things, opting to run them over with the lawn mower every few days instead—turning them into hacked-up mulch.

Olivia braced herself as she approached the cemetery gate. She took a deep breath, squared her shoulders, and sat up straight. She had a few more minutes to prepare herself. Nate's headstone was on the opposite end of the grounds from the gate, and she'd have to meander her way through for a bit to get there. Park Cemetery was a maze of paved lanes that ran along immaculate plots, small ponds, and mature maple trees. Wooden benches dotted the landscape for family members of the deceased who wanted to sit and soak in the serenity of the place. Even people with no loved ones lain to rest here came to walk, feed the ducks, or simply *be*. Olivia had to admit, this place was beautiful. It had been costly, but it was worth it to have Nate here.

Olivia pulled up behind Karl's Subaru. Bright sunshine reflected off the hatchback, causing Olivia to see spots once she looked away. God had given them another beautiful October sixteenth. On this day last year, they'd buried Nate under the same warm sunlight gracing them today. That sunny day was a stark contrast to the day Nate died, when a fierce series of thunderstorms had taken out trees, power, and a young man in his prime of life.

Nate had been driving too fast for conditions when he hit that bad patch at the Outcrop. The police report said he'd lost control when he hydroplaned and crossed into the path of an oncoming semi-truck. The officials said it happened so fast that Nate wouldn't have known what hit him. Olivia supposed she should be grateful he hadn't suffered, but honestly, she mostly tried not to think about it at all. The violence of the accident was just too terrible. Maybe that's why his parents had chosen today to get together. To remember the peaceful day of Nate's burial instead of the awful day of his death.

Olivia tried to open and close her door as quietly as possible, hoping to give Nora a few more minutes of sleep, but a squeal from inside the car told her that her sleeping beauty was very much awake.

She slid the rear door open. "You little stinker," Olivia said as she worked to unlock the five-point harness. "That wasn't a very long nap."

Nora replied by blowing raspberries. She smiled a wet, gummy, three-toothed smile, delighted with the newly discovered sound she could make.

"Come on, you goof. Let's go see Grandma and Grandpa." Olivia grunted as she hefted Nora out of her car seat. At a dainty five feet two inches, the petite Olivia marveled that her "little" girl was in the ninety-sixth percentile for both weight and height. Especially considering how tiny she'd been when she was born. Deciding to arrive several weeks early, Nora had only weighed four pounds, three ounces at birth. She would probably be tall, like Nate.

It was remarkable how much Nora looked like her father, and Olivia wondered again if that's why Nate's parents kept distance between themselves and their only grandchild. Maybe it was too painful for them to be reminded of him. Or maybe that was just their way. After all, they'd never completely warmed up to Olivia either.

Olivia continued to talk gibberish to Nora as she carried her and made her way towards Nate's parents down at the base of the gradual hill. Janet and Karl were talking quietly as they stood over their son's gravestone, which was made from a gorgeous, light gray granite.

When Janet, who held an enormous and beautiful bouquet of sunflowers and mums, spotted Olivia walking towards them, she visibly stiffened. Olivia pretended not to notice and smiled in greeting as she approached them. Karl smiled back, but she could see that his eyes were red—and wet. Janet, too, had swollen eyes and a slightly pink nose, but she did not wear a smile. No surprise there.

"I'm so sorry I'm late," Olivia said breathlessly.

Karl was the first to respond. "Olivia," he said kindly, "How nice to see you. And Nora!" His eyes widened as he reached out to touch the baby's cheek. "My goodness, you've gotten big." He looked at Olivia in surprise, and Olivia thought back to the last time he'd seen his granddaughter. It had been three months ago. A lot changed in three months for an infant.

"She's a big girl, alright," Olivia responded lamely. What else could she say? *Maybe if you came around once in a while, this wouldn't be such a surprise?*

"Hello, Janet," Olivia said, addressing Janet over Karl's shoulder as he held Nora's little hand. "Those are beautiful flowers."

Janet looked pointedly at Olivia's hands, which held all baby and no flowers, and replied, "Yes, well my Nathan deserves at least that much."

Used to handling Janet's little jabs, Olivia smiled and replied, "Of course he does. And the roadside memorial looks lovely too. I drove past it today."

Janet held Olivia's gaze a half-second too long before she sniffed and turned away to put the flowers in the granite vase alongside the headstone. When it became apparent that Janet wasn't planning to respond, Karl jumped in. "Oh, you know Janet, she's always had an eye for what looks nice. And it helps us to keep these sites looking good for our boy. There's some comfort in that, you know." He gave a sad smile.

Olivia resisted the impulse to put a hand on his shoulder. Karl wasn't touchy-feely and had never been one for showing emotion. He'd always been one of those dads whose head was perpetually hidden behind his newspaper. A few grunts here and there were really about all he had contributed to conversations when she and Nate visited the house. After all these years, Olivia and Karl still felt like strangers.

"No, she wouldn't know," Janet corrected bitterly. "Because she never *ever* visits her husband's grave. She doesn't bring flowers. She doesn't care. She comes here today looking . . . *happy*!"

Olivia was shocked speechless, her mouth hanging open in a suspended *O*. Janet thought she didn't care? Of course she cared! Nate had been her husband!

Olivia's cheeks flushed hot, and she worked to find her voice, "Janet, I . . ." she began before faltering, not knowing how to organize her thoughts and emotions into something coherent.

"Now Janet," Karl said soothingly as he patted her awkwardly on the shoulder. "Olivia's got to be happy—for the baby, you know? She can't spend her days crying. She has Nate's baby to raise."

Janet lifted her eyes to look up at Nora, who was blessedly quiet at the moment, perhaps sensing that something important was happening. For a second, Olivia thought Janet was finally seeing her granddaughter. Her icy blue eyes seemed to thaw a touch, but when Janet set her mouth into a hard line and looked away a moment later, Olivia knew she was as hardened as ever towards them both. Maybe she always would be.

"I'm sorry I've hurt you," Olivia said quietly. "You should know that I might smile on the outside, but I have a lot of pain too."

"Hmph," Janet replied, turning away abruptly, her back now to Olivia.

Olivia had known this would be uncomfortable, but she really hadn't expected it to be quite this bad. Nate's parents asked that they all come together today to honor Nate. It had both surprised her and caused her to feel a bit of hope for the future of their relationship. She felt those hopes being dashed to pieces now. She truly should have thought about buying flowers, but she'd forgotten.

Of course, she couldn't admit to Janet that she'd forgotten to bring flowers to her dead husband's grave on the one-year anniversary of his burial, so she said nothing about the flowers. She wanted to set the record straight on one thing, though.

"Janet. Karl. I need you to know that I do come here. Nora and I come sometimes on Sundays, and I . . . I talk to Nate. I talk to him and think about him all the time, whether I'm here or not. He was my husband, and I miss him every single day. I do." Olivia cleared her throat to get rid of the ache that she felt there.

Janet turned her body away from Olivia and hugged her arms around herself, but she maintained eye contact, and Olivia saw a world of hurt and accusation in her mother-in-law's expression. "I wish I could believe you," she said tonelessly.

The three of them stood awkwardly in front of Nate's grave. After a few minutes of absolute silence, Olivia decided she would only stay another few minutes. She could handle this thoroughly uncomfortable situation for that long, surely, and she was about to suggest they each say a few words when she heard footsteps approaching from behind them.

All three of them turned around to see Sean, Nate's best friend, striding towards them. Now it was Olivia's turn to stiffen. Who had invited Sean?

She hadn't spoken to him in a year, although she spotted him in town from time to time. He greeted them as a whole before sweeping Janet up in a hug. It was startling, frankly, this show of affection by a woman who showed none of her own. But Olivia watched in amazement as Janet positively melted in Sean's embrace. Olivia spotted the small bouquet he held in his right hand.

Crap. He'd remembered flowers.

Shaking hands with Karl first, Sean stooped down to the headstone and set his bouquet there at the base of the granite slab. He paused for a few moments on one knee, his head bowed and his back to Olivia. She was still angry with him, but she had to admit—it was nice to see him again. Sort of . . . comforting.

He looked good, she noted. Sean was one of those guys with effortless good looks. He didn't seem to try real hard, but then he didn't have to. In that sense, he'd been Nate's opposite. Jokingly, he'd always referred to Nate as a *poser*.

It was true, and, honestly, that should have been her first clue.

Nate had as many hair products on his side of the vanity as she'd had on hers. But Sean had no need of that stuff. She'd never seen his hair in anything other than a crew cut, and he kept his stubbled beard short and neat as well.

When she had first met him years ago, she'd immediately liked him and trusted him. He was Nate's closest friend, but he became her close friend as well. She'd spent countless hours with Nate, Sean, and Susan, Sean's fiancée. They'd even gone on vacations, the four of them. They'd been like a family, and that strong bond made Sean's betrayal of her trust even more painful.

On the night of Nate's accident, Olivia had told Sean she never wanted to see him again, and that she had no room in her life for liars. He'd left several minutes before Nate had, giving them privacy for the most explosive and ugly fight of their marriage. She couldn't bear to think of the words they'd said to each other before she ordered him out of the house. The police had come knocking some time after that.

Of course, Olivia saw Sean and Suze again at the funeral, although she did her best to ignore them both. Susan's pleading with her had barely registered, but then Olivia had been so dazed and numb, so walled-off, that nothing penetrated. In fact, even now, Olivia didn't have a very clear recollection of the funeral or the days immediately following; she'd felt like she was walking around in a fog of confusion, but as the haze slowly lifted, she knew the loss she'd suffered had been a terrible one. She'd lost her husband and her friends. She was a pregnant woman all alone in the world, and she'd never before felt such despair.

After a minute or two, Sean pulled himself up to his full height. He towered over Janet and Karl and over Olivia, especially. Olivia pretended to fix Nora's fly-away hair to avoid looking at him, but out of the corner of her eye, she could see him staring at her uncertainly. He stroked the stubble at his chin before finally speaking to her. "Hi, Livvy . . . How are you?"

Her face flushed for a second time. Only her parents, Nate, and Sean had ever called her by this pet name, and since her parents and Nate were gone, and she hadn't spoken to Sean at all since the burial, she hadn't heard it said in a full year. She experienced a small ripple of joy at the sound of that name, though it shouldn't bring her any kind of pleasure to hear it. Sean had lost the privilege of using it the day he'd lied to her, but it conjured up warm, fuzzy feelings of the past, and she felt a momentary longing for what used to be.

"I–I'm good," she stammered. Janet whipped around and looked at her incredulously.

Olivia quickly attempted to clarify. "I mean, I'm sad, you know, but, well . . ." she trailed off lamely, as Janet's frown grew.

Sean looked at her sympathetically. "I know what you mean."

Nora began tugging at Olivia's hair. She had a death grip, and by the time Olivia had extracted her hair from her daughter's tight fist, several auburn strands had been yanked out.

"Ouch, Nora. Be gentle with Mommy." Since she was holding Nora on her right hip, she used her left hand to sweep the hairs out of Nora's clenched fist.

Janet made a small, startled sound, and Olivia looked up to see the expression of outraged surprise on her mother-in-law's face. She said nothing, but continued to stare at Olivia with accusation in her eyes.

"What is it?" Olivia asked. She couldn't help adding, "What have I done now?"

Janet set her jaw and pointed at Olivia's hand. "Where is it?" she demanded.

It took half a second for Olivia to understand. Her ring, or rather, the absence of it. She'd recently put it away in her mother's old jewelry box. In fact, she'd put it away on the anniversary of the accident only a few days ago. It had seemed like it was time, and she was testing it out. So far, her finger felt strange and bare without it. But this was none of Janet's business, and Olivia straightened her posture to stand a little taller and a little stronger.

"It's at home," she said, simply, not offering any other details. She forced herself to hold Janet's gaze.

"You're not going to wear it anymore?"

"I don't know. Maybe not."

"Well, then I want it back."

Olivia's mouth fell open. "What?"

"My mother's ring. I want it back."

"You can't be serious." Olivia swallowed. Her mouth had suddenly gone dry. "You want to take my wedding ring?"

"Now, Janet—" Karl started.

"You stay out of this, Karl!"

Karl took a full step back, careful to keep his eyes trained on the ground. Obviously, he would be no help.

But Olivia wasn't a redhead for nothing, and she could feel the anger rising inside—threatening to boil over. "What is the matter with you? You think you can just take my ring?"

Janet answered with one raised eyebrow and a smirk.

"Well, you can't. That's my *wedding* ring. A gift from my *husband*." Olivia's voice shook with righteous indignation.

"Oh, stop!" Janet spat. "Just stop. We all know you were going to leave Nate. Nobody talks about it, but we all know it."

"Why do you—?" Olivia began before Janet cut her off.

"That marriage was over, and you know it too. You're the reason Nate got in the car that night. He called us. He was coming over to talk about his crumbling marriage. You forced him out into that storm. You killed my son, and yet you come here pretending that you loved him—pretending that ring means something to you. Well, it means something to *me*. That was my mother's ring, and I'll be damned if I let you keep it in some box somewhere like an old, forgotten souvenir."

Olivia's face felt almost unbearably hot, and she was shaking so violently that Nora began to cry. She had worked for a solid year to convince herself that Nate's death wasn't her fault. She could now, in all honesty, say that it wasn't. It had been a freak accident and unspeakable tragedy, no matter what Janet said.

Karl was no longer looking at the ground. Instead, he was looking at Olivia—sad accusation in his eyes. Janet, well, she was shaking as badly as Olivia was, and Sean looked to be suspended in the action of physically coming to her rescue only to find that his feet were glued to the ground. She could see he was horrified for her sake, but unsure of how to help.

Olivia willed herself to calm down. She gave Nora a few reassuring pats and whispered soothing nonsense in her ear. It settled her down and gave Olivia just enough time to pull herself together.

"Janet," Olivia began with a forced calm she didn't feel. "You have no idea what you're talking about. You've made a whole lot of false assumptions, apparently, and I'm not about to sit here and disabuse you of whatever ugly notions have filled your head about my marriage to Nate."

"Listen to her," Janet said, looking at Karl incredulously before directing her attention back to Olivia. "*Disabuse*? All that fancy talk doesn't erase what you did to my son."

"Think what you want, but just know that you don't have all the facts. You know the details of one terrible night of our marriage, and probably not even all of those. I owe you no explanations, but if you want to know the truth, I will tell you out of respect for our shared love of Nate."

"The truth," Janet scoffed.

"Yeah, the truth. If you want to know the truth about what happened, ask me, and I'll tell you."

Janet looked like she'd sucked on a lemon. Karl was looking longingly up the hill at his car, and Olivia looked to Sean for a support she desperately needed, even if it had to be from him. She'd take what she could get. He gave her a slow, encouraging nod.

Olivia took a deep breath before fixing her eyes back on Janet. It seemed like now was the time to say the hard things. "These are the facts, Janet, whether you like them or not. You have *never* liked me. Never. But Nate was my husband, and I was his wife. This is his daughter, though you've chosen to barely acknowledge her. That's your loss. Our marriage was real. We sealed our vows with rings that we gave to each other. The ring he gave me was and will remain mine. We didn't have a perfect marriage, it's true. But we loved each other. Nate's gone, but Nora and I are still here. If you want to be a part of our lives and lay this . . . this hatred and animosity to rest, my arms are open to you. But I will not listen to your accusations another minute. I will *not* put up with your meanness anymore. You choose how you want it to be between us."

For a moment Olivia thought perhaps she'd finally gotten through to her mother-in-law. Each woman stared at the other, unspeaking.

But then Janet spat out, "Well, you're right about one thing. I *never* liked you. And I never will. My Nate was too good for you." And with that, she brushed past Olivia and stormed up the hill to the old Subaru, leaving Karl to follow meekly behind her. He didn't make eye contact with Olivia as he passed, but he hesitated briefly, seeming unsure of what to do, before finally trudging up the hill after his wife.

They'd made their choice. Even though it wasn't like they'd been an active part of her and Nora's life, Olivia still felt a staggering sense of loss and a loneliness that was almost crippling. Her eyes stung, but since she'd resolved never to cry about Nate or anything having to do with him again, she worked valiantly to keep the tears at bay.

Olivia swallowed hard twice before turning to Sean, who had drawn closer to her. She studied his handsome face and saw nothing but sympathy there before he pulled her into a strong, silent hug. She let him hold her for a minute, although she remained stiff in his arms, and Nora wriggled between them in protest. Awkwardness aside, it felt good to be held in the strong arms of a man again.

Chapter 2

Sunday nights were always a little depressing, this one even more so because of the earlier drama at the cemetery. Olivia didn't want to think about that anymore today. It had been so ugly. The only good thing that had come from going there, although she hated to admit it, was the reconnection that had occurred with Sean. But she didn't even want to think about that right now. Olivia's jumbled and twisted feelings towards him only made her feel confused. There was a lot to sort through there, and it couldn't be accomplished tonight, anyway, so she closed the book on all thoughts of Sean.

Even though Olivia loved her job, Sunday night marked the end of the "Nora time" she looked forward to all throughout the work week. It didn't help that she felt terribly guilty about taking her sweet baby to daycare five days a week for nine hours a day. She couldn't shake the suspicion that she was paying somebody else to raise her child. But what choice did she have? None. No choice at all.

Maybe the feminists had sold them all a lie, Olivia thought, not for the first time. They'd said that women could have it all: career and family. And while that was true—women could absolutely do both—it was a juggling act that nobody could do perfectly. At least she couldn't. It seemed like if you gave one hundred percent at your career, the home front went all to pieces, and if you gave your all at home, your work performance suffered.

So, what had to happen, at least in her case, was the career mom had to resign herself to being mediocre at both, and Olivia could not abide being just mediocre at anything. Sometimes, when she lay awake at night, as she was now, with her thoughts whirring round and round, she thought that maybe everybody else had it figured out. Maybe she was the only woman who couldn't seem to pull it off.

Realizing that she was several miles down this path of negativity, Olivia forced herself to call to mind all of her blessings. Was her situation as a single mom perfect? No, it wasn't. But it was pretty good, and there was plenty to be grateful for. She'd found Shirley and her in-home daycare about a month before she'd had to head back to work. Having called all the daycare phone numbers on the list the hospital had given her, Olivia despaired of ever finding one that would take an infant. It turned out that daycare regulations were pretty strict, and as a result, there were few openings for young babies.

Shirley's home daycare was small. She didn't advertise, and Olivia had only found her by sheer luck and word-of-mouth. God had really come through for her in a big way—one hundred percent. Olivia had resorted to desperate prayers and pleading before bumping into a coworker at the grocery store who has listened sympathetically to Olivia's struggles and suggested Shirley.

Nora fit into the daily routine at Shirley's house beautifully. It was a warm and inviting place, and Nora was happy there, and that's all that really mattered anyway. It didn't matter, or at least it shouldn't, that sometimes Nora seemed a little too willing to be plopped down into the lives of Shirley and her family. A little too eager to leave Olivia's arms for Shirley's. Olivia knew it would be far worse if Nora cried at drop-off, but sometimes she thought a few tears might be a little gratifying. What a terrible thing to wish for!

Shirley's household was a busy one. And a loving one. One that had a father and a mother and lots of kids running around. There was even a dalmatian dog named Pongo in the mix. The environment was loud and fun and lived in and so very different from Olivia's house, which was far too quiet, tidy, and still.

What if she couldn't give Nora enough? She had no father to give her, and there would be no siblings. She wouldn't ever be able to provide a Shirley-esque home for her daughter.

Olivia punched her pillow and flopped over to face the wall. Wasn't she supposed to be counting blessings? How had she slipped back into the negative zone without even realizing it?

"Okay, Olivia—five blessings. Go," she said out loud. This was a count-your-blessings game she played to reframe her thinking when she was anxious. The first four were always so easy, always the same. One—Nora. Two—her job. Three—her neighbor, Anna. Four—good health. And usually number five was something like the new friendship she was developing with her building principal, or her house, or living in Nicolet. But tonight's number five surprised her when it came to her, and when she realized just how true it was, she couldn't help the small smile that tugged at the corners of her mouth.

Five—she'd turned the page on a chapter of her life today. It had been an unbelievably painful year. Even now she fought against the fear of what else life might throw at her, but she also knew she was at the start of a brand new chapter—one so full of promise she could almost feel it. It was time to write it, time to start living again. It was time to take joy in the small things in life. She was ready to begin anew, and she fell asleep with a smile on her face and hope in her heart.

Chapter 3

It was third period English, and Anna's hands were shaking as she peeled her orange over the garbage can next to the pencil sharpener. Announcements had just begun over Nicolet High School's PA system, and she knew the homecoming court was going to be announced any second. She wasn't sure what she hoped to hear.

In the grand scheme of things, she knew it really didn't matter all that much. On the one hand, Anna wasn't exactly comfortable in the spotlight, but on the other, she felt excited about the possibility.

It wouldn't be the first time they spoke the name *Anna Davis* over the school's PA system, but it always gave her a little thrill to hear it. Announcements, including sports stats, were made every day at the start of third period, and during cross country season in the fall and track in the spring, it wasn't uncommon to hear her name spoken over the loudspeaker. She had helped lead her school to many track and cross country victories over the years, and she hoped to be scouted by a few universities for next year.

Anna took a deep breath and returned to her seat. They'd already announced the cross country win from the meet over the weekend. She was used to running in all kinds of horrible weather—it was to be expected in the U.P. in the fall and spring—but the weather had been so amazing, and she'd felt so strong and so good as she raced. Her time, a personal best time of 16:51.3, had been less than one second away from the school record held by some unfortunate girl named Mildred in 1983. She'd been so close!

Popping a section of orange into her mouth, Anna willed herself to relax. She heard the voice announce the loss of the varsity football team last Friday night before she let her mind drift off to the events that had occurred after that game.

It had been hotter than usual the last few days, and after the football game, a bunch of seniors had gone down to McCreaty's Cove for one last swim. Winters in Michigan's Upper Peninsula always lasted half the year, and that wasn't an exaggeration. Kids wore snow suits and winter boots over their Halloween costumes—Anna honestly didn't know why anyone bothered dressing up at all—and snow and ice still dotted the landscape as late as mid-May, sometimes even into early June. There was a picture of Anna and her brother, Mitch, when they were little, swimming at the beach with small ice chunks floating in the surrounding water. The photo had been taken on June first.

Mother Nature must have known they needed one last swim in Superior, and students of Nicolet High seized the opportunity. The football team had lost—nothing new there—but after they'd made plans to head to the beach, nobody cared very much about the loss. Anna's boyfriend, Alex, had driven a group of them down to the sandy cove. She'd thought it was shaping up to be a pretty fun U.P. night, but as they pulled into the lot that overlooked the beach, a feeling of dread washed over her as she noticed a certain freshman girl and her posse on the sand below, and she was looking up at Alex's truck expectantly.

Blythe Severin had been a thorn in Anna's side from the first day of school a few weeks ago. This freshman girl had set her sights on Alex, and she had no scruples whatsoever about letting Anna know she was making herself the competition. She most definitely was *not* following the unspoken high school hierarchy. Freshmen were supposed to have a healthy fear of upperclassmen, weren't they? That's how Anna had been as a freshman. She never would have dreamed of trying to steal a senior girl's boyfriend right out from under her nose. The nerve of that girl! But there she was, in all her gorgeous glory, with two of her friends flanking her on either side as she closed the distance between them. "Please let them not be coming over here," Anna muttered to herself.

"What'd you say?" Alex asked from inside the truck through the open window.

"Nothing," Anna replied quickly. She'd learned not to talk about Blythe to Alex. It annoyed him.

Watching the girls discreetly from under her lashes, Anna noted Blythe was never alone. Everywhere she went, she had friends with her, even in the hallways at school. Anna wondered if she was afraid to be alone. Maybe the friends were the true source of her power—she couldn't seem to go anywhere without them. It was pathetic, but Anna wasn't able to draw up much sympathy.

Blythe was tall, at least five foot nine, and everything about her was perfect. Her rich, dark hair was thick and shiny. Her olive-toned skin was flawless underneath her expertly applied makeup. She was pencil slim, her visible hip bones protruding out like can-opener blades above her low-slung short shorts. Even her eyes were striking, although they were cold and turned up at the corners like an evil cat's.

Anna wished she could climb back into the truck and tell Alex to go somewhere else. It wasn't like they lacked for beaches around here. But everyone from their group, including Jess, Anna's best friend, had already unloaded, and they were halfway down the steps to the sand. Ignoring Blythe as best she could, Anna waited for Alex to finish doing whatever he was doing in the truck. She tapped her foot impatiently and looked out over the cove just in time to see Alex's best friend, Jared, catch Jess and lift her up in the air, spinning her around while she squealed with mock indignation—her tawny ponytail whipping in the wind. They weren't dating, but Jared flirted with Jess a lot. All the boys did, but Jess seemed mostly oblivious to it. Anna couldn't remember the last time Alex had flirted with her.

Alex shut the driver's side door and moved around the front of the truck. "Can you hold my towel?" he asked. Her arms were already full. She was carrying her sandals, water bottle, and three towels, but she nodded anyway, and Alex threw his towel on top of the pile before hoisting the cooler out of the truck bed.

Anna turned to head down the stairs to the sand, taking care not to miss her footing on the concrete steps. Out of the corner of her eye, she could see the three freshman girls continue to make their way towards them. *Here we go again,* she thought with a sigh. By the time she reached the bottom stair, she'd worked up enough courage to reason with Alex one last time. Nodding her head in Blythe's direction, she said, "You need to show her you're not interested, or she's going to keep bothering you—and me." She wiggled her toes in the still-warm sand.

Alex rolled his eyes. "She's harmless, Anna. It's no big deal, like I keep saying. Let her say hello and do her thing, and then we'll swim." Jess and Jared had already joined a large group out in the water in front of them, and more cars were arriving in the lot behind them. Alex took a second to scan the scene. "Looks like the entire school's here," he said, shifting the subject.

Anna shrugged and stayed silent. Why wouldn't Alex put Blythe in her place? She'd told him all about how Blythe made her feel. The way she stared Anna down in the halls. And he'd seen for himself the way Blythe threw herself at him. Alex was a nice guy, Anna knew that, and she was glad for it. It was the reason she'd stayed with him for two years. He was down to earth, funny, and sweet. That he was such a hottie was just a bonus.

Until the last few months, they'd never even had any big fights—only a couple of petty tiffs here and there. But since the summer, things had changed. In July, they'd had their first real, heated fight, which had ended with him peeling out of Anna's gravel driveway. There'd been five or six more since then, and while they always made up, Anna felt things shifting. More and more, Alex seemed . . . almost indifferent to her. Not all the time, but enough for her to notice. Maybe it was normal and maybe it wasn't—she didn't know for sure. All she knew for certain was that she loved him so much that sometimes she couldn't breathe.

Anna forced her mouth into a small smile as Blythe and her friends covered the last few feet of ground that remained between them. She stopped and stood *right* smack-dab in front of them, and while Anna didn't consider herself an unfriendly person in need of loads of personal space, somehow she felt Blythe had invaded hers, and it galled her so much that she retreated a step to put some distance between the two of them. Anna could see in Blythe's expression that she considered it a victory. Alex hadn't moved an inch, so Anna had essentially stepped herself right out of this little meet-and-greet. She'd made herself the outsider. Too late to change that, she supposed.

"Hey, Alex," Blythe cooed in a slightly nasal voice as she fingered the charm on the end of her necklace. Anna realized she'd never heard her talk before. One more thing to add to the list of stuff that bugged her about Blythe. It sounded like she had one of those swimming plugs pinched around her nose. "It's so hot out, isn't it?" She let go of the charm and trailed her index finger all the way down to her impressive cleavage.

Anna almost choked as she watched, and she looked from Blythe to Alex to see what his reaction would be. He smiled easily back at the stacked stick insect, in all her pink bikini-topped glory, and then, unbelievably, performed a slow, appreciative scan. Anna couldn't believe her eyes. Blythe was stunning; it was true. Compared to her, Anna felt dowdy and hopelessly flat-chested in her black cutout one-piece. But still, Alex was being a total pig. She realized with a start that he hadn't looked at her like that . . . maybe ever, and she felt her hands tremble as she kept her grip on the towels.

"Hey there, girls," Alex said easily. "How's it going?" The three of them smiled adoringly at him.

"Better now that you're here," Blythe replied. "I was hoping you'd show up." She spoke these words to Alex alone, and when she shifted her gaze to Anna, it was obvious she wished Alex *was* alone. She'd given Anna this look so many times now—the slow head to toe inspection that mean girls the world over seemed to know how to do. Anna would have thought she'd be immune to it by now.

She wasn't.

It was a critical, calculated look, meant to make her feel small and inadequate, and boy oh boy, did it work. Every. Single. Time.

Blythe's dislike of her seemed almost visceral, and Anna still hadn't quite come to terms with it. This was a first for her. Generally, she was well-liked by everyone, and she'd never encountered such meanness before. For the first time in her life, she felt completely insecure, and that was saying something. Anna's life hadn't exactly been a walk in the park.

Oh, she knew she was pretty, but she was no knock-out, not like Blythe was. Blythe was model beautiful. Anna also knew that Alex had finally witnessed "the look" for himself. She'd been telling him about this for weeks now, but he always said he couldn't judge something he hadn't seen. Well, now he had. There was no way he could have missed what Blythe had just done to her. Maybe now he'd put this girl in her place. Anna waited for him to do or say something, but he was looking over Blythe's shoulder at one of his friends, who was motioning for him to come over.

"Jace wants us to head down the beach a bit. You guys want to come with us?" he asked them.

No. Fricken. Way. Alex was inviting Anna's one and only enemy in the world to come and hang out with them? Did he really think they were all going to swim and splash around together? Not in a million years.

"Whatever," Anna said to him, shaking her head. "You go on. I'm gonna stay back here with Jess and Jared and the others." She waited a few seconds before turning around, giving him time to choose to stay with her. But no. He said that it was fine, and he'd catch later. *What the heck?*

"Better take your towel," she told him stiffly.

He grabbed it without a word, without a "thank you," and ran off through the sand with the three girls. Anna stood there watching them, feeling equal parts embarrassed and angry. He'd abandoned her without even a thought.

Honestly, though, she didn't want to be near him right now anyway, and not just because he'd checked Blythe out in front of her, although that was bad enough. What bothered her more than anything was that he hadn't stood up for her when Blythe had done her best to make Anna feel small. Alex used to be kind of protective of her. Once, he'd even called Mitch out for yelling at her. She couldn't imagine him doing anything close to that now.

It was probably best that Alex *had* left. If he'd stayed with her, she wouldn't have trusted herself not to go off on him right there in front of half the school. The way she felt right now, she wouldn't have held anything back. Standing in place, she took five slow, deep breaths to get control of herself. Just before Anna turned to join Jess, Blythe whipped her head around to glance back at her, and Anna couldn't miss the smug smile on Blythe's face. Round One—Blythe.

Anna was quiet for the rest of the night. Jess asked her about it at one point, but Anna told her she'd tell her later. Jess accepted that and moved on, trying to give an appearance that everything was normal. She carried on the conversations with the others for the two of them and kept Anna right beside her. Anna loved that about her. Jess was loyal, and she never pried.

Alex, who eventually came back to hang out with their group, behaved as though everything was just fine, although Anna had a feeling he knew better. He was just a little too loud and a little too smiley, like he was overcompensating.

The ride home in his truck confirmed that he wasn't oblivious to her feelings at all.

After dropping off Jess and Jared, Anna remained quiet. Even though she hated playing games, she couldn't help herself. Alex's forced attempts at conversation didn't budge her into talking, and after several minutes, he sighed heavily.

"Come on, Anna. Don't be mad."

She was immediately defensive.

"How can you say that? How can you say 'don't be mad?' You didn't stick up for me, Alex! Plus, you ogled her right in front of me! And I had to listen to her little shrieks as you splashed and chased her down the beach like two actors in some ridiculous movie montage. I could *see* you, Alex! I mean, I have eyes. How am I supposed to feel right now?" She was getting louder and more worked up.

"Calm down," he said, taking his eyes off the road briefly to look at her.

"Calm down?" Anna's temper ignited. This was not a real common occurrence for her. Usually she was pretty even-keeled, but she felt betrayed, misunderstood, and out of control of the situation. It was bad enough that this girl was after her boyfriend, but she had Anna nervous to turn corners in her school's hallways—the school she'd called home for over three years. She seemed to be perpetually in Anna's path, and being so routinely confronted by a group of girls who stared daggers at her as she walked by was getting harder and harder for Anna to handle.

It was her senior year, and Anna felt more insecure than she had felt even as a freshman. With Mitch newly out of the house and her dad always gone, she was more lonely now than she'd ever been before. And now, this ninth-grade *toxin*, who Anna hadn't even known existed a few weeks ago, was playing with her mind in a big way, and she was almost as angry at herself for letting Blythe get to her as she was at Alex.

"Don't tell me to calm down. You say you love me, but you're not showing it. You didn't stick up for me, and you should have. You stayed with her when you should have stayed with me. How can you not see what a jerk you were tonight?"

"Oh, I'm a jerk now? I see. I'm a jerk for being nice to someone? I'm a jerk for hanging out with another female *and* her friends? It's not like we went off together! I'm a jerk because I didn't spend every second with you down at the beach? You know what? I did come back to spend time with you, Anna, and you *ignored* me. Stop being so petty and sensitive!"

An embarrassed flush crept up Anna's neck. She wanted to win just one of these fights with Alex. Just one. Lately, he never saw things her way. She always felt so sure she was in the right, and then he'd yell and say stuff that made her feel like maybe she was the wrong one after all. But she couldn't be wrong about this, could she?

Maybe she was being a *little* petty. And she already knew she was sensitive. That much was true. Her Aunt Heidi always said she wore her heart on her sleeve. But if Anna was sensitive, then Alex was *in*sensitive, and that's what she told him.

They remained quiet the rest of the trip to her house. She lived ten minutes outside of town, but the silence that stretched out between them made the trip seem three times as long. Normally, she would have caved by now and apologized, but this time, she dug in her heels.

When they finally pulled into her driveway, she opened her door, prepared to leave the car without a word. Alex reached for her arm.

"Wait," he said with an aggravated sigh. "I don't want to fight with you, okay? I *hate* fighting with you. You need to know that I would *never* cheat on you. Never. I love you." He moved his hand from her arm to her hair, tucking it behind her ear in a gesture that was as familiar and comforting as a warm, soft blanket on a cold night, but even that couldn't prevent the chill that crept over Anna as she heard the word *cheat*.

Looking up into his face, she felt a little better. He was sincere, and at the moment he seemed more like the Alex she'd known for years and less like the Alex she'd experienced over the last few months. She didn't know that Alex. *Her* Alex could be trusted, no matter what. He'd more than proven that over the years. This was just a rough patch. It wouldn't last. Anna felt most of the resentment and anger dissolve as she looked into his big brown eyes.

It was hard to pinpoint Alex's best feature since he was built to perfection all over, but Anna supposed if she had to choose, she'd pick his eyes. They weren't merely brown. They were the color of espresso with flecks of gold. Alex's eyes had always communicated something to her. They spoke of kindness and love, honesty and trust. She let them speak to her again in this moment and allowed them to soothe her. Alex pulled her into a hug, and she melted into it and let the rest of the anger go.

"I love you too. I'm sorry." In that moment, Anna told herself not to worry. But later that night, when she'd turned off the bedside lamp and stared into the darkness of her room, she still did, and even her sleep was troubled.

Anna had awoken this morning with the same butterflies in her stomach that she'd finally fallen asleep with, and they were still with her now as she waited on the announcements. She took a deep breath as she tuned in again and listened to the familiar voice of their class president, Adam Diedrich.

He announced the freshman court followed by the sophomores and juniors and, finally, the seniors. "And your senior homecoming court is as follows. For the ladies—Julie Harland, Rachel Beecher, Dannie Stiles, Rebecca Simms, and Anna Davis."

Anna felt her stomach do a funny little flip as she heard her name, and everyone in the room turned and congratulated her before hushing to listen to the boys' names.

". . . David Harris, Charlie Avery, Alex Anderson, Jared Yates, and Ben Thompson." Anna's stomach did another flip. Alex was on the court. How fun! And Jared too.

Anna looked up to see Miss Josten's smile of congratulations, and Anna smiled back. A fresh-faced brunette with a cute bob haircut and great taste in clothes, Sarah Josten was a brand new teacher this year, and she was brand new to Nicolet too. Nobody really knew much about her, other than that she was young and sweet and from the South, and the only reason they knew that was because of her accent. Anna didn't know where in the South Miss Josten was from, but she thought it must be a lovely place. Her young teacher sounded genteel and sophisticated, and Anna could listen to her talk all day long.

Miss Josten pronounced *I* as *aah*, and she called a pen a *pin*. She also said *y'all*, which was Anna's absolute favorite. The best was when she put all three together, as in, "Aah'd like y'all to take out a pin." Her other teachers would have said, "Hey, guys, grab a pen."

Even though Miss Josten was private about her life and her past, she was enthusiastic and fun, and she'd quickly become Anna's favorite teacher. It helped that English was her best subject. Today, they were going to share the memoirs they'd written. Anna was looking forward to it and pulled her paper out of her folder as Adam began wrapping up the homecoming announcements.

Float building would go on until Thursday night at the bus garage, he said, and they needed all hands on deck to help make the floats spectacular. This year's homecoming theme was Egyptian Mysteries, and the senior float was supposed to feature King Tut. Anna had been so busy with cross country that she hadn't helped with the float at all this year. She felt guilty about that and decided she had to make some time this week.

Homecoming was a big deal in Nicolet, and loads of people would come out for the parade and the game. The town was named after Jean Nicolet, a French explorer who spent a lot of time in the Great Lakes region in the early seventeenth century. Many of the area's streets were named for French explorers and priests, although now there were more Finnish Americans here than French Americans. In Nicolet, Finnish culture was alive and well. Cars were adorned with *Sisu* bumper stickers, and every second or third house had a sauna in the basement or backyard. Anna was part Finn herself—on her mother's side. Over the years, Aunt Heidi had made it a point to teach her and Mitch all about their Finnish heritage so they could learn to "appreciate" the culture and know where they came from.

Aunt Heidi always expressed such regret that Anna would never know her Grandpa Sepi and Grandma Maggie. Anna hadn't yet been born when her grandmother passed away. Her grandfather had joined Grandma Maggie a year later when Anna was just a small baby. They'd both drifted away, peacefully, in their sleep. Dad and Aunt Heidi took a lot of comfort in that.

Even though she had never met them, thanks to Aunt Heidi and her dad, she almost felt like she *had* known them. She even had a letter her Grandpa Sepi had written to her before he died. He'd written one to Mitch too. Although Mitch might not cop to it, Anna was pretty sure he treasured his letter just as much as Anna treasured hers. She'd seen it once, unfolded and resting on his nightstand.

Grandpa Sepi had grown up here in this place. Anna liked to imagine stepping over the very footprints he and her grandmother had left behind from their days walking through the downtown and harbor area. She thought of her mother's footprints left behind too. The idea that she was literally following in each of their footsteps helped Anna feel connected to them.

Nicolet was a small town of twenty-four thousand, not counting the students at the local university. Some kids talked about blowing out of there as soon as they had their high school diplomas in hand, but Anna loved her hometown. The community was tight-knit and took a lot of pride in its high school, even its perpetually losing football team.

Really more of a hockey town, Nicolet's best male athletes competed in ice arenas, not on football fields, but despite that, the whole town got involved with Nicolet High's homecoming each year. The parade and game would be packed. Convertibles, which were always donated for the day by wealthy families, ensured that the homecoming court appeared at the parade in style, and Anna wondered what kind of car she'd get to ride in. Later at the game, at halftime, Adam would announce the court. She was already looking forward to all of it.

Adam finished the announcements by reminding students they would cast their final vote for the senior homecoming king and queen on Thursday morning, and he'd reveal the results at the assembly on Friday. That was days away! It felt like a long time to wait.

Chapter 4

In reality, the week went by pretty quickly. Between cross country practice and a meet on Tuesday plus float-building on Wednesday, Anna stayed busy. It was an unusual week in that her dad was at home. Steven Davis spent a lot of time traveling for work and really wasn't around much, but even when he was home, he wasn't really *there*. It had been that way her whole life, but Anna had seen enough parents interacting with their kids to know that her situation wasn't at all normal. She knew her dad must love her, because that's what dads did, but she wished he'd tell her sometimes, or even better, show her. Mostly, he was just the guy who provided money for groceries, clothes, a warm house, and a car.

Speaking of her car, it was a good thing her dad was around right now. Her car was out of commission, and she needed her dad's help to get it to a mechanic. Although he promised he'd get it in for her earlier in the week, it still sat parked in the garage. For the past several days, she'd had to catch a ride to school with her neighbor, Olivia. For everything else, she was at the mercy of Jess or Alex—or Mitch, in a pinch.

Anna couldn't believe tomorrow would already be Friday. She'd mention the car again to her dad tonight over dinner, which would be ready soon. She expected Mitch and Alex anytime. Somehow, she'd managed to get them all together for a meal. It had been too long, so she'd made her specialty, which was a favorite of all three of the men in her life. While the lasagna finished baking, she worked quickly to get the table set and the kitchen cleaned up.

Over the years, she'd become the family cook. It had happened out of necessity, and it hadn't been pretty—or edible—at first. But someone had to do it. If Anna hadn't stepped up, they would have been stuck eating mac and cheese or takeout pizza for every meal.

Sometime around the eighth or ninth grade, Anna's cooking skills had gone from adequate to top-notch. And even though she'd found it stressful sometimes to juggle school, sports, and meal prep, lately she'd missed it. Ever since Mitch started college and moved into the dorms, Anna hadn't really had much opportunity to cook like this. With her dad on the road all the time, it was just her, and it made little sense to go to all the trouble for one person.

It would have been unbearably lonely for Anna if not for her neighbor, Olivia—and Alex and Jess, of course. Often, she ended up eating at her neighbor's house. Olivia Reeves lived next door with her young daughter, and Anna spent a lot of time over there, actually. Sometimes it felt like more of a home to her than her own house did, and she was grateful for the close friendship that had developed between Olivia and herself. Plus, it was a relief to know she had someone close by if she needed anything. Anna hated sleeping alone in her big house. She didn't even have a dog to keep her company.

Once the boys had arrived, Anna dragged her dad out of his office and dished up the lasagna, bread, and side salad she'd made. In under a minute they were all digging in, all except Anna, who looked on for a moment, pleased by their obvious satisfaction with her efforts.

Mitch grunted his approval. "Anna, this is amazing. You would not believe how bad dorm food is," he said with a mouthful of the homemade garlic bread she'd kneaded and baked to perfection.

Anna smiled with pleasure. "Good, I'm glad."

She had briefly considered buying frozen garlic bread to save time, but in the end, she went all out and make it from scratch. It wasn't every day that her dad *and* Mitch *and* Alex were there for dinner. It needed to be special.

She looked to her dad, who was attacking his plate with a gusto that was enormously gratifying, and smiled. She didn't expect that he would say anything about the meal one way or the other—he would be too distracted for that—but Anna knew he was enjoying it, and that was enough for her. He worked so hard and spent so much time on the road. She worried about him.

Steven Davis was only forty-four, but with his deep worry lines and graying hair at his temples, he didn't look quite that young. Oh, he was still handsome—all of Anna's friends said he was the hottest dad in town—but he looked tired, and she was fairly certain he was growing a little thicker around the middle.

"How's work, Dad?" Mitch asked.

Steven nodded as he finished his mouthful. "Good. I gotta say, though, it's nice to be home for a change."

Anna beamed at him.

"Although I've got to fly out again tomorrow morning, but only for a quick twenty-four hours. I'll be back Saturday morning."

"How's that new cagey thing working out?" Alex asked. "I remember you talking about that last time I saw you."

"Oh, that," Steven gave a dismissive wave of his hand. "We've been putting those in for half a year now, probably. It's doing great. The docs love them."

Steven was a biomedical engineer, and he worked for a big medical device company called Chester Biotechnologies. His job was to travel and train doctors all over the Midwest in how to use and place various medical devices in spine and joint surgeries. He seemed to love his work, maybe a little too much, but living in hotels and eating out in restaurants was taking its toll on him. Those dark smudges under his eyes and his growing tummy were only two of the most obvious signs, and Anna wished she could take better care of him. She'd cook meals like this for him all the time if he were home more. Not that lasagna was a low-calorie meal. But home-cooked meals were a lot healthier than all that fast food. And she was sure he'd sleep better in his own bed.

"How's hockey going, Mitch?" Alex asked.

"Awesome. But dryland is kicking my a—my butt," he amended, catching himself just in time. Steven Davis, in a sad attempt to be a good father, had a strict "no swearing" policy for his kids.

"When's your first game?" Anna asked.

"Not for a few weeks. We play Anchorage first."

"Home or away?"

Mitch perked up at this question, asked by his father. Wiping his mouth with his napkin first, he answered, "Uh, home. Are you going to make it, do you think? I mean, that'd be awesome if you could . . ."

Almost everything with her brother was *awesome,* but in this case, Anna knew the word was appropriate. It would mean everything to Mitch to have their dad there in the stands watching his first Division One college hockey game. Mitch had gotten a full-ride scholarship for his freshman year. He played wing on the first line, and Anna couldn't wait to watch him play again.

"I'll try," their dad answered as he tackled his salad.

Mitch nodded, clearly having hoped for something more definitive but settling for what he'd been given, which at least was not an outright *no.*

"Dad, you got us season tickets, right?" Anna asked.

Steven nodded and popped a crouton into his mouth.

"I'll be there for sure," Anna reassured Mitch. She turned to Alex. "I've said it before, but I practically grew up in ice rinks. I followed Mitch to hockey tournaments in at least four states growing up. Plus Canada. Whenever I could tag along with some family, I would."

"And you still love the game," Alex added, before taking a large bite of lasagna.

"What I love is watching Mitch play," Anna clarified, looking at her brother affectionately.

Mitch cleared his throat. "Well . . . good, then." He glanced at her before turning his attention back to his plate.

Fortunately, Anna was mostly secure in the love of the men in her family, but she did a mental eye roll. Neither one of them was comfortable expressing any kind of deep emotion. She knew they were both horribly scarred from what had happened to them so long ago, and she wished she could help somehow. But they had always held something back with her. It was as if they'd both walled off a part of themselves—the part she most wanted to connect with, and no matter how she'd tried over the years, those walls weren't budging. Anna felt Alex squeeze her knee in support.

"Did Anna tell you about homecoming?" Alex asked both the Davis men.

"Yeah, that's awesome," Mitch responded at the exact moment their father said, "No, what?"

"What about homecoming?" Steven asked again.

Anna smiled. "Alex and I are both on the court."

"What does that mean?" Steven asked, looking mildly interested.

"Man, I know it's been a long time since you were in high school, but really. You don't remember homecoming? How old are you?" Mitch teased.

Steven stopped and stared at Mitch for a few seconds, his expression inscrutable. After a few uncomfortable seconds, Mitch looked at Anna nervously, and she gave a tiny shrug of her shoulders.

She was wondering if her dad would say anything at all in return when his face relaxed and he smiled at Mitch. "Oh, come on. Give your old man a break." With a small twinkle in his eye, he added, "Refresh my memory."

Anna would have said that she lived for moments like these, but this was the first one of its kind—ever. She wanted to enjoy it fully, but she found she couldn't. It was bittersweet. Maybe in another family, this bit of light banter would have been no big deal, but teasing and joking and laughing weren't really things her dad did. She felt her eyes burn with the threat of happy tears and was horrified. If she cried now, she'd ruin the moment. Anna shot Alex a brief but pointed look as she hopped to her feet with her water glass. He got the message and took over for her.

"No, yeah. What it means is that we're, you know, homecoming royalty, or whatever, and tomorrow they'll name the king and queen. We'll all ride in the parade tomorrow afternoon, and then they'll announce us at the football game that night. Right Anna?" he asked as she returned with her fresh water. "Did I get it all?" he asked, winking at her.

"Mostly. We'll get announced at the assembly tomorrow too," she said casually. She sat back down in her chair and pulled her legs up underneath her. She'd had just enough time to regain control of herself. "Oh, and the best part. We get to ride in convertibles in the parade too, and . . ." Anna stopped talking as she realized her father was now staring at her with the same expression he'd worn a moment ago with Mitch.

She shifted in her seat as he slowly set his napkin down on the table. "Why didn't you tell me this?" he asked quietly.

Anna looked at Mitch and Alex first before replying. "Well, I mean, I just found out on Monday."

"It's Thursday," he said simply.

"I know. I—I didn't want to bother you with it when you were working. It's just stupid high school stuff." She scrambled to give any other explanation than the obvious one, which was that she simply hadn't thought he would care. He never had in the past, so why would anything be different now? "I told you about the race, though," she pointed out.

"I want to know what's happening in your life," Steven said simply, looking at Anna before turning and addressing Mitch. "Yours too."

When Steven turned his focus back to his plate, the siblings looked at one another questioningly. This had never happened before either. Their father had been oblivious to them, more or less, for years. What was going on?

Everyone was quiet for a moment, but soon the sound of silverware clanking against plates returned as they resumed eating again, and Anna listened absently to the male conversation that occurred around her. She, however, was lost in thought.

Alex helped Anna clean up afterwards. She sent Mitch back to the dorms, ostensibly so he could get some studying done. He thanked her for the "awesome" lasagna, some of which she'd sent home with him in a small Tupperware container. She was threading the dish towel through the dishwasher handle when her dad came back into the kitchen.

"You said the parade is tomorrow?"

She turned. "Yeah. After school."

"What time?"

She looked at Alex. "Four o'clock?"

Alex nodded. "I'm pretty sure."

"Four o'clock," she repeated.

He paused as he studied her. "I wish I could be there," he said. He gave a sad smile before turning and leaving the kitchen.

Anna waited a few beats before turning to Alex with a bewildered smile of her own. He simply opened his arms for her to step into.

Later that night, the two of them were eating a plate of the oatmeal cookies Anna had made earlier in the week. It was late, and Anna realized she'd forgotten to remind her dad about her car. He was already asleep, so it would have to wait.

"I can help you. Give you rides and stuff." Alex offered.

Anna gave her second cookie a slow dunk in her milk. "It's okay. I've got rides for the next few days."

Alex shrugged and stuffed an entire cookie in his mouth. Anna smiled. He was as bad as Mitch.

"So . . . how's work been this week?" Anna asked. Alex had a job at a local sporting goods store. He'd had to work every day this week until closing, so she was glad they could spend some time together tonight.

"Good," he answered through a mouthful of cookie before washing it down with a gulp of milk. "On Tuesday, I sold an elliptical to some lady who didn't even know she wanted one," he joked with pride. "Too bad I don't get commission."

"You really are great at sales. I'm sure you'll have a bright future selling used cars," Anna teased. "Seriously, though, congrats on the sale, although I wish you'd been able to come to the meet on Tuesday. I did really well. I won."

"Oh, yeah. I heard that. Sorry. Good job."

Alex had once admitted that he would rather watch paint dry than watch a cross country meet. Even though Anna understood, it still bugged her. He hadn't seen her run all season. Even Mitch had made it to two meets.

Alex had torn his ACL sophomore year playing football, and even though he stayed fit by going to the gym, he wasn't a high school athlete anymore. If he had been, Anna would have been there for as many games as she could make, cheering him on.

Her phone dinged. Seeing that Alex was taking a peek at his phone too, she opened the message. It was from a freshman girl named Laura, one of Blythe's friends.

Alex looked up at her sharp intake of breath. "What?"

Anna turned her phone slowly to show him. "That girl, Laura, just sent me this."

She watched Alex's expression, which didn't change, but a red flush was creeping up his neck.

Anna's heart pounded up in her ears. "Alex," she began, looking a second time at the photo of him with his arm around a smiling Blythe Severin, "when was this? Tuesday? It looks like you're at the freshman football game here."

Alex let out a whoosh of air as he dashed a hand through his dark blond hair. He was now red up to his hairline.

"Well, yeah. Okay. I went to the football game."

"What, with Blythe? I thought you were working. You know, foisting ellipticals on all those unsuspecting women."

Alex put his hands up defensively, even as he held his third cookie. "Look, Anna. I knew you would get like this, so I didn't say anything. I got off work early, so I went to the game. By myself. I bumped into some people there. Blythe was one of them. That's it."

"Why didn't you tell me you got off early?" Anna asked, unable to keep from looking repeatedly at the picture in front of her, which she'd captured with a screen shot. Alex looked amazing, as always, his smile just slightly lopsided. Blythe had her arm around his shoulders and she'd tipped her head towards his so that their temples were touching. She looked gorgeous. Together, they were an impossibly good-looking pair.

"Well, I—" he started. "You know. I told you I couldn't come to the meet because of work, and I just . . ." he shook his head, trying to find the right words to break it to Anna gently that he'd chosen to go to the football game instead of to her meet.

"What time did you get off?" Anna asked.

"Look, Anna. I'm sorry. I should've watched you run."

"What time?" Anna demanded.

He sighed in exasperation. For a second, she thought he might not answer. "Five," he said, finally.

"Five. You got off that early, and you didn't think you could come and watch me cross the finish line at least? Listen, I know we've talked about this. And I get it. It's boring to stand around waiting for runners to go by. But you could have been there at the end to watch me finish. My meets are usually over by five thirty. Couldn't you give me even a half hour of your time? You know how much I—" Anna's voice broke, and she bit down on her lip to keep from crying.

Alex knew how hard it was for her to see her teammates cheered on by their families, but as much as she wanted him there, what she really wanted was for him to *want* to be there.

"And then to see you with . . . *her*. If I'd known you were going to the game, I would have come for the second half. Unless . . ." she added slowly, "maybe you didn't want me to be there." Anna's voice tipped up slightly so that her words ended in a question.

Alex shook his head slowly as he watched her. “What’s that supposed to mean?”

“Nothing,” she muttered. “Just—never mind.”

An awkward silence followed. After several seconds, Alex dropped his cookie back on the plate. “It’s time for me to go.”

“Yeah,” Anna said, her voice hard and foreign to her own ears. “It is.”

Chapter 5

Anna woke up the next morning puffy-eyed. She'd called and messaged Alex countless times last night, but he hadn't answered. She'd checked, and he wasn't sharing his location with her anymore, which was upsetting by itself. It had been an agonizing night, and when she finally fell asleep, it wasn't good sleep.

Anna had never been a pretty crier. She turned all red and puffy before the first tear even fell, and the effects of the cry lasted long after it was all over. Unfortunately, she wasn't particularly gifted with makeup, and she knew she looked a wreck. She did what she could and headed downstairs for breakfast.

Anna sat in the kitchen and scrolled through Instagram on her phone. Why did so many girls in her class insist on posting pictures of themselves in bikinis? Anna felt a little sorry for them. They really needed those *likes*.

She hadn't put much of a dent in her bowl of Cheerios when she heard footfalls heading towards the kitchen. Who was here? She turned to look right as her dad walked into the kitchen. He was wearing a pair of jeans and a plain black t-shirt. Not his usual business attire.

"Morning," he said with the wide-awake voice of a man who had been up and talking for hours. He most likely had been.

"Hey!" she said with surprise and wiped her mouth with her napkin. "Good morning. I didn't think you would still be here. Aren't you supposed to be on an airplane headed to Chicago right now?"

"Uh, yeah. Slight change of plans. I've been on a call with the president of the company, and I'm going to be working from home the rest of this week and part of the next." Steven's gaze didn't quite meet his daughter's eyes.

"Wait, what?" This was yet another new one. Steven Davis's entire job was to teach surgeons in the operating room how to use the medical equipment his company engineered. "How will that work?" she asked.

"I'm just going to be working on some reports. Maybe do some virtual instruction." He poured himself a cup of coffee.

"Wow. So, you're actually going to be around for a while? That's really nice." She smiled at her dad, who looked at the tile floor and shuffled his feet. He seemed to be on the verge of saying something, but then changed his mind. "You good?" she asked, eyebrows raised.

"Yep," he said simply, giving a quick nod before turning to leave the kitchen.

Conversation over. She watched his retreating form until he turned the corner that led to his office. What was going on with him?

Anna sighed and slowly sipped her orange juice, grateful she had awoken earlier than usual and wasn't in her typical rush to get out the door to school. Her brain felt sluggish, and she worked to clear the fog. One thing she knew for certain—she couldn't solve the mysteries of her father or Alex right then. She was not at all in the right frame of mind. She felt all discombobulated and emotionally fried.

Plus, after all these recent fights with Alex and all the stupid tears she'd cried through the night, she had the sneaking suspicion she just might be turning into a teenage drama queen. Anna had always prided herself on how well she avoided drama. Now look at her. If she wasn't careful, she would become what she'd always loathed. It was time to switch her focus. No more drama this morning. Instead, she focused her thoughts on what the day might bring.

Nicolet High School's tradition was to hold an assembly before lunch on homecoming day. The football captains would say a few words. Then the senior class president would introduce the homecoming court one boy and one girl at a time. As Adam announced them, the boys would walk in through one set of doors, and the girls from the other set. They would meet in the middle of the gym and walk down the center of the gymnasium to a grouping of chairs at the far end.

It was customary that the boy would hand the girl a single red rose before escorting her down the center of the gym. Anna wondered how Adam would pair them off. She wanted to walk with Alex.

Smiling to herself, ruefully, Anna wondered how Alex had sneaked his way back into her thoughts. She took a few more bites of cereal. Maybe she could catch him between morning classes to see if they were okay.

Obviously, she was still upset with him, but now that she thought about it, she hadn't really let him explain. And was it really his fault that he didn't enjoy watching cross country? Truth be told, she probably wouldn't enjoy watching it either. Now, running cross country? That was another story.

Hopefully, they'd be able to kiss and make up, so to speak, before the assembly. That thought made her feel better. There was still a good chance of salvaging the day, and Anna really wanted to make the most of it. Homecoming was one of the best days of the year; she didn't want anything to ruin it. And she truly didn't care if her school voted her queen or not. It would be nice, but it wouldn't upset her if they didn't.

Once the king and queen were announced, the four classes would compete against each other in the assembly games—relays, pie-eating contests, and skits—before being dismissed for lunch. Anna would be all dressed up, so she wouldn't be able to compete in any events this year, but it would still be a ton of fun. After school, there would be the parade and then the football game. She was excited about all of it, and she looked forward to spending the time with Alex.

Hearing two short beeps of a car horn, signaling Jess's early arrival, Anna quickly rinsed out her cereal bowl and loaded her dishes into the dishwasher. She'd have to skip brushing her teeth this morning, so she grabbed a stick of gum out of the kitchen junk drawer before sliding her feet into her flip-flops and grabbing her backpack.

Olivia had planned to drive Anna in to school, but she had an early meeting this morning. Thankfully, Jess didn't mind carting her all over town. At least Anna knew she could get to school and back home again. Although, if she'd known her dad was going to be around, she could have asked him for a ride.

Quickly glancing at her feet, Anna wiggled her toes. She'd painted her toenails an alternating red and white, her school colors. It was supposed to be another warm day, so she was wearing jean cut-offs with a white t-shirt. Her red flip-flops completed her ensemble. Taking one last look in the mirror next to the door, Anna realized with a start that this was going to be her last homecoming. In that moment, she determined to enjoy every minute. She had been far too mopey lately, and if she spent even one more day like that, she didn't think she'd be able to stand herself.

"Time to suck it up, buttercup," she said aloud to her reflection before opening the door and waving to Jess.

"Dad, I'm heading out!" she yelled across the house. "Love you!"

"Okay!" he yelled back. "Mitch and I will be at the parade!" he added.

Anna smiled from ear to ear. Maybe this was why he'd stuck around. "Alright! I'll look for you!" She opened the door before closing it again. "Oh, and Dad? Will you remember to get my car in?"

She waited a second, listening. "Dad?" she yelled again.

"I'll get it," he hollered back.

She swung her backpack up and over her shoulder, grabbed the garment bag that held her dress, and walked out.

Jess's parents had given her the cutest yellow Jeep for her birthday last year. It was a few years old, but there was hardly even a scratch on it. It was a stick shift, and Jess had tried to teach Anna how to drive it. She'd long since given up, but they'd had a lot of laughs along the way. Arguably, with its removable hardtop, the Jeep wasn't the most practical vehicle for the U.P., but it sure was fun to ride in. Especially with the top off, like it was today. Anna threw her bag into the back and then carefully laid the dress flat before hopping in.

From the moment they backed out of the driveway, Jess chatted happily about this and that. Anna was content to listen. Jess's enthusiasm over homecoming was contagious, and Anna was smiling and laughing within minutes. The two of them were supposed to have done the leap frog relay race together with two other boys from their class, but when Anna was named to the court, Jess had to replace her with someone else. She'd recruited their friend, Emily, and together they'd developed a strategy Jess felt sure would win them the race.

In a stroke of genius, Jess purchased knee pads, the kind used for cleaning, for their team. The idea was, as they leapt over one another, they would fling themselves forward and down to the floor. The knee pads were going to allow them to slide without worrying about hitting too hard. It was going to give them the edge, Jess was sure of it.

"Let's just hope the boys hold up their end of the deal," she said with a laugh. "We're gonna win the assembly," she said confidently. "The seniors always do. It's, like, our right as upperclassmen."

Anna listened on, content in the moment and basking in the remarkably warm breeze that whipped her hair around her face. She'd need a brush when she got to school, but seated there next to her best friend, with the warmer-than-normal breeze rushing by and the eastern sky glowing orange and pink, it was worth a few snarls.

When she had woken up that morning, she'd been prepared to talk to Jess about Alex and Blythe ad nauseam—driveway to high school parking lot—but she realized with some surprise she no longer needed to.

They were nearly to the school, and Jess hadn't lost any steam. She was still chattering on about the day's plans and the events of the week. Her thick hair was pulled up in her signature messy ponytail. Jess was gorgeous in a natural, sporty kind of way with the body of a gymnast—small, lean, and strong. At five foot one, she was the shortest player on the varsity basketball team, but she was indisputably the quickest and strongest. She was fast on the track too. Track was the one sport the two girls shared in common, though they ran different races. It was fun to cheer each other on.

They cheered each other on in life, not only at meets, and Anna knew she couldn't have asked for a better bestie. Technically, they'd never fought. They bickered from time to time, sure, but mostly their friendship was free of the drama that seemed to plague a lot of the other girls. They loved each other like sisters, or at least the way Anna imagined sisters would love each other.

Jess had moved on to a new thread of conversation. She was like that. A whirlwind. "You know how he is," she was saying. "I'll never be good enough, you know? No matter what I do."

Even though Anna had missed the first part of this conversation, there was no doubt who Jess was talking about. Her dad was incredibly tough on her.

"He gave me today off for homecoming, which I still can't believe, but I'm going to be stuck in my driveway doing ball handling drills and shooting threes all weekend."

"Geesh! Lucky you."

Jess gave her a sidelong glance. "You know, your dad should definitely do better, so don't get me wrong, but sometimes I wonder what it might be like to have my dad be just a little more like yours. Less . . . *involved*." She shot Anna a sardonic smile.

"They're complete opposites, that's for sure. I can't even get my dad to come to a meet, let alone help me get ready for one. Although, he is coming to the parade today."

"No way!"

"Yeah, I don't know what happened, but he was super chatty at dinner last night. I mean, he even joked around. And then he basically told us he wants to be a part of our lives."

Jess arched her brow. "Hmm. Do you think it will last?"

"I'm not sure. I was wondering if maybe having Mitch in college now and me at the end of high school has shaken him up a little. Like maybe he knows time is running out. I don't know if it'll stick, but I guess we'll see."

Jess's comment was interesting, because Anna was also slightly jealous of Jess's situation. She knew the pressure on Jess was real, but at least her dad *was* involved in her life. On the weekends and in the off-season, not that she really had much of one, Mr. Swanson created Jess's workouts for her. He'd have her run on the back roads near their house for training. With the Jeep's top down, he'd drive alongside her—chatting with her, yelling at her, and playing her favorite songs. It was certainly over the top, but Anna still found it kind of sweet in a misguided sort of way.

"I'll come over and rebound for you on Saturday. I have nothing going on until later in the afternoon at four. Mitch has a scrimmage, and I think my dad might be going. Do you wanna come with us?"

Jess's face visibly brightened. "Yes! I'd for sure love to go, but I'll have to check with Dad first. Is Alex going?"

"He can't." Anna pressed her lips together.

Jess gave her a look, but Anna didn't elaborate. She really couldn't. When she'd asked him earlier in the week, he'd said he was busy. She'd wanted to ask what he was doing, but she worried he'd think she was controlling.

"So, things are still a little off?"

"Yep." Anna nodded. "Definitely off, and maybe more than a little."

She filled Jess in, even though she hadn't planned to, and when she finished, Jess shook her head in disgust. "He shouldn't be giving that Blythe girl the time of day. Especially knowing that she's so awful to you."

"You know what's weird? I actually worry I'm going to bump into her every time I round a corner at school. How pathetic is that?"

"Well, she's definitely got way too much power over you, if that's the case. You're gonna laugh, but you should try what my mom's always telling me."

"Which is?"

"Kill her with kindness." Jess giggled.

"What? Is that even a thing?" Anna joined her friend in laughing. "Ahh," she sighed when they had settled down. "I love your mom. The things she says, sometimes. It just kills me!"

"With kindness?" Jess asked with a wink.

Anna groaned. "That's so bad!"

"I just love it when I'm witty."

The two of them were still laughing when they entered the school, and they hugged quickly before parting ways.

Olivia—or *Mrs. Reeves* when they were at school—had told Anna she could leave her dress and other things in her office until it was time to change for the assembly. Anna stopped in before first period, but Olivia wasn't there, which was a little disappointing. Olivia was one of Anna's favorite people. She was sort of like a cool mom slash older sister, who doubled as Anna's guidance counselor. They were also neighbors.

They confided in one another often, and Anna knew Olivia had been going through some tough times. It had been just over a year since her husband's death. Anna hadn't known Olivia then the way she did now, having only met with her to discuss course options and college plans, but she remembered the details of that accident well. It had shaken the entire town, and Olivia had moved in next door to the Davises not long after.

Several months pregnant with her daughter, Nora, Olivia rarely felt well, and Anna had made some meals for her to help and welcome her to the neighborhood. It hadn't taken long for them to become close, and although Anna knew Olivia might not see it, she had come a long way from the sad, haunted woman she'd been when she first arrived next door. Anna was glad to see her friend looking happy and healthy again.

She was lost in thought as she headed to first period physics—not her favorite. Who could focus on kinematics at seven-thirty in the morning? Just as she got near the door, she looked up to see Blythe and her little group of friends. What were they doing standing outside of her class?

Anna knew the answer.

There was no reason for Blythe to be in this hallway because no freshman classes were held over here. She was simply here to stir up trouble. Anna wasn't sure how Blythe knew she had first period physics in the first place, yet here she was. She wondered again at the younger girl's boldness. She sure had guts.

Annoyed at herself for feeling nervous, Anna pressed her lips together in a grim line. This was getting ridiculous. She was letting a fourteen-year-old stranger make her uncomfortable. Forcing herself to meet Blythe's withering stare, Anna stood up a little taller and smiled brightly. "Morning, girls. Hi, Blythe," she said with exaggerated cheerfulness. Blythe's friends rolled their eyes, but Anna had the satisfaction of watching Blythe's expression change from haughty to uncertain before she entered the room. In that instant, Blythe lost some of the power she had over Anna, and Anna was almost giddy as she took her seat. *Thank you, Mrs. Swanson.* Maybe there was more to killing with kindness and catching flies with honey than she'd realized.

Chapter 6

First and second period physics and calculus flew by. Third period dragged, but only because they had a sub who gave them mindless worksheets to do the whole time. It was a good thing they'd shortened morning classes for the assembly. Anna was an office aide fourth period. Her work there was easy since all they had her doing was making copies for an upcoming professional development day. The copier jammed only once, and Anna was well-versed in how to fix it. She had thrown away the ruined paper and was just hitting the resume button when Olivia came in.

Although she knew Olivia was in her mid-twenties, Anna thought she looked more like a well-dressed high school student than a guidance counselor. The boys all thought she was hot, which she hoped Olivia was oblivious to. The last thing Olivia needed was the complication of half her students crushing on her. Anna supposed it was inevitable, though. Olivia just had that certain *something* that made her a knockout. It went far beyond her gorgeous hair and striking green eyes, which Anna noted with concern looked a little tired today.

She experienced a flash of guilt. Normally, she spent a significant amount of time with Olivia and the baby, but this week had really kicked her butt. The homework volume alone was enough to stress her out, although she knew her stress level was nothing compared to what Olivia must have been experiencing these last few days. She imagined her neighbor was still struggling with the recent anniversary of her husband's accident, and Anna resolved to make it a point to get over for a visit soon.

The young counselor's face lit up when she saw Anna.

"Anna!" she exclaimed as she wrapped her in a hug. "I was hoping you'd be in here."

Anna wasn't super tall at five feet six inches, but she towered over the petite Olivia, who sometimes seemed so fragile, Anna thought she might break. She squeezed her back gently and wondered why she always smelled faintly of fresh lemons.

"Hey Oliv—I mean, Mrs. Reeves."

"Oh, when nobody's around just call me Olivia. *Mrs. Reeves* sounds so weird when you say it."

Anna laughed. It did feel weird to call her *Mrs. Reeves*. It was way too formal for two people who knew each other as well as they did.

"I saw your stuff in my office, and I hope you don't mind, but I peeked at the dress. Anna, it's the most beautiful dress I think I've ever seen!"

"Thanks. I told you my aunt picked it out. She's got an eye for clothes and stuff. I would have walked right past that dress."

"Well, you're lucky, because it's one of a kind. You'll want to hang on to it."

Anna nodded. Aunt Heidi had said the same thing.

"So, I'm sorry I missed you this morning. My meeting ran long. How are you? Nervous?"

"Off and on," Anna admitted. "Alex and I are sort of fighting again too, so I'm stressing about that."

Olivia sighed. "That boy."

"Anyway, so long as I don't trip when I walk across the gym, I'll be fine," Anna joked, moving the subject away from Alex. She knew Olivia walked a fine line when talking about Alex, since he was in her section of the alphabet. Olivia's case load comprised all students whose last names began with the letters *A* through *K*.

Olivia laughed and squeezed Anna's warm hands with her own cool ones. "Don't be silly. You'll be great. Ooh, you're so warm. I'm always freezing."

"Well, you know what they say, 'Cold hands, warm heart.'"

Olivia shook her head and smiled. "Anna. I can't wait to see you named homecoming queen today."

Anna flinched. "Oh gosh, don't say that!"

"Oh, but you will be! You deserve this honor so much, Anna," she continued earnestly.

"Well, thanks but—" Anna began, not wanting to make a big deal of it and feeling her face turn even redder. She didn't know if the other girls on the court felt this same embarrassment that she did, but Anna really didn't want people to think she had her heart set on being homecoming queen, or worse, that she thought she had it in the bag. Being in the spotlight kind of sucked, honestly. There was just too much pressure.

"No, no, hear me out," Olivia said with a smile, still holding Anna's hand. "You're the kind of girl who deserves this honor. There are plenty of girls out there who get nominated for this sort of thing. These . . .

popularity contests"—she gave a careless flick of her wrist—"who aren't deserving. They're just silly gossips. Too busy posting all their filtered selfies on the internet to even think about anybody else. They're all so shallow. You, my dear, are the opposite. And it's refreshing. You just keep doing you, no matter what." She squeezed Anna's hand.

"Thanks, Olivia." Anna gave Olivia a quick hug before pulling back and adding with a cheeky grin, "But you should know. Even though I'm not much for social media, I post selfies sometimes too. And sometimes"—she gasped in mock horror—"I even use filters."

Olivia grinned back and gave another dismissive wave. "You know what I mean." She squeezed Anna's hand one last time. "Good luck, honey. I've gotta run, but a bunch of us from the office are going to come and watch. See you there!" And then she was off.

Olivia may have looked a little tired around the eyes, but Anna thought she'd sensed a new sort of energy about her just now. She'd flitted in and then out again, just like the kaleidoscope of hyperactive butterflies that came and went in Anna's stomach. She wondered if they might lift her off the ground and carry her away too. A silly thought, but she sort of wished they would.

The gym was noisy and crowded. The cacophony of the band warming up and the voices of hundreds of students talking and hollering to each other as they moved around to find their seats strangely helped settle Anna's nerves. She hadn't been able to connect with Alex, and she knew she'd feel better now if she had. Standing outside of the side doors with the rest of the girls, Anna wondered if it would be weird when they saw each other.

Eight of them waited there at the doors together. The freshman, sophomore, and junior classes had one girl each to represent them, while the seniors had five. The freshman girl, who Anna recognized from Snapchat, as Jill something-or-other, looked ready to faint. She was pale, and Anna could see a few beads of sweat on her upper lip.

"I'm nervous too," she whispered to her. "You'll do great, don't worry."

"Thanks," she smiled back weakly. "It's just . . . how many people do you think are in there?"

"I dunno. About fifteen hundred, maybe?"

She paled even further. Maybe honesty wasn't always the best policy. Anna gave her shoulder an awkward little pat before turning to Julie Harland, who had just said something to her.

"Sorry, what?" Anna asked.

She moved a little closer. "I guess we missed the memo," Julie repeated, glancing toward the other senior girls standing just off to the side of them. Anna followed her gaze.

"Did you know they were all going to skip morning classes to get their hair done?" Julie asked.

"No, I didn't," Anna admitted.

"They all went to Salon Six together. Don't you think they should have asked us to go?" "Yeah, probably. But are you really all that surprised they didn't?"

The other three girls were all varsity cheerleaders, and they stuck together pretty tight. Anna thought it was interesting that they turned up their noses to anybody else who wasn't a cheerleader. She wondered where they got their confidence. Honestly, they weren't all that well-liked by anyone. Girls thought they were mean, and the boys had begun to wonder if they weren't a little too much trouble.

Anna didn't say this out loud to Julie, but personally, she thought they looked ridiculous. With their elaborate updos and overdone makeup, they looked like they were headed off to prom, and it wasn't even eleven o'clock in the morning.

Anna wore her hair down. She'd brushed the golden locks to a smooth sheen back in Olivia's office, where she'd gotten ready, and she knew it looked soft and full. Julie's hair was in a high, messy bun. She was a dancer, and she and the other girls on the dance team usually wore their hair up like that. She looked natural and pretty.

"No, I guess not," Julie answered. "I'm just annoyed, I guess. And I probably wouldn't have gone even if they had asked," she admitted. "I think we look *way* better than they do anyway."

Anna gave a small smile. She wondered again where other people got their confidence.

"Where did you get that dress, Anna? It's *so* gorgeous!" Julie exclaimed, as if she hadn't quite noticed it until just then.

Anna looked down at her long, flowy dress. "Oh, thanks. My Aunt Heidi got it for me when I was visiting her this summer. She thought I could wear it to prom."

"Is that . . . your mom's sister?"

Anna tried to keep from showing her surprise. "Uh, yeah. They were twins, actually."

"No way! Identical?"

"Yep."

"Whoa. That must be so cool."

"Well, I guess it would be if my mom was still alive."

Julie winced and covered her face with her hands. "Anna! I'm sorry. I'm such an idiot."

Anna heard the echo of her words. "No, no, no. *I'm* sorry."

Julie peeked out from behind her hands. "I shouldn't have brought up your mom."

Anna reached out and placed her hands on Julie's shoulders. "I *love* that you brought up my mom. Nobody ever does, and I—I *need* to talk about her sometimes. That came out totally wrong. I just meant that I think it's hard for Aunt Heidi. A long time ago, she told me it feels like she lost a piece of herself, and I know Mitch, and maybe even my dad, had a hard time looking at her without being reminded of my mom, so that's been hard." Why was she babbling on and sharing even more awkward information?

Julie bit down on her lip. "I'm sorry," she said again.

"No! It's okay. Really. I probably said too much. It's just that I never get to talk about her, so I'm probably a little clumsy about it when I do. It feels good though, actually. To talk about my mom, I mean."

"Oh. Well, that's good," Julie said, twisting her bracelet round and round, not quite meeting Anna's gaze. "I do really like the dress, though. I bet everyone's jealous of it," she added, meeting Anna's eyes briefly, before turning and moving several feet away.

Anna thanked her, though she couldn't be sure Julie had heard her. She sighed and wondered why people had such a hard time talking about her mom being dead. Didn't they know she wanted to talk about her? If *she* didn't, who would? Certainly not Mitch or her dad. She'd given up trying to draw them out long ago. Talking about her mom seemed like a good way to honor her memory, to reassert that she'd lived, she'd died, she'd mattered.

Anna knew the circumstances of her mom's death were cause for gossip, but that couldn't be helped. It didn't mean that they should all just go around pretending it hadn't happened. Although, she conceded, maybe this hadn't been the best moment to dive into conversation about her. It made a strange kind of sense that her mom was at the front of her mind right now, though. This was a moment any girl would want her mother to be a part of.

She looked down at her dress and fingered it lovingly. At least she had Aunt Heidi. Anna wished she would visit sometimes, but they talked on the phone regularly, and that was better than nothing. Years ago, Anna used to wish she could just move to Minnesota and live with her there. She'd even come close to asking her dad's permission once, but then she'd immediately felt guilty and selfish. If she left, who would take care of him and Mitch? They needed her too much.

No. Visits to Minneapolis with Aunt Heidi had to be enough. She relished those times they spent together, especially the longer summer visits. Her aunt was the one who had encouraged and nurtured Anna's love of running. Heidi had been a marathon runner for as long as Anna could remember. She'd been ten years old the first time Heidi took her on a long run. They'd chosen a path along the Mississippi, and Anna had lasted two whole miles. She'd loved it, and better yet, she'd impressed her aunt.

Heidi liked to do other cool things too, like going out to fancy dinners and the theater. By the age of fourteen, Anna had seen *High School Musical*, *Hamilton* (twice), and *Wicked*. This coming summer, they had plans to see *Cats*.

The two of them always had a ton of fun together. Even though Anna wasn't much of a shopper, her aunt had turned it into something of an art form, and Anna found she truly looked forward to hitting the stores, so long as it was with Aunt Heidi. She had such amazing style. She was the type of woman who had shoes to match every outfit. Purses too.

Looking down at her dress now, Anna had to admit: It really was something special, and it made her feel like Aunt Heidi was here with her today. Maybe that was stupid, but she couldn't help it. When they'd spotted the dress, Heidi had literally squealed in a rare outward display of excitement. Anna squealed too, but for a different reason. This dress had come with a hefty price tag—six hundred bucks. There was no way she was even going to try it on, she told her aunt. But Heidi had insisted. And now, here she was, feeling prettier than she could ever remember feeling, and Aunt Heidi wasn't there to see it.

At least she'd begged for Anna to send her pictures. Heidi had already sent her two reminder texts over the course of the morning. Mostly, Anna was fine with her aunt watching from afar, but a small part of her had wanted to tell her aunt to get over herself and come back to Nicolet already. Then she wouldn't need pictures and texts.

Aunt Heidi was tricky to figure out, and although Anna had tried to discover what the problem was, it remained a mystery. Heidi wasn't talking. At least not about the past, and not about the reason she hadn't been home in over fifteen years. But she was a wonderful aunt, and Anna loved her. They were tight, even with four hundred miles between them.

She continued to play with the soft material of the dress. It was really more of a Grecian gown, pleated in lightweight crinkled silver lamé with floral shoulder appliqués. It had a V-neckline with strap detailing and a slit that traveled up to Anna's mid thigh. The fitted bodice and empire waist reminded her of something a Greek goddess might have worn—maybe Aphrodite. Slipping into it in the dressing room that first time had been a real thrill, and she felt that same thrill as she'd put it on again today.

With her skin still lightly tanned from the summer, the silver color of the gown really popped. It even enhanced her eyes, which people had always found striking under ordinary circumstances. She knew her amber eyes were considered a rarity, and they were her favorite feature, though not for that reason. Her mother's eyes had been the same coppery hue. Anna loved knowing she shared that remarkable feature with her mother. With her aunt too, of course.

The voice of their principal welcoming everyone to the assembly cut through Anna's thoughts, and she took a deep breath as Mrs. Hennings turned the mike over to Adam. It was the senior class president's job to run the assembly, which was a good thing because Adam was a natural at being the center of attention. He was always smiling and cracking jokes. Everybody liked him. Easygoing as he was, Anna thought she could hear a nervous tremble in his voice as he got things underway.

Adam laid out the order of events, which would be the announcement of the court, followed by a few words from the varsity football team captain. After that, classes would perform their skits. Then the games would begin, and students from each class would cheer on their teams from the stands. The assembly would end with Anna's favorite part—the yell fest. Mrs. Hennings would use a decibel meter to measure which class yelled the loudest. Honestly, for whatever reason, the yell fest was everyone's favorite part of the homecoming assembly. There was a technique to this, believe it or not, it wasn't just haphazard yelling, and the freshmen never knew how to execute it. The seniors always nailed it. This would be Anna's fourth and final yell fest.

Adam began by announcing the freshman court. A boy Anna didn't recognize and the nervous girl from earlier walked out to the middle of the gym from their separate sides. They locked arms uncertainly and continued to their chairs, set up on a small stage at the far end of the gym. The poor kid hadn't known to give her a rose. Oh well, their class cheered wildly anyway, and Anna was glad to see the girl smiling happily. Adam announced the sophomores, the juniors, and then the seniors.

Julie and David Harris were the first seniors to walk out. Much to Anna's delight, she saw that she and Alex were both next. He looked great in a crisp white dress shirt, a red tie, and black dress slacks, and he beat Anna to the center by a few seconds—getting down on one knee and offering her the red rose with a tight smile that didn't quite meet his eyes.

He was putting on a show.

Deciding to play along, she laughed as she accepted it from him before they, too, locked arms and continued up the center of the court to their places. Anna listened to the cheers and looked up at the sports deck to see Olivia waving and smiling happily.

Once all the names had been called and everyone on the court had taken their seats, the principal handed Adam a white envelope. The gym grew quiet as he tore it open.

His speech was smooth, with no lingering trace of nerves. "Ladies and gentlemen," he began in an exaggerated announcer voice, "I would like to introduce you to this year's king and queen."

He paused for effect, and Anna felt her heart jump up into her throat. She could feel the tension radiating off of Alex too.

". . . David Harris and . . . Anna Davis!"

The student body erupted in cheers and applause, and Anna could feel her heart beating all the way up in her cheeks as she stood and put a hand over her mouth in a reflexive gesture of surprised excitement. She saw, with some humor, that David was also standing, but with his arms outstretched above his head in triumph.

"Come thither, your royal highnesses, and receive your crowns," Adam beckoned them over with one hand.

David, chest puffed out in comical exaggeration, strutted over. Anna hoped her walk looked slightly more humble. Adam crowned David first, before awkwardly attempting to place the other crown on her head. It was too big and kept slipping down over her eyes. She tried for a few moments to center it before giving up with a shrug and a laugh. Her class laughed along with her and cheered as she and David walked their victory lap, waving to each class of students. Anna, who kept one hand on her crown to keep it on top of her head, smiled so widely that her face ached. It didn't matter. She was loving every minute of this. Maybe the spotlight wasn't so bad after all.

Who would have thought *she* would be voted homecoming queen? She wasn't the prettiest or most popular girl in her class. Not by far. In fact, sometimes Anna didn't even feel like she was on the same wavelength as the other kids in school. They were carefree, fun-loving party animals where Anna was an old soul, according to her Aunt Heidi. Anna had always wondered if that was code for *boring*.

As they passed the others on the court, Anna stole a quick glance at Alex. He was standing up with the others, but he wasn't clapping, and he wasn't smiling. Their eyes met briefly before he looked away. With some effort, Anna continued to smile, but she felt some of her joy evaporate.

The rest of the assembly went by in a flash. Jess, Emily, and the boys won the leap frog relay by a mile. The skits were stupid but fun. The seniors, of course, won the yell fest, but it was the junior class who won the assembly games overall. It all ended fifteen minutes early, which was nice because it gave students an extended lunch. The seniors ate up on the sports deck, and Anna looked for Alex, but he wasn't there. He'd bolted from the gym after the assembly before she'd been able to break away from David, but she was eager to talk to him.

She didn't get the chance until the end of the day when she spotted him under the canopy on her way out of school. Leaning up against one pillar, he was obviously waiting for her. As she walked towards him, he watched her, his expression inscrutable.

"Hey," she said as she drew near. From the look on his face, something was very wrong.

He took a deep breath and looked away. "Hey."

A short, uncomfortable silence ensued.

"Um," Anna began, unsure of what to say. "I'm sorry about yesterday. Are you still mad at me?"

He sighed. "No, I'm not mad at you." He sounded tired. "Look, congratulations on being queen, or whatever, but I gotta go. I'll see you at the parade." He pushed off of the pillar and turned to go.

"Wait," Anna said, grabbing his arm, bewildered. "What's the ma—"

He shook her off. "Just leave me alone, alright?" he snapped. "I'll—" He ran an agitated hand through his hair. "I'll see you later."

Anna watched him walk away and out to the parking lot. Although the sting of tears threatened, she blinked them back, watching his retreating form as she leaned back against the pillar. It was warm, she noted. Probably from the sunshine, and not from Alex's residual body heat. She tried to soak in the warmth as she waited for Jess.

"What an asshole!" Jess exclaimed in the car, on the way to grab a quick snack for the two of them. They had about a half hour before Anna would have to change back into her dress for the parade. She looked in her mirror and changed lanes to pass the slow, rusted out truck in front of them. "I can't even believe him. We all watched him pout like a baby when he lost to David. He just stood there. I was almost embarrassed for him. Seriously, people are talking about it."

Anna had to admit, that was a little gratifying, at least. Out loud she said, "He was just disappointed."

Jess kept her eyes on the road, but she pursed her lips and gave a small shake of her head. "You can't be serious. Anna, why are you always defending him or giving him a pass? He doesn't deserve it. I don't know what's wrong with him, but I swear, you've got blinders on. If I hear you defend him again, I might just throw up."

Anna looked at Jess's profile and scoffed. "Come on."

"I can't! Why did you apologize today? What are you sorry for? He's the one who lied. He's the one who went off with Blythe and her boobs. You did nothing wrong."

Anna chuckled. "Blythe and her boobs? Seriously?"

Jess grinned, but Anna could hear the frustration in her voice. "I just wish you could stick up for yourself."

"I know how to do that. I was just trying to smooth things over."

"Lately, that's all you do with him."

Anna sighed and looked quietly out the window. Jess was right. "I know. I just don't know what to do anymore."

Jess raised her eyebrows. "Are you asking for my advice?"

Anna laughed in spite of herself. "No. Not yet."

"Okay, then. You just let me know when you *are* ready."

"I will."

Chapter 7

What a day it had been! Olivia was still smiling as she filed the last bit of paperwork off her desk. It was one of those days where she felt like she'd made a difference. Sadly, not every day was like that. Today, she'd gotten a young and dangerously thin girl some help for an eating disorder. The sophomore had finally confided in Olivia after having met with her in her office for several days running. Olivia had conferenced with the girl's parents and recommended some professionals, so the ball was now rolling and help was on the way. It was heartbreaking and exhilarating at the same time.

She'd also met with a certain young man whose parents were going through a divorce. He'd allowed himself to cry for the very first time over it in the privacy of her office. She felt he was now on the path to healing, though it wouldn't be easy. He'd asked if he could see her a few more times. Another student, a senior, had spoken with an air force recruiter, a decision she had been vacillating back and forth on since the previous year.

Olivia loved her job. She loved her students, and she loved helping them. But the brightest spot of her day had been watching Anna be crowned homecoming queen. Olivia knew it wasn't all that big a deal when placed in the greater context of life, but she had laughed to the point of tears as she watched Anna walk the lap around the gym with her big, beautiful smile and oversized crown. Olivia had a huge soft spot in her heart for her neighbor. She was one of a kind.

Knowing that Anna spent a lot of time alone at home, Olivia tried to keep a close eye on her. As a result, Anna virtually lived at Olivia's house when she wasn't in the middle of her busy cross country season. Months ago, Olivia had asked her other neighbor, Harry Niemi, an old Finnish Yooper who didn't seem to own anything that wasn't flannel, if he would mind helping her make a path between her house and Anna's. They lived out in the country, and the lots were large. She wanted Anna to feel that she was close by. After a few hours, Harry and his chainsaw had made a nice, wide path from Olivia's property line to Anna's, and it had only taken a few weeks for the path to look like it had been there forever.

Olivia checked the clock and saw it was time to pick up Nora from daycare. She powered down her computer, gathered her things, and closed the door behind her.

Regrettably—maybe even tragically—Olivia wouldn't have much time with Nora today. By the time she'd picked her up from daycare and gotten home, there'd only been fifteen minutes for her to spend with her daughter before the babysitter arrived. Not nearly enough time, and Olivia felt horribly guilty.

But it's not like this happened all the time, Olivia reminded herself. Today was special. It was homecoming, and the school liked to have one of their guidance counselors in attendance at homecoming. It was Olivia's turn this year, which in some ways worked out well since she would have come to support Anna anyway.

The downside was that she couldn't have Nora with her, and since Anna was her usual babysitter, Olivia had to scramble to find someone else, although *scramble* wasn't exactly accurate. One perk of her job was that she knew many, many responsible would-be babysitters, and she'd found someone for tonight without too much trouble—a junior girl who helped in the office sixth period. Luckily for Olivia, Meredith wasn't particularly keen on going to homecoming anyway since she'd just broken up with her boyfriend. She was no Anna, but she'd still be good with Nora.

Olivia was just reviewing the instructions with Meredith when her phone rang. Apologizing, she fished it out of her purse and nearly dropped it when she saw who it was. *Sean.* Several days had gone by since she'd seen him in the cemetery. That had been on Sunday, and it was now Friday. She'd wondered all week if he might call, maybe even hoped, if she was being honest.

Something had seemed to shiver awake between them that day when he'd held her. Once she'd allowed herself to relax, she recognized how perfectly she fit against him, even with a baby on her hip. And right then, with her head tucked against the solid warmth of him, she'd become aware of Sean in a whole new way. She wondered if he had felt it too. She kept having to remind herself that he was a liar and a traitor. Still, she felt a tightening in her chest whenever she thought about him. At the moment, that tightening was accompanied by the pounding of her heart as she reluctantly silenced her phone and dropped it back in her bag.

Meredith was a quick study and had no questions, so Olivia gave the baby one last hug before handing her off to the sitter, along with a bottle to keep Nora distracted while she left. She absolutely hated leaving her baby, especially after not seeing her all day, so as she pulled out of the driveway, Olivia tried to distract herself by singing along with a song on the radio. She must have been gifted as a multi-tasker, because she could harmonize with George Strait, worry about Nora, wonder about Sean, and drive her car—all at the same time.

She hadn't been in the car long when her phone rang again. Even before she glanced at the screen, she knew who it would be. Sighing, Olivia turned down the radio. She had to answer. She knew Sean well enough to know he was persistent in all things. It had taken him months to give up calling after Nate's death. She hadn't blocked his phone number, but she refused to answer every time he reached out. Once, he'd even come to the house, but she had pretended not to be home. After that, he gave up. Now, he was trying again, and whether or not she wanted to admit it, she thought she might be ready.

"Hi, Sean."

"Livvy . . . hey." His deep baritone voice greeted her, tinged with a touch of surprise. He must not have expected her to answer. There was a long pause. Olivia quickly glanced at her phone to make sure they hadn't been disconnected. They hadn't. She put the phone back to her ear and spoke at the same time he did.

"Sorry," she said. "What was that?"

"Oh, well, I just . . . I was hoping we might talk. I know, at the beginning, you weren't ready, but maybe now . . ."

Olivia let go of the breath she'd been holding. "Listen Sean, I'm just not sure what more there is to say. I think—"

"But that's just it. There's so much left to say, Livvy. I've needed to explain some things for a long time, and I thought that, you know, after the cemetery last week, that maybe you'd be open to it."

"Sean, I—"

"Please."

Olivia wasn't sure what it was exactly. The simple *please*, the faintly pleading quality of his voice, a desire on her part to reconcile this piece of her past, or maybe even a slight curiosity to understand whatever had happened between them on Sunday. Whatever the reason, she agreed.

"When?" he asked.

Better get it over with, she thought.

"This weekend, if you're around. Even tonight could work. I'm chaperoning homecoming at the school, but during the game, I'll mostly just be a spectator. You could meet me there. By the fence in front of the bleachers."

She could hear him shuffling some things around in the background before he answered. "Yeah, that'll work, I think. Those games start at seven, right?

"They do."

"Okay. I'll get there as soon as I can after practice. I'll look for you, probably around seven-thirty. And Olivia?"

"Yeah?"

"Thank you."

"Okay. Bye, Sean." Olivia dropped the phone in her lap and frowned at the clock on the dashboard. The game was hours away, and the anticipation was going to make the time between now and then seem twice as long. Ugh, she'd never been good at handling nervous energy. Let's hope she didn't allow herself to stay too tightly wound. She had hundreds of teenagers to monitor for the next several hours, which wasn't an easy task at the best of times.

Driving on the rest of the way to the high school, Olivia let her thoughts drift. She knew she'd turned a corner the last few days. That perpetual heaviness in her chest had lightened, and she finally felt like she could breathe. Even the fiasco with her in-laws at the cemetery had done more to help than harm, oddly enough. Miraculously, she was making peace with the past. A year ago, or even six months ago, she wouldn't have believed it was possible. She was moving forward. Writing that new chapter.

This healing had actually been going on for a long time, she realized with some surprise. She was only just noticing it now, but it had been happening so gradually, so steadily, that it had crept up on her. When she thought about it, she knew she hadn't been truly lonely for several months now.

It was no accident that she'd moved in right next door to the Davises. It was providence. Olivia remembered the day Anna had come by to welcome her to the neighborhood. What kind of teenager baked cookies and brought meals for a new neighbor? But there Anna had stood on her porch, a tray of chocolate chip cookies in hand and a box full of casserole dishes at her feet.

Of course, they'd been acquainted through Olivia's work at the school, but it took no time at all for that acquaintance to grow into a solid friendship. Right away, each one found something special in the other—a missing piece, really—and Olivia knew that didn't come around every day. She had needed Anna just as much as Anna needed her, and after just a few short months, Olivia felt closer to her young neighbor than she did to anyone else in the world.

And then there was Nora. Although the conversations were completely one-sided for the time being, they were in this life together for the long haul. The baby snuggles went a long way to filling Olivia's cup to overflowing. Added to all that, she'd been getting to know Erin Hennings, the high school principal, a little better. Erin was single, and they had a lot of fun together. Although Erin was high-strung, and her larger-than-life personality could be overwhelming, Olivia enjoyed their growing friendship and trusted her as a confidant.

As if on cue, Erin called. "Olivia, are you here?"

"Not yet. I'm only about five minutes away, though."

"Oh good! I might need you to drive one convertible. I'm looking at old Al Randell, and I'm not real sure he should drive anyone anywhere. Ever. The poor guy is practically blind!"

"Didn't he donate his Camaro for today?"

"Yes," she stretched the one-word answer out as if to say, "What's your point?"

"Erin, he's going to want to drive his own car. What am I supposed to do, fight his keys away from him?"

"No, no. Of course not. I'll do that. I just need you to drive his car."

Olivia laughed. "Well, do me a favor and wait for me. I want to see you try to pry poor Mr. Randell's keys out of his hands. It's not going to work. That guy is almost as stubborn as you are. Just ask the booster club. They love his money, but not so much the man."

"*Almost* is the key word here. And I won't have to force anything. You'll see. I'm a master at this stuff. That's why I'm such an amazing principal. I know every trick in the book. Hell, I could've written the damn book."

"Oh, to have your hubris." Olivia laughed. "I'll be there in a few."

It took Olivia several minutes to park and find Erin in the throng of students preparing to march in the parade. Kids and adults crowded the parking lot, and they all wore smiles and chatted noisily. Olivia noticed three of the four floats were all ready to go and in the lineup.

It looked like just the senior float was missing. Leave it to the seniors to be last minute. They'd always been a bit disorganized as a class. Their class president, Adam, was a pretty laid back kid, so it made sense.

The cars for the homecoming court were all lined up and ready too. The first car was Al Randell's, and he stood proudly beside it, talking to Erin as he stroked the hood. He was not holding his keys. Erin had them in hand.

Olivia grinned. She would never underestimate her friend again. Not only had she gotten Mr. Randell to give up his keys, he looked downright happy about it. Erin spotted Olivia and waved, pointing her out to Mr. Randell, who squinted at her and then, rather oddly, turned pink up to the tips of his ears. But he smiled widely at her as she approached.

"Olivia, you remember Al, don't you?"

"Of course. Mr. Randell, how are you today?"

"Oh, it's a good day, young lady. A good day." He rubbed his hands together vigorously.

Erin looked back and forth between Mr. Randell and Olivia. "Olivia, I was just telling Al how excited you are to drive his amazing car."

"Oh, yes. Thank—"

"You know," he interrupted, "I've got more where this came from. Wait till you see my BMW. Didn't want these hooligans scratching that one up though. I keep her tucked away pretty tight."

"Probably smart," Olivia responded.

"Yep. And I hear you're a single gal. That's very interesting. Very interesting. You know, I'm a single guy."

"Er, well . . . that *is* interesting," Olivia replied helplessly, darting a glance at Erin, who was struggling to hold back her laughter.

"I've been a bit lonely, truth be told," he went on as he looked her up and down, in an obvious, squinty-eyed perusal. "Forgot you're a red head. I guess that's all right."

Erin choked on a laugh. Olivia felt a blush creeping into her cheeks.

"Um, okay." What was happening?

Thankfully, a booster approached Mr. Randell right then, and while he was distracted, Olivia turned on Erin. "What on earth did you tell him, Erin? Is he hitting on me?" Olivia asked in a low whisper-yell.

Erin smiled widely. "I just told him you're hard up for male companionship and that it'd float your boat to drive a hot car with a hot stud next to you in the passenger side."

"What?!"

"Well, okay, maybe not the stud part. Look, I just told him you were single and looking for some fun today. I can't help that he misunderstood my meaning," Erin said innocently. But her smile gave her away.

"Ugh! Erin!"

She handed Olivia the keys, rolling her eyes. "Come on. Hop in. Get acquainted."

Olivia shook her head incredulously and opened her mouth to complain.

"With the car, not the man. C'mon, Olivia. He's a harmless old guy. Relax. Have some fun." Erin glanced down at her watch. "Listen, I gotta run. You okay here?"

Olivia sighed. "I'll be just great. Thanks."

Erin hugged her quickly. "You're the best."

Olivia watched her run off into the crowd, shaking her head in amazement. Erin was a force of nature.

"You ready, missy?" Mr. Randell asked her from the other side of the car.

"I'm ready, sir."

He joined her inside and buckled up. "Sorry about that just now. That Erin Hennings thinks I'm an old fool. All she had to do was tell me she didn't want me driving. Hear that enough from my own kids, that's for sure."

"You mean—?" Olivia asked in dawning realization.

"Oh, I knew what she was up to. I'm young at heart, but not *that* young. Jeepers. A fiery red head five decades younger than me? I guess I'm flattered." He chuckled.

Olivia laughed. "She thinks she's so smart."

"It'll be our little secret. Now, where are these kids we're driving? Damn hooligans! Don't kids know how to tell time anymore? They better not scuff up my seats."

Chapter 8

Anna quietly surveyed the senior float. It was the last one that remained in the bus garage, and only a few small groups of seniors remained along with it, frantically folding, tying, affixing, and spraying the napkins. It would shock a person unfamiliar with float-building to see just how many napkins it took to decorate a float—probably thousands. They had to be folded and secured a certain way before they were tied on to the float's skeleton and spray-painted the right color.

The senior float's "sand" base was a little sparse, and that was being kind. Large patches of chicken wire were exposed all over the place, and it was easily the "fugliest" float Anna had ever seen in four years of float building. Still, Adam was running around frantically, shouting instructions at the small groups as they worked.

"We've got ten minutes, people. Ten!" he shouted, glancing at his watch. His face brightened when he spotted her from across the bus garage. "Anna Bear!" Anna had known Adam since before she could walk. Their moms had been friends, and they'd spent a lot of time together as babies and toddlers. Anna had the pictures to prove it. He'd been calling her Anna Bear for as long as she could remember. Unfortunately, it had caught on with a few classmates over the years, and now Anna was "Anna Bear" even to people she didn't really know.

"I mean, Your Majesty," he corrected with a grin. He hurried over to her and gave her a quick hug. "This is such a mess," he said in a low, anxious voice. "We don't have enough people to pull this float off."

"I've never seen you quite this . . . excitable."

"Yeah, well, I've never had to build and launch a float almost single handedly. And look at it? Why did I bother? Our class is made up of a bunch of slackers."

Anna winced. "Sorry, Adam." She hadn't helped as much this year as she should have. "Where's everybody else?"

"Probably sleeping off Ben's party last night." Adam narrowed his eyes.

"There was a party? On a Thursday?" The senior class had a reputation for being a little wild, but a party on a Thursday was impressive, even for them. Although their class had its share of lushes, Adam wasn't one of them. In fact, Anna felt lucky that there was a pretty large group of them who didn't drink. It made it easier to pass on the alcohol when a bunch of them did. She peered at Adam closely, noticing the dark circles under his eyes. "Did you go?"

"Yeah. Everybody was there." He coughed into his fist. "Well, almost everybody," he amended. "Where were you?"

"Home," she said simply. Why hadn't she even heard a whisper about this party today at school?

He put down his napkin and twisty tie. "Anna," he began slowly. "Alex was there."

They strolled around the front of the float, and Anna passed her hand over the fluffy napkins as she moved. "Was he?" she asked, keeping her voice as nonchalant as possible.

"Yeah, he was." He cleared his throat.

Since it was highly unusual for Adam to be this serious for this long about anything, Anna braced herself for some bad news.

"He got there kinda late and, uh . . . he came with someone."

She stopped and looked up at him. His cheeks had turned bright pink, and she could see that this was awkward for him. "Blythe?"

Knitting his brows together, he answered, "I think that's her name. She's a freshman. Tall, brownish hair . . ."

"And beautiful?"

He squirmed uncomfortably. "Well, maybe, if you like that sort of girl. Which I don't," he was quick to add. "She wears enough makeup to spackle an entire wall."

Anna pulled out her phone from the small clutch she was carrying. She found the picture she'd saved of Blythe and Alex just to torture herself. "This girl?" she asked.

He peered over her shoulder at her phone. "Yep, that's her."

Anna shook her head. "What is he doing?" she asked to nobody in particular, but Adam answered anyway.

"I don't know. Sorry, Anna. I just . . . I thought you should know. But listen, Alex is a tool. I've always thought that. You'll be better off without him."

Without Alex? Who said anything about her being without Alex? Anna couldn't even picture it. He'd been a major part of her life for so long. She organized her days, as much as she was able, around seeing him. Registering that Adam looked worried, she rushed to reassure him.

"It's okay, Adam. It's fine. Thanks for telling me," her voice didn't sound nearly as strong as she had hoped it would, and Adam seemed to pick up on the slight tremble. He pulled her into a sturdy hug. Anna hugged him back briefly before pulling away. If she allowed herself to be comforted, she was afraid she'd break down.

Even the concerned look on his face was almost enough to undo her, and she looked away as she explained, "Things with Alex have been . . . different lately. And Blythe . . ." she trailed off, not knowing how to sum her up in just a few words. She didn't want to talk about Blythe. At the same time that she wanted to pepper Adam with questions to find out exactly what he'd seen, she wasn't sure she wanted to know. At least not right now when she was supposed to be in a parade, all happy and smiling. Anna took a deep, lung-expanding breath and slowly let it out, allowing a silence to extend between them.

Adam broke it, gently. "Uh, Anna. There's more. I wasn't going to tell you this, but they seemed together, if you know what I mean."

Anna felt the blood drain out of her face. She just couldn't do this right now. Swallowing a few times before speaking, she answered simply, "Okay."

Adam went on. "They just seemed really close, you know? I mean, I looked over, and they were—"

Anna put her hand out for Adam to stop and shook her head. "Yeah, Adam, I'm getting the picture, but I just—I can't talk about this right now. Okay? I'm sorry."

He looked stricken. "Oh, shi—I shouldn't have said anything."

"No. No, I'm grateful you did. It's just . . . hard to hear, and I can't . . . I can't think about it right now. The parade is about to start." She gave him another quick hug. "It's okay, Adam." Pushing back the tears and the hurt as best she could, Anna, using her most chipper voice, said, "Well, I'd better get over to the cars."

"Yeah, okay. I'm right behind you, just as soon as I get everything ready here. Five minutes."

Students, cars, and floats packed the parking lot. The band was warming up, and a few teachers and parents scurried around trying to make some kind of order out of the chaos. Anna spotted Jess. She looked super cute in her knee-high socks with red and white stripes, red shorts, a white t-shirt, and NHS in red and white lettering painted on each cheek. Seeing Anna, she waved and started towards her.

"Anna Bear, you are rockin' that dress!" She held Anna out at arm's length as she looked her over appreciatively. "I still can't believe how awesome you look in it!"

Anna forced the corners of her mouth up, but it took some effort.

"Hey, you okay?"

"Did you know there was a party last night?"

Jess nodded. "I heard about it today. And I could smell the hangovers all around me. I feel like half our class went home to nap. Makes me glad I don't drink."

Anna agreed. Hangovers didn't look worth it to her either.

"Why?"

"I'll tell you later. I just have to find the car I'm riding in. Do you know which one it is?"

Jess grinned. "It won't be too hard to find. Just look for a red Corvette."

"I get to ride in a Corvette?" Anna couldn't believe her luck. At least she'd be fancy and flashy on the outside, even if she was dull and depressed on the inside.

In the end, it *was* hard to find because a throng of admiring teenage boys surrounded it. Working her way through them, Anna could see David already seated in the back. Someone had spread a red blanket down to protect the leather, since the two of them would sit up on the back of the car with their feet down on the seats.

"There she is!" David shouted. "My queen!" He reached for Anna's hand, and with exaggerated gallantry, he helped her in. David was always the life of the party, usually in a good way these days. Anna thought he might be trying to patch up his reputation. In past years, he had been a little out of control—a little too loud, a little too drunk, and a little too combative at parties. But so far this year, he seemed to have straightened out. Regardless, for as long as she'd known him, he'd been sweet to her, and Anna had always liked him immensely, even if he rubbed Alex the wrong way. After she settled in next to him, he gave her a one-armed, platonic hug.

"One thing's for sure. We are riding in style to-day." He gave a loud whoop, which was echoed by the rest of the surrounding boys.

Anna laughed, feeling her mood improve a little. "Boys and their cars," she said with a small shake of her head.

They had about a fifteen-minute wait before the parade got underway. Anna talked to David the entire time, so she missed seeing Alex and the other seniors pile into the two cars directly in front of them in line.

Alex and Julie were sitting in the white mustang ahead of them. He sat with his back turned to her, so Anna couldn't get his attention. She felt the now all-too-familiar sinking feeling take hold, but as she closed her eyes and said a little prayer for strength to get through the next hour, the feeling subsided and was replaced with a different feeling, one of resignation that was new to her.

Deciding to analyze it all later, she smiled at Mr. Benninger, who had turned to ask if they were ready to go. Benny, as the student body called him affectionately, was a tenth-grade biology teacher and the high school hockey coach.

"Let's do this thing!" David said enthusiastically.

"Right on, Dave-o," Benny said with a salute. He was such a dork. Anna loved him.

"So, David," she said with mock seriousness. "Do you know how to do the beauty queen wave?"

He looked at her as if she'd grown horns. "Uh . . . that would be a *no*."

"Okay," Anna instructed. "You can either screw the lightbulb, like this." She demonstrated, twisting only her wrist. "Or, you can wash the window, like this." She showed him, making sweeping motions from her elbow. His overly dramatic attempts at both waves left the two of them in stitches, and as Anna recovered, she saw Alex turned around in the car ahead, watching her with an inscrutable expression. Anna gave a tentative wave, but he simply stared at her for a second longer before turning back around.

"What's with him lately?" David asked, turning serious.

"I don't really know," Anna answered honestly. "You were at the party last night, right?"

David squirmed, and he cleared his throat. "Uh, yeah."

"So then you know we aren't doing great right now," she prompted.

"I guessed as much. Sorry, Anna. He's a lucky guy, but he's too stupid to realize it. You deserve better than that. "You're money, and we all know it." Anna watched the mischievous sparkle re-enter his eyes as he added, "You deserve a fly guy like me." He bumped her playfully with his shoulder.

"You're right." She giggled. "You are just what I need. A total player who's the life of every party. I don't think I could keep up."

They both knew they'd never date. How? She wasn't sure. Sometimes you just know things like that. He was a safe flirtation, and vice versa. And while she'd never heard anyone called "money" before, she knew it was a compliment, and it soothed her battered heart.

"Well," he said as he put his arm around her, serious once more. "I've got your back today. You just stick with me."

"Thanks," Anna said gratefully, leaning into him and giving him a little bump in return. "I will."

The parade went from four o'clock to quarter after five, and by the time it was over, Anna's face hurt from smiling, and her arm was sore from waving and holding it up for so long. As they returned to the school parking lot, she breathed a sigh of relief.

It had been fun waving and throwing candy to the little kids. But maybe the best part had been seeing her dad and Mitch, along with someone else she didn't recognize, sitting in chairs in front of the historic downtown movie theater, which was about halfway through the parade route.

Mitch wore a Nicolet State hoodie up over his head, but a few blond locks were visible along the edges. He was determined to have "hockey hair" despite Anna's advice that he should keep it short. Oh, well. He'd waved and yelled and whistled obnoxiously, as every good brother should, but it was her dad's reaction that Anna was still thinking about. As she passed by, he watched her with that same intent expression he'd worn last night at dinner. After years of feeling more or less invisible to him, Anna didn't quite know how to react to this shift. She'd always been able to think about their relationship dispassionately because it had been dysfunctional for as long as she could remember. Were there times she wanted it to be different? Of course. Had she cried tears over her dad's lack of interest in her? Most definitely, at least when she was younger. Less so now.

But today, he had looked so . . . proud, and yet so devastated as she waved and rode by. And seeing his face like that, Anna had to fight the urge to climb out of the car and run to him. But then what would she have done once she reached him? Hugged him? She couldn't remember the last time they'd hugged. Maybe his birthday. What a realization. His birthday had been months ago. Anna didn't know what to make of the change in her father, so she pushed it out of her mind. She was good at that.

Another puzzle was the guy with Mitch. She'd never seen him before. Whoever he was, Anna knew one thing for certain—she'd never seen a more gorgeous male. Aunt Heidi would have called him a Baldwin, and Anna still felt a little zip of electricity run through her now, just at the mere thought of him. Immediately, she felt sheepish. It had been a while since she'd noticed another boy in this way, and she knew it must be wrong. As far as she knew, she was still with Alex, although by the sounds of it, that may not be the case for much longer. If he was cheating on her, that was it. She'd have to break things off. Maybe.

Anna tried to get close to Alex once the car had parked, but too many people stopped her for hugs or congratulations that by the time she'd broken free, he was gone. This freeze-out by him was so baffling, and she felt both bewildered and betrayed. The Alex she knew, or thought she knew, wasn't this cold. She felt like he was being deliberately cruel. Was he trying to make her hate him? Was this his way of breaking things off?

The game wouldn't start for a few hours, so Jess dropped Anna off at her house and went home herself to change. They all knew the warm temperature wouldn't hold once the sun went down. Anna would have to wear her dress until halftime when the court would be presented on the field. After that, it would be the leggings, Birkenstocks, and cross country sweatshirt she was going to pack into a small drawstring backpack.

After the game, the school would host a homecoming dance, which was the only informal dance of the year. The rest were formal. While lots of people thought informal dances were stupid, Anna preferred them. She was more of a jeans and t-shirt kind of girl than a fancy dress girl by far.

Letting herself into the house with her key, she could see her dad hadn't made it home yet. Maybe he was out grabbing some food for them, Anna thought hopefully. And maybe he'd come to the game tonight to see her announced. The thought made her smile.

Looking around the quiet, dark kitchen, she realized she knew where everything was in every single drawer and cupboard. She knew because she was the one who put stuff away and kept things organized. She kept a running grocery list and monitored perishable expiration dates. How many teenage girls could say that?

That reminded her of one of her more recent fights with Alex. He'd basically told her she was no fun, and then he accused her of being more like a forty-year-old woman—paying bills, buying groceries, and getting oil changes instead of going to parties and keeping up her Snap streaks. Anna flushed at the memory. Alex was right. But what choice did she have? Snap streaks were fun, but they didn't fill the pantry or lubricate the engine.

Anna knew it disgusted Olivia that her father allowed her to take on so much responsibility. But Anna was eighteen now and used to it. And honestly, her peers weren't too far behind her. They'd be figuring out the real world for themselves soon enough. She was just way ahead of the curve, and she took a lot of pride in her ability to make meals and more or less run the household. But with Mitch gone now, there was a lot less to do.

She set her house key down on the countertop and noticed a note had fallen to the floor. She picked it up and read it.

Anna,

I had to leave for Chicago after all. I'm driving this time, and I don't think I'll be back until next Wednesday. Call if you need me.

Dad

P.S. Congratulations on homecoming. You made me proud.

Conflicting emotions swept over Anna. He was gone. Again. She poked her head out the door and into the garage. Sure enough, there her car sat—languishing in disrepair. She swallowed down the disappointment of knowing she'd have to keep begging rides off people.

But . . . he was proud of her. Her dad was proud of her. Even though she had already assumed he was, it was still so nice to read the words. She didn't think he'd ever expressed that before now, and she wished he hadn't left again so she could hear it directly from his mouth.

Why had he left? It almost seemed like he'd run away. That's how it felt. Anna had been looking forward to having him at home for a stretch. She always preferred him at least in the house, even if he shut himself away in his office most of the time. She didn't like being alone. Plus, she really wanted to find out if she had imagined what happened at the parade. That look. Now she'd have to wait. She was tired of waiting.

Actually, she was just plain tired. Anna decided to lie down for a few minutes on the couch in the living room. Jess was going to pick her up again, but not for another forty-five minutes. She set her phone alarm so she wouldn't rest too long and allowed herself to drift in and out of blissful sleep as the sun slanted through the front window, warming her body with stripes of heat.

After what could only have been a few minutes, Anna awoke to the ding of a message from Jess, who had bad news. Her father, deciding that she hadn't practiced or exercised enough that week, was making her squeeze in a quick run and a few drills before the game. He'd also taken her car keys for the night to punish her for slacking off. Luckily, Jess's mom was more reasonable and had promised her a ride in to the game once she finished her workout.

Anna wished Jess's dad would go a little easier on her friend. His expectations were way too high. That Jess had made it almost all the way through high school without cracking under the pressure was impressive.

Jess thought she'd be able to get to the game by halftime, but she couldn't be sure. Either way, Anna would have to find another ride. This was just great. Who was going to drive her into town? Anna was pretty sure Olivia had stayed at the school, so she was out. She didn't want to annoy Alex any further, but she didn't know who else to call.

She texted him. *I don't have a ride. Long story. Can you come and pick me up? Please? I don't know how else I'll get in.*

Waiting for his response with a pounding heart, Anna wondered how she could be this nervous to send Alex a message. She was getting to be more pathetic than even she herself could stand. It took a few minutes for the phone to ping back his message, and what she read sent a flash of heat through her body.

Can't.

That was it? That was all he could bother to write to her? What a jerk! She was flying through the grieving process at lightning speed, she thought to herself sardonically. Wasn't it first denial, then sadness, then anger? Something like that. Well, now she was angry.

Earlier that day, she and Jess joked that they'd be each other's date to the dance. If she was honest, Anna already felt embarrassed about that. She didn't have an actual date for her own homecoming. But it had been a minor consolation that she'd at least arrive with someone else and not alone, and now . . . now she didn't even know if she could get there. It wasn't like she could walk into town from way out here where she lived. She glanced at her watch. She'd try Olivia anyway, just in case.

Getting Olivia's voicemail, Anna disconnected without leaving a message. Who else could she call?

Mitch!

She'd forgotten about Mitch. He answered on the fifth ring. "Hey," he answered groggily.

"Are you sleeping?"

"Well, not anymore."

Strange. Mitch was not a napper. "Sorry. Listen, Dad left, and—"

"Where'd he go?" He was alert now.

"Chicago. He's driving."

"What? That's weird."

"I know."

"He told me he'd be home for a while. He was gonna come to the scrimmage this weekend." Mitch sighed loudly. "But, hey. Why am I even surprised? You know Dad."

"Yeah."

They were both quiet for a moment. They didn't need words to share their disappointment with one another. On this, at least, they were on the same wavelength.

"Anyway," Anna went on, "I need a favor. My car's still out of commission, and I have to get to the game tonight."

Anna could hear him fumbling around on his end of the line. "When?"

"Um, like right now," she said sheepishly.

Mitch swore.

"I'm sorry, I'm sorry. I can be a little late. If you leave in ten minutes . . ." Anna quickly calculated in her head, "I'd be there in about half an hour, which gives me plenty of time before the half-time show."

Mitch sighed and reluctantly agreed. "But only because it's homecoming, and you're gonna have to get yourself a ride home. I have plans tonight. I'm meeting up with some ladies at a party."

Anna rolled her eyes. He'd said *ladies*, plural. "That's fine. I'm sure I can get a ride from someone afterward. Thanks, Mitch."

"Yep," he answered before disconnecting.

Anna quickly packed her bag. She put the dress back on, reapplied some blush, and brushed her hair. It took her all of five minutes. She grabbed a slice of leftover pizza from the fridge and stood, bag slung over her right shoulder, in front of the large bay window in the living room, so she'd see when Mitch arrived. What should have been a five-minute wait turned into a fifteen-minute wait, and Anna had to fight her growing annoyance. He was doing her a favor, she reminded herself.

When he finally pulled into the driveway, she grabbed her house key, locked up, and ran, as much as her dress would allow, out to the passenger side door, only to find that somebody was already sitting there—the hot guy from the parade.

Her heart skipped a beat as he grinned at her through the window, and she flashed him a quick smile in return before getting into the back and sliding to the middle seat of Mitch's little Camry. It was a bone of contention between them that he was stuck driving a compact sedan while she had a Ford Escape to ride around in. Dad had bought Mitch's car first, used of course, but he'd decided Anna needed something a little larger for safety. Some might say their father had spoiled them by giving them their own cars at sixteen, but it had been out of necessity since they were responsible for getting themselves everywhere they needed to go.

"Thanks for picking me up, even if you are insanely late," Anna said, slightly breathless.

Mitch shook his head. "You're such a pain," he said as he backed out of the driveway, the gravel crunching under the car's tires.

"What do you mean? I told you I needed to be there for halftime. I'm going to miss it at this rate."

"Stop worrying. I said I'd get you there, and I will. You're lucky I came all the way out here at all."

Anna bit down on her lip to keep from snapping at him. When Mitch was cranky like this, it was best not to poke the bear.

In the next second, Mitch's friend turned almost fully around and introduced himself. "I'm Landon LaFleur," he said, giving her his right hand to shake, though at a somewhat awkward angle. Anna took it, noting that it was warm and strong. "Mitch's roommate," he added.

"I'm Anna," she returned smoothly, though she was not nearly as calm on the inside as she was on the outside.

"Nice to meet you," he said with a smile that caused his eyes to crinkle at the corners.

There was still enough daylight to see well, and Anna felt suddenly tongue-tied as she took in those eyes, which were a deep, striking blue and framed by impossibly long, dark lashes. His hair, nearly black, was straight and thick and slightly on the longer side, just brushing the collar of his jacket. She had the absurd impulse to run her fingers through the ends where they flipped up.

It was hard to tell sitting down, but he looked to be almost Mitch's height, although he was much more muscled than her brother. And he had a strong, squared-off jawline, high cheekbones that carried just a hint of color, and a straight, perfect nose. Her earlier assessment at the parade had been accurate. He was the hottest male she'd ever set eyes on. It was almost unfair to all the other men out there.

"Well, lady-killer. Looks like you've smitten another one," Mitch said sarcastically, breaking the prolonged silence. Looking at Anna in the rearview mirror, he added, "He's gifted like that."

"Stop," Landon said with a laugh.

Anna felt the heat creep up into her face, and it only intensified when she realized she was still holding Landon's hand and had yet to respond. His smile widened. "Nice to meet you too," she replied, quickly releasing his hand and wishing she could bash Mitch over the head with a blunt object.

Landon looked at her for another long second, and Anna forced herself to hold his gaze, even though what she really wanted was to be swallowed up by the floor of the car. Something happened in that moment, and Anna felt a tingling surge that started in her chest and spread outward through all her nerve endings. Slowly, he turned back around, but she found, like an idiot, that she couldn't stop smiling. But then, she could see from Landon's profile that he was smiling too.

The ride hadn't lasted nearly long enough, Anna decided, after Mitch and Landon had pulled away and left her near the path to the football field. She and Mitch had spoken a bit, and Mitch and Landon had talked, but she and Landon hadn't said another word to one another the entire car ride. Not because she hadn't wanted to. She wanted to know more about him . . . just not with Mitch listening in. For that brief time in the car, staring at Landon's profile, she forgot all about Alex.

As she had known she would be, Anna was a little late to the game. Okay, she was very late to the game. There were only four minutes left until halftime, and she had to carry her heeled shoes and run up the path and to the far end of the field where the homecoming court and band had gathered. Olivia was there helping to organize everyone.

"There you are, Anna! You cut this pretty close, kiddo," she said, a frazzled edge to her voice. "I was just about to have someone call you," she added, as she pointed to where she wanted her to stand, behind the band and next to David.

"Sorry about that," Anna said, still breathless.

Olivia blew her a kiss before turning to continue her coordination efforts.

Anna, knowing she'd be walking past Alex but not wanting to see him, fixed her eyes on David as she headed his way. She thought she could feel Alex's eyes on her, but she couldn't be sure. David expressed his relief that he wouldn't be walking all alone, and she apologized again for being late. "I didn't have a ride," she explained, telling him a condensed version of the story, and his eyes flashed when she got to the part where she'd reached out to Alex.

David shook his head. "You should've messaged me. I would've picked you up."

"I didn't think to. Sorry. But I'm here now, so it's all good."

Olivia worked to reshuffle them into correct order, and by the time it was all said and done, Anna and David stood at the very back of the line. As Alex and Julie moved to the spot in front of them, Alex worked hard not to make eye contact, and Anna reflected again just how bizarre this all was. She wished it wasn't happening and that things could go back to normal again, but there wasn't anything she could do. It was out of her control.

The halftime show went without a hitch, and afterwards Anna realized she truly had enjoyed it, despite the underlying negative energy between herself and Alex. Walking across the field, arm and arm with David, and hearing the cheers from the stands had distracted her from all her troubles. It helped that David was so unaffected by everything. Some people might think he had a big ego, but it wasn't that at all. His personality was simply larger-than-life, and he didn't take anything too seriously, especially himself. Anna wanted to be more like that. More carefree.

David had something funny to say at every turn, and as a result, he'd kept the whole experience light and entertaining for Anna. When it was all done, they both found places to change, and he waited for her to put her dress in Olivia's van before they headed to the student section together. After returning Olivia's keys to her, they found seats with Jess, who had barely made it in time to see the show. Adam and Emily and some of their other friends moved up to join them. Alex wasn't anywhere to be seen.

Chapter 9

Phew! They pulled it off. The halftime show had gone perfectly. Having expected to be only a chaperone tonight, it surprised Olivia when Erin asked her to help with the halftime show at the last minute. She'd been standing at the fence behind the Nicolet bench with Sarah Josten while keeping an eye out for Sean. Sarah was a new English teacher this year, but beyond welcoming her at the beginning of the school year, Olivia hadn't talked with her much. The little she discovered in the few minutes they'd stood together left Olivia wanting to know more about her.

Sarah had a slight southern accent, and Olivia had just asked her where she was from when a frantic Erin interrupted them. She told them Brian Benninger was supposed to be organizing the homecoming court across the field, but he was a no-show. Could they both fill in? The look Sarah shot her told Olivia that Sarah was about as thrilled at the idea of corralling and organizing teenagers again as she was.

But now that halftime was over, and the two of them were back in their spot along the fence, they could breathe easy. Olivia remembered they'd ended their conversation with her question about Sarah's background, but she'd gotten the sense that Sarah didn't want to talk about it. Not wanting to pry, Olivia decided not to ask any more questions of her new friend tonight. Instead, she thought she might offer some information about herself. She felt the need to unload some of the anxiety that had built up inside of her over the impending meeting with Sean, and sometimes that was the best way to break the ice with somebody new anyway.

"So, listen. I have an old friend meeting me here tonight. He's a little late," Olivia said, glancing at her watch, "but I think he's still coming. When he gets here, would you mind keeping an eye on things while we talk?" she asked.

"Of course," Sarah replied, looking at her curiously, but not asking questions. Olivia could tell she wanted to, but she got the sense that the new teacher had a certain need for privacy. She probably wanted to respect Olivia's as well.

Olivia had decided not to confide in many people the painful details of her life over the past year. Basically, there were only two people who had the inside scoop on her story: Erin and Anna. At first, Erin was only included because she was Anna's boss. She needed to know certain things. But over time, Olivia shared more and more with her, and of course, now she was a friend in the truest sense. And although some might find it strange because of their difference in age, Olivia had her young neighbor, Anna, as well. Until now, she hadn't really needed anyone else in her inner circle.

But there was something about Sarah that made Olivia want to open up to her. Maybe once she shared a bit of her life, Sarah would want to do the same. Olivia had always had such a curiosity about people and a need to connect with them on a deeper level. That was probably the reason she was drawn to guidance counseling in the first place. She hadn't experienced this feeling, this interest in getting to know someone new, in a long time, and Olivia felt relieved to have it back.

"His name is Sean. We used to be close, but I haven't spoken to him in over a year."

"Why?" Sarah asked tentatively. "What happened?

"I know you're new here, but it's a small town, so people talk. I imagine you've heard about what happened to my husband," Olivia said with a question in her voice.

"Yes. I have," Sarah admitted, shaking her head. "I'm so sorry."

"Thanks. It was a . . . difficult time," Olivia said. "But did you also know that he . . . Did you know he was unfaithful?"

Sarah looked down and shifted her feet, having the grace to look uncomfortable.

"That's okay," Olivia said quickly, not wanting to put her on the spot. "I wasn't sure if that was common knowledge around town or not. I suppose I shouldn't be surprised. I used to feel so embarrassed about it, you know? But why? Why do women who are cheated on feel embarrassed?" It was a rhetorical question, but Sarah responded anyway.

"I'm not sure. I know what you mean, though. I had that happen to me back in college, and I felt the same way. As if I was afraid to show my face around our friends."

"Yes! Exactly!" Olivia exclaimed, glad to have that never-before-mentioned feeling validated.

"Anyway, I found out about the cheating the night of Nate's accident, but I knew something was off for a long time before that. I just tried harder to be the perfect wife. I did ask Sean, the guy who's meeting me here, about it. I had a feeling something was going on, and I knew that if there was, Sean would know about it. I trusted him when he told me nothing was. It turns out there were many, *many* women. Sean lied, and I just . . . I haven't been able to forgive him."

Sarah nodded in understanding.

"And I don't know if I could trust him ever again," she added. "But he wants to talk tonight, so . . ."

"Why are you so sure Sean would have known?" Sarah asked gently.

"Well, I guess, let me back up. Nate coached college hockey, so he was away on road trips a lot with the team, and Sean was the assistant coach. And Nate's best friend too. They played together at Michigan State, and then they both ended up here as coaches. Anyway, Nate had someone at every stop. I don't know how Sean couldn't have known. Of course he knew," she said with a frown.

"I found out the night Nate died, like I said. He'd just gotten home from an away game, and he was in the shower. His phone rang, and I answered it, even though he didn't like it when I did that. That should've been enough of a clue right there that something wasn't right. Anyway, the phone rang, and it was some woman. He'd stood her up that visit, and she was mad. I don't know why, maybe just to be cruel, but she told me everything. They'd been, you know, *together* for months, I guess."

"Hmm. And you said there were others?"

Olivia nodded.

"How do you know?"

Olivia sighed. "See, even now I feel embarrassed."

Sarah put her hands up. "Oh, please. You don't have to tell me. I'm sorry to be pokin' around in your personal business."

Olivia shook her head. "You're not poking at all. I'm the one who brought it up. After Nate's accident, everything was such a mess. *I* was such a mess. I wasn't feeling the greatest, and I was three months pregnant with my daughter, Nora. It wasn't an easy pregnancy. So, I shut myself away for a while. During that time, I figured out Nate's phone password, and I went through all his contacts and messages. I know that makes me sound like a lunatic. I guess I was a little crazy. I was just so sad, and I was so *angry*. I called the numbers of the female names I didn't recognize. I guess I just needed to know. I needed to know just how big a fool I'd been."

Sarah nodded. "I understand. But you're not a fool."

Olivia sighed. "So that's it. That's my sad, little story."

Sarah looked thoughtful. "Are you still sad?"

Olivia considered the question for a second before answering. "Yes," she said slowly, "but not like before. Something changed for me, just recently, in fact, and I feel . . . different. Better."

"Good for you," Sarah said softly. Olivia didn't miss the wistful look in her brown eyes, but she didn't feel now was the right time to dig into why.

"And you know what else?" Olivia added, moving past the moment. "I'm not really angry anymore. At Nate."

"And what about his friend . . . Sean?" Sarah asked.

"You know, I guess maybe I'm not really that mad at him anymore either, but I don't trust him, and I don't know if I want him in my life. But this needs to happen. How can I move on if I'm still holding on to a piece of the past?"

Sarah nodded slowly, seeming to think that over. "What do you suppose he'll say tonight? If he shows?"

"Well," Olivia answered, scanning the crowd of faces for him, "we had a 'moment' last week."

"You mean—?" Sarah asked with raised brows.

"Oh no. Nothing happened. Just, I was sad, and he hugged me, and things felt almost like the old days. Sean was a *huge* part of my life . . . before."

Sarah allowed Olivia's silence to go on for a few seconds before she commented. "I hope you don't mind. I wouldn't normally weigh in on somethin' like this with someone I only just met, but I feel very comfortable with you. Like I've known you a long time." She smiled shyly.

Sarah's hand was resting on top of the fence in front of them, and Olivia placed her hand over hers and gave a quick little squeeze. "I feel that too." She smiled warmly. "What advice do you have for me?"

"I think you should have an open mind tonight with Sean. It seems as though you miss him."

Olivia weighed Sarah's words carefully. It was true. She did miss him. The intense anger that had burned so hot all those months had faded down to one little glowing ember, although she hadn't really even been aware of the change. So, could she have an open mind towards him? She thought she could. She could at least try.

Two hands suddenly grabbed Olivia by the shoulders and whirled her around. "What the—!" she exclaimed in surprise.

"Olivia, that guy, Sean, is here," Erin hissed, hands still on Olivia's shoulders as she glanced back at the ticket window.

Olivia put her hand on her chest as her heart returned to its normal rhythm. "Erin, you almost made me pee my pants."

Sarah laughed delicately beside her.

Taking in Olivia's lack of concern about her news, Erin asked, "Did you know he was coming?"

Olivia nodded.

"Why didn't you tell me? I thought you hated him!" she added in a loud whisper.

"When would I have told you? I didn't know he was coming until I was already on my way here, and you've been too busy setting me up with old geezers and forcing me to do your bidding since I got here." She paused. "And I don't hate him," she felt the need to add.

"Huh," Erin said, angling her head to the side. "Well, don't look now, but he's heading our way." Of course, all three of them looked.

"Boy, he's hot," Erin said appreciatively with a low whistle. "He's the whole reason I go to those college hockey games."

"We'll give you two some privacy," Sarah said, giving Erin a pointed look.

Erin scowled, but reluctantly followed Sarah's lead, turning back to Olivia to mouth, "Good luck."

Olivia merely nodded. Sean was making his way toward her at a rapid clip. He had a strong, purposeful stride, and she had to admit, he looked pretty amazing. It had always been annoying to Nate that Sean was deemed the better-looking of the two. Even so, Nate was the more cocky one, at least on the surface.

Olivia was one of the few allowed to see beneath Nate's carefully constructed exterior, and the vulnerability she found there was what had endeared him to her in the first place. In fact, if she hadn't glimpsed that, she would have dismissed Nate as not her type at all. Instead, she felt special and privileged that he allowed her to see the real him because he'd invited very few people to do so. Many times since his death, Olivia had wondered if all his affairs hadn't been some messed up attempt on his part to feed his underlying insecurity. She supposed she'd never really know.

Sean wasn't at all cocky—not on the surface and not down deep. She'd never seen even a hint of anything other than a genuine kindness and gentleness that seemed to completely defy the tough-guy impression his large size could easily give someone. Olivia had always found him to be very down-to-earth. Self-deprecating even. Having believed so unwaveringly in his goodness only made his betrayal that much more difficult to understand and accept, and as she was reminded of the reason for his appearance there tonight, Olivia felt a small resurgence of the old indignation taking on new life. Recalling Sarah's words, she did her best to cool the emotions down and be open to what he had to say.

Sean silently took the place next to her that Sarah had just vacated, and they studied each other for several seconds without speaking. Looking up into his face, Olivia catalogued each of his features and felt dismay when her heart rate picked up. He really was impossibly handsome.

She considered the reasons she had never truly noticed his attractiveness before. For one thing, she'd been accustomed to seeing Sean so regularly that she'd probably stopped truly *seeing* him. He'd simply been her friend, Sean. And for another, she'd been a faithful wife without a wandering eye, unlike her husband. She'd noticed Sean's looks, of course, but they hadn't quite computed in the same way. Not the way they were computing now, that was for sure. Olivia shifted her weight uncomfortably, and when Sean cleared his throat, she thought she saw a muscle flex in his jaw. "Sorry I'm late. Tom showed up out of the blue, and it took some time to get away. You remember."

Tom was the athletic director and a total headache to deal with. Nate had butted heads with him countless times.

"It's okay. I wasn't free until a few minutes ago anyway. I had to help out with halftime stuff."

He nodded, still studying her.

"What is it?" she finally asked, as she self-consciously smoothed her hair with both hands.

Sean gave a quick shake of his head. "No. Sorry, it's nothing. You just— You look great. Happy," he clarified. "I've been worried about you, but maybe I don't need to be anymore."

"I'm fine," she said, and then gave a small laugh. "You know, it's funny. I've said those two words so many times without truly meaning them. But today, I do. I really am fine. You don't need to worry about me."

"That's good, although it'll be a tough habit to break. I haven't stopped thinking about you for over a year." He broke eye contact suddenly and stuffed his hands into the pockets of his jeans.

An interminable silence followed before both of them spoke at once.

"Sean—" she began.

"Look—" he started.

Olivia chuckled, looking away for a second. Then she met his gaze and said, "You first."

He nodded. "Okay. I guess I'll start at the beginning." Sean looked around them at the crowd in the stands and the students milling around the sidelines, going back and forth from bleachers to concessions. "Is this okay to do here?" he asked, seeming to rethink the location of their meeting.

"It's okay. It's noisy. Nobody'll hear us."

Sean nodded and took a deep breath, holding it a moment before beginning. He was looking straight ahead, but not at the game in front of them, rather somewhere beyond it.

"Livvy, we were family. You, me, Nate, and Suze. I lost you all. I lost you and Nate in an instant, and Suze not long after that. I don't have any other family. They're all gone now. I know you probably get that better than anybody. Some people lose friends, and yeah, it's sad, but you move on. But when your friends *are* your family, and you have nobody else . . ."

Olivia waited for him to continue. She wasn't ready to talk yet. Mostly because she wasn't sure she'd be able to get anything past the lump that had formed in her throat. She knew exactly what it was like to feel all alone in the world. She had been so focused on her own pain and anger, and she felt the beginnings of a deep shame that she hadn't even stopped to consider how Sean might be faring. She'd been so angry with him for so long that it was jarring to feel anything other than that, and as she stood here beside him tonight, she found herself confused by her own jumbled emotions toward him.

It was a good thing she was comfortable with silences. She'd learned, through her work, not to rush to fill them. Silences truly were golden. They gave her students time to gather their thoughts, as both she and Sean were doing now.

He continued. "It's been a hard year. Grieving Nate. Grieving Susan and other . . . stuff. And I've been worried about you, wondering if you're okay. If Nora's okay. But Livvy, if I'm honest? I've also been mad as hell. At you. There, I said it."

Olivia flinched. That was unexpected. She'd just assumed she'd be the one doing the forgiving tonight. She'd felt ready to move on. But now it seemed like she'd entered the twilight zone and the tables were weirdly turned. "*You* were mad? At *me*?" she squeaked. "What do you mean *you* were mad?"

"Olivia, you wouldn't even talk to me. You wouldn't let me explain anything. I lost my best friend, and on the day of his funeral, you wouldn't even look at me." Sean's voice broke, and he looked away for a moment before continuing. "We could have helped each other through that, and instead—"

"Well, that's because—"

He put out his hand. "Hold on a minute. Just wait. I'm not done yet." He shook his head and smiled ruefully. "Don't give me that look, Livvy. I know that look. Yeah, yeah, you're mad. Fine. You'll get your turn in a minute. I've waited a year to say this, and I've got to get it out."

A voice in her head shouted at her that *she* was the wronged party here, but she told it to simmer down and forced herself to listen to what Sean had to say.

"That night when I came back to the house to give Nate his phone charger, and you two were having it out, you asked me again if I knew about Nate and the, ah, women. And you didn't really even ask, you accused."

"That's because you had guilt written all over your face. Plus, your silence told me everything I needed to know. I *know* you, Sean. I could tell just by looking at you that night that you knew. How could you have kept that from me? Especially since I'd already asked you if Nate was having an affair not long before that."

A month or so before she'd gotten pregnant, Olivia approached Sean to ask him if her worries were founded. Things between her and Nate were going from bad to worse, and she'd been desperate for answers. He reassured her that everything was on the up and up.

"You looked me in the eye and said that he wasn't having an affair. I could feel something was off with us, and I went to you for help. And you lied. And you lied again that night by not coming clean."

"See, you're doing it again. If you'll give me a chance, I'll explain everything."

She gestured for him to go ahead with an exaggerated sweep of her hands.

"About a year after you guys moved here, the team was down in Ann Arbor for a weekend game. On Sunday morning, I got up early for coffee, and I saw a woman leaving Nate's room." Sean shook his head. "I called Nate out over it, and then I punched him in the face. That's how furious I was. Remember that black eye? I forget what he told you about that. Anyway, you guys were already family to me by then, and I felt literally sick to my stomach that he would do that to you."

Olivia thought back and remembered Nate coming home with a black eye long ago and the explanation that he'd taken an elbow to the face during a line change. "Go on," she prompted.

"Well Nate, he cried. I couldn't believe it. First and only time I ever saw him do that. He told me he must've been out of his mind. Begged me to never tell you. He told me things had been a little tough for you guys lately, but that he loved you and he would fight for you. He said he'd never step out on you again. I was furious, but I believed him."

"And you didn't tell me."

Sean gave an exasperated sigh. "Olivia, I promised I wouldn't. And I believed it would never happen again. I didn't want to be the one responsible for ruining things between you. It wasn't my information to share. That was up to Nate. I thought he should tell you. I told him he should. I don't think there should be secrets like that in a marriage. But it wasn't up to me. And like I said, I thought it was over."

She scoffed. "So you just took his word for it."

"Actually, I did believe him, but I watched. I watched closely for the next several months, at least. I never saw any signs." Sean kicked at the dirt with the toe of his shoe. "After he died, it bothered me a lot that I could've missed the affair he admitted to that night, so I called around. It turns out that on the road, Nate would always reserve two hotel rooms. The one next to mine, and another one far away, usually on a different floor. That's why I never saw anything."

Olivia chewed her lip. This changed things some. Oh, it still upset her that Sean hadn't told her about the first time, but she studied his face and knew he was telling her the truth now. She felt a niggling of regret for how she'd handled things. In her defense, during their time apart, she'd been grieving, dealing with pregnancy hormones and unrelenting morning sickness, and then after that, the exhaustion of new motherhood. She'd had a lot on her plate the last year. But she should have given Sean a chance to explain. She'd been selfish. Too busy wallowing in her own pain to see that her friend was suffering too. He hadn't had it easy either.

But what now? She knew she could forgive him. In fact, she realized she already had. But she didn't know how to move forward with any kind of relationship with him. Maybe it just wasn't possible. Gone was the easy friendship that used to exist between them. It had been replaced by something else, something she was afraid to define. All she knew was that she was aware of him in a brand new way, and it left her feeling a little unsteady, a little unsure of herself.

Sean seemed to hold his breath as he looked at Olivia expectantly. She met his eyes and gave a nod. "Okay."

"Okay . . . ?" He drew the word out in a question.

"Okay. I believe you."

He raised his eyebrows, waiting for more.

She sighed. "And I'm sorry. I should have listened to you. I was angry and sad and confused."

He ran a hand back over his crewcut. "Yeah. That makes two of us."

They were both quiet. The noise of the game played in the background as they retreated into their respective thoughts for a time.

"Sean?"

"Yeah."

"I really am sorry. I shut you out. It wasn't right."

He turned slowly to face Olivia, squaring up his body with hers and hesitating only briefly before reaching for her and enfolding her in his arms, surrounding her with all his warmth and strength. "Thank you. I'm sorry too. I'm so sorry."

Olivia wrapped her own arms around Sean's waist and closed her eyes, allowing herself to relax against the solid length of him in a way she hadn't been able to just a few days before. She breathed him in. He smelled wonderful—like some kind of outdoorsy soap with notes of sandalwood and sage and some other indefinable masculine scent she guessed was simply him.

She'd hugged Sean countless times over the years, but never like this. Every inch of her was pressed against every inch of him. Her thoughts and feelings warred against each other in a mad scramble for sanity. This felt so right, but it must be wrong. It had to be. How could she be feeling these things for Sean Lacombe? They'd been friends in the truest and purest sense for years. More importantly, he'd been Nate's very best friend in the whole world.

Yet this sudden, deep ache in her chest and the unmistakable response of her body as he pulled her even more tightly against him spoke of an attraction that was very real and very powerful.

And very scary.

Olivia couldn't stop the tremble that came over her. She wanted to pull him even closer. She wanted to push him away. She wanted to stay in his arms forever.

A loud blow of a whistle reminded Olivia of where she was, and she pulled away reluctantly. Gazing up into Sean's face, she noticed an odd light in his deep-set, mocha-brown eyes as he stared down at her, and in that moment something changed profoundly between them. The air around them was suddenly charged with an energy Olivia didn't care to analyze. Instead, she searched for a safe topic to return things back to normal. She needed to find her footing again, and she took a literal step back.

"What happened with Suze?" she finally asked. "I always wondered. I never saw her again after the funeral. We messaged a few times, but mostly she just . . . disappeared. I feel bad about that."

Sean seemed to shake off the moment as well before answering, "It's a little complicated, but the long story short is that she . . . did something. A while back. I found out about it not long after the funeral. I tried to forgive and forget, I really did, but in the end, I just couldn't."

Olivia wanted to ask more, but she wasn't sure Sean wanted to share more.

He looked thoughtful. "You know, Suze reminded me a little of Nate. They lived life out loud, you know? And people were drawn to that, and to them. They were both a little too into themselves, and somehow so insecure at the same time.

"Anyway, those are just a few of the similarities I noticed, and it made me nervous. I was trying to figure out how I could've been so blind and so duped by my best friend, and then I found out that Susan—" He cut himself off before he shared too much. "And then suddenly I just couldn't trust her anymore. So that's that. Last I heard, she was in Colorado."

Had Suze cheated too? It sounded that way. Olivia so desperately wanted to know what Suze had done, but now wasn't the time. Instead she said, "That's too bad. I'm sorry things didn't work out. But you did say we were like a family, and you know what they say about families: They're all dysfunctional."

Sean chuckled.

Smiling softly, she added, "But seriously, I'm sorry she left."

"Oh, don't be. I'm not. At least not anymore. She wasn't right for me. Or I wasn't right for her. Either way. These things, they work out for the best sometimes. You know, God's planning and timing, and all that." He cleared his throat, and Olivia saw that muscle tighten in his jaw again.

"Livvy. Do you think you and I could—Do you think we could maybe try . . . ?" He didn't seem able to get the words out, so Olivia helped him.

"You want to start over?"

He blew out a puff of air and rocked back on his heels. "Yes." He looked gratefully at her for articulating the question for him. "I mean, if you want to. I don't want to pressure you or anything. But, you're very . . . special . . . to me, and I want you in my life."

He'd just laid it all out there. She liked that about Sean. No games. "Well," she said cautiously, "we can try."

"Maybe we've already started." He smiled at her in a way that made her experience a weird little jolt inside. It wasn't unpleasant.

Chapter 10

Nicolet was down fourteen to nothing, and it was the end of the third quarter. Their boys were giving it their all, but everyone knew this wouldn't be a win tonight. Anna couldn't remember the last time varsity had won a football game, but a person wouldn't know it based on fan enthusiasm. The cheerleaders were leading the Nicolet section in their favorite cheer, *Knock 'em Down,* when Anna spotted Alex again.

He hadn't come back to the stands with them after halftime. Instead, Jess told her, he'd headed in the direction of the parking lot, and Anna had just spent the last twenty minutes obsessively watching for any sign of him. Now he was returning to the game, and he was walking hand-in-hand with Blythe around the fencing near the ticket window.

Anna felt her pulse race. There was no question any longer. They were together. And he hadn't bothered to tell Anna that they no longer were. Sensing Anna's body go rigid, Jess looked at her friend questioningly and then turned to follow Anna's gaze. It took half a second for Jess to read the situation, and she grabbed Anna by the arm.

"What the hell!" she hissed. "I can't even believe him! What is *wrong* with him?"

To Anna's horror, she began to cry.

Jess looked at her in alarm. "No, no. Don't do that. You're alright. You can cry later, but not right now, okay?" She put a protective arm around her, and Anna nodded, wiping frantically at her tears and trying valiantly to keep herself calm. This wasn't her. She didn't cry in public. She was no attention seeker, unlike most of the other girls at their school. Except that Alex seemed to have turned her into a bit of a nut these last few days—or weeks. She hated it.

Anna had almost gotten herself under control, blinking rapidly to stop the flow of tears, when David, who was sitting directly in front of her, turned around. Evidently, he'd seen Alex too. He took one look at Anna's red eyes and runny nose and cursed under his breath.

"This is *so* not cool of him. I'm gonna go talk to him, Anna." He was already making a move down the bleachers.

"No!" She grabbed his arm. "Please don't, David."

"He's being an ass, and not just to you. He's been all weird with me today too. He should *not* be doing this to you, especially today." He shook his head. "This is *your* day. He's just pissed off because *I* was king with you, and not him. Someone needs to set the guy straight. Might as well be me."

Anna lost her grip on his arm, and she looked at Jess in paralyzed horror as David continued down the bleachers.

"Oh no! There's going to be a scene. Should we leave? I think we should leave," Anna prattled on nervously. But Jess wasn't really listening. She just held on tightly to Anna and watched what was about to unfold. Unfortunately, the two girls weren't the only ones whose attention had been captured. Everyone in the student section was looking back and forth between Anna and the trio down below. Anna couldn't hear what was being said, but she could see plenty, and the angry gesturing by both boys and the smug look on Blythe's heavily made-up face spoke more loudly than words ever could.

As if things couldn't get worse, Adam touched Anna's shoulder on his way down to the confrontation, telling her he, too, was going to give Alex a piece of his mind. Before long, Jared and Jace had joined in to defend Alex.

Things escalated quickly from there, and before Anna knew what was happening, other boys appeared out of nowhere, all crowding around the base of the bleachers, and yelling at each other. This was quickly becoming a bigger event than the halftime show had been, and all eyes were riveted on it. The game had even come to a stop as the boys on the field noticed the commotion. In complete disbelief, Anna watched Alex shout something at David. He was right up in his face. In response, David gave Alex a hard shove, and Blythe screamed. After that, all hell broke loose.

Jess let out a strangled yelp and yanked Anna up to standing beside her. "What are we supposed to do?" Jess's expression was one of utter dismay, and Anna stared back at her with wide eyes before directing her attention back to the fight below. She brought her hand up over her mouth and watched helplessly as fists flew.

"That's it. I'm getting you out of here." Jess dragged Anna down the bleachers, but she hadn't really thought it all the way through, because the only way out required them to walk into the fracas themselves. And that's where they were when the school principal and other adults came running to break up what could now only be described as a brawl.

Maybe it would delight some girls to know they could start a brawl without even trying, but not Anna. She was completely mortified. Not only was she dealing with the raw emotion that flooded over her at seeing Alex and Blythe together, but the entire school had now witnessed her humiliation. The cherry on top was that she felt completely responsible for such a violent scene, so much so that she was literally shaking. David and Alex were bleeding profusely from their noses, and even Adam was staggering around blindly, holding a hand over his right eye.

If she hadn't been so traumatized, Anna might have found it comical to see their diminutive principal grab Alex by the collar and lead him away to the office. Alex wasn't all that tall for a guy, but Erin Hennings was at least a whole head shorter than he was, and if Alex had wanted to, he could have broken free at any time. But their principal's power didn't come from her size. It came from her personality.

Mr. Benninger had magically appeared out of nowhere to help, and he had David by the upper arm, and was guiding him away as well. As the space cleared, Anna could see kids she didn't even know nursing their wounds and answering the questions being shouted at them by the parents, teachers, and even the football coaches.

Jess and Anna stood against the side of the bleachers, still clutching each other, for long minutes until Olivia and a man Anna didn't recognize appeared next to them. Olivia asked the girls if they were alright. They nodded silently. She asked if they would come with her. They nodded again.

When they stepped through the doors of the guidance office, which was attached to and just down from the main office, the shouting voice of the principal greeted them. Jess and Anna exchanged a nervous glance.

"Never mind that, girls. You're not in any trouble," Olivia reassured.

"Then why are we here in the office?" Jess whispered to Anna.

Once they'd sat in the two chairs opposite Olivia's desk, she closed the door and moved around them to her own chair. It was a small office, but Olivia made the space inviting and non-threatening. There were three live plants in different locations, as well as a framed photo on the wall of the famous Nicolet Lighthouse with the blue waters of Lake Superior stretching out for miles behind it. She had several motivational posters framed and hung on the walls as well, and Anna's favorite said, *Today is a good day for a good day*. If only that were true of this day, she mused.

"So," Olivia began, "can either of you tell me what that was all about back there?"

Jess and Anna looked at each other, wondering how or where to begin.

"Let me start over," Olivia said gently. "Are you girls truly okay? Anna? I get the sense this has been a tough day for you." That's all it took. When Olivia's gaze moved to focus solely on her, Anna absolutely lost it. She sobbed. Body-wracking sobs. And she couldn't stop. Jess tried to comfort her, but Anna turned away, gripping her arms around herself. She glimpsed the bewildered hurt in her friend's eyes, but she just couldn't be comforted right then. She needed to cry. She was so angry and so hurt. Not to mention so embarrassed.

Anna had always said Jess was her best friend, and she was her best *girl* friend. But Alex had been her best friend for a long time, and she knew tonight, without a shred of a doubt, that she'd lost him for good. She'd lost her best friend and her boyfriend in one fell swoop with the entire school looking on, and she couldn't be consoled.

Vaguely, Anna was aware of Olivia speaking to Jess in low tones and Jess leaving quietly. Olivia came to sit in Jess's chair, close but not touching. She seemed to know Anna needed more time to release everything. She cried with ugly abandon, just like she would have if she'd been all alone. When the tears slowed and the sobs became small hiccups, Olivia tapped her arm and handed her a tissue. Anna stared at the wall as she wiped at her eyes and nose, needing a moment to compose herself before turning to meet Olivia's concerned gaze.

Anna filled her guidance counselor in. It didn't take long since Olivia knew most of the story. Anna just filled in the holes, and once it was all out, she took a deep, restorative breath and waited for Olivia's feedback.

Olivia took her time, gathering her thoughts before speaking. "Anna," she began thoughtfully, "I know you're terribly hurt, and my heart aches for you, honey. It really does. But listen. You've been open with me about the changes you've seen in Alex recently. I've known Alex for years also, and he is not at all himself. Now, you know I can't share certain . . . things with you, but I can tell you that Alex is going through some troubles of his own right now. That said, he's been treating you very poorly lately, and there's no excuse in the world for that. As hard as it might be for you, I think you need to put some space between yourself and him."

"You mean, break up? I'm pretty sure that's already happened. He just forgot to tell me," Anna said in a wobbly voice. It sounded so final. She didn't feel ready to say goodbye to him. And what Olivia had said worried her. What troubles was Alex dealing with? Was he okay? At least he had Olivia in his corner, whatever it was.

"Well, first, I think the two of you need to sit down and talk to one another. But yes, I do think that some time apart would be good for you both."

"But how can I talk to him when he's avoiding me?" Anna asked. "He won't take my calls, and I can't seem to get close enough to him to say two words, let alone have a deep discussion. He's ghosting me, and it's like he's written me off. I don't even know what I did wrong. Did I do something wrong?"

"No, honey. I don't think you did anything wrong. What I think is that you two have been in a very serious relationship for a long time. Sometimes that can be scary for one or the other in the couple, and they pull away. I think that's what's been happening. Alex has been pulling away from you, and that's caused you to hold on a little tighter. But I think, at the same time, Alex became jealous at the thought of you moving on without him.

"You being named homecoming queen without him being voted king brought that home for him in a big way today. He probably had a hurt ego on top of that. But I doubt he's been able to name these emotions, and right now he's just feeling anger and directing it at you, which isn't fair, of course. Now listen, that's really all I can say about that. But you can talk as much as you need to."

Anna knew Olivia had to be careful, so she didn't press her.

"Would you like an opportunity to talk to Alex now?" Olivia asked. "I think I could arrange it."

The idea of finally being able to talk to Alex filled Anna with hope and dread at the same time. But she knew she needed to clear the air with him before she could move on in any real way.

"Yes, please. I think that'd be good."

"Okay. I'll just be a minute. Sit tight."

Olivia was gone for some time, during which Anna had to talk herself down off the ledge once or twice. Whether she wanted to or not, the bottom line was that she had to talk to Alex eventually. Better to get it done now than to put it off and agonize over it.

Just as Anna began to wonder if Olivia was ever coming back, she poked her head into her office. "I'll be right out here if you need me." Anna spotted the same man Olivia was with earlier hanging back on the other side of the room. He was pretending to read college pamphlets.

Anna nodded because she knew her voice wouldn't work. A few seconds later, Alex appeared in the doorway. He had the beginnings of two horrible black eyes, and he still had some dried blood at the base of his nose and smattered on the front of his shirt. Despite that, he looked amazing to her, and Anna felt her heart break a little further to know that he was probably no longer hers. The words hadn't been said yet, but at this point, it was just a formality.

Alex sat down in the chair next to hers and stared ahead. She could see the tension in his face as he clenched and unclenched his jaw. Realizing that she was going to have to be the one to speak first, Anna tried to remember Olivia's words to keep herself from becoming too emotional. Anna had known Alex so well for so long. The fact that she didn't recognize him now and even thought of him in terms of old Alex and new Alex meant that he must be going through a really tough time.

"Are you okay?" she asked.

Silence.

She tried again. "You need to know that I didn't ask David to do that. That fight had nothing to do with me."

"*Really.*" It wasn't a question, and the sarcasm was thick.

"Really. Alex, look at me."

He finally met her eyes after a few seconds, and when he did, Anna saw a hostility there that shocked her. She tried to think of what to say next. In the end, she was straightforward.

"Are you breaking up with me?" She held her breath as she waited for him to answer. He didn't look at her when he finally responded.

"Yeah. It's time."

Anna didn't miss a beat. "Okay." She spoke with a finality and acceptance that seemed to catch them both off guard.

He looked at her then, really looked, and for a second he was his old self. Gone was the hostility and anger. Instead, he appeared uncertain. Insecure. Sad, even. The moment didn't last, though, and the chip reappeared on his shoulder as suddenly as it had left.

"Fine. That's it, then," he said.

"That's it, then," Anna echoed sadly. She felt stunned that this was how it was going to end. Surely they should have had something more to say to one another after two years. But no. That was it.

Alex got up and left the office, and Anna sat in the chair, wondering how in the world she was going to go on without him. She hadn't realized it, but being Alex's girlfriend was partly how she had defined herself. Alex Anderson's girlfriend. Without that piece, who was she?

Aunt Heidi's advice of a few months ago replayed itself, and now Anna wished she'd listened. They'd been out running during Anna's last visit in early June, and they were several miles down their favorite path along the Mississippi. Anna was sharing her summer plans, which had apparently included too much Alex because after several minutes of Anna's chatter,

Aunt Heidi had brought them both to a stop and placed her hand on Anna's shoulder.

There they had stood, off on the side of the trail, bent over slightly with their heads together, catching their breath. When Aunt Heidi straightened up, she looked Anna in the eye and said, "Anna, listen. I'm glad you have Alex in your life. I really am. But I'm speaking from experience here. Don't get so wrapped up in another person that you lose yourself, okay? Because if anything ever happens, like if you and Alex break up, you'll be really, really lost, honey."

Aunt Heidi had looked so worried that Anna held back what she really wanted to say, which was that her aunt had no idea what she was talking about. Maybe if she visited once in a while, met Alex, saw them as a couple, she might understand. They were rock solid. Neither one of them was going anywhere. But instead, Anna held Aunt Heidi's gaze and nodded.

"Good girl." She rewarded Anna with a small pat on her shoulder. "Trust me, losing someone is painful enough on its own. Losing your own identity along with them is almost unbearable."

Anna was fairly certain she knew what her aunt was referring to, but she didn't dare ask. She'd learned long ago not to be the one to bring up her mother with Aunt Heidi. It left her aunt with a haunted sort of look, and she'd shut down. Instead, Anna waited for Heidi to talk about her. It didn't happen often, but when it did, Anna gobbled it up. She was like a dog who sat in wait under the dinner table, happy to be thrown a few scraps of information every now and again.

That day out on the path, Anna had thought her aunt was overreacting about Alex. She'd even felt a little defensive. A relationship with a boyfriend was different than a relationship with a twin sister. Anna was just a committed girlfriend who loved her boyfriend. That's what she'd thought then. But now she could see it, and she understood.

She really had placed Alex first, ahead of everything and everyone, including herself. And it had worked for a while, back when he reciprocated, unhealthy as it still may have been. But as he'd grown more and more moody and more distant through the summer and fall, she'd just tried harder and harder to keep him happy. She'd become the giver, and he'd become the taker, and Anna could see now that she'd lost herself and become a doormat in the process.

It sounded like Mrs. Reeves was speaking to Alex on the other side of the door, but Anna couldn't make out what was being said. Soon it grew quiet. Still, Anna continued to sit and stare, unseeingly, at the spider plant behind Olivia's desk. A few minutes later, Olivia returned to check on Anna, and they talked for several minutes more.

Olivia asked, "What do you want to do? Are you going to stay for the dance?"

"No. I think I just want to go home."

Olivia looked at her young friend dubiously. "Is anybody even there? I hate to think of you home all alone right now. I'm not sure that's the best thing for you."

She had a point, Anna thought. She didn't really want to be alone in her big, dark house tonight. "I'll call Mitch to come get me. He won't be happy, but he'll come, and if I ask, he'll stay with me."

"Are you sure?" Olivia looked doubtful. So far, she hadn't been all that impressed with Anna's brother. Anna could tell. She'd told Olivia enough over the last year for her to have developed a pretty poor opinion of the men in Anna's family, but Anna couldn't help feeling protective of them, even though she knew Olivia was right. Her dad and brother left a lot to be desired.

"No, he will," she said definitively.

"I'd take you home myself, but I have to stay to chaperone. When will your car be fixed?"

Anna sighed. "Soon, I hope. It's becoming harder and harder to get places."

Olivia looked worried, and Anna loved her for that. Knowing she had someone right here in town—right next door even—who cared enough to worry about her, filled her with gratitude, and she hopped up and flung herself into Olivia's arms, knocking her slightly off balance.

"Whoa!" Olivia exclaimed as she steadied herself and put her arms around Anna. She rubbed her back in soothing strokes.

"I'm sorry," Anna said over Olivia's head. "I always forget you're so tiny."

Olivia chuckled. "Must be my oversized personality."

Anna laughed at that, and somehow that small act made her feel better. "Thanks. For everything."

"Oh, kiddo. Everything's going to be okay. It really is."

Anna stepped back. "I know, but it still sucks."

"It does."

Digging her phone out, Anna dialed Mitch's number. "I'll just call Mitch now." After giving her a thumbs up, Olivia slipped out the door again.

Mitch answered on the third ring, and hearing his voice on the line inexplicably caused Anna to experience a fresh wave of emotion. "Mitch?" she croaked out past the painful lump in her throat. "Can you come get me? I really need you."

Chapter 11

Anna left Olivia and her hot mystery man behind in the office and walked out into the quiet, low-lit hallway. The composite vinyl flooring gleamed with a fresh coat of polish, and although the industrial-grade chemical smell was strong, she could still make out the faint and familiar scent of pencil shavings and old books. Out of the corner of her eye, she saw movement, and she turned to watch Jess get up off the floor. She'd been sitting with her back against the wall, waiting for her. Dusting herself off, she gave Anna an assessing glance.

Anna knew what Jess was seeing. She was barely holding it together. If Jess hugged her now, she'd lose it again. Jess seemed to know it too, so she simply fell into step beside Anna instead, careful not to make eye contact. That would have done it too. Jess waited until they were in the foreign language hall before speaking. "We aren't staying, are we?"

The *we* she'd used meant more to Anna than Jess would ever know, and she thanked God for her, right then and there. Not a lot of girls had a true friend who could be trusted one hundred percent. A lot of back-biting went on with girls in their high school who claimed to be close friends. They'd do things to each other, like post ugly pictures to social media just to embarrass one another, or blab each other's secrets to the world just for the fun of it. They'd even steal each other's boyfriends. Anna and Jess were different. They were there for each other. Loyal.

"I talked to my mom and told her what's going on. She said to tell you all men are fools and to hang in there."

"Aw. That's nice."

"And she said I should stay the night with you. She'll smooth it over with Dad. She'll have to pick me up early, though. Gotta get that workout in, you know? The sky might fall otherwise." Jess rolled her eyes.

Anna gave her a sympathetic smile. "I called Mitch. He's on his way."

Jess looked at her in surprise. "Wow! Mitch is really coming through for you today. Who knew he could think of anyone other than himself?"

"He's not that bad," Anna defended.

"You know I love your brother, but you have to admit, he hasn't been that *good* either."

Anna shrugged. "Mitch is Mitch."

The girls waited together at the front canopy for Mitch to arrive. Luckily, the game wasn't over yet, so the covered entrance was empty, except for them. Anna felt relieved that she wouldn't have to see anyone else from school tonight. Jess allowed her to be silent, knowing Anna needed to get out of there first before she'd be able to speak about what had happened. Silences with Jess weren't weird, and it didn't seem like they'd been waiting too long before Mitch pulled up in his little car. Oddly, he waved to her from the passenger seat.

Jess squinted. "Who's driving his car?"

Anna thought she might know, but it was too dark to tell for certain.

Just as the two girls hopped off from the bike rack they'd been sitting on, the doors to the school opened, and Olivia and her male friend walked out.

"Just seeing you off!" Olivia called out. Anna smiled and felt warmed from the inside out. She might have just had one of the worst nights of her life, but here she was, being tended to by Olivia, Jess, and Mitch. She was lucky.

Anna studied Olivia as she walked towards her. Could it be that the heightened color in her neighbor's cheeks was a result of the man walking beside her? She wondered again who he was. Whoever he was, he was the epitome of the old romance novel cliché. But *tall*, *dark*, and *handsome* weren't remotely descriptive enough words to do this guy justice. Added to that was the air of mystery those deep-set eyes suggested. His size made Olivia look even more dainty than she usually did, and Anna had to admit, they made a striking pair.

Olivia peered past Anna to Mitch's car. "Oh, good! Mitch came. Who's driving?" Olivia's friend seemed to take an interest in the answer to that question too, and he craned his neck to get a look.

A second later, the driver's door opened, and Landon got out. He looked at Anna over the roof of the car, but then his gaze moved past her.

"Hey there, Coach!" he hollered with obvious surprise.

"LaFleur!" the mystery man exclaimed. "And who's that with you? That you, Davis?" He peered through the darkness.

Noting Anna's dawning realization, Olivia made the introductions. "Anna, this is Mitch's coach, Sean Lacombe. Sean, this is Anna. She's my neighbor and good friend. And Mitch's sister."

"Ah. Small world." Sean smiled, and Anna, even in her depressed state, nearly melted into the concrete. So this was the infamous Sean she'd heard so much about. She had to say, he and Olivia didn't look like enemies any longer. She'd have to get the scoop later. *Way to go, Olivia,* she thought with a smile.

"It's good to meet you," she said instead.

"Yeah, you too, kid, although I'm sorry for the night you're having," he said kindly. Then he turned to Olivia. "Did you say this is Mitch's car?"

Olivia nodded.

"Hmm." The two of them exchanged a meaningful glance, and that's when Anna realized she'd just inadvertently gotten Mitch into trouble. Maybe even big trouble. There could only be one reason for Landon to be in the driver's seat of Mitch's car on a Friday night. It might not have been such a big deal if Mitch were older, but he was only nineteen—two years away from being twenty-one. If he'd been drinking, he was in violation of the athletic code, not to mention the law. *Crap.* What else could go wrong tonight?

"Gimme just a minute, will you ladies?" Sean asked before strolling over to Mitch's window. Though she tried, Anna couldn't hear what was being said. Landon remained standing awkwardly next to the open driver's side door, looking like he wanted the earth to swallow him up whole.

"Oops," Olivia said, pulling a face.

"He's screwed, right?" Jess asked nobody in particular.

Anna turned to Olivia beseechingly. "I don't want Mitch to get in trouble, Olivia. Please. This has been such an awful day, and he's only here to do me a favor." She folded her hands together like she would if she were praying. "He was just trying to be a good brother. He said he'd stay the night at home and everything," she added, hoping Olivia might have some pull with the coach.

Olivia was pensive for a moment and then gave a long-suffering sigh. "I'll be right back," she said, and then she winked at Anna over her shoulder.

"Oh, Olivia, thank you!" Anna called after her.

Linking arms, Jess and Anna waited anxiously and tried to hear what was going on. Olivia had pulled Sean away from the car and was talking to him quietly while Mitch stared murderously at Anna. She ignored him. After a few moments, Sean nodded and bent back down to the window. He said something more to Mitch, then to Landon, and then he called to Jess and Anna, gesturing for them to get into the back seat through the door he held open for them.

Anna quickly hugged Olivia before getting in and smiled at Mitch's coach as he held the door for her. She scooched all the way over to make room for Jess and waved goodbye to Olivia once she'd buckled up.

"Well, that was—" Landon began, after he'd pulled away from the curb.

"What the *hell,* Anna?" Mitch interrupted. "A heads up my coach was here would've been nice!"

"Don't yell at me. And I didn't know he was your coach," she said defensively.

Mitch dropped his face into his hands and held it there for a few seconds before looking back at her. "This is just the last thing I need. I've been playing like shit all week, and now my coach knows I've been out drinking. Thanks a lot."

"Mitch, it's not her fault," Jess said in Anna's defense.

"I wasn't talking to you, *Jessica,*" Mitch snapped.

Jess stiffened next to her. "Mitch!" Anna admonished. Mitch and Jess had always gotten along. They were almost honorary siblings. Jess had been in their lives since elementary school, and throughout high school, she'd used the Davis house as an escape from the dictator she called *Dad.* The time they'd spent together, the three of them, had resulted in a solid friendship between Jess and her brother, even if they had little spats here and there, as they were having now.

Anna knew for a fact that Mitch confided things in Jess that he never told her, his own sister, about. So many times over the years, she'd wanted to ask Jess what they talked about together, but she could never bring herself to. She was glad Mitch and Jess were close, but it would be a lie to say she wasn't sometimes jealous.

"Jerk," Jess muttered under her breath, but not quietly enough, apparently, because Mitch whipped around again to glare at her.

Anna intervened. "Listen. I don't know why you guys are suddenly at each other, but please, just stop. Tonight's been bad enough without the two of you fighting on top of it all."

Neither of them responded. Mitch continued to look straight ahead, and Jess stared out the side window. Well, so much for that.

Anna continued, "Mitch, I'm sorry about your coach. I didn't know who he was until after you pulled up. And I didn't know you'd been drinking either. To be honest, I didn't even know you drank, but I guess we'll save *that* talk for another time."

Mitch turned halfway around to look at her, brows lowered and eyes narrowed to warn her away from bringing the subject up again. Was that supposed to be his intimidating hockey face? If it was, he needed to practice in the mirror some more.

"I've had a horrible, terrible, very bad, no good day . . . or whatever, and I'm sorry I ruined yours too. It wasn't on purpose." Anna closed her eyes before adding, "I just want to go home."

Mitch sighed heavily and turned back around, and then all was blessedly quiet. The only noise was the sound of the turn signal as Landon prepared to head west towards the Davis home. Landon was the one who broke the silence several minutes later. “Are you okay, Anna?”

Anna was touched he would ask. “I’m okay.”

“What happened?” he asked gently.

Anna had been replaying the events of the day, and she opened her eyes to look at Jess, nodding to indicate that she could go ahead with the story. That was all the prompting Jess needed, and she didn’t hold back her opinion of Alex as she recounted his treatment of Anna over the last few days. She retold the details of the fight with stunning accuracy, along with a few embellishments, and Anna could see it impressed the boys.

Hockey players loved a good fight.

Jess ended the tale with their visit to the office. “That’s the end of what I know. Anna will have to tell you the rest.”

Anna was tired of this entire ordeal. She felt strangely detached from it. No tears threatened her now, no lumps in her throat, no nervous stomach. Lately, she seemed to ping pong between feeling far too much and feeling next to nothing at all, like she was numb. She wondered if that was normal.

Massaging her temples, she explained, “Well, long story short, Alex dumped me after the fight. Olivia found him for me, and we talked.” She said this so matter-of-factly that Jess looked stunned.

“Oh, Anna!” She clutched her friend’s hand. “Are you okay?”

Aware that there was a stranger in the car, listening—an extremely good-looking stranger—Anna didn’t want to go into it any further. Her humiliation was now complete.

“I’ll be fine,” she reassured her. “It’s not like I didn’t know it was coming. In a weird way, I feel relieved that it’s done. I’m not waiting for the other shoe to drop anymore. I was on edge all day.”

“You want me and Landon to kick his ass?” her brother asked, turning to look at her again. This time, he succeeded in looking menacing.

“No!” she laughed nervously.

“Because we will,” Landon added, looking in the mirror at her with smiling eyes and a quick wink.

“Well, thanks,” she said. “But there’s been enough bashing in of people’s faces already tonight. You guys can save it for the ice.” If this boy, Landon, was anything like her brother, then he capitalized on any opportunity to drop his gloves.

Mitch remained indignant about the way Alex had treated her, which Anna thought was sweet. She sensed he was winning Jess over again. He may not have been the world’s greatest brother, but he was loyal, and he was saying all the right things.

Once he got past his desire to pummel Alex to within an inch of his life, he told Anna she could do better, that Alex was a loser and that he'd never really liked him, and on and on. When Mitch finally ran out of steam, Landon chimed in on a serious note. "Hey, Anna? Just know something, okay? It gets better. You won't feel like this forever."

Again, they made eye contact in the mirror, and Anna treated him to a smile. She found she wanted to talk to him some more. She wanted to ask him how he knew that. It sounded like he was speaking from experience.

"Thanks, Landon."

Mitch must not have had *that* much to drink because he trudged to the house in a straight line and was coordinated enough to unlock the front door on the first try. He flipped on the lights in the kitchen and went immediately to the refrigerator, where he helped himself to a few sips from a jug of orange juice. He had a gross habit of drinking it straight out of the container—he did it with the milk too—and no amount of complaining by Anna had changed that. She'd stopped trying long ago.

Anna grabbed a glass out of the cupboard for herself and got one for Landon when he asked. She filled them both with ice, followed by some tap water.

Jess, slumped on a stool at the kitchen island with her chin resting on one hand, wrinkled her nose as she watched Mitch continue to gulp down orange juice. "You're an animal," she said. "Get a glass."

Mitch pulled a face at her before replacing the cap and wiping his mouth with the back of his hand.

"Man, I'm beat," he said as he closed the refrigerator door. Anna studied him and noticed that he did look tired. He had dark smudges under his eyes that hadn't been there earlier in the week. "Really, it's a good thing we're staying here tonight. The dorm gets crazy on the weekends, and I need to get some sleep. I gotta be up early tomorrow."

"Why?" Anna asked. "Do you guys have practice in the morning?"

"*I* do. Dryland. By myself. Just me and Coach," Mitch said, clearly annoyed and clearly still placing at least some of the blame directly at her feet.

"Hey, you got off easy, bud," Landon reminded him. "I thought Coach would for sure bench you the first couple games. That's what he's always done before. But then he talked to that lady and must have changed his mind."

"Mitch has Anna to thank for that," Jess informed Landon. "She asked Mrs. Reeves to step in."

Mitch looked at his sister in surprise. "Yeah?"

Anna nodded.

Mitch at least had the good grace to look sheepish. "Er, well, thanks for that. I guess maybe I shouldn't have yelled earlier. And look, I'm sorry about Alex. But he's no good for you, so don't be sad too long."

Anna rolled her eyes. "Okay. I'll get over it tomorrow."

Landon smiled from behind his water glass, but her sarcasm was lost on Mitch. "Awesome. Okay, I'm heading to bed. Landon, you can take the guest room. Anna or Jess will show you."

Jess looked over at the clock on the microwave and then back at Mitch. "It's nine-thirty," she said with eyebrows raised.

Mitch looked surprised. "Huh. Feels later. Anyway, I'm still going to bed."

Anna was concerned. Mitch didn't look well to her. "Are you feeling okay?"

Thinking about it a minute, he answered, "I don't know. I had a scratchy throat earlier this week, but then it went away. Now I just feel kinda weak. It's probably just stress."

Jess snorted. "Too many girls and too many parties will do that to a guy."

Mitch cracked a smile. "It's all worth it."

She chuckled. "Get some sleep, Romeo."

When Mitch left the kitchen, the three of them looked at one another wordlessly. The clock ticking above the sink was the only sound to be heard, and a speculative gleam entered Jess's eyes as she glanced back and forth between Anna and Landon. She cocked her head at Anna. "You know, I'm a little tired out too, so I think I'll get ready for bed. Can I borrow your moose pajamas? They're my faves."

Anna felt her cheeks go pink. "Uh, sure. You know where they are. And your blue toothbrush is still in the drawer."

"Great. Thank you," Jess said a little too formally. Anna could see her friend fighting an amused grin as she left the kitchen. Once she was in the living room and out of Landon's sight, she turned around and mouthed, "He's so hot!" She gestured with her hand, also, in case Anna hadn't caught the words.

Pressing her lips tightly together so she wouldn't smile, Anna quickly looked away. Out of the corner of her eye, she saw Jess turn around and head up the stairs.

Landon was still leaning casually against the kitchen sink, observing her. "Looks like everyone's going to bed," he remarked.

Anna knew Jess wasn't going to sleep right away. She was a night owl. She'd watch Netflix on Anna's laptop until Anna came up. Then they would unpack everything that had happened tonight. Anna was eager to get Jess's take on it all and hear her list all the reasons she'd be better off without Alex.

But she also felt a powerful pull to stay in the kitchen with Landon. Wasn't it her job as a hostess to make him feel comfortable and at home anyway? She couldn't go upstairs without spending at least a little time with their guest. Sure, that was all that was motivating her—good manners.

Anna pulled her phone out of the side pocket of her leggings and set it on the counter. It had blown up with messages in the car, so she'd turned it off. She figured she'd just leave it off for the night.

Now that it was just Anna and Landon in the kitchen, they openly studied each other. Even after all the angst of the day, Anna could appreciate his good looks. He was a full-on *man*, and his five o'clock shadow proved it. The small crescent-shaped scar over his left eye didn't detract from the overall package, she noted. Somehow, even an imperfection looked perfect on him. Anna suddenly felt shy and out of her element in her own kitchen.

What kind of guy was he? A player? He didn't seem like one, although he undoubtedly attracted a fair amount of female attention.

"If you're tired, I'll show you to your room," Anna offered, cutting into the silence.

"I'm not tired." His blue eyes penetrated hers with an intensity that caused her to look away, and when she glanced back at him, one corner of his mouth had lifted in amusement.

When it became obvious he wasn't planning on saying anything more, Anna spoke again. "Landon," she began nervously, "thanks for picking me up. I'm sorry you had to cut your night short. It sounded like you and Mitch were at a party when I called."

He shrugged. "It's okay. I'm not really into that scene anyway."

"You're not?" Anna found this surprising. She had just assumed a good-looking college hockey player would be whooping it up on a fairly regular basis.

"I'm not," he said simply.

"How come?"

He studied her a moment before tipping his head to the side. "Well, you're not either, right? Into that scene, I mean."

How had he guessed that?

"Mitch has told me some things about you," he admitted.

Interesting. "He has? Like what?"

"Well, he says you're a 'good girl,' among other things."

Anna laughed. "Well, I don't know how *good* I am. I mean, I try but . . . yeah, I've never been a part of all that either. I go out, but I'm more like a bystander than anything else."

"Speaking from experience, I can tell you, you're not missing anything."

"I know. I've seen a lot of . . . not-so-good stuff happen to drunk people over the years."

He nodded in agreement.

Curious about his story, she asked, "What changed for you?"

He shrugged again, this time in the way people do when they're trying to minimize the importance of something. "I don't know. I guess I saw myself turning into my old man. I didn't like it."

Anna felt goosebumps pop up on her skin. This was turning into the kind of conversation she lived for. The deep stuff. She nodded and waited for him to go on.

But instead of offering more information about himself, he turned the tables. "Why don't you? Do the party scene, I mean?"

She thought for a moment. "Lots of reasons, really."

"Name one."

She chose the biggest of them all. "I don't like feeling out of control. It reminds me of how I used to feel as a kid."

"You felt out of control as a kid?"

She nodded.

"How so? Did you get a little too crazy on your tricycle?" he teased, eliciting a laugh and a denial from Anna before she turned serious again.

Anna toyed with the drawstring of her hoodie. "Did Mitch tell you about our mother?"

"A little. Probably not everything. I know she died in an accident when you were both young."

"There's a lot more to it, but honestly, I'm surprised he told you that much. Mitch doesn't talk about her. I wish he would. Our mom was amazing. She grew up here, and people in town loved her. When I was younger, a friend of my Grandpa Sepi would sometimes tell me stories about her. He knew my mom from the time she was in diapers, so he definitely had some good ones to share. He died a long time ago, but I wrote down the stuff he told me so I wouldn't forget."

Landon nodded for her to go on.

"My mom was beautiful and fun and feisty, but she . . . struggled after I was born. They thought she had postpartum depression—and maybe she did—but then she was diagnosed with bipolar disorder a few years later."

"Oh, man. That's too bad."

"Yeah. I mean, it's totally treatable and everything, and tons of people live with it and do really well, but she felt like her meds changed her personality. Made her too numb. So, she didn't always take her pills, which meant her condition went untreated a lot of the time. I guess it was bad. She would get kind of . . . wild. Reckless, even."

"You guess?"

How was she going to explain all this? While it was refreshing to have bypassed polite conversation and jumped right into the nitty-gritty, it was a little jarring. Instead of warming up with something inane, like the weather, here they were starting out by sharing their respective childhood traumas.

While Anna got the sense she could trust Landon, she reminded herself that she didn't actually know him at all. Maybe it would be best to dial this back a notch. She waved a hand dismissively. "It doesn't matter," she said. "I'm sure you don't want to hear about my mom. It was years ago anyway."

He nodded slowly, his eyes focused intently on hers. It was almost like he was reading her, and after a few seconds, Anna had the ridiculous thought that maybe he really could read her. Wouldn't that be something? It would be so wonderful, such a relief actually, if someone could truly have a look inside her head, to the deep recesses of her mind, and help her untangle the confounding web of disconnected memories and unsettled feelings she had never been able to completely sort out.

These and other absurd thoughts were interrupted when Landon replied, "I guess I get it if you don't want to talk about stuff from the past. But if you do, I definitely want to hear it."

And she realized then that she really did. Anna wanted to open herself up to him. She wouldn't try to figure out why.

"I like to talk about her. Most of the things I know are secondhand, of course. The little I do remember about her is . . . confusing. My dad and my aunt, the two people who could best help me figure it all out, are still grieving her, which I know seems crazy after all this time, but I just can't ask them. I only have two clear memories that I know are mine, and then lots of fuzzy little snapshots that don't make any sense.

"Honestly, half the time I don't know if the things I *think* I remember about her are my own memories at all, or if they were planted in my head from pictures or stories I've heard. And a lot of times, I don't even know how to express . . . how to put into words, the things I *feel* in connection to those memories."

"Some emotions don't have words," he said simply.

Anna's eyes grew wide and her mouth fell open. "I've always thought that!" How had Landon known just the right thing to say? He'd hit the nail on the head. In her experience, people their age didn't really think too much about this kind of stuff. Where had he come up with that? She asked him.

"When you grow up in the mess I did, and you get out, you have a few scars, but as a result you can see things pretty clearly."

"Oh." It was another stupid reply.

His handsome face looked sincere when he said, "But you can try to tell me, and I can try to understand."

Anna blinked. Twice. She was standing here in her kitchen trying to make sense of her life with a Nicolet State University hockey star she hadn't even known the name of yesterday. It was absolutely surreal.

"Are you sure?" Anna asked doubtfully.

In answer, he hopped up on the counter near the sink and crossed his arms. Anna laughed and lifted herself up to sit on the island across from him. "All these kitchen chairs and an entire living room with comfy furniture, and we sit here."

He smiled. "The best conversations happen in the kitchen."

"You know, you're right."

He nodded. "So back to these memories."

"Well, like I said, there are two memories I know are mine. In the first one, Mitch was at school and my mom had gone back to bed, which she did a lot, I think. The sunshine coming through the window was so bright, I had to squint every time I looked up to check on her. I was playing with my dolls on the floor next to the bed, and I remember I got hungry for lunch.

"I was afraid to tell her, so I made myself a peanut butter sandwich. My hands were sticky, so I pulled a chair over to reach the wipes behind the sink. The chair I stood on tipped and crashed to the floor with me on it. I wasn't really hurt, just scared and crying on the floor. My mom came running and pulled me into her lap, and I remember her sitting there with me in the kitchen, still in her nightgown. She was crying too."

Anna looked at him and waited for his reaction. "That's it."

He gave her a small, encouraging smile. "And the second memory?"

"The second one must have been when she was manic. We were out in the lake in this blue kayak, the kind you sit down inside of. I was on her lap, and I was upset because my legs were getting pinched. We were wedged in really, really tight.

"I must have squirmed too much or something because we flipped. I remember the water was so cold, and I didn't have a life jacket on. My mom held on to me with one hand, and she held the kayak with the other. She kept me calm by singing 'You Give Love a Bad Name.'"

Landon broke in with a grin. "Wait a minute. Bon Jovi kept you calm?"

"I know, right? Anyway, I don't remember much else. I heard more about it years later. Some guy I bumped into in the grocery store found out who I was, and he remembered me. He was retired from the Coast Guard by then, but he was one of the guys who rescued us. I guess a strong, south wind blew us out pretty far. They took us to the hospital, but I don't remember that part. I'm sure I must have been terrified, but I don't remember that either."

"You must have been," Landon agreed. "I'm sure your mom was too."

Anna was quiet for several beats before she asked, "Can I tell you something else? Just one more thing?"

"You can tell me anything," Landon answered simply.

Anna hesitated. She was talking a lot tonight, and as good as it felt, she wondered if she should stop. In a snap decision, she plowed ahead. "I have this recurring dream, and it really bothers me. I haven't ever shared this before, not even with Olivia. Maybe I should, because I'm dreaming it more and more. I've had it twice just this last week. Anyway, in the dream, I'm standing in front of my mom. She's completely hysterical. In real life, she was so pretty, with this absolutely gorgeous, curly hair that she let grow down to her lower back, but in this dream, she's just a total disaster. Her mascara's running down her cheeks, and her hair is all sweaty and tangled.

"I'm standing there, not sure what to do. Finally, I decide to hug her, but I'm super nervous to try because I think she might push me away. When I work up the guts to reach out to her, she mirrors me, and I'm confused for a second. She looks confused too. And that's when I realize that I *am* her. I'm standing in front of a mirror. *I'm* the one who's hysterical and out of control. And then I wake up."

Anna shook her head and looked down at the floor, needing to break eye contact for a moment.

They were both quiet for several seconds before Landon spoke up. "Yeah, I don't think you need Joseph to interpret the meaning of that dream."

Anna was confused. "Joseph?"

Landon smiled. "Yeah, you know. The guy whose brothers sold him into slavery in Egypt, but he gets out by interpreting the pharaoh's dreams. I just read about it."

Nodding, Anna pretended to know what he was talking about, but he must have seen right through it because he grinned and explained, "Coach gave me a Bible and gives me ideas of what to read."

"Oh right," Anna said, her eyes lighting up. "*That* Joseph—with the colored coat. I always loved that story as a kid." She laughed before stopping to think about what he'd said. "Wait, your *hockey* coach gave you a Bible?"

He shrugged again in that way he had. "He's a PK."

"What's a PK?"

"Preacher's kid. He knows a lot about that kind of stuff, so I ask him questions sometimes."

"This is Sean you're talking about?" she clarified.

"Yep."

"Huh. That's . . . really nice," Anna marveled. "I'm used to hearing Mitch drop half a dozen *f-bombs* in just one shift on the ice. I guess I figured you were all like that. I didn't know hockey coaches . . . or players, could be so . . . wholesome."

Landon gave her a slow smile that didn't exactly feel *un*wholesome, but it did something interesting to her insides. She brought them back on track. "So, if you're Joseph, what does this dream mean?"

He sobered quickly. "It means I think you and I might have a very similar fear."

"Which is?" she prompted.

"Becoming just like our parents," he said softly, his gaze penetrating hers once more.

In that moment, Anna realized the truth of his words. She'd never given voice to this worry before. Not even to herself. What if she did end up like her mother? From what she'd been told, her mom hadn't shown any signs of bipolar disorder before Anna was born.

Taking a moment, Anna wondered about herself. She had always been afraid of feeling things too strongly. The last few weeks with Alex had been a roller coaster, and the intensity of emotion she'd felt had unsettled her. How much teenage angst was normal? Of course, she wasn't under any illusions. A girl whose bipolar mother had died in an "accident of her own making"—as she'd, unfortunately, overheard someone say once—was bound to be at least a little messed up. But maybe tonight wasn't the best time to go digging too deeply into it. She was already so raw.

She hopped down off the island. "You know, it's been a long day. Would you mind if I headed up to bed?"

Landon looked surprised and then concerned. "Of course," he said, jumping down himself. "I'm sure you're tired. You've had a rough day. And look, I'm sorry if I said too much."

"No, no. You didn't. I loved talking to you. Honestly, I hope we can talk again. I'm just feeling a little . . . Well, I don't even know the word, to be honest. I feel . . ."

"Exposed?" he offered.

That hadn't been the word at all, but as he said it, she realized it fit too. "Yes, almost naked, even," she added without thinking.

Oh no! Where had that come from? *Naked?* Landon looked at his feet and cleared his throat, a small smile playing on his lips.

"Let me show you the guest room," she said quickly, gesturing for him to follow her. "The sheets are clean, and there's a bathroom connected. Towels are in the vanity drawers. You've got your own TV in there, if you don't want to go to sleep right away. And if you get hungry, we have leftover pizza and lasagna in the fridge. Help yourself. There's a ton of pop on the shelves in the garage, so feel free."

She was talking too much—she knew she was—but it was soothing her nerves and so she continued to point out amenities as she flicked the light switch on in the spare room. But when she turned to say goodnight to Landon, she was startled into silence. She hadn't realized he'd followed so closely behind her to the threshold of the room, and even after pressing her back all the way up against the doorjamb, Landon was still mere inches away. She could feel his warm breath on her forehead as he thanked her. She didn't miss the laughter in his voice.

Anna forced herself to look up and meet his eyes. While his sparkled with amusement, she was afraid of what hers might reveal, so she quickly looked away and wished him a good night. She couldn't get to her room fast enough.

Chapter 12

The transom window over her bed was east facing, and Olivia awoke to the sun shining in, blanketing her with its light. She kept her eyes closed and stretched luxuriously—relishing in the thought that she had absolutely no reason to hop out of bed this morning. There was no place she had to be today. She could take it nice and easy, or at least as nice and easy as Nora would allow.

Listening closely, Olivia smiled as she realized Nora was still quiet. It was eight o'clock in the morning. They'd both slept in. She got up quietly and peeked into the nursery just to make sure, and then closed the door most of the way as she turned to head to the kitchen. She'd put the coffee on a timer last night. Nothing like waking up to fresh coffee, brewed all on its own—as if by magic.

She sipped quietly as she thought back to the night before. She hadn't gotten home until after midnight. The rest of the game and the dance had been uneventful, thank goodness. She hadn't wanted any more excitement after that huge fight had broken out. At least ten suspensions had been meted out because of that fight.

Olivia was worried about Anna. Alex too, truth be told. At least she could check on Anna over the weekend. She'd have to wait to see Alex. He wouldn't be able to come back to school until Wednesday of next week. She would call on Monday, she decided, just to make sure he was doing okay. It was hard not to be angry with him for hurting Anna, but she needed to remain objective if she was going to do her job well where he was concerned.

Olivia let her thoughts drift to Sean. He'd stuck around a lot longer than she thought he would. They finished watching the game and talked some more during that time, and it surprised her when he followed her back into the building and stayed for about an hour of the dance. He'd stood by her side almost the entire time, and they chatted comfortably about topics that were sort of surface and safe.

He'd brushed up against her a few times, as groups of students moved around them, and her reaction to those moments of contact embarrassed her. There was a big difference between finding someone attractive and actually being attracted *to* them. By the end of last night, Olivia realized she fell into the second category.

She had no idea what to do with that knowledge. Sean had been Nate's friend. Her friend too. Wouldn't it be weird to move into unfamiliar territory with him? And would it dishonor Nate's memory somehow? And then there was the question of whether Sean even felt anything more for her than a sort of brotherly affection. If she were honest, she got the sense that he might be interested, but she wasn't sure she could trust her male-interest radar anymore. It hadn't been used in a while, so it might not be all that reliable.

No—she didn't have any answers. In fact, before yesterday, she hadn't even wanted friendship with Sean. And now . . . now her brain hurt just trying to figure out her own mind and what she wanted. She might as well be a teenage girl again for all the distress she was feeling—and all over a boy. Maybe a woman never really outgrew her boy-crazy phase, and it just lay dormant, like a sleeping giant, until awakened again. Olivia was definitely awake.

An hour later, she was still in the kitchen cleaning up from breakfast when a knock came at the back slider door off the deck. Anna was the only one who would come to this door, so Olivia wasn't at all surprised to see her neighbor standing there in jeans, flip flops, and an oversized sweatshirt. She had a travel coffee mug in hand and wore a soft smile. Olivia was relieved. Anna looked well-rested and maybe even happy. She hadn't expected that.

"Morning," she said through the screen as she slid the door over. "You're up early."

"Yeah, I got up when Mitch and Landon left. Jess's mom came over early to pick her up too, so it's just been me for the last half hour."

"Hmm," Olivia said before taking a sip of her own coffee. "You had a houseful. Early practice for your brother this morning, huh?"

"He did not look good when he left."

"I'm sure he didn't. Hangovers will do that to you," Olivia said wryly.

"Oh, it wasn't that," Anna clarified, putting down her mug so she could lift Nora out of her playpen. The baby immediately grabbed a fistful of

Anna's hair. This was becoming a nasty habit, Olivia realized in dismay.

Anna worked to free her hair with Olivia's help before continuing. "I don't think he really had all that much to drink. I actually think he's coming down with something."

"Oh no! That's too bad."

"I'm sure he'll be fine. If he gets a cold, I still have some of your frozen chicken noodle soup I can give him. That stuff can cure anything." Anna switched gears. "So, how did the rest of your night go?"

"I was going to ask you the same thing. Are you okay? You look better than I thought you would."

"You know, I'm surprised, but I'm doing alright. I feel like I should be devastated and laying in bed with a box of chocolates and tissues right now." She shrugged. "It's not like I'm happy about what happened or anything. I miss Alex already, and I feel sad when I really stop and think about it, but I think I was ready to get off the roller coaster. I'm not so anxious anymore. I'm sure when I see him around at school and other places, it'll be hard. But right now, I'm okay. It helps that I turned off Snapchat notifications. I think I'll keep it off for a while. I'm taking a break from Instagram too."

"Good plan." Olivia pressed her palm to her heart. "And I'm relieved you're okay. I guess I'm glad you had a houseful, so you weren't alone last night. If it were anyone else, I'd be less than thrilled about four unchaperoned teenagers staying the night together, but you and Mitch have always been so grown up. You've had to be, I guess."

"Wow. You're calling Mitch a grown up. Your opinion of him is improving."

"Oh, you know I like Mitch. He's a good kid. I just don't like your family situation for your sake. That's all."

"Well, I'm fine, but thanks for caring. And you should know, there were only three teenagers at my house last night. Landon is twenty." She wiggled her eyebrows.

Olivia laughed. "Do I detect some interest here?"

"Oh, I don't know." Anna moved to put Nora back down in her playpen. "I just broke up with Alex, so I'm really not looking for anything. But I have eyes, you know? He's cute. And he's super nice."

"Hmm."

"I'm going to the scrimmage this afternoon. I'm excited to watch Mitch, and now I know one of his teammates too. He's number twelve. I asked this morning."

"Hmm," Olivia said again, smiling from behind her coffee mug.

"Do you think maybe you'd want to go? You and Nora? Jess can't come. Her dad's being weird."

"Her dad *is* weird." Olivia rolled her eyes.

"I know. Anyway, do you want to go?"

No, not really, she thought to herself. To Anna she said, "I'm not sure. I have nothing else going on, but . . ."

Anna picked up on her reluctance. "Have you been back to a hockey game since . . . ?"

"No, I haven't," Olivia admitted. "And I've always really loved hockey. I've missed it, but—"

"Great, so you'll go with me?" Anna interrupted excitedly.

Olivia sighed. "I'm not sure I want to see Sean there." More accurately, she didn't want Sean to see her. She'd look like she was stalking him. Or something.

"Oh no! So you guys didn't make up last night?" Before Olivia could answer, she added, "I can't believe he was there. I didn't know you were meeting up, but I was so glad to finally meet him. He's really something else in the looks department, Olivia. And did you know he reads the Bible?"

Olivia laughed. "I guess I assumed, with his background."

"Didn't you make up?" Anna asked a second time.

"No, no, we did."

Anna looked confused. "So what then?"

This was getting uncomfortable. She felt like she was fifteen years old. Olivia began arranging the vase of flowers on the island to avoid having to look at the all-too-perceptive Anna. It took her all of two seconds to read Olivia's mind.

"Olivia! Do you have feelings for?—"

"Don't say it!" Olivia held her hand up defensively. "Don't say it," she repeated, this time less forcefully. "I'm not ready for this, for any of this."

Anna rested her hip against the edge of the island countertop. "What do you mean by *this*?"

"You know. *Feelings*."

"Feelings for someone else, or feelings for Sean?"

"I don't know, Anna. I really don't."

Anna studied her for a moment.

"I think you should come."

"Oh yeah? And why's that?"

"Because I need a ride." Anna grinned.

***

"Are you sure Mr. Niemi didn't mind towing my car to the dealership?" Anna asked for the second time from the passenger seat of Olivia's van.

"No. Like I said, Harry loves to help people out. That's one reason he keeps all that equipment and all those tools around. He's retired and lonely now that he's a widower. His kids have gone off to the four corners, and I don't think they visit much. Any time he can do a little work for someone, he's all over it. Really, he's just the best neighbor." She looked at Anna and winked. "After you, I mean."

Olivia's flannel-wearing neighbor was a true godsend and had helped her out countless times. She always returned the favor with something home-cooked or home-baked. Otherwise, Olivia knew Harry lived off of takeout and frozen dinners. He was always so happy to get some homemade cookies or hearty soup. "It thrilled Harry to make that path between our houses, you know. He's a real sweetheart that way."

"I know. I just feel bad."

Your dad's the one who should feel bad. That's what Olivia wanted to say. What kind of father abandoned his daughter without a working vehicle? How was Anna supposed to get to school? Or practice? Or any place else she needed to be? She wanted to slap that man awake. Steven Davis was basically going through life asleep, and he was missing everything. He had two great kids, but half the time it seemed like he'd simply forgotten they existed.

"They said your car should be ready by Monday afternoon. I can get you to school and then drive you over there afterwards, before your meet. Will you have money to pay for the work?"

"Thanks, Olivia. And yeah, I've got the credit card for this kind of stuff."

"Do you have practice tomorrow?"

"Yep, but Mitch said he'd drive me."

"If anything changes, let me know. I'm around."

"Okay, thanks. And thanks for coming with me today. Sorry if I pressured you."

"*If* you pressured me?"

Anna laughed.

"Who are they scrimmaging against?" Olivia asked.

"Michigan Tech."

Michigan Technological University was another Division One school over in Houghton, about two hours away from Nicolet. The school had a great reputation for churning out well-trained engineers of all stripes. They were also well known for their hockey program, and there was a nice rivalry between Michigan Tech and Nicolet State.

"This will be a good game, then. I hope Nora loves it." Olivia felt the familiar surge of excitement that she always used to experience before watching a game. Its unexpected return was as gratifying as a surprise visit from a long-lost friend.

Anna peered into the back seat. "If she wakes up for it."

Nora was awake all right, thanks to the loud noise of the buzzer. Once she got accustomed to that new sound, she was surprisingly content to sit and watch the game from Anna's lap. The three of them sat directly behind the glass at center ice—best seats in the house. Playing had already begun by the time they got there, and they were only among a handful of other spectators. They observed the play on the ice in silence for a short time before Olivia asked if Mitch had been out yet. Anna, who had been watching for her brother for the last several minutes, replied in disappointment, "No. Not yet."

"What number is he?"

"Twenty-four. I'll let you know when he's out on the ice. I'm looking for him."

"I noticed your Landon. He's quite the defenseman. Big guy."

"He's not *my* Landon."

"So you say," Olivia said with a sly smile.

"Oh, come on," Anna said, rolling her eyes as she laughed. But the truth was, she had looked for Landon almost immediately upon entering the arena. When she first spotted him, she experienced a body-wide tingling sensation. She didn't like thinking about why that happened whenever she looked at him. Because if she was already over Alex and ready to move on, what did that say about her? That she was just a fickle teenager with no emotional depth? What if it was something worse, like a mood disorder? She'd lain awake last night, worrying that maybe she'd inherited one from her mother. She needed some reassurance on that front, and who better than Olivia to ask. She knew all about this stuff. Anna glanced at Olivia, who was watching the game intently.

"Can I ask you something?" Anna asked, playing with the seam on the hood of Nora's coat.

"Shoot," Olivia said, without taking her eyes off the ice.

"Can bipolar disorder be hereditary?"

Olivia sucked in a breath and turned to look at her. Anna chuckled. She had her full attention now. "I'm sorry, I know that was a big shift in conversation."

Olivia, having recovered from her surprise, touched Anna's arm gently. "To be honest with you, I've wondered when we'd have this conversation. Are you worrying about it?"

Anna nodded. "Especially after this week. I've been all over the map with how I'm feeling."

"Honey, I think that's completely normal. You suffered a big breakup this week. A big change to your life."

Anna turned to face her more fully and nodded. "But that's just it," she said earnestly. "It was a huge deal, right? And look at me today. I'm not even sad at the moment. How can that be? I felt, almost . . . overwrought last night at the school, and today I'm fine? I don't think that's normal."

Olivia chuckled. "Well, *normal* for people and *normal* for teenagers are two completely different things, Anna." At Anna's frown, she rushed to continue and moved her hand up to Anna's shoulder. "I'm sorry. I don't mean to make light of this. This is a serious question, and I want to give you a serious answer. I have absolutely no concerns about you having bipolar disorder at this time. I think what you're feeling is one hundred percent in the realm of normal." At Anna's dubious expression, she repeated, "One hundred percent."

Anna let out a whoosh of air. "Okay, so right now I'm normal. What about in the future?"

Olivia weighed her words before speaking, which made Anna squirm a little.

"It is true that bipolar disorder is more common in people who have a first-degree relative with the diagnosis. But it doesn't mean it will affect you too. Look at your Aunt Heidi. I think I read once that the DNA of identical twins is something like 99.99 percent the same, and yet your aunt doesn't have bipolar disorder. So, yes, there's a genetic component, but there are other factors, and the bottom line is that there's treatment."

"Yeah, but look how that worked out for my mom," Anna pointed out.

"I can't speak to your mom specifically, but there are millions of Americans living with bipolar disorder and managing it really well. They have successful careers, they have loving families and healthy friendships . . ."

That was true. Anna had done enough research over the years to know that. "Olivia, I'm just scared. I don't want to hurt people. My mom's illness, it hurt my dad. It hurt Mitch and Aunt Heidi."

"And *you*, Anna. It hurt you too." Olivia spoke gently.

Anna nodded. She knew it was true.

Olivia continued, "But we can't live life worrying about all the 'what ifs.' We'd make ourselves crazy. Instead, educate yourself. Know the signs. Don't fret and obsess over them, though. Cross that bridge if you have to, armed with knowledge, but not before. If something happens, you'll get treatment."

Anna was silent as she bounced Nora up and down on her knee. The future probably had enough trouble of its own. It made little sense to bring it into the present, which had its own share of problems. Aunt Heidi had told her something like that once. Anna just wished she could know for certain if she would end up having to battle the disorder whose effects had always loomed so large in her life.

Olivia broke into her thoughts. “Anna, I *know* you. If it comes to that, you’ll handle it the way you do everything else: with strength and dignity and determination.” She put her arm around Anna’s shoulders and added, “And you’ll always have me to lean on. No matter what.”

Anna pressed into Olivia, trying to absorb some of the rock-solid strength she always exuded. “Thanks, Olivia.”

“You’re welcome.” She gave Anna one last squeeze before saying, “Your boy’s out again.”

Anna and Olivia spent the next period cheering on Nicolet’s team together, taking turns holding Nora and keeping her entertained. Anna knew the game of hockey, and Landon was a very, very good defenseman and all-round player. He was lightning fast, seemingly everywhere at once, and he had an explosive slapshot that he’d already used to score from his position near the blue line.

“Look at him go,” Olivia marveled in the third period. “He’s quick for how tall he is.”

“Who, Landon?” Anna asked, even though she knew exactly who Olivia was referring to. Olivia gave her a knowing look but said nothing. Instead, she adjusted one of Nora’s little booties she’d kicked halfway off.

“I wonder if Mitch is even going to play. There’s only five minutes left in the period,” Anna mused, adjusting the baby in her lap. “Maybe Coach is teaching him a lesson or something.”

“Could be,” Olivia answered distractedly, still trying to tie the laces on the booty as Nora kicked her legs and squealed with delight, sweetly oblivious to the difficulty she was adding to the task.

Anna looked around the arena and spotted Mr. Benninger. “Oh look, Benny’s here,” she said, waving up at him.

“Goody,” Olivia muttered, but she turned also to look and smiled a greeting at Mr. Benninger. But the smile disappeared a little too quickly once she turned back around, and Anna knew it hadn’t been genuine.

“What? You don’t like Benny?”

Olivia bobbed her head from side to side before answering. “It’s not that I don’t like him, exactly.”

“Well, what then?”

“I don’t know. I just find him a little irritating, I guess. He tries too hard. He’s too smooth. Like a used car salesman, and I definitely don’t want what he’s selling.”

“Huh,” Anna said, flabbergasted by this revelation. Everyone loved Benny, or so she’d thought. “He’s single, you know.”

"Yes. I do know this."

"Oh," Anna said slowly, drawing out the *o*. "He must have hit on you or something."

"Or something. Let's just say I did my best to avoid him. He was just a little too eager."

Anna wasn't having it. "Well, I think he's great."

"Alright. In a few years, you can date him."

"Olivia! Gross! He's, like, old."

"Hey! He's *my* age!"

"Exactly," Anna smiled mischievously.

Olivia gave Anna a small shove. "You'd better watch out. I'm your ride the next few days."

Anna laughed.

"Anyway," Olivia continued, "he's moved on. He's busy making Erin Hennings uncomfortable now."

"Our principal? Wow!" Anna thought on this a moment. "You know, I can see them together. They'd be cute."

Now it was Olivia's turn to be revolted; she pulled a face.

"Seriously, Olivia. I don't get it. Benny's hot for an old guy, and he's so sweet. What am I missing here?"

"A lot, apparently. He was pretty persistent with me, mostly because I just couldn't bring myself to come right out and tell him to leave me alone. But Erin has no filter. She says exactly what she thinks. If she's not interested, she'll put the kibosh on it right away."

"If she wants to," Anna said doubtfully. It was surprising, really. Olivia usually seemed to read people really well, but she was dead wrong about Benny. Too bad. Anna could kind of see them together. Although, by the looks of things, Olivia wouldn't be interested in anyone who wasn't a hot college hockey coach with a crew cut. Anna had been sneaking peeks at her friend off and on throughout the game, and Olivia had been doing more watching of the coaching than she was of the playing.

She'd been right. Olivia had it bad, and Anna was thrilled.

It was definitely time for Olivia to move on. Anna had teased her earlier about being old, but really, she was still so young and had so much to offer. She was gorgeous and kind, and the playful and funny part of herself that she'd told Anna might never come back had reemerged in a big way over the last few months—the last few weeks especially. She was like a tulip. She'd been lying dormant over a long, dark winter, but now spring was here, and she seemed ready to bloom. It was beautiful to see, Anna thought as she studied her neighbor.

"You're staring at me," Olivia accused without taking her eyes off the game.

"Sorry," Anna said quickly, suddenly embarrassed.

Olivia turned and looked at her then. "I was just teasing. What is it?"

"I was just thinking that I'm really happy you're here with me." It was the truth.

"Aww, kiddo. I'm happy too." Olivia put an arm around her again, allowing her head to rest briefly against Anna's.

Anna felt a lump growing in her throat and was grateful that Nora chose that moment to squirm in her lap and cry. Olivia scooped her daughter up and kissed her nose. Nora calmed immediately and flashed a drooly smile, first at Olivia and then at Anna.

"Faker," Anna teased.

"She knows just how to get what she wants, I'll tell you that."

The buzzer sounded, signaling the end of the game. The score was four to two—Nicolet. Anna was standing up to stretch her legs when number twelve skated by and pounded the glass in greeting. She hadn't been watching, so she flinched in surprise and then laughed at the sight of Landon smiling at her from around his mouth guard as he skated backwards towards the bench.

Anna felt a surge of . . . *something*, and it kept a smile on her face long after he'd skated away. Her heart felt unexpectedly full at the moment. That really was the only way she could describe it. She was so busy basking in the glory of the moment that she missed Olivia's knowing smirk.

Chapter 13

Mitch never made it onto the ice. Olivia was fairly certain this was a direct result of last night's choices, and she respected Sean for going a little easy on Mitch while making sure he didn't get off scot-free. But as they walked away from the bleacher seats, Anna voiced her disappointment over not having been able to watch her brother play.

"Dad was supposed to come, or at least he planned to at one point. I'm really glad he didn't. Mitch would have hated to sit the bench with Dad watching. I'm sure he's upset enough as it is. Do you mind if we hang around so I can say hi to him quick?"

Olivia had a sneaking suspicion Mitch wasn't the only one Anna wanted to say hello to, but she didn't mention that. She really didn't want to wait around herself, though, because she feared it might look like she was some kind of groupie just hoping to get a glimpse of the team's gorgeous coach. Although, it'd be pretty hard to mistake her for a groupie these days. If the wrinkles around her eyes didn't give her away, the diaper bag on one arm and baby on the other definitely would. Suddenly, she felt ridiculous.

"Actually, Nora and I will just head back to the car and wait for you there, but you take your time."

"Are you sure? 'Cause I don't have to wait."

Olivia reassured her several times before making her way through the arena towards the exit. It felt really strange being back in this place, especially when she'd first walked in. Somehow, it felt both like a lifetime ago and just yesterday that she'd sat in these stands, game after game, cheering for her husband's team. It was a relief to have this behind her now. She'd done it. She'd come back into this place, Nate's place, and had made it through a game without feeling overwhelmed by sadness.

At first it had been jarring to see Sean standing in Nate's spot, shouting Nate's orders, and managing Nate's team. Yet she'd found that she could hardly look away. The more she watched Sean, the more he seemed to fit perfectly in that role and the harder it was to picture Nate ever having filled it himself. The mind was an odd thing. So, too, were memories.

Until fairly recently, Olivia had often felt distraught and panicked when a memory appeared to be fading. Sometimes she'd find she couldn't clearly recall all the features of Nate's face, and she'd have to find a picture of him to reassure herself that she wasn't forgetting him.

But now something had shifted. She wasn't even sure what it was exactly, but she found she wasn't holding on so tightly anymore, and it was okay that her recollections were starting to resemble images done in soft focus. They'd jabbed at her with their sharp edges for so long that it was a welcome change. She truly hadn't believed that she'd ever be able to find peace, and yet here it was, staring her in the face. She was ready to grab on to it with both hands.

The trophy case was near the entrance to the arena, and Olivia stopped to look at the display. She'd been there when some of those trophies had been awarded. Seemed like a lifetime ago. There were pictures too. She recognized faces of players she hadn't thought about in years.

While she was studying the last team picture that included Nate, she heard heavy, fast footfalls approaching from the corridor behind her. She turned in time to see Sean round the corner at a rapid clip, but he stopped short when he saw her. A look of uncertainty crossed his handsome features as he hesitated before continuing forward, closing the rest of the distance between them.

"I thought maybe I'd missed you," he said.

"No," she answered simply, and then added, "Aren't you supposed to be in the middle of your post game pep talk right about now?"

"I left them with Jackson for a second."

Olivia assumed that was the name of his assistant coach. She nodded and then searched for something more to say. "Your boys played well."

"Yeah, they did. Thanks," he returned. They continued to stare at one another, neither one knowing what to say next. Sean broke the silence.

"How was it, being back here? It's been a while."

"You know, it actually feels okay."

"You sound surprised."

"I might've built it up in my mind a little. I didn't really know what to expect, I guess, but I'm trying new things these days."

He nodded, silently rocking back on his heels as he studied her. "Well, I'm really glad you came. It was nice looking across the ice and seeing you there. Felt like old times." He looked down at the floor as he shuffled his feet.

She smiled ruefully, remembering how she hadn't been able to stop staring at him. Had he noticed? "Maybe not quite like old times," she said.

Sean looked up at that. “Maybe not quite,” he agreed, his eyes locking on hers once more. He cleared his throat. “Listen, some of us are heading over to 906 Pizza when we finish here. If you don’t have plans . . .”

“Oh, thanks, but I’ve got Nora.” She lifted the baby higher on her hip.

“I’ll help you with her.”

“Well, I also have to give Mitch’s sister a ride home. We came together, and I’m sure she needs to get going and finish up homework and . . . stuff.” Of course, that was the moment Anna appeared from around the corner.

“Oh! Hey, Coach,” she said breathlessly. Sean nodded at her in greeting.

“Olivia, do you think maybe we could grab some pizza with the team? We’re invited.” Anna schooled her features into a caricature of hopeful pleading, and Olivia realized she would not be able to say no.

Sean’s lips curved into a slow, satisfied smile.

The popular pizza parlor was a short drive away, which was good because it didn’t give Olivia enough time to lose her nerve. Anna chatted happily—for the most part—in the seat beside her the entire way there. The only thing that tempered her enthusiasm was that she still hadn’t seen her brother, and she openly wondered what kind of mood he’d be in when she did. She wasn’t even sure Mitch knew she was joining the team for pizza and worried that he might not like it. It turned out that Landon had zipped out of the locker room with his skates still on to ask her if she wanted to go.

“What is this, Olivia? Is this, like, a date? How will I know where to sit? I don’t want to assume that he wants to sit with me, but he must if he asked me, right?” she fretted.

“Just take his lead,” Olivia advised absently. The truth was, she was wondering the same thing. Had Sean invited her out on a date? What was this exactly?

“What does that even mean, ‘take his lead?’” Anna wondered out loud. “Do I sit with him or not?”

“Don’t worry so much. It will work out just fine. You can start out sitting with me if you’re not sure.”

“Alright,” Anna answered, slightly mollified.

“And if you feel nervous, you can always hide behind Nora. She’s going to need to eat and have a bottle while we’re there. You can keep busy feeding her if you need to. I’m glad I brought a jar of baby food and some formula, just in case.”

“Yeah. If you hadn’t, we wouldn’t have been able to join them.”

Olivia frowned. This was true. If only she *had* been a little less prepared, she'd be driving home right now where her favorite sweatpants were just waiting for her to slide them on. Instead, she was heading over to 906 Pizza for what may or may not be a date with Sean and actively sweating through the armpits of her blouse as she tried to figure it all out.

Speaking of active, Anna was nearly bouncing out of her seat with excitement. "We're almost there. I think we'll beat the team," she said.

"I'm sure we will. Hopefully they're still showering away that awful hockey smell." Olivia wrinkled her nose. "The gear alone is bad enough. Especially the gloves."

"It really *is* bad," Anna agreed. "I remember driving home from Fargo with Mitch and his friend and the friend's parents after a tournament. I can't even describe the smell. It was nine hours of olfactory torture."

Olivia was still laughing at Anna's wit when she pulled into the parking lot of the pizzeria. Claiming a space next to a red Mini Cooper, she reminded herself she was just like that sweet little car—compact, but with loads of spunk. Or at least she used to have loads of spunk. She could really use some tonight. Continuing to admire the Mini, Olivia opened her door and stepped out into the dappled streaks of sunshine that cut through the distant hedge of tree branches beyond Grimsby's Park off to the west. There was no question: The days were getting shorter now. Soon the snow would fly.

Anna beat her to Nora's car seat and hoisted the baby out, so Olivia grabbed the diaper bag and her purse, and the three of them headed inside. They'd just gotten the baby situated in one of the restaurant's high chairs on the end of a booth when Olivia heard the bell on the door jingle, and she turned to see Sean and several players filing through.

"I'm ridiculously nervous," Anna muttered under her breath as she shook out some puffy finger-food treats on Nora's tray.

"You're not the only one," Olivia admitted, giving Anna's shoulder a light squeeze.

Anna looked at Olivia in surprise. "Thanks! That actually makes me feel better."

"Oh, sure. Anytime," Olivia joked.

The two friends hadn't sat down yet. Rather, they flanked the baby on either side of the high chair. 906 Pizza was one of those places where you placed your order up at the counter and waited for your food to be brought out to you. Olivia had chosen a double booth near the front counter with a divider that could be lowered or raised. It was all the way down at the moment. She smiled at Sean as he greeted her from the end of the booth on the opposite side of the divider.

"You haven't ordered yet, I hope?" he asked. Olivia shook her head. "Good, because this is on me tonight. Do you still like the Pizza Margherita?"

Olivia must have shown her surprise because he chuckled and said, "You didn't think I'd forget that, did you?" He flashed a wide grin before turning to place their order at the counter.

Olivia loved Margherita Pizza because of the huge chunks of garlic found on every slice, but it had always annoyed Nate when she ordered it. He could not abide the smell of garlic, which she inevitably smelled like for hours after indulging in a few slices of the delicious pizza. As a result, she had rarely allowed herself to eat it, and when she did, Nate would grumble about it. They'd had a big, ridiculous fight over it once, right here in this restaurant, with Sean and Suze looking on. Sean must have remembered, and Olivia looked down at her hands as she thought back to that incident.

Nate really had been a world-class jerk sometimes. She'd been so embarrassed that night. She recalled that she barely spoke to him the rest of the evening afterward, and they'd even gone to bed angry—over pizza. Except that, of course, it hadn't really been about the pizza.

Sean was getting input on the order from the dozen or so young men who had joined him near the counter. Olivia recognized Landon from last night, and she watched as he headed over towards herself and Anna.

Smiling, he nodded a greeting to her before addressing Anna. "Do you want to sit over there on the other side of this booth?" He pointed to the booth that adjoined the one Olivia was now seated in.

"Sure," Anna said. She winked at Olivia before following him around to the other side. She sat on the same side as Olivia and slid to the middle of the bench seat. "I can still help with Nora if you need me," she said, leaning closer to the divider. "We can just pass her back and forth."

Olivia smiled. "I'm sure I'll be fine. You have fun." She didn't bother to ask before she slid over and raised the divider so that it was halfway up. That way, if Anna needed her, she was still accessible, but it would give her and Landon a little privacy. Anna shot her a grateful look.

By the time Olivia had dug the jar of prunes and a baby spoon out of the diaper bag, Sean appeared with a pitcher of root beer and two glasses. He set them down on the table before sliding in across from her. Her heart gave a brief flutter. How he could look this good in a white t-shirt and jeans, she had no idea.

"There. That's done. It always amazes me how much pizza hockey players can eat," he said, shaking his head with a baffled grin. "I just ordered ten large pizzas, and now I'm wondering if it'll be enough. It's a good thing Zach Jackson, my assistant coach, couldn't come tonight. That guy can eat a whole pizza by himself."

Olivia laughed. "Impressive. I'm sure ten pizzas will be more than enough. You'll be eating leftovers for a week."

"You'd be surprised," he said, watching as Olivia reached over and snapped a bib around Nora's neck. Nora must have decided she'd been patient long enough, and she let out a series of angry howls, arching her back the way all angry babies seemed to know how to do. People in the restaurant were looking at them, but Olivia kept her composure. In fact, focusing on the baby helped settle her nerves.

Sean looked impressed. "She's madder than a hornet. Better get her fed." He eyed up the spoonful of prunes and shook his head. "I'm not sure I'd be too excited about eating that either. Poor kid wants a pizza."

"That may be, but prunes it is for tonight. Gotta keep her regular, you know." She cringed on the inside. Leave it to her to bring up baby poop on a dinner date.

Sean wrinkled his nose. "I guess."

He watched as Nora calmed down and ate what Olivia fed her. After a minute of silence, Olivia looked at him and asked, "Do you want to do it?" What had started out as an almost fascinated expression turned quickly to one of terror, and it was so absurd that it made Olivia laugh out loud, erasing any lingering nerves she may have had.

"It's not hard. Here," she said, handing him the spoon and the jar of prunes, still chuckling. He took the spoon awkwardly and dipped it in the jar, loading it up with the purple mash—maybe too much—because most of the spoonful fell with a decisive *splat* on Nora's tray before he could reach her mouth, which remained open in comical anticipation of the delicious bite.

Sean laughed ruefully. "I can manage a team of twenty young men, but I can't manage to feed a baby prunes. Go figure."

"Try again," Olivia said once she'd regained control of herself. She wiped tears from her eyes. One of Sean's players nudged the guy sitting next to him, and gestured towards them with a wide grin.

Nora wailed again as she waited for Sean to reload. Now, all the players were watching the scene play out, and one of them yelled, "Come on, Coach! Fast and furious!" Another one chimed in, "Yeah, eye on the target, and just remember . . . It's not worth doing if you don't do it right."

Sean gave them a look of mock exasperation. "Are you gonna throw all my one-liners back at me? Let me tell ya, this is a lot harder than it looks. But hey, at least I know you're paying attention."

The guys laughed good-naturedly and began to chant, "Coach! Coach! Coach!" Sean grinned broadly and tried again, this time successfully transporting the contents of the spoon into Nora's waiting mouth. "Goal!" one of them yelled, fist raised.

Olivia's face hurt from laughing, and she looked at Anna to see that she was enjoying it all too. Once everyone turned back to their own conversations at their tables, and Sean had delivered several more bites, Olivia became serious. "So what happened with Mitch today? I noticed he didn't play, and now he's not here tonight."

Sean scraped the bottom of the jar. "I imagine he's pretty miffed about being sat. There was last night, which you already know about, and then he showed up fifteen minutes late for dry land this morning. I was prepared to let him play today, but he had a baditude and seemed pretty sluggish, even though I only gave him a light workout. I'd say he gave about fifty percent, and I just couldn't reward that."

Baditude. Olivia smiled. She'd have to remember that one. "I get it. It's all about the life lessons, right?"

He cocked his head in Anna's direction. "Was she disappointed?"

"Only a little. He was only half the reason she was there."

"I suppose the other half is sitting across from her?"

"You nailed it," Olivia said. She leaned forward to sip out of her straw, feeling completely at ease now. Her nerves had settled and been replaced with that old feeling of camaraderie she'd always felt with Sean. But that wasn't all she felt. This new awareness of him was definitely a big part of the mix too.

"Landon's a great kid. Hard worker. Comes from a bad home situation. I think he's got a lot to prove. To himself, I mean. I think that's probably what drives him the most."

"It always amazes me when kids with backgrounds like that turn out as well as they do," Olivia admitted.

"He's asking a lot of questions lately. Meaning-of-life type questions. He's different this year. Last year, we weren't all that close. I think he was partying pretty hard. Just looking for a good time and trying to fill a void. He'll tell you he came away feeling emptier than ever. It taught him something, though. He and I are pretty tight these days. And you know me, I never miss an opportunity to preach." He winked.

"But you're never *preachy*. Nate loved that about you. He always knew where you stood on things, but he never felt judged. I'm glad this boy has you in his life. He's lucky. And I'm really glad he's a good kid because she's already halfway to smitten by the looks of it." Olivia peeked over at Anna and Landon. They were absorbed in conversation. Anna must have said something funny because Landon threw his head back and laughed.

"She could do worse."

"And she has," Olivia said wryly.

"That guy last night? The bloody one?"

Olivia nodded.

"Yeah. He looked like a chump to me."

"He's actually not a bad kid, just too into himself to be good boyfriend material. It doesn't help that he's a little messed up right now."

"Messed up. I think that description would apply to Mitch at the moment too."

"Really? What's going on? Besides what I already know."

Sean worked at the last remaining bit of food at the bottom of the jar and fed it to Nora, who was now happily playing with the liquid prunes on the tray. She lifted her smeared hands up to her face and hair, leaving a trail of purple, wet mess behind. She was absolutely delighted with herself. Sean smiled sheepishly. "Sorry about that."

"Never fear," Olivia said, reaching into her bag. "I come prepared." She held up the packet of travel wipes.

Still grinning, he filled her in as she cleaned up the mess. "I don't know if you've ever seen him play. I guess you could say Mitch is a bit of a phenom. Players like him don't come around every day, so we're lucky to have him, but he worries me. I think he's let it all go to his head. Some of these kids, they adjust just fine to the little taste of celebrity they get when they play for this school. Everyone knows who they are. I don't have to tell you how it is. The girls. The parties. The hero worship from the town."

Olivia nodded. She remembered.

"He's not handling it well. Plus, and maybe you can help me with this since you know the family, but there's something about his dynamic with his dad that I think might be messing with his head." Sean shrugged. "I could be wrong, but I don't think I am."

"No. You're not wrong." Olivia glanced at Anna and saw that she was engaged in conversation with Landon before she filled Sean in on what she knew about the Davis family dynamics. She spoke in a low voice, and he listened quietly, shaking his head regretfully from time to time.

When she finished, he said, "I knew about the mom, and I figured something was up with the dad. I just didn't know what."

"It's sad."

"She seems to do okay, no?" he said, tipping his head in Anna's direction.

"She does, but she has her own scars. They do what they can to cope and get through the day, you know? They've gotten by, doing what they're doing, for fifteen years."

Sean shook his head again. "I just hope we don't watch Mitch go off the deep end and throw it all away. He's got some things going for him, though. A sister who cares, a coach who cares, and a roommate who's already learned from some of the same mistakes he's making. Landon will watch out for him."

Olivia sighed. "I guess time will tell."

"Always does."

Nora started to make some more noise. She was used to having a bottle directly after her evening meal. "If you can just give me a minute, I'm going to ask for some warm water to make her a bottle. Can you keep an eye on her for me?"

"Sure. We're old friends now." He took hold of Nora's hand, and Olivia watched her daughter squeeze his pointer finger and gaze up at him with an innocent smile. She felt a reverberation of that squeeze deep in her chest, and she turned away with a wistful smile on her lips.

She loved how Nora and Sean looked together. They made a sweet picture, and for a moment she wondered how the three of them might appear to some stranger looking their way. She bet they would look like a family. Two parents out with their baby on a Saturday night. Olivia felt a twinge of longing.

There wasn't a wait at the counter, so it didn't take long for her to get what she needed. When she turned back, she saw that Sean had taken Nora out of the high chair and was holding her hands in his and standing her up, facing him, on his thighs. His smile was wide, and she could hear Nora give a happy little gurgle. A picture of Nate flashed into her mind. He'd never hold his daughter like his best friend was doing now, and that was an unspeakably sad reality.

Anna stopped her before Olivia got back to her table, which helped bring her thoughts around. "I can give Nora her bottle if that's what you're about to do."

"It's okay. I can do it. Unless you want to?"

"Yeah. I do, and Landon wants to meet her."

"Hand her over, Coach," Landon said, reaching over the divide for the baby. Sean looked at Olivia for permission, which she gave with a nod.

She handed Anna the bottle with the pre-measured formula inside, followed by the glass of warm water. "Just fill it up to six ounces, " she instructed. Nora was happily bouncing in Landon's lap as Olivia took her seat. She smiled contentedly. "I love her, of course," she said, referring to Nora, "but it's so nice to have help sometimes."

Sean observed Landon and Nora together and laughed when he witnessed her reach out and bat at Landon's nose. He turned his attention back to Olivia. "I'm sure it gets tough, but I know you wouldn't trade it."

"Never," she agreed, and then noticing the look of wistfulness that crossed his face, she tipped her head and asked, "What is it?"

He just shook his head. "A story for another time, I think."

But Olivia's curiosity was piqued.

"Is that the ticking of a biological clock I'm hearing?" she asked, working to strike a teasing tone. Of course Sean must think about having a family of his own one day, but the idea of it made her heart sink. She didn't want to think about him sitting here with his beautiful wife and two kids. She would never have that with him.

He smiled ruefully, but said nothing. This wasn't quite the response she'd expected.

"Sean? You can talk to me, you know."

Looking up, he met her eyes and held her gaze. "I do know," he said simply.

He glanced around a second to make sure nobody was close enough to hear him. He needn't have worried. The place was abuzz with numerous conversations happening all at once.

"Suze was pregnant," he said quietly.

Olivia's mouth fell open. "What? When?"

"Around the time of the accident. I didn't know."

"What happened?" Olivia put her hands over her mouth. "Oh no. Did she lose the baby?"

He didn't answer right away, fiddling instead with the napkin in front of him. For a second Olivia thought he might not give an answer at all, but then he said, "It was . . . by choice, Olivia. Hers."

"Oh, Sean."

He went on. "She said she wasn't ready yet. To be a mother. You know Suze. She wanted things done in a certain way. First, she wanted to finish her master's degree. She was less than a year away from that. Then we were supposed to get married and settle into our new house with our new dog, a friggin' *poodle*, by the way. And she wanted to be married for two years—just the three of us, me, her, and the dumb dog, before trying to have a kid. So you see, it wasn't that she didn't want to have a baby with me, it just wasn't in the right order, and I didn't get to have a say. It's just a fluke I even found out about it at all . . . afterward." His voice was bitter, and the look of raw pain when he met her eyes made Olivia's own eyes sting.

"That just shouldn't be," she whispered.

"Well, it *is* all the same. That was my kid too, *my* baby. You know? I know it's not a popular opinion to have these days, and it's definitely not how she saw it." He looked over at Nora with a longing that made Olivia's heart break.

"I'm so sorry, Sean."

"Yeah, well . . ." He cleared his throat and dropped his gaze. "Thanks. Me too."

"And afterwards, you and Suze . . ."

"I just couldn't go on, Livvy. I just couldn't stay with her after that. It was over."

Olivia nodded. "I get it." She placed a comforting hand over his, not realizing how intimate the gesture would be. He flipped his hand over and held on to hers, gently but firmly, and Olivia blushed profusely as she stared at their intertwined hands.

Sean cleared his throat again, this time holding her gaze. "Livvy, can I just ask—do you feel it? This *thing* between us? It can't just be me . . . right?"

She looked down at the table and smiled. Sean had never been one to beat around the bush. "It's not," she admitted. "I feel it too."

"And do you feel a little guilty about it?"

"Yes."

"What do you think he'd say?"

"Get away from my woman?" she suggested, with a hollow laugh. "Sorry, that's not funny."

He sighed heavily and absentmindedly played with her hand. "I like to think we'd have his blessing."

Olivia leaned forward in the booth. "Sean. What is it that you feel exactly?"

He thought for a moment before answering her. "I'm almost afraid to say it, but it's strong and true, and it's not going to go away. I felt it in the cemetery that day, I felt it the other night, and now again today, and all the moments in between. You were the best kind of distraction during the scrimmage, so don't get me wrong, but seeing you come in, I couldn't focus on what I was there to do. I even drew a blank on a couple of plays for a minute." He chuckled. "I felt about fifteen years old."

He continued to caress her hand, sending shivers up her arm and down her spine. Olivia couldn't believe she was feeling this again, and she was so relieved he was feeling it too.

"I didn't watch much of the game myself, to be honest."

The pizza arrived just then, interrupting the conversation just when it was getting interesting and forcing their hands apart. The perky blond waitress stayed to chat them up for a few minutes too long, mostly directing her attention at Sean, and Olivia noted her look of appreciation as she gave Sean one last, slow perusal before turning reluctantly to leave.

Olivia supposed this was a common occurrence for him. He was an amazing-looking and extremely nice person. Of course he'd attract women. Olivia had never been the jealous sort in the past, and she was dismayed to find that, for a moment anyway, she'd wanted to claw the poor girl's eyes out. Had Nate ruined her ability to shrug off a harmless flirtation by some random woman with a man Olivia wasn't even in a relationship with? She might have some work to do, she realized. The last thing she wanted to bring into any future relationship was jealousy and insecurity. That would be pure poison.

Her thoughts must have reflected outwardly on her face, because she looked up to see Sean staring at her with concern. "I don't know what you were thinking just now, but I might be able to guess."

She quickly tucked those poisonous thoughts away. "Oh, it's nothing. Sorry."

But Sean knew her too well, and after he'd dished them both up a slice of pizza he said, "You would never have cause to worry with me, Liv."

"Oh, I wasn't—"

"Wait, just listen a sec. Look, I know you got a raw deal with Nate, and that's putting it mildly. I know it would take some time to get comfortable again. To trust again. I'll be patient. But I need you to know that you can trust me. You *can*."

She thought on his words for a moment. "I know," she said finally, and she meant it.

It wasn't easy to admit to herself that the warning signs had been everywhere with Nate. She'd just ignored them—chosen not to see them. Instead, she'd focused on how fun and exciting he was. How exceptionally *hot*—in looks, but also in the bedroom. The man had been insatiable in the real sense of the word, obviously. Back when she'd thought she was the only one, it had thrilled her to be desired like that.

So, she focused on how she felt when she was with him, like she was so lucky that he'd chosen *her*, out of all the women out there, and she'd felt so privileged that she was one of the few people in his life he could be his true self with. But he'd always been selfish. Always. And he'd cared way too much about appearances. A memory came to mind.

Switching gears slightly, Olivia asked, "Do you remember the time we went out for my birthday, and Nate spilled a little beer on his shirt?" If Sean noticed the shift in conversation, he didn't let on.

He laughed, "Oh, yeah. The tiny little drop of beer heard round the world. He had to go home and change."

"He *insisted* on it. I begged him to stay. We were about to go dancing at the Blue Moon."

"Yeah, that's right."

"Do you remember, he promised he'd come back and meet us there?"

He looked at her, nodding perceptively. "He didn't."

"And then he wouldn't pick up his phone, said he had it on silent, or whatever. But you and Suze insisted on taking me out dancing anyway. You were both so sweet. You knew that's what I really wanted for my birthday—a night of dancing." She shook her head and smiled at the memory. "You let me be a third wheel."

"What can I say? It worked out really well for me. I had a beautiful woman on each arm. I was the envy of every guy at the Blue Moon that night." Sean smiled mischievously.

Olivia laughed and then sobered. She traced over a name that was carved in the wooden tabletop in front of her with her pointer finger. "You know, when you dropped me off, and I asked Nate why he hadn't come back, he told me there wasn't any point in going back out once he was already home. No point! It was my birthday."

Sean shook his head ruefully. "You were always begging him to take you dancing."

"He hated it."

"That's because he was a terrible, terrible dancer," Sean said. He chuckled and shook his head. "He wasn't any good at it, and Nate didn't like doing things he wasn't good at. You know, Nate acted like a cocky, tough guy, but he was really pretty insecure. Not many people knew that about him."

Olivia smiled. "You were a good friend to him."

Sean shook his head. "I miss him every day. I know he was far from perfect, but I loved him like a brother. A pain-in-the-ass brother, but still . . . a brother."

"I know he felt the same way about you." Olivia had thought many times over the years that the two men were an unlikely pairing. They were so different from each other, but somehow their friendship had worked. It had been strong. Both men would have thrown themselves in front of a bus if it meant saving the other, and that wasn't an exaggeration.

"How did you guys keep from competing against each other?" Olivia asked. "I've always wondered that. I mean, you played the same position at Michigan State, and then you both went on to coach. You were up here as an assistant before Nate came. Didn't it bother you that he got the head coach position? Maybe you should have been offered it first."

Sean stroked his chin before responding. "I've always said that it's pretty hard to have a competition with someone who refuses to compete."

"So you're saying because you didn't engage in that with Nate, that's why there was never any jealousy?"

"I didn't say there wasn't jealousy. I'll admit, it rankled to be overlooked for the head coach position, but I just decided I had to let it go. And I did."

"And you did," Olivia echoed. "Just like that?"

"Yeah," Sean said with a shrug. "I decided to just be happy that my best friend was coming to town, and we'd be able to work together. I knew my time would come eventually somehow. Some way."

"Huh. I don't know if Nate would have been quite so gracious if he'd been the one in your shoes."

Sean laughed. "You're right about that. But look," he said seriously, "the truth is, Nate was a better coach than I was at that time."

Olivia protested, but he put up his hands, leaning back against the booth. "It's true. It was hard to swallow at first, but once I admitted it to myself, I was able to learn a lot from him during the time we worked together. He never gloated or tried to rub it in. Honestly, he made me a better coach; he taught me a lot, and I'm grateful to him for that, I really am."

Olivia recalled the last time she'd seen Nate and Sean together as coaches with their team. It had been after the WCHA championship game in the spring, six months before Nate had died. The entire team had rushed the ice at the buzzer to celebrate a nail-biting victory against Bowling Green. She smiled as she remembered the expression of sheer joy on the faces of both men. They'd looked like young boys to her in that moment as they hugged each other, and she and Suze had been both laughing and crying as they cheered from their spot behind the glass. Just the memory of it now brought a smile to her lips.

Sean looked at her with his head cocked to one side. "What are you thinking about?"

"Oh, just memories of you and Nate," she replied, still smiling.

He reached for her hand again, never taking his eyes off hers. In a thick voice he said, "That smile. I swear, it could launch a thousand ships."

She laughed and rolled her eyes. "I forgot you were a lit major," she said, downplaying his compliment even though she was secretly delighted. "But I'm no Helen of Troy."

He smiled, still caressing her hand. "I'm impressed you recognized that."

"I may not have majored in literature, but I'm pretty well read. Give me another one."

"Okay, let me think . . ." It took him a second, but the sparkle that entered his eyes told her when he'd thought of one. "Here we go. 'Shall I compare thee to a summer's day? Thou art more lovely and more temperate.'"

"That's easy. Shakespeare. Give me a harder one, and something a little less cheesy."

"Less cheesy, huh? I'm literally quoting Shakespeare here, and you think it's cheesy. I'm just totally deflated."

"Stop," she said, laughing.

"Okay, let's see." He thought for a minute. "Here's one. 'Stay gold, Ponyboy.'"

Olivia chuckled. "Oh, come on. That's not a hard one. It's S.E. Hinton—*The Outsiders*, although I can't remember who said it."

"Nice," he said, nodding with approval. "But you're right. Too easy. Try this one: 'You never really understand a person until you consider things from his point of view . . . Until you climb inside of his skin and walk around in it.'"

"I know this one!" Olivia whisper-shouted and slapped the table. She recognized it, but she couldn't quite place it. "Don't tell me," she warned him, holding up a finger. "I'm thinking."

Sean tapped his fingers on the wooden tabletop with exaggerated impatience and grinned at her. He seemed to know she wasn't going to get it.

"Ugh!" Olivia said, disgusted with herself. "I can't."

"*To Kill a Mockingbird*," Sean informed her with a self-satisfied smile.

"One more," she insisted.

"Okay, last one. I don't think you'll get this one either. 'Hope is the thing with feathers that perches in the soul and sings the tune without the words and never stops at all.'"

"Ooh, I like that one. I don't know if I've ever heard it. Frost?"

"Nope, Dickenson."

"Dickenson?" Olivia questioned with raised brows. "Wow. I always think of her poetry as sad and depressed."

"Yeah, that's one of her nicer ones."

"It's perfect. That's how I feel tonight—hopeful."

Chapter 14

The drive home started out as a quiet one. Nora had fallen asleep promptly, and Olivia was busy playing back the evening's conversation and basking in the afterglow of her time with Sean. A quick glance at Anna told her she was doing the same. A contented little smile played on the younger girl's lips. It wasn't until they were about five minutes away from their neighborhood that Anna spoke.

"Do you think I'm shallow?"

What questions this child was asking today! "Why in the world would you ask that? Of course you're not shallow!"

"Well, I know we sorta already talked about this, but don't you think it's pretty shallow that I've already moved on from Alex? In my mind I have anyway. At one point, yesterday, I wished the world would just end, and now . . . well I didn't want the night to end. I'm feeling all kinds of things."

Olivia smiled. "Like what? What are you feeling?"

"I feel all jittery and like I can't catch my breath, and look at me—I can't stop smiling. I'm so excited I doubt I'll even be able to sleep tonight."

Olivia reached over and patted Anna on the knee without taking her eyes off the road. "That's really, really wonderful, and I'm so happy for you. You are not in the least bit shallow, so you can take that worry and toss it."

"Okay." Anna rolled down the window and pretended to throw something out. "Done." The two women grinned at each other for a second before returning to their respective thoughts.

A full minute ticked by before Olivia admitted, "You know, I'm feeling some of those same things myself, actually."

"I know, I can tell," Anna said happily. "How did you leave it with the coach?"

"We don't have any plans. He mentioned he's going to New Hope tomorrow morning since he has the day off."

"Is that a church?"

"Mm-hmm. Over by the crossroads. I was thinking I might go and surprise him. I've been wanting to get back to church anyway. I haven't been in so long, I might be a heathen now."

"Me too," Anna said with a grin.

Olivia drove in silence for another minute. They were nearly home. "What about you?" she asked. "How did you and Landon leave things?"

"He asked if he could call me tonight," Anna said with a sigh of contentment. "I said yes, of course. I love talking to him. He's sweet and funny, and it feels like I've known him forever. How can someone so hot be so down-to-earth?" She sighed again. "He's just such a good person, Olivia. I honestly didn't know guys like him existed in real life."

Olivia glanced over at her, this time placing her hand on top of Anna's head. She smoothed her hair in a motherly gesture. Hearing the happiness in Anna's voice made her smile, but after pressing the back of her hand against Anna's forehead, it faded into a frown. "You feel warm to me. Are you feeling okay?"

"Mostly. I have a small headache, and I'm a little tired, but it's been a big week."

"Huh. That's true, but that wouldn't cause a fever. Do me a favor, and take your temperature when you get home. Let me know what it is, or I'll worry."

"Okay, *Mom*," Anna muttered playfully. But after a few seconds, she turned to face Olivia. "You know, I sorta wish you *were* my mom. I mean, I know you're not old enough to be, or anything, but . . ." She trailed off. "Never mind, that was stupid."

Olivia pulled into Anna's driveway. She always enjoyed the crunch of gravel under her wheels. It helped give Anna's house a friendly country feel. She barely heard it this time, however, as she took in the sweet words of her friend. She put the car in park and turned to face Anna.

"It's not stupid at all. Of course you want a mother figure in your life, and I want to be that for you. I'm honored, really." Olivia chuckled. "I just hope I don't *look* old enough to be your mother." She grabbed hold of Anna's hand, and though she still smiled, she spoke gently, "You know I love you, right?"

Anna nodded, but she didn't quite meet Olivia's eyes, and her features looked unnaturally tight. While Olivia didn't want to make Anna uncomfortable, she needed to be very, very clear on this. It was important.

"Anna, look at me." The brightness of her eyes was obvious, even in the nearly dark car. Olivia continued, "I couldn't love you more if we really *were* family. There is nothing I wouldn't do for you. Nothing. You need to know that you will always have me in your life. No matter where you go or how much time goes by. I will be there. I will always show up for you. I will push and shove and jostle my way into your life, even if you want me out. Just like a mother would. Know that."

Anna nodded, and Olivia reached over to wipe a tear off her too-warm cheek.

"Now, go take that temperature, because I'm certain you have a fever, and I'm already worried."

Anna moved so quickly that Olivia didn't see her coming, and she let out a little *oof* as Anna squeezed her in a powerful hug. "I love you, Olivia. And Nora too." She leaned back and wiped at her eyes. "Thanks for the ride. Thanks for the whole night. It was the best. I'll text you my temperature after I take it."

"Good girl." Olivia smiled as Anna got out of the car and ran up to her front door. As always, Olivia waited to be sure she was in before she backed out of the driveway. She wiped at her own eyes before putting the car in reverse.

Chapter 15

Anna did have a fever. She texted Olivia to let her know, and Olivia immediately called back. Apparently, it was considered low grade, so she wasn't too concerned. By Sunday morning, Anna's throat hurt, and her temperature remained a little high at 100.8 degrees. She spent the morning on the couch, watching TV. She hardly ever lazed around like that, but she found she didn't have a lot of energy.

Still, she refused to miss practice. If she didn't go, she wouldn't be able to compete on Monday, in the Great Northern U.P. Conference. Tons of scouts would be there, and Anna knew she could walk away from that meet with a scholarship if she did well.

But if her performance at practice foreshadowed what was to come at the meet, Anna was in trouble. Practices the day before meets were always on the light side, but she hadn't been able to finish the easy workout. She was completely gassed. When she climbed into Mitch's car after practice, he spoke the truth like only a brother could.

"You look like hell."

She cocked her head at him before buckling up. "Nice. Thanks."

"No, seriously. I thought you looked bad when I picked you up, but now . . . you look *really* bad. As in, awful. Are you okay?"

"*Hmph.*" Someone needed to give Mitch a clue. Telling any female she looked awful under any circumstances was a no-no, but it wouldn't be her, at least not today. "I don't really feel well, to be honest," she admitted. "My throat's on fire, my head's pounding, and I have a little bit of a fever."

He looked at her like she was crazy. "Why did you go to practice? You're sick."

Anna shrugged as she scrolled through her messages.

"You shouldn't have gone, Anna." He put the car in gear.

"It's fine," she said, trying not to sound annoyed.

"When's Dad coming home?"

"Tuesday."

"Are you going to be okay at home alone?"

"Mitch, I'm always home alone."

"Yeah, but now you're sick."

Anna gave a long-suffering sigh and put her phone down. "I'll be fine. I'm used to it. But right now I just want to close my eyes, okay? Talking hurts."

She saw his look of concern and treated him to a reassuring smile before she shut her eyes. If she'd felt better, she would have been gratified that he cared and was worried about her, but as it was, just the effort of pulling up the corners of her mouth had depleted what remained of her energy. She couldn't remember the last time she had felt this rotten. Even her skin seemed to hurt. She needed a distraction, so she let her thoughts roam.

On the way to practice, she'd talked to Mitch about sitting the bench during the scrimmage. He'd been ticked, as she'd known he would be. Although he went on and on about his coach, Anna could read between the lines enough to know that, mostly, he was upset with himself. They'd avoided any talk about Landon, but it was the elephant in the . . . car, and she imagined it'd come up sooner or later.

Landon. She had an amazing time with him last night. It might even go down in history as one of the best nights of her life. While she might not be wise in years, Anna knew that the powerful and almost instantaneous connection she felt with him was rare and special. The cherry on top of the evening had been the sweet moment she'd shared with Olivia afterwards. Some people might feel sorry for her—she had a dead mom and a deadbeat dad—but Anna knew she was lucky, and when she'd finally gone to sleep, it was with a deep feeling of gratitude, even though she hadn't felt the greatest.

Anna decided right then, with her eyes still closed, to let go of any hang-ups she had about moving on too soon with someone new. That would be a stupid reason to miss an opportunity to get to know someone as amazing as Landon. If they ever dated, and she hoped they would, she knew it would be different. She wouldn't lose sight of herself this time. She didn't think something like that would be possible in a relationship with someone like Landon anyway.

She'd thought Alex was a terrific boyfriend, but he'd been the only one she'd ever had, so she hadn't been able to compare him to anybody else. Now that she could, it was no contest. When it came to being good boyfriend material, Landon was a ten. Alex, she could now see, was maybe a six, and that was the old Alex. The new Alex probably hung out somewhere around a three.

Landon wanted to know her. What made her tick. Alex hadn't paid a lot of attention to that—some, but not a lot. Landon made her feel . . . special. Important. It was a nice change.

He was super easy to talk to and a superb listener, but he shared openly about himself too. He could be serious and contemplative as well as light-hearted and funny. Anna had experienced each of those sides of him last night, both at the pizza parlor and later on the phone.

About an hour after she'd gotten in, he called, and they talked until the wee hours. She opened up more about her family, and the near-constant disappointment she felt about her lack of relationship with her dad. She told him about the interest he'd taken in her homecoming, and the change she thought she'd seen in him before he bolted off to Chicago like a wounded deer.

They talked about Mitch and their shared concerns over him. Landon was careful not to give too much away, which Anna respected, but he said enough for her to put two and two together. Mitch was drinking and partying a ton, and it was spilling over and affecting his grades and his game. Although she wished she could talk to her brother about it, she didn't really know how to bring it up. At least Landon promised he would keep an eye on him. That made her feel a little better. He could relate to what Mitch was doing, where Anna could not.

Prior to coming to Nicolet State, Landon's girlfriend of nearly four years broke up with him. They'd planned to make the move to Michigan together, and then she'd completely blindsided him. She'd found someone else. He told Anna, with painful honesty, about how hollow he'd felt all last year, and no matter how many parties he went to, how many keg stands he did or puck bunnies he brought home to his dorm, nothing had worked to fill the void.

Towards the end of freshman year, he made a decision to live his life differently. He stopped drinking altogether, which at first he thought might be hard but had turned out to be pretty easy when it came right down to it. His team still razzed him from time to time, but he wasn't going back. Everything in his life had improved with that one decision: his sleep, his grades, his game, his ability to look at himself in the mirror and like who he saw reflected back at him . . . so much so that now he wouldn't change it for anything.

Landon also shared stories from his childhood, some of which had broken her heart, like the story about the time his parents left him in the back of their locked car for hours while they had drinks with friends inside a local bar. He'd been just six years old. They hadn't been able to afford a sitter, so they dressed him warmly and left him in the backseat with some books and two blankets to keep warm. But it was Alaska in November, and the temperature had dipped dangerously low that night.

Young as he was, Landon knew he was in trouble. Afraid that his parents would be angry with him, he'd gone to a house across the street for help instead of into the bar to look for them. The people in the house called the police, and Landon had been removed from his parents' home for a few weeks while Child Protective Services investigated. Anna had felt genuine sadness for his six-year-old self.

But she had also laughed to the point of tears at some of the other stories he'd told. Once, when he'd been in the fifth grade, he ran up behind his mother, who was standing in line at the grocery store, and goosed her before giving her a big hug from behind. When she turned around, he saw it was actually Mrs. Willis, his perpetually cranky and wart-nosed math teacher, who—as it turned out—looked a whole lot like his mother from behind. That was where their similarities ended, however, and even before the horrible woman had fully turned around, Landon realized his mistake.

Mrs. Willis was so irate, she clocked him upside the head with her purse, knocking him into the candy display. Landon's mom witnessed the entire thing and abandoned her cart in the cereal aisle to valiantly defend her son. She gave Mrs. Willis a hard shove, and things went downhill in a hurry. Wide-eyed, Landon watched his mother and school teacher roll around in a sea of candy on the supermarket floor, grunting and shrieking and pulling each other's hair until a manager arrived to break them apart. He escorted the two angry women and the mortified Landon from the little IGA with instructions not to come back for a month.

According to Landon, it wasn't all bad. The silver lining to the awful ordeal was that Mrs. Willis refused to talk to him, or even look at him, for the rest of the school year. That meant Landon, unlike the rest of his classmates, was spared from being put on the spot with her trick questions. He no longer had to worry about incurring her wrath and ridicule by answering incorrectly, and he attended math class with a light heart until the end of the year.

Anna had laughed so long and hard at that story that her stomach muscles actually ached. She found it to be just as hysterical now as when she first heard it, and she made a mental note to share it with Mitch sometime when she had the energy. That time was definitely not now. She was so depleted, she didn't even react when her phone dinged with a message.

"Aren't you going to get that?" Mitch asked her in surprise. Everyone knew there wasn't a whole lot that would keep a teenage girl from her phone. She'd heard once that phone alerts caused a dopamine release. It was technology's version of cocaine. She believed it, but today even her dopamine was toast.

"I'll look later," she said, eyes still closed.

"What if it's your new boy?" On the surface, his tone was teasing, but her eyes flew open at the subtle edge she detected.

Anna hesitated before asking, "Mitch, are you okay with me and Landon talking?" Her voice sounded huskier than it normally did, and the deep burn in her throat made her eyes sting.

He exhaled heavily before responding. "Oh, I dunno. I guess. I don't have a reason not to be. He's a good guy, so it's not that. It's just weird."

She swallowed painfully. "I should've asked you first," she said by way of an apology.

He treated her to a reluctant smile. "It's okay. Just . . . be careful."

"I will," she assured him.

He looked at her. "Your voice sounds different."

"I know. It hurts. My throat, I mean."

"I had that a few days ago. Maybe not as bad, though. I wonder if I gave it to you."

"Maybe," Anna said. She moved lower in her seat to get comfortable. Her body ached all over.

She wanted to talk more about Landon. She wanted to hear more about Mitch's conversation with the coach. And she still hadn't told him about how cozy Olivia and Sean had been at the restaurant. But it would all have to wait. For now, she just wanted to close her eyes again. And she did.

When Mitch got Anna home, he initially refused to leave her there. It took some work, but she finally convinced him she'd be fine. Once she got inside, she didn't bother to stop at the shower; she didn't even think about eating. She just went straight to her unmade, queen-sized bed and crawled under the rumpled covers.

In Anna's opinion, there was almost nothing worse than getting into an unmade bed—call her a perfectionist—but that morning she hadn't been motivated enough to make it up like she usually did. It didn't matter; she fell asleep immediately, awaking some indeterminate amount of time later with massive body chills that had her shaking violently. Grabbing the quilt she kept folded on the end of the bed, she pulled it over herself and tried to get warm.

It didn't work, and she slept fitfully. Although marginally aware of things happening around her, like the darkening of her room as the sun set, and her phone ringing and alerting her to new texts, Anna didn't really register those things in any meaningful way.

The dream/wake cycle was so fast and so frequent that she could no longer tell which was what. She was out at Sable Rocks, an area on the edge of town where people liked to cliff jump into Lake Superior. It was a favorite hangout for families and students alike. The tourists especially loved it. But there was no cliff diving happening in her dream. Instead, she stood by as a sledgehammer worked to break up the vast amounts of black, volcanic rock that gave the area its name. She screamed at the man running the equipment, telling him to stop.

He had to stop! He was ruining one of her favorite places. Pieces of rock were flying everywhere as the heavy machinery knocked out a steady beat.

Anna awoke confused. She was in her bed, yet she was still hearing the beat. She felt completely disoriented, and it took a moment before she realized the beat was actually the awful pounding in her head. And her left shoulder was radiating a terrible, searing pain. Some of the flying rock kicked up by that sledgehammer must have hit her. But why was she all wet? She was completely soaked through. She must have jumped into Superior, she reasoned.

No, that made no sense. She was in her bedroom. The familiar popcorn ceiling was right overhead, complete with the small water stain from a roof leak several years ago. She tried to sit up, but it was as if she were being pressed down by some unseeable force into the wet sheets. The weight was almost rib-crushing, and for a moment Anna felt like she couldn't breathe. Something was really wrong with her.

Chapter 16

Olivia was still flying high from all that had happened over the weekend, and she lay wide awake as she thought back over her day. What a great day it had been! She'd made it to church—that was something in and of itself—and the fact that Sean had been there with her was icing on the cake.

Surprising Sean had been fun. She'd planned to arrive early so she could find him and sit with him, but Nora had had a dirty diaper at the last minute, and they'd arrived late. When she entered the sanctuary, she could see the church was packed, and the band was already playing a song she recognized from one of the Christian radio stations she sometimes listened to on her way to work. Disappointed, she figured she'd have to find Sean after the service was over. She slipped into the last pew, which was the only one not stuffed full of people.

After bending down to stash her purse on the floor under her seat, Olivia straightened and began to sing the lyrics that were projected in the front on a screen. She'd sung a few lines when she felt the hairs on the back of her neck stand on end, and she scanned the singing heads, but nobody in the congregation was looking her way. As her gaze swept across the front of the church, she saw a member of the praise band, the tall, gorgeous one playing the keyboard, staring at her with a wide smile. She'd felt her cheeks grow warm as she smiled back.

Sean gave her a quick wink before turning his attention back to the sheet music in front of him, but the smile that lingered on his lips as he played mirrored her own. How could she have forgotten? Hockey, literature, and music. Those were his passions. Music was the one he'd always bemoaned lacking the time for.

Because hockey took him out of town too frequently, he wasn't able to play with the church band very often, but when he *was* in town, he lived for it. On those rare Sunday mornings off, Nate used to kick his feet up on the coffee table, hot mug in hand, and laugh, saying, "Here I sit with my hot wife and hot coffee while Sean's off jamming with the Christians."

After several more songs, the pastor invited the congregation to be seated, and a few minutes into the Scripture reading, Sean appeared at the end of her row with two steaming cups of coffee in hand. Coffee at church was nothing new, but coffee *during* church? That was a new one for Olivia. She grabbed the cup with a whispered thanks and scooched down to make room for him, careful not to wake Nora, who had immediately fallen asleep to the music.

Olivia had experienced a small thrill as he settled in beside her. Even though there was plenty of room in their row, Sean sat so close to her that their shoulders touched. And when he stretched an arm behind her, resting it on the back of the pew, she thought maybe she'd died and gone to heaven. Feeling the warmth of his body seep into her skin, she'd had an almost irresistible urge to lean more closely into him. Honestly, Olivia couldn't remember the last time she'd felt such a rush.

As they'd sat together, listening to the same message and praying the same prayers, Olivia realized how much she had craved doing that with Nate. They'd never explored spirituality together. She and Sean had now connected on a level that she and her late husband never had. Towards the end of their marriage, their strongest connecting had taken place in the bedroom, but even that must have been a lie if he'd had a woman stashed in every city the team visited.

Olivia hadn't expected to feel these things for Sean, and yet here she was, lying in bed at 11pm on a Sunday and not sleeping because she couldn't stop thinking about him. Want and need pooled low in that nearly forgotten place she'd been afraid had died right along with Nate. But now, it was roaring awake with a vengeance, reminding her she was still a woman with needs and desires that were very much alive. This reawakening was both a blessing and a curse, and she punched her pillow in frustration before turning over on her side.

The yearning wasn't only physical. Afraid to acknowledge the thought that hung suspended at the front of her mind, but knowing it would be dishonest to pretend she wasn't thinking it, Olivia decided she needed to address it head on. What if she got everything she'd ever wanted after all? A family and a man who cherished her. A man she could love *and* respect. A man who wanted only her and her alone, and who met all her needs—intimate and otherwise. What if the greatest tragedy of her life actually brought about a happiness she hadn't even known was possible?

Olivia wasn't naïve. She knew it was a little early to be making such a leap, but she couldn't shake the feeling that today something important had snapped into place. All those hollow, dry places inside of herself had been given a healthy drink, and she was determined to soak up every last drop. She recognized what it was, this feeling, although she wasn't quite ready to name it out loud.

That night, she dreamed of Sean.

Olivia never overslept. Never. But she'd turned her ringer off at church, and she'd forgotten to turn it back on again. She completely missed the alarm as well as calls from the school and a call from Shirley, who wondered if Nora was still coming today. Who she hadn't missed a call from, curiously, was Anna, who had been depending on her for a ride to school today.

Foregoing a shower, Olivia did her best with her hair, brushed on a bit of powder foundation and blush, and grabbed Nora out of her crib and the diaper bag off the changing table. It was a mad dash, and she'd had Siri call Anna multiple times with no answer. She really didn't have time to go over there, late as she was, especially if Anna had gotten to school another way. She looked at her watch. First hour was already ten minutes in.

"I'm sure she's already there," Olivia said to a sleepy-eyed Nora. She scooped her daughter out of the crib and carried her, along with the diaper bag, messenger bag, and purse, out to the car. By the time she'd gotten Nora in her seat and their things in the trunk, Olivia's arms were burning from the combined weight of all their belongings. Babies sure came with a lot of stuff, especially considering how little they were.

"I'm so late, I'm so late, I'm so late," she said to herself as she carefully backed her car out of the garage. Her driveway was a circle, which she always appreciated. It was long and tree-lined, and trying to back out of it in a hurry would have been almost impossible without running into one of the massive sugar maples.

The ability to back out in a straight line, even with the help of a back-up camera, was something Olivia had yet to master. It had been a standing joke between herself and Nate. He used to stand outside of their old house and watch her back up, zigging and zagging from one side of the driveway to the other, often stopping to correct herself, and he'd laugh and point while she did her best to ignore him. Once she made it to the road, she'd flip him the bird with a smile as she drove off, and he'd laugh even harder as he waved.

At the end of the driveway, she unnecessarily signaled to the empty air behind her the right-hand turn she'd need to make to head into town—that would have gotten Nate going too—but something made her hesitate.

“Crap,” she said out loud, before turning left instead. Olivia revved her engine to get to Anna’s driveway as fast as her van would take her, and she ordered Siri to call her again—still no answer.

“I don’t have time for this!” she yelled and pounded the steering wheel. Nonetheless, she put the car in park and ran up to the front door. She was about to ring the bell when she saw the door wasn’t latched. The sight of that small gap between the door and the jamb caused a wave of dread to wash over Olivia. Something wasn’t right.

Wasting no time, she pushed through the door, shouting Anna’s name. Nothing. Olivia moved through the first floor of the house, looking in the kitchen, living room, and laundry room. The lights were all turned off, and the house was immaculate, which was how it always looked. Nothing amiss there. Anna defied all odds when it came to housekeeping. Most teenagers couldn’t even keep their rooms clean, but Anna, who never left even a dish in the sink, had already mastered the art of tidiness.

Olivia breathed a sigh of relief. Everything seemed to be on the up and up, minus the front door. Anna must have already left for school and had just been careless about closing it. Olivia would lock it on her way out. Turning back towards the kitchen, Olivia retraced her steps out of the house when an object at the base of the stairs caught her eye.

Anna’s backpack.

If her backpack was here, Olivia reasoned, then so must Anna be. Olivia’s heart pounded, and the hairs on the back of her neck stood on end. She dialed 911 on her phone as she walked up the stairs, just in case she needed to press send in a hurry. She hoped to God she was overreacting and could laugh about this in a minute, but for now, she had a terrible, terrible feeling.

“Anna? Anna, are you up here?”

Olivia hadn’t ever been upstairs in this house, and she wasn’t sure which room was Anna’s. She did a quick search of the first three rooms before pushing the door open to the last room on the left.

“Anna!” she gasped. The young girl lay lifeless and ashen on the bed at the far end of the room, and as Olivia rushed forward, she looked instinctively for the rise and fall of her chest. She was breathing, albeit shallowly. When Olivia smoothed Anna’s limp hair away from her eyes, her panic grew. She’d never felt anyone this hot to the touch in all her life. The heat was literally radiating off her young friend. Her t-shirt and sheets were drenched with sweat, which explained the acrid smell that had greeted her when she’d opened the door. “Anna,” she said, frantically shaking her in an effort to rouse her. “Anna, wake up,” she tried again. After one final attempt, Olivia knew she needed to get help, and her hand shook as she hit the *send* button.

Chapter 17

"Anna . . . hear me? . . . Wake up . . . Open . . . honey. That's right. Open your eyes, Anna."

"Dad?" Anna's voice sounded foreign to her own ears. It was weak and raspy. Was her dad calling from Chicago? His voice seemed to travel on the clouds. Where was her phone? She needed to call him. He had to come home.

Anna's thoughts seemed to make perfect sense and no sense at the same time. Something was very wrong with her, and she was scared. Absolutely everything hurt.

"Dad?" she repeated. She struggled to see, to open her eyes, but her lids were so heavy that at first she wasn't sure she could manage the task. After several attempts and then a few repeated blinks, she was able to open her eyes and keep them open. A small victory.

For a few seconds, everything was blurry and out of focus, but soon she could see clearly. The room she was in was terribly bright, and at first it pained her. But once she'd allowed her eyes to adjust, she took in her surroundings. Her father was standing over her, and she was lying in a narrow bed. A bed with rails. An intermittent beeping sound was coming from a small machine to her right, and a dry erase board was mounted just below a TV on the wall in front of her. Written on it were the words: *Nurse Tina*.

This was a hospital room, Anna quickly realized. What the heck was she doing in the hospital? A panic threatened to overcome her senses, and she quickly looked to her dad for an explanation. Her eyes must have communicated the question, because he began to talk, and the more he spoke, the calmer she began to feel.

She'd been sick, he said. She'd been very sick, but she was okay now. Olivia had found her at home and called for an ambulance. That was all

Anna heard before her heavy lids closed again of their own accord, and she was pulled back down into a deep sleep.

It went on like that for several hours—short stints of wake time followed by long stretches of sleep. Each time she roused, she reached for her father, and each time she drifted back off again, she was holding his hand. When Anna finally awoke for good some time later, her father was still standing watch by her bedside. He looked dead on his feet.

She asked again what had happened.

"You weren't ready Monday morning. Olivia was giving you a ride to school because . . . well . . . because you had no other way to get there." He ran an agitated hand through his already unkempt hair. His voice shook as he continued, "When you didn't come out or answer your phone, Olivia went to the front door, which wasn't even closed. Obviously, you were sicker than you or Mitch realized. I know you usually check and double check all the doors when you're . . . alone."

He was taking forever to get to the point. "Dad, what hap—?"

"Sorry, sorry." He held up his hands. "I'm just a little . . ."

He didn't finish his sentence, but Anna knew what he'd been about to say. He was a little strung out. She could see it in his face. Normally more youthful in appearance, it now carried deep grooves, both on his forehead and around his mouth, and his dark blond hair was sticking out in tufts. He looked like he'd aged ten years.

"Anyway, she went inside and found you, and you didn't respond when —" He brought his fist to his mouth to regain some control. Anna had never seen him show this kind of emotion. She waited quietly, not knowing quite what to say or do.

After taking a few shaky breaths, Steven continued. "She couldn't get you to wake up, Anna, so she called for an ambulance. You were in bad shape. Your spleen had ruptured."

Anna's heart skipped a beat. "My spleen?" she repeated in horror. Could you even live without your spleen?

Reading her mind, her dad patted her head reassuringly and answered, "It's okay, honey. Don't worry. They fixed it. You're going to recover from this completely. Believe me. I've asked a hundred times."

"But—"

Just then, the door to her room opened, and a man came in wearing a white lab coat. He was an older guy, probably in his late sixties, and he held a clipboard with what she assumed was her chart fastened to it.

"Anna," he said with warmth and a smile. "It's good to see you looking so chipper."

She didn't feel in the least bit chipper, but she smiled up at him anyway.

"I'm Dr. Lindsey, and I've been taking care of you these last few days."

Last few *days*? How long had she slept? "What day is it?" she croaked.

"Wednesday," he said matter-of-factly. "You've been getting some much-needed rest. I know just how much sleep you teenagers like to get, and I guess you were entitled to a little extra after all you've been through." He smiled at her kindly. "Has your father explained everything to you?"

"Well, not everything, I don't think. If he did, I don't remember."

"That's okay. You've been on some heavy painkillers, so I'm not surprised if the last two days feel like a blur. Let me start from the beginning. You have something called mononucleosis. Have you heard of it?"

Anna shook her head.

"It's also called *mono*, or even the *kissing disease*."

"Oh, yeah." She had heard of it, actually.

"Turns out, your brother has it too. Probably how you picked it up."

Anna was indignant. "I don't kiss my brother!"

Dr. Lindsey threw his head back and roared with laughter, but when he saw she was serious and in some distress, he became serious too. "No, no, of course not." He patted her hand. "Your brother . . . Mitch, is it?" He turned to question her father, who nodded. "Mitch. Okay. Well, you see, your dear brother, Mitch, indicated that he sometimes drinks out of the milk jug at home." He slanted his head and squinted his eyes. "Or maybe it was the juice bottle. No matter. Nasty habit, either way. Especially since mono spreads through saliva. I'd bet money that's how you got it. Now, some people get mono and have no symptoms whatsoever. Some have mild symptoms, like your brother did, and some can get very sick." He pointed at her.

Well, that figured. Of course she'd be the one to have the bad case. Just when things had looked up in her life, *bam*, an attack of the kissing disease. And she hadn't even had the pleasure of actually kissing anyone to make it all worthwhile. Stupid Mitch and his stupid, filthy habits.

Anna forced herself to tune back in to the doctor.

"Mono can cause your spleen to become enlarged. We can get into the nitty gritty if you're curious, but the bottom line is that when the spleen becomes enlarged, it's at an increased risk of injury. That's why kids who are recovering from mono can't play contact sports for a while, as a precaution. If it gets bumped or has any trauma to it, it can rupture."

He read the confusion in her eyes, and continued. "Very rarely, an enlarged spleen can rupture without trauma to it. You see, as it stretches, it can tear a little bit, or a lot. That's what happened in your case. Now, it can be life threatening if left untreated because . . . well . . . the spleen, it's a bleeder."

Anna grimaced. If her memory of anatomy and physiology was correct, the spleen was normally about the size of a fist. Unwillingly, she pictured her spleen, bloated to twice that size, spurting out massive amounts of blood, and she closed her eyes tightly against the disturbing image.

Unaware of her distress, Dr. Lindsey continued. "You are very fortunate, young lady, very fortunate that you were brought to the hospital in time. You had some significant internal bleeding, and you did require a transfusion."

This was almost too much. Anna felt dizzy. She had someone else's blood running through her veins? That was . . . gross. She looked down at the inside of her wrist and the delicate blue lines there, as if she'd be able to notice a difference.

Continuing on, Dr. Lindsey explained, "Sometimes, in cases like this, a splenectomy, a removal of the spleen, is required. But in your case, I was able to repair it. You still have your spleen." He said this last part with a sort of staccato voice and a great deal of pride as he rocked back on his heels.

Anna blinked twice before responding. "Thank you so much." She was sincerely grateful, even though she still felt queasy about the somewhat graphic information she'd just been given. She ruled out a future career as a surgeon.

"You're most welcome, my dear. Now, do you have any questions for me?"

She had several. "Am I still sick? My throat's on fire, and I feel really hot." Ironically, a chill ran through her, and she shivered. She must still have a fever.

Dr. Lindsey nodded. "You've got a pretty severe case. When you came in, your temperature was just under one hundred and five degrees." He whistled and shook his head. Anna guessed that must be an impressive number. "And your blood pressure had dropped dangerously low. The transfusion has addressed the blood pressure, and we're keeping your fever down as much as possible with ibuprofen and acetaminophen, but as for the rest, unfortunately, you'll just have to ride it out."

Anna felt tears well up in her eyes. She didn't want to "ride it out." She wanted to feel well again.

"Your throat will feel better in a few days, I expect. You're also on some painkillers, through your I.V. there, to keep you comfortable, although we've adjusted those down now. Soon, we'll remove it and get you some pills to help with pain control. Those, as well as the ibuprofen, will help your throat some. You'll be pretty tender in your belly for a while. Speaking of which, is it okay if I check your incision?"

Anna nodded and her dad stepped away to give her a bit of privacy.

She helped the doctor open her gown once he'd donned a pair of rubber gloves, and as he worked to peel back the bandage, she asked the question that had been bouncing in her brain for the last several minutes. "Dr. Lindsey, is my cross country season over?"

He stopped what he was doing and met her gaze. "Yes, dear heart. And I'm right sorry about that. Right sorry, indeed."

She blinked through the sting of tears.

"Your father mentioned to me that you're a real talent. I know this must be a heavy blow."

She gave a quick nod, and he patted her hand a second time before continuing to look over her incision.

"The good news is everything looks to be healing up just fine."

"And the bad news?" Steven Davis piped in with a frown as he turned from the window on the far side of the room.

Removing his gloves, Dr. Lindsey replied, "Well, there really isn't much bad news, other than what I've already mentioned. I suppose the bad news is that we'll have to keep a close watch on the spleen. It will remain enlarged for several weeks to months. We'll need to have regular follow-ups to check it."

Her dad nodded, but Anna noticed he'd grown paler.

"We'll get Anna discharged later today, and you'll get a sheet with instructions that will tell you what to watch for. She'll be weak for some time, I would imagine. Mono can do that, even once the symptoms are gone."

Dr. Lindsey returned his attention to Anna. "This may be a long haul, young lady, but I think you're up to the task. You're a strong one."

"Thank you, Doctor," her dad said, reaching out to shake Dr. Lindsey's hand.

Anna echoed her thanks, but she wondered if she really was strong enough.

It took forever to be discharged, and Anna was dressed and ready to go a full three hours before the paperwork came through. By the time she'd been wheeled outside and helped into her dad's car, the sun was setting, and she was tired to the bone. She listened as her dad told her for the umpteenth time how lucky she'd been and how sorry he was that he hadn't been there for her. Though she was quickly growing weary of reassuring him, she told him again that it was fine, even though they both knew it wasn't.

Several minutes into the ride home, he told her about Heidi.

"Aunt Heidi's *here*? In Nicolet?" She furrowed her brow. "But I don't remember seeing her. Did she come to the hospital? Where is she now? Is she at the house?"

Steven was slow to answer her rapid-fire questions. "You were pretty out of it, so I'm not surprised you don't remember, but she spent a lot of time sitting with you." He chuckled. "You should have seen her. She literally quizzed your doctor. The nurses too."

Anna groaned. Leave it to Aunt Heidi.

"You know how she gets. She wanted to make sure you were being taken care of, and she was actually pretty impressed. Reluctantly so, but still impressed." He shot her a small smile.

Anna smiled back. Aunt Heidi could be a real pill, but she had a heart of gold, even if she did sometimes come off as a little too . . . intense.

"I wondered why I didn't have any texts or calls from her. I was gonna ask you what was up with that."

"Yeah, she was here almost the whole time, but she had to fly back to Minnesota to take care of a few things yesterday. She'll be back again late tonight."

"Is she staying with us?" Anna asked. She thought she knew the answer to that question, but still, she hoped.

Steven shifted uncomfortably. "No. A hotel."

Anna sighed her disappointment.

Her dad said nothing.

It was past time for some answers, but now wasn't the best time to ask the questions. For one thing, Anna felt a little off from the medication, and for another, it hurt her throat to talk. But if circumstances were different, if she hadn't been on her way home from a two-day stint in the hospital after one of her organs basically exploded, Anna would have finally asked her dad some questions: Why isn't Aunt Heidi staying with us? Why can't you guys get along? Why won't she ever visit Nicolet? Why can't any of us talk about Mom together? And what about Mitch? Does anyone really know how he's doing? Does anyone care?

These questions and countless others filled the space between them—unasked and unanswered. Finally, the sound of the blinker punctuated the silence as Steven made the turn onto the highway toward home. Once he'd accelerated to speed, he spoke. "So, Anna . . ."

"Yeah?" She turned her head and watched him shift in his seat once again.

He cleared his throat before saying, "Heidi and I don't get along real well, which I'm sure you already know."

Anna gaped at him. Where had that come from? "I wish I knew why," she said in response, not trusting herself to say more than that. She wasn't at her best, and this was uncharted territory.

"Lots of reasons, some complicated and some not. This situation is just the latest." He pressed his lips together in a grim line. "Can't say I blame her."

Anna watched a muscle flex in his jaw. "She's mad at you." She said this as a statement and not a question.

"Yes."

"Because you weren't here when I got sick." This wasn't a question either. They all knew he should have been there. He should have been there for a lot of things.

"Anna, I'm a flawed—" The car hit a pothole with a heavy *thud*, interrupting him and causing Anna to grimace in pain. Thrusting a hand out toward her reflexively, Steven pulled a face too. "Ugh! These roads! Why do we even pay taxes? Are you okay?"

She nodded and relaxed the muscles near her incision.

He shot her a look of remorse. "I'm sorry, and not just for the pothole. I'm a broken record, I know, but I can't say it enough." After a few beats of quiet, he continued, "I seem to hurt you and Mitch without even trying. From the time your mother died, I haven't done anything right." He shook his head in disgust.

Anna didn't make a sound. Didn't move. Not even to scratch the itch that suddenly materialized below her left eye.

"You were in the middle of potty training, and Mitch had just started kindergarten, and I was just so clueless about everything. I didn't know how to . . . I mean, I had to *hire* someone to show me how to take care of you, for Pete's sake. Your mom, she did all that stuff. She cooked the meals; she read the child-rearing books. I didn't even know your diaper size, and I definitely didn't know you were allergic to amoxicillin—learned that one the hard way. I had no clue what time Mitch's school started or the name of his teacher, or how school drop-off worked.

"And it's no exaggeration to say I could hardly feed you two. Not proper food, anyway. I'd never even used the stove before. Shelly ran the household. Took care of you kids. She did all the hard stuff, and she made it look so easy. I just got to come home from work and have fun with my family, not a care in the world. But she's the one . . ." Anna watched that same muscle in his jaw twitch as he searched for what to say next.

"I couldn't do it without her. I was a mess, and I knew I'd keep being a mess. I *knew* it just like I knew it was my fault she died. The guilt I felt. The guilt I still feel . . . I *tried*, Anna. I really did. But I failed. I failed my wife, and I failed my kids. I figured I couldn't screw you and Mitch up too badly if I wasn't around, so I kept my distance." He tapped his thumb on the steering wheel in agitation before he went on. "And then the other day, it just hit me like a ton of bricks. You kids are all grown up now, an inch away from adulthood. How did that happen? And where was I when it happened? Not here. Not where I should have been."

Anna put a hand out on his shoulder. "Dad . . ."

He shot her a startled glance, almost as if he'd forgotten he wasn't alone, and then he sighed heavily. "Sorry, kiddo. I didn't mean to say all that. It's not right to unload on you, especially right now."

Anna shook her head slowly as she stared at his profile. "No, it's okay. I've . . . ah . . . I've kinda been waiting for this, actually. I've been wanting you to *unload*, as you say, for years."

He spoke quietly. "I know, and I wish I could start over. Do things differently. At your dinner that night, for the first time, I thought maybe I *could* start over. I went to your parade. You have no idea how proud I was to see my daughter riding through town—homecoming queen."

He looked at her with sparkling eyes. "And I was going to go to Mitch's scrimmage. I felt like I could finally do it, you know? Watch my boy play without feeling . . ."

Feeling what? Anna wanted to ask, but she held back.

"And then I choked. I just . . . couldn't. It's almost like I've forgotten how to be—" He stopped himself, and then, pushing a hand through his hair, he tried again. "I guess I don't know how to . . ."

"How to what, Dad?" she asked tentatively.

He drew a frustrated breath and released it. "You know what? Never mind. I'm not making any sense."

Definitely, there were holes to this explanation, but Anna knew the gist of what he was trying to say. Her dad had regrets, wanted to change, but got scared. She'd known that when he'd left for Chicago. But there was more to it. There had to be. Details that would help fill the gaps. What had happened that made him blame himself for her mom's death? And why had he thought he needed to stay away from her and Mitch? He went on again before she could figure out what to ask or how to ask it.

"You're eighteen years old, Anna, and I still don't know how to be your dad. Maybe it's just too late now. Too damn late." His fingers flexed around the steering wheel.

Bewildered, Anna told him it wasn't too late, and she would have said more, but where to begin? She was trying to get over the shock of having heard a curse word fly out of his mouth. And then to have him string so many other words together at one time, and with so much emotion . . . She'd always just assumed he didn't feel much of anything. To know he'd been living his life with all this guilt, feeling things this intensely—she was overcome with compassion for him. For years, he must have been all twisted up in knots on the inside. How had he lived out every day like that?

She wondered again why he would blame himself for her mother's death. And he must have been out of his mind to think it would be better to withdraw from his own children—for years—in an effort to protect them. Protect them from what, exactly? She wanted to ask him, but she was afraid of saying the wrong thing. A deep regret settled over her that she couldn't be at her best for what was turning out to be the most important conversation of her life.

Misreading Anna's silence, Steven said, "I don't expect you to forgive me. Not yet, at least. I'll have to earn it, and that'll take time."

Anna gave a slow shake of her head. "How could I not forgive you? Of course I do. I love you, Dad," she said simply, artlessly.

When he looked at her, his face appeared unnaturally tight, and he glanced back at the road before again meeting her eyes and saying hoarsely, "I love you too, honey."

Anna swallowed twice past the pain in her throat. She would not cry. If she did, her dad might feel sad, and there was no way she was going to pile on by shedding tears, not even happy ones. She'd known he loved her, of course, but it was so nice to hear the words, and she blinked back the evidence of her joy.

The ding of her phone alerted Anna to a message. Figuring both she and her dad could use a minute, she grabbed it out of the console. It was Landon checking in—again. Tired as she was, Anna smiled softly.

He'd been in to see her today, and they'd played a few rounds of cards to pass the time while she waited for the hospital to complete her discharge. He'd even stuck around for a horrid hospital lunch of overcooked meatloaf and dry mashed potatoes before heading off to practice. Anna had eaten little off her plate, but Landon nearly licked his clean. Maybe dorm food really *was* bad!

"I take it from your smile that's Landon?" her dad asked, appearing grateful for the distraction.

"Mm-hmm," she murmured, quickly shooting off a text back.

"You know, he wasn't allowed to see you that first day, but he stayed in the waiting room overnight anyway."

Anna's stomach fluttered, and she put down her phone. "He did?"

Steven nodded. "So did your brother."

Warmth spread over her, and not from her fever. "Hmm. That's really nice."

"They let Landon see you the next morning. He was in and out of your room a few times."

Anna sat up straighter and winced at the pain the movement caused over her incision. "While I was sleeping?"

Picking up on the change in her voice, her dad looked at her quizzically.

"What did I look like? Did I look awful?"

Steven cocked his head to one side. "Well . . . I wouldn't—"

"Oh no!" Anna groaned and covered her face. "Of *course* I looked awful. Nobody can look good in a hospital gown, even when they're well." By the time Landon had come in today, she'd changed into her street clothes. She wished he hadn't seen her when she'd been all gorked out and wearing the most unattractive garment known to mankind.

Her dad was quiet before saying, "Well, if anyone could, it'd be you."

It was a touching lie. "Thanks, Dad." Embarrassing as it was, there was nothing to do about it now, and she couldn't have looked too terrible because Landon had come back. Anna smiled at the thought and then yawned. "My eyelids feel like they weigh ten pounds apiece." She fought against the sleep that threatened to overtake her and looked at him for a long minute. "I'm just gonna close my eyes a minute. Please don't go away, Dad. Okay?" she whispered.

"Honey, don't worry. I'm not leaving again for a good, long while. I've . . . taken some time off."

She shook her head. "I meant, please stay like this. Don't change back. We can't go back to . . . before. I want to talk more . . . about everything. Please, don't go away."

He patted her knee. "I'm not going anywhere."

As she lost the battle against sleep, and her eyes finally closed, she was fairly sure she heard him say, "I promise."

Chapter 18

It was the end of the school day on Wednesday, and Olivia, having taken the rest of the week off, was tidying up her office as if it were already the start of the weekend. Tomorrow and Friday were half days anyway, so when Erin had suggested she take the rest of the week to recover from Monday's scare, Olivia took her advice, experiencing only a smidgen of guilt.

She called Shirley from the school to let her know the change of plans for the rest of the week and asked if she'd mind keeping Nora for an extra half hour so she could run to the store. Olivia wanted to make a few meals for the Davis family tonight, and she had a shopping list a mile long.

It amazed Olivia at how quickly grocery shopping went without the baby along. She was in and out in record time, and it was barely five o'clock when she pulled into her driveway with Nora and the groceries. When the house came into view, she broke into a happy smile. Sean's truck was parked out front again. This was becoming a bit of a routine, one she could definitely get used to. From the moment she'd called him that morning two days ago, Sean had been there for her.

She didn't know why, but she'd called him first—as soon as she'd seen Anna tucked away in the ambulance. The only thing she could remember from that conversation is that Sean had said, "Hold on. I'm coming."

Overwrought and unable to think clearly, Olivia allowed him to take over completely. He called Mitch to explain the situation and directed him to call his father. He called Erin to explain why Olivia wouldn't be at work. He dropped Nora off at daycare—driving Olivia's van while she stared off blindly in the passenger seat. And then he had driven them both to the hospital to await news about Anna.

Mitch had beaten them there, and they found him in the ER's waiting room, pacing. He was a total mess. His eyes were swollen from crying, and he shook uncontrollably as he told them that Anna had been rushed to the operating room for emergency surgery. That was all he knew. Seeing Mitch so visibly shaken helped Olivia push aside her own fears and worries so she could be strong for him, and when she'd hugged him, he held on to her for dear life. She and Sean had walked with him to the OR waiting room on the second floor.

They hadn't been there more than a few seconds before Landon appeared in the doorway, windblown, winded, and wide-eyed. He hadn't seen her seated in the corner, and instead made a beeline for Sean and Mitch, who were getting checked in at the front desk by a silver-haired clerk. Olivia had watched as Sean finished speaking with the kind, old woman and then pulled both boys aside near the windows opposite the desk, whispering to them and laying a strong, comforting hand on each of their shoulders.

Whatever he said appeared to calm them, at least to some extent, and they joined her in the corner section, where they were afforded a modicum of privacy. The four of them waited there together for several hours until the surgeon, at last, came out to give an update.

Once the doctor had reassured them that Anna was in recovery and was going to be just fine, Mitch had put his head in his hands and wept while Olivia stroked soothing circles on his back. She promised she would stay with him until Steven arrived from Chicago.

About an hour later, Olivia accompanied Mitch to Anna's in-patient room on the fifth floor. Sean and Landon hadn't been allowed up, but they made an exception for Olivia at Mitch's request. She'd helped Mitch understand what was happening, asked questions of the doctors and nurses on his behalf, and worked to calm his lingering fears. She'd also had to reassure him that Anna's condition was not his fault. Over the course of conversation with Dr. Lindsey, Anna's surgeon, it had been determined that Mitch had most probably given her mono. It hadn't sat well with him, and that was putting it mildly. As a result, he could barely look at his sister as she laid there in the hospital bed.

Olivia knew Anna wouldn't remember, but she sat with her young friend and held her hand while Mitch stood and looked out the window. Never coming into full awareness, Anna didn't register any kind of recognition when she briefly opened her eyes, but Olivia liked to think Anna could feel her calming presence beside her. At least Olivia hoped her presence was calming. She had to work very hard, repeatedly, not to think of those terrifying moments just a few hours earlier.

Olivia stayed until Steven arrived, which hadn't taken as long as she'd expected. He'd gotten there so quickly, Olivia shuddered to think of how fast he must have driven. Luckily, he'd arrived in time to catch Dr. Lindsey at the nurse's station. Accompanying Steven into Anna's room, Dr. Lindsey went through everything all over again, but Olivia wondered how much Anna's father actually heard. Steven Davis appeared to be out of his mind with worry and could not take his stricken eyes off his daughter for even a second.

Before the doctor left, he spoke to Mitch and warned him that if his mononucleosis test came back positive, as he expected it would, Mitch would have to stay off the ice for a few weeks as a precaution to protect his own spleen.

Under normal circumstances, Mitch probably would have been indignant over that, but the poor kid couldn't muster any reaction at all to the news—he was simply too distraught over Anna and his perceived blame over her current circumstance. Olivia knew the last thing Mitch needed was more guilt loading him down.

She had never gotten him to open up to her, even though she'd tried many times when he'd sat across from her as a student in her office at Nicolet High. Olivia knew the signs, though, and she believed Mitch carried a lot of unresolved emotions over the death of his mother, including guilt for not having been able to save her.

What it must have been like for him as a small child to watch his mother get swept off the breakwall that day! Olivia knew about Shelly Davis and what had happened during that early November storm. Of course, she'd learned small bits and pieces from Anna, but Anna had been a small toddler at the time and only knew what she'd been told. The bulk of what Olivia knew came from her neighbor, Harry, whose late wife, Lucy, had been an eyewitness. She and a friend of hers had driven to the overlook above the breakwall to be awed by mother nature.

The waves that day were said to have topped out somewhere between twenty and twenty-five feet. In fact, Olivia was pretty sure Lake Superior had broken records, not that anybody focused on that in the aftermath. According to Harry, a handful of other people had had the same idea as Lucy and had gone to experience the "gales of November" for which Lake Superior was so famous—or infamous.

Everyone there that day had known to stay at the top of the embankment, and most had even remained inside their cars, sheltered from the high winds and well away from the violent water's reach. All but one. Lucy saw Shelly Davis get out of the car next to hers. She also noticed little Mitch, unbuckled in the back seat—hands and nose pressed against the window—as he watched his mother's retreating form head down the embankment towards the breakwall.

In alarm, Lucy and many others had gotten out of their cars, yelling out their warnings to Shelly and pleading with her to come back. Shelly had turned back to them and simply laughed and waved before continuing out onto the breakwall and straight into harm's way. According to Lucy, the waves soaked her within seconds, and she turned back to give the crowd a huge smile and a thumbs up before continuing further out. She made it about fifty yards before a massive wave swept her off the concrete wall and into the churning water.

Little Mitch, all of five years old, had watched it happen and jumped out of the car, quick as lightning, to rescue his mother. It had taken two equally quick men to catch and restrain him as he yelled, kicked, and screamed. Tragically, there was nothing anybody could do to save Shelly Davis. No one dared enter the water themselves—it would have been a death sentence—and by the time the police and coast guard arrived, it was far too late.

Over the years, Olivia had unwittingly created a vivid image in her mind of Mitch-the-child, impossibly young and innocent, fighting against those men to save his mother. It was so upsetting to her, she tried not to think of it. But now, days after Anna's emergency, Olivia couldn't quite shake the new and equally upsetting image of Mitch-the-man looking for all the world like that frightened, broken child of her imagination as he waited for news of his sister that day in the hospital. She was grateful she and Sean had been able to lend some support to him, but she knew it would take more than that to save him from his own demons. To start with, it would take his family coming together to support him, as they were doing now for Anna.

Olivia brought flowers to the hospital on Tuesday, although Anna hadn't been awake to receive them. Both Steven and Heidi, Anna's aunt, had been there. Steven hovered and doted on Anna, even as she slept. Olivia had spotted him fixing Anna's blankets, completely unnecessarily, twice while she spoke with Heidi. She would bet money that things were about to change at the Davis house, although she couldn't say for certain if the relationship between Steven and Heidi would ever be anything other than frosty. That was too bad.

Olivia liked Heidi, which wasn't any great surprise. She'd heard enough from Anna about her over the years to know Heidi was good people. She was certainly very pretty. In fact, she looked a lot like Anna, or Anna looked a lot like her, which—of course—really meant that Anna strongly resembled her mother.

She and Heidi talked for the better part of an hour while Steven paced and fidgeted and watched over his daughter. Several times, Heidi thanked Olivia for being there for Anna. She credited her with saving Anna's life, and while her thanks were genuine, the pent-up hostility she obviously felt towards Steven for *not* being there seemed close to bubbling over, and Olivia just hoped Steven could take it when it happened.

He had been so humble and so broken and so grateful to Olivia, that it had been impossible for her to stay angry with him, and not only that—she found she was willing to do whatever she could to help him begin the healing process with his children. At the very least, she could make a few measly meals. Something to start with anyway.

Maybe she'd put Sean to work in the kitchen tonight. That might be fun. He seemed as eager to spend time with her as she was to spend time with him. Yesterday, Tuesday, he'd come over after practice to check on her. They'd sat out on the back deck with a glass of wine and the baby monitor, and he'd let her tell him all over again about what she'd stumbled upon Monday morning and how scared she'd been. Then they'd spent the rest of the evening sharing old stories from the past. They had reminisced well into the night. And now, here he was again.

She parked beside him and got out.

"Hey! Have you been here long?"

"Not long. I was going to call you in another five minutes."

"Sorry, I stopped off at the grocery store."

She hadn't asked him to, but Sean moved to unload her groceries for her. Noticing Nora asleep in the backseat, he smiled before carefully and quietly grabbing the grocery bags. Olivia followed him into the house, carrying the infant car seat. Nora didn't even stir.

"No practice today?" she whispered as they headed inside.

"Jackson's running the first half for me." He followed her into the kitchen and set the bags down on the counter.

"It's not like you to miss even half a practice. Everything okay?" she asked, turning her head in his direction as she set Nora's seat down on the kitchen table. She searched his face for hints that something was wrong.

"Everything's fine. I just—I had to see you." The way he stared at her caused her stomach to do somersaults. He continued to watch her another few seconds, a look of uncertainty crossing his features before it was replaced with one of determination, and then he reached for her—drawing her into his arms and sweetly kissing the top of her head. She smiled into his t-shirt as she sensed him sniffing her hair. He let out a sigh of contentment at the same time that she gave one of her own, and she laughed softly.

She loved how this felt, snuggled up against him. They were spending a lot of time together, getting reacquainted and reestablishing their friendship, but beyond little touches here and there, each one shamelessly thrilling her, their relationship had not gotten physical. Standing here now, completely engulfed by him, Olivia realized just how much she'd been craving this. She never wanted to stop touching him.

Sean's hard-muscled body pressed intimately against her softer, smaller one. They held each other, both unaware of how many seconds or minutes had gone by. And then there it was again, or rather, there it was *still*—that emotion Olivia was so afraid to name because it was just too soon to be feeling it.

But who cared about the timing? And since when had Olivia become such a coward? Where was her tenacity when she really needed it? Her mother had always marveled at her feistiness. "I guess you're not a redhead for nothing," she used to say with a laugh and a shake of her head.

Resolved to reclaim the spunk she knew must still be there inside her, and willing to accept whatever consequences might follow, Olivia decided. She was going to take the plunge, cross the Rubicon, and say what needed to be said to go after what she wanted. Reluctantly, she pulled herself out of his arms so she could see him. Something this important needed to be said face to face. She gazed up at him.

"Sean, I have to talk to you about something, and it might seem a little crazy or rushed, or . . . crazy." She wrung her fingers together, wondering if red hair wasn't actually more of a curse. Unfortunately, feistiness didn't equal finesse, but then that never had been her claim to fame.

"O-kay," he said, slowly releasing her. His voice tipped up at the end in a question. He reached down to calm her anxious hands, rubbing his thumb over one of them in gentle circles.

Olivia took a deep breath. "We've gotten older," she blurted.

Sean gave a slightly puzzled smile. "Speak for yourself. I'm still a young buck," he joked and waggled his eyebrows.

She shook her head, her face serious. This was harder than she'd thought. "I just mean, we've had a lot of life experience. More than we did when we were younger."

He tipped his head to the side and smiled quizzically. "True."

"And so we can trust ourselves more now, don't you think?"

"Compared to when we were younger? I'd say so."

"Aah," she said, her voice shaking slightly. "I don't even know how to say this to you," she said, bringing her hands up to her temples as if to help straighten out her thinking. "I mean, we haven't even kissed yet." Sean's eyes grew wide, and Olivia's face turned the color of beets after she realized what she'd just said.

Sean recovered quickly and chuckled, moving closer to her again. "Is that what you want, Livvy?" he asked softly. "For me to kiss you?"

She bit down hard on her lip and nodded. Sean moved closer. He ran a hand through Olivia's hair and then tucked it behind her ear. "How long have you wanted me to kiss you?" he whispered, his eyes twinkling.

"Too long, and probably longer than that," she whispered back, knowing that made no sense at all.

He smiled and caressed her face from her temple down her jawline. "I never let myself think about kissing you . . . before. But lately, it's been all I can think about."

"Good. Do it."

Sean threw his head back and laughed.

"Ah, Livvy. I love you." This was said on the echo of laughter and probably wasn't meant to be serious, but Olivia grabbed hold of the words anyway.

"That's what I wanted to tell you," she said earnestly. She looked up into his warm, brown eyes and held his gaze.

"What?" he asked, still smiling.

She took a deep, stabilizing breath and found her courage. "That I love you."

Sean stilled. He stared at her, his smile fading into something else, something serious.

"I know it's crazy," she heard herself saying. "I know it. But it's true. I can *feel* it, and it's real. I swear, it's real. I know what love is, and I . . . I love you, Sean," she repeated. The more she said it, the more confident she felt about it. There was no embarrassment now. No desire to take back her words. "You don't have to say it back," she added quickly, putting a hand up to his chest. "But I had to tell you how I feel."

Sean stared at her, stunned. For a second, Olivia wondered if he was going to speak at all, but then he gave his head a quick shake, the way hockey players sometimes do after taking a hard check against the boards. "That's . . . Livvy, come here."

He brought her against him in a crushing embrace, lifting her onto her toes and bringing his mouth down on hers with a bruising force that delighted her. His hands were everywhere all at once—in her hair, on her face, gliding up and down her back, pressing her even more firmly against him. Their mouths melded together as one, and Olivia sank into him as he deepened the kiss. She'd forgotten what this felt like. He tasted faintly of peppermint and more powerfully of something else, something rich and sweet and sensual.

Olivia couldn't get enough. While he kept her mouth occupied, she explored the powerful muscles of his body, running her hands up and down the planes of his back and then along the ridges of his biceps and down to his forearms. When she reached his hands, which rested on her hips, she marveled at the contrast between her own soft fingers and his harder, calloused ones. She moved her fingertips up and down his hands in feather-light touches, like strokes of a paint brush on canvas.

Sean moved his mouth to her neck, leaving a trail of kisses. She shivered and felt him smile against her sensitive skin. Eyes still closed, Olivia placed her hands on either side of his face and guided his mouth back to hers. She lost all track of time and place and allowed herself to simply *feel*. Only the sound of Nora's cheerful babble from the car seat some time later brought her back to reality, and she began to pull away, but Sean kept her close. She settled back against him, and he rested his chin on the top of her head. He was breathing in shallow pants, as if he'd just run a sprint, and she could feel his hot breath in her hair.

When she'd caught her own breath, she whispered, "Thank you. That was lovely." Olivia giggled over her exaggerated politeness.

Sean pulled away to look at her, his pupils dilated. "You do not know how long . . ." he began.

"Tell me."

"Livvy, I've loved you forever, I think, although I might not have known it at the time. I've been dying to say it to you all week, but I was afraid to scare you off. I love you. I love you more than my own life, and Nora too," he said, looking at the baby who was watching them alertly, as if she knew something profound was happening. "I want things for us I'm not sure you're ready to hear yet."

Olivia laughed, her eyes shining with happiness. "Let me get Nora out, and then you can tell us both."

He did.

Chapter 19

"No way! Are you telling me you're engaged? Like, to be married?" Anna stared wide-eyed from her bed at Olivia, who looked happily back at her from the chair by the bedside. It was Friday morning, and Olivia had taken Nora to Shirley's after all—just for a few hours—so she could stay with Anna while her dad was out.

"Technically, no, I'm not. But like I said, we talked about it, and it's what we both want. There are a few things left to . . . discuss first, and it wasn't a bended-knee proposal or anything like that, so you can just settle down." Olivia was still smiling as she got up to adjust the blinds in Anna's bedroom to let in a little more sunlight. Anna sighed happily. There was definitely plenty of good mixed in with the bad in life, that was for sure.

"What a week. I nearly die, you get pseudo-engaged, my dad becomes a human again . . . What else could happen?" Anna mused with a smile.

Olivia laughed and sat back down. "I'm glad you can have a sense of humor about it all, honey."

"What else is there to do? Otherwise I'd just have to throw my head back and cry."

"Well, you can do that too. It might not be a bad idea, actually."

"Yeah, okay," Anna joked.

"Hey, I'm serious. You've had a lot happen. This," she said, gesturing towards Anna's prostrate form in the bed, "is a big deal."

Running her fingers across the tiny embroidered flowers on the quilt covering her from the waist down, Anna knew Olivia was right. Although there were definite bright spots in her life, she felt the loss of her sport acutely and worried that cross country might be over for her for good. These last three missed meets would have been the most important for her in terms of being scouted. Even knowing track season still awaited her and could also be an option for college, Anna had her heart set on a cross country scholarship. Running a track just wasn't the same as running through the woods on a trail. It didn't feed her soul in the same way. Added to that disappointment, Anna had never handled illness well. She didn't like being sidelined by anything, and feeling crummy was no fun.

So she did cry. She'd cried the last two nights when she was alone and knew her dad couldn't hear her. She didn't want to make anything harder for him than it already was. He was walking on eggshells with both Mitch and Aunt Heidi, and she could see from the way he looked at her that he still felt tremendous guilt for not being available when she'd gotten sick.

Dr. Lindsey had told her she could return to school in another week if she felt up to it. He suggested she start back slowly, going for only a few classes at the beginning and then gradually building from there. Anna wondered how she'd have the energy to get through a school day, and she worried about how it would go for the first few weeks. At the same time, she couldn't wait to get back. She missed having structure to her day. She missed running and going to practice. She missed her friends.

Jess had been by, of course; Landon too, although her dad wouldn't allow them to stay long for fear she'd wear herself out. And her other friends had left her messages wishing her well. Even Alex had texted, asking if she was okay. She hadn't written him back yet. Not that she was playing games, she just wasn't sure she could handle a back and forth with Alex right now. Not only was she weak physically, but she also felt sort of emotionally frail as well. Dr. Lindsey assured her that her strength would come back, but he'd warned her it would be a slow process.

"I told you about cross country," Anna said, not looking up from the quilt as she spoke.

Olivia leaned forward, elbows on her knees. "You did. I'm so sorry. All your hard work," she shook her head. "But, you never know, that last race of yours, the one that broke the school record—"

"*Almost* broke the record," Anna corrected.

"Close enough," Olivia said dismissively. "That's bound to be noticed by somebody. Your coach will say something. Scouts are always contacting coaches. Plus, there's still track season. You'll catch an eye or two there, I'm sure."

"Maybe," Anna said doubtfully. She had her heart set on a scholarship to Nicolet State, and they didn't have a track team, only cross country. She didn't think their coach scouted runners at track events.

Olivia patted her knee through the covers. "Hang in there, honey. I know it must be hard."

Anna sighed. It *was* hard. She comforted herself that the silver lining to all of this was that she might have gained a better dad out of the deal. And maybe, just maybe, his relationships with Heidi and Mitch would get better too. He and Mitch were going to have lunch today. Anna hoped it would go well.

Mitch texted her yesterday to check on her and apologize for not coming by. Anna hadn't seen him since the hospital. He had a lame excuse, but she knew the real reason, or at least she thought she did. According to Olivia, he blamed himself for what had happened. He'd unwittingly given her mono and then left her all alone when he knew she was sick. He shared that guilt in common with their father.

But Steven wasn't wallowing in *his* guilt. He was trying to make real changes, and Anna could only hope that Mitch would follow suit. It seemed a little "Cats in the Cradle" that Mitch had pined after their dad's attention for so long, and now that he had it, he might reject it. Word was, he'd been reluctant to agree to this lunch.

As for Aunt Heidi, Anna supposed she should be happy that she was at least speaking to her dad now. This seemed to be an opportunity for a fresh start, and Steven had seized it, asking Heidi to take a hike with him up Mt. Joliet on Saturday, which was tomorrow already. How was that possible? The minutes dragged and yet the days flew by. Time was a funny thing.

Anna suggested the hike to her father since Aunt Heidi had spoken about that trail to her so often, and Landon said he'd keep her company since her dad would have insisted somebody stay behind with her. Aunt Heidi used to hike to the top of Mt. Joliet regularly growing up, sometimes even running most of the three-mile trek. Aunt Heidi had given no particular reason, but Anna knew it was a place of special significance for her. It had become special to Anna as well. Not only was it absolutely gorgeous, but it was a great workout. From base to peak there was almost a six hundred-foot gain in elevation. It made Anna tired just thinking about it.

It usually took Anna about an hour and a half to hike up to the top and come back down again. More if she lingered up at the peak. She hoped this outing would give her dad and Aunt Heidi plenty of time to talk. She had known her aunt wouldn't be able to say no to the opportunity to revisit one of her favorite places in the area. Added to that, Aunt Heidi could never resist a physical challenge, and the hike was one of the most difficult in the entire state of Michigan. It was probably also the prettiest.

Perhaps the beautiful view might inspire them to focus on all that was good and right in the world so they could leave behind past wrongs. From the top, a person could see for miles around. The town of Nicolet looked so tiny from up there, and both the lake and the forest below stretched on and on, in opposite directions, all the way to the horizon. Anna had often thought it would be the perfect spot for a proposal, and that led her back around to thinking about Olivia's news.

"So, tell me more about this non-proposal," she instructed Olivia, adjusting her covers up a little higher. She still had a fever, and she went back and forth between being too hot and too cold.

Olivia hopped up to help her. "There's really not a lot more to tell," she said. "It was kind of spontaneous, so there was no getting down on one knee, like I said. No ring. But I don't need all that anyway. We just talked about how that's what we both want. To be together. To be married."

Anna scrunched up her face. "Well, that's not very romantic. Come on, Coach! You can do better than that."

Olivia laughed. "Except that it was, Anna. Romantic, I mean."

Anna sighed at the wistful expression on Olivia's face.

"But there's a lot we still have to talk about," Olivia said a little too casually.

Anna tilted her head. "That's twice you've mentioned needing to talk about things first. What things do you need to talk about?" Anna pulled another face. "I'm being nosy."

Olivia studied her. "You're not being nosy, or if you are, I don't mind. But you *are* tired, and I think you should rest now."

"I *am* really tired," Anna admitted through a yawn. Under normal circumstances, she would push harder to satisfy her curiosity, but these weren't normal circumstances.

"Let's get you some rest, then. You'll need your beauty sleep for later. What time did you say Landon was coming?"

"He has class until two, and then he'll be over."

Olivia looked at her watch. "Why don't you sleep for an hour, and I'll wake you for lunch. After that, you can rest up some more until he gets here. Maybe then you'll feel up to moving downstairs to the living room before I go. I'll help you get set up on the couch."

"I love you, Olivia," Anna said with feeling. And she really, really did. She loved Olivia just as much as she loved Aunt Heidi.

Olivia smiled affectionately. "I love you too, honey. I'll get you some more water and let you rest."

"Thanks," Anna said, but her eyes were already closed.

Chapter 20

Instead of waking up to Olivia an hour later, Anna awoke to Landon seated in the chair near her bed, ankle resting casually on the opposite knee as he scrolled through his phone. She watched him for a few moments without his knowledge, noticing the way a lock of dark hair fell forward over his left eye. He reached up to brush it back without taking his eyes off the phone. He looked relaxed and happy and ridiculously hot, and her heart picked up its rhythm as she continued to study him.

It was strange to think he was only a year older than Mitch. He seemed far older—far more mature. He had such a powerful drive to succeed, yet he possessed the type of gentle spirit that moved her unlike anyone else ever had. He constantly impressed her, but he never bragged. And she had yet to hear him complain about anything. Not even his past.

Sometimes Landon seemed too good to be true, and yet Anna knew without a doubt that he was completely and one hundred percent genuine. She only hoped she could be such a good person herself. He made her want to try. She smiled at the thought, and that one tiny movement alerted Landon that she was awake.

"Hey there, sleeping beauty," he said, getting up and kissing her on the forehead.

Her smile grew. Could he be any sweeter? "Hi! This is a nice surprise. I didn't know you were coming so early."

"Neither did I, but one of my professors canceled class, so I thought we could have a little lunch together before my next class."

"Lucky me! Olivia made soup. We could have that, if you want. Is she still here?"

"No, she went home when I showed up. Is it in the fridge? I can heat a couple of bowls and bring them up."

She nodded and moved to sit up. "Perfect."

"Alright. Sit tight, and I'll be back."

He headed out of the room, but before he made it to the hallway Anna called after him, "Hey, did Mitch say anything to you about having lunch with my dad today?"

Landon paused in the doorway and turned around. "Yeah, he did."

"And?" she pressed.

"I guess you could say he was a little worked up about it. He wanted to cancel, but I talked him into going."

She was simultaneously disappointed with Mitch and thrilled with Landon. "Thank you. This needs to go well today, Landon. It really does." Anna glanced at the clock on the nightstand. It was after noon. "Maybe they're at the restaurant now." If they hadn't met up yet, they would soon.

"They might be. I'll send good vibes while I put the mad culinary skills I've learned in college to good use," he said with a grin.

After finishing their own lunch, Anna felt fortified and ambitious. "No, honestly, the doctor said it's important for me to get up and move around." Anna had been working for the last several minutes, without success, to convince Landon that a short walk to the end of the driveway would do her good.

He looked back at her doubtfully. "I just don't think you're ready for that yet. It's too far."

But Anna was stubborn. "Will you help me?" She reached out to him with one hand.

Landon scrambled to put their soup bowls aside on the nightstand and reached for Anna's hand to help her sit up all the way. When she winced, he went still. "You okay?"

"It's just my incision," she reassured him. "Obviously, they had to cut through some muscle, so every time I use my abs, it hurts a little. I never realized how much you use your abs, even just rolling over in bed."

"You're right. You use your core muscles all the time—abs and back. My mom has a bad back, and it was the same thing for her when I was growing up. Just standing up would hurt her sometimes."

"But she's a hairdresser."

Landon pushed the covers away, helping Anna free her legs from the tangle of sheets and blankets. "I know. Makes it hard for her, being on her feet all day."

"So, I know you said you don't really talk to your dad anymore, but what about your mom?" Anna asked, getting slowly to her feet as Landon helped her keep her balance.

"We write to each other."

"Emails?"

He smiled. "No. We do it the old-fashioned way. We write letters. You know, the kind with envelopes and stamps."

"Wow," Anna said, impressed.

Landon chuckled. He helped her across her bedroom and out into the hallway. Anna knew her progress was slow, and she could already feel herself tiring, but she continued on. When they got to the steps, Landon spoke again. "I send the letters to the salon. Not my house."

She stopped and gave him a questioning look before tackling the first step down.

"If my dad found out she wrote me, he wouldn't like it."

Anna shook her head. "Wow," she said again, at a loss. It seemed Landon's dad was not at all a nice man. Landon had been giving her little snippets here and there into what his life in Alaska had been like. She concluded that his dad was a drunken bully, and his mother was too weak-willed to stand up to him. She almost didn't know which of his parents to be more upset with.

Anna made it down four more steps before she cried *uncle*. She just couldn't do it. She had really wanted to make it to the mailbox. Then she could collect the mail and feel like she'd accomplished something with her day.

Landon, to his credit, only looked relieved and didn't say *I told you so* as he helped her back to her room. With his help, Anna gingerly crawled back into bed, and when she was comfortable again, she asked him the question she'd been afraid to ask but really wanted the answer to. "Landon, did your dad ever hurt you? You know . . . physically?"

He didn't answer right away, instead fiddling with her covers to get her all tucked in. Then he sat back down in the chair she typically used at her desk but which had found a new home and purpose by her bedside.

"Only once," he finally said. "My mom made sure it only happened the one time and never again."

"How?"

"She left him . . . after." Landon broke eye contact and stared off out the window. "She took me to her best friend, Marjorie's, house. We stayed there for a couple of weeks. Honestly those were some of the best weeks of my entire childhood." He met her eyes again. "I didn't want to go back home."

Anna's opinion of his mother improved a couple of degrees. "Did things get better when you did go back?"

"He never hit me again, if that's what you mean, but no, things didn't get better. He was a mean drunk and even meaner when he was hung over, which meant I was pretty much out of luck. I spent as little time at home as possible as I got older."

Anna made a sympathetic hum in the back of her throat and waited for him to go on.

"You know what's sad is that as bad as it was, some kids have it even worse. I mean, my mom wouldn't have won any parenting awards, that's for sure, but at least I knew she loved me. But my dad, I never have figured out why he is the way he is. He has no room in his life for me, and he never did.

"At least I had hockey. It's what got me out, and I think my mom knew it would. I think that's what her goal was all along. It's why she pushed. It's why she fought for those need-based scholarships and showed up for all my home games. Do you know my dad has literally never seen me play? Not once. He wanted nothing to do with it."

Anna studied him. "You talk about all this so matter-of-factly, but it must still hurt."

"It does," he admitted. "It hurts, but I'm doing fine. I have a good life. Would I have preferred a dad who didn't hate my guts? Who didn't gamble away the mortgage payments every month? Sure. But, honestly? I don't think about him much anymore."

"I'm sorry, Landon," Anna said, reaching out a hand.

He took it and shrugged. "It is what it is." The sympathy and regret she felt for him must have shown on her face because he shot her a reassuring smile and said, "I'm doing just fine, Anna. Honest."

Anna admired him more than she admired anyone else in the world. Landon was tough. He'd had to be. She thought about her dad and Mitch. She hoped it wasn't too late for their relationship. "I hope my family can be fixed," she said. "I think it can happen. My dad is more than willing to work at it, and I'm open to it. I'm not sure about Mitch and Aunt Heidi, though."

Landon seemed to choose his words carefully. "Mitch is working some stuff out right now. The emergency with you really shook him up. I know it goes even deeper than that, but what your family has going for it is your dad seems to care, at least. He seems to want to change. It's just up to Mitch and your aunt to decide what they want."

As if on cue, Anna heard Aunt Heidi's voice calling her name from the bottom of the steps.

"Come on up!" Anna hollered back, her voice just strong enough to travel down the stairs. Anna could hear the telltale noise of her aunt's knees cracking and popping as she made her way up, which is what they always did on steps, and Anna cringed, just as she always did when she heard it.

Aunt Heidi had terrible knees, but she continued to run marathons. She was stubborn that way.

When Heidi entered the bedroom, she looked first at Landon and then at Anna with some surprise. Landon hopped up out of his chair.

"I wondered whose car that was," she said. She shot Landon a small smile. Looking at Anna, she asked, "Are you allowed to have boys up here in your bedroom?"

Anna was taken aback by the question. *Was* she allowed?

"I'm pretty sure. At least, I don't think Dad made a rule about that, specifically," Anna said.

Heidi rolled her eyes. "Of course not."

"Come on, Aunt Heidi, lighten up a little. Dad's trying. Anyway, I'm too tired and too weak to get into any trouble, and even if I wasn't, Landon's a good guy."

"But still a guy," Aunt Heidi muttered.

The corners of Landon's mouth twitched as he looked down at his feet. Heidi seemed to remember her manners and extended her hand. "Landon. It's nice to meet you. I'm surprised our paths haven't crossed until now. I guess we must be on opposite visitation schedules. Anna's told me lots of good things about you."

Landon looked Heidi in the eye and shook her hand. "I've heard a lot about you too. It's nice to finally meet you."

Aunt Heidi nodded slowly, and the gleam that entered her eyes told Anna that Landon had made a good first impression. Anna breathed a sigh of relief. She hadn't realized how important it would be to her that her aunt like him. This spoke well of Landon because Aunt Heidi's approval wasn't always easy to obtain. Trusting people didn't come easily to her.

"Looks like you're taking good care of our Anna. I appreciate that. She's my favorite niece, you know," Heidi said and winked at Anna. They both knew she had no other nieces or nephews besides her and Mitch.

"Aren't you supposed to be at Allison's?"

"I finished up early." She gave the keys in her left hand a little toss in the air. "Thanks for letting me use your car. You'll be happy to know it's all fixed up and running smoothly."

"Oh, good. Now if only I could drive."

Heidi smiled. "All in good time." Addressing Landon, she explained, "I was visiting one of my old friends from school. She has *eight* kids, if you can believe it, and the youngest drank bubble solution and threw up all over the couch. That was my cue to leave."

Landon wrinkled his nose. "Poor kid."

"He's cute as a button, but he's a holy terror, let me tell you. Allison definitely has her hands full. Did I mention six of the eight are boys? Just last week, her twins spray painted two of their chickens, put them on the trampoline, and took turns bouncing them as high as they could. Allison looked out the kitchen window and saw blue chickens and feathers flying through the air."

Anna burst out laughing at the image. "No way!"

Heidi laughed too. "I swear. Anyway, I wasn't supposed to be here for another few hours, so I'll just be downstairs in the kitchen while you two visit. Your friend, Olivia, made some nice dinners for you, but I thought I'd add a couple of casseroles to the freezer for when I'm gone. You know your dad couldn't cook if his life depended on it."

Anna didn't like it when Heidi said things like that about her dad, but she let it slide. Instead, she focused on what her aunt had said just before knocking her dad's cooking skills. "Don't talk about leaving, Aunt Heidi," Anna pleaded. "I feel like you just got here."

"I'm not going anywhere just yet, not for a few more days, at least. We'll have to watch that chick flick you mentioned before I go."

Anna brightened. "And maybe more than just that one," she suggested.

"I'll start a list," Aunt Heidi said before turning to leave. Over her shoulder she added, "You two behave up here."

Anna and Landon looked at each other and shared a smile. Once they could hear Heidi's knees cracking again, Landon sat back down and spoke quietly. "Like you said, she's a little intense, but she's really nice."

He looked at his watch. "I should probably go now that your aunt's here. She's not comfortable with me being up here. And anyway, I need an oil change, and it should probably happen before the weekend. I can come back after practice tonight if you're up for it. I don't want to overwhelm you too much."

Anna scoffed. As if she'd say no to seeing Landon, no matter how tired she was.

He grinned. "Why don't you just text me later and let me know. I'm free most of the weekend since we don't have games, just a few practices to work around."

"Okay, but I can already tell you I'm up for it," Anna said, just before a jaw-cracking yawn overtook her. "And don't worry about being up here," she added. "Aunt Heidi doesn't make the rules."

Landon looked doubtful but nodded anyway. "You're cold," he observed, and Anna realized she was shivering. He got up to pull the quilt over her, but this time, he sat back down beside her on the bed and took her hand in his, giving it a gentle squeeze, and she felt a corresponding squeeze in her chest.

"I wish you could kiss me," she whispered. Her words surprised her and made her blush—it wasn't like her to put herself out there like that—and she was grateful that Landon didn't react in a way that would further embarrass her.

He smiled and said simply, "Me too." A small twinkle entered his blue eyes before he added, "But it's not the mono keeping me away, it's your aunt." They both laughed before Landon grew serious. "I think there'll be plenty of time for kissing in our future, Anna. Don't you?"

"I hope so," she said honestly.

"I know so. In fact, I've got big plans for it, but in the meantime, I suppose this will have to do." He raised himself up over her and gave her another gentle kiss on the forehead. The sweetness of it spoke to her heart. Pulling back, his blue eyes stared into hers, and he rubbed a thumb along her jawline. "You have soft, girl skin," he whispered.

Anna touched his jaw in return and let her hand slide over his lightly stubbled chin. The prickly sensation traveled from the tips of her fingers all the way to her spine, causing a small shiver to form there. She could touch him all day. From his expression, the feeling was mutual.

"I can't wait to take you on a proper date," he said, straightening up.

Anna let her hand fall back to the bed. "Soon," she promised. "As soon as I'm cured of the plague."

Landon chuckled and grabbed her hand for one last squeeze. Reluctantly, he let go and stood. "Okay," he said, and he took several steps back. "I'll see you tonight." Just before he made it to the doorway, he spotted their dirty bowls and went to retrieve them. "I'll just take these down to the kitchen."

"Thanks," Anna said. It would impress her aunt that he was clearing dishes.

"I'll talk to you soon, then." Landon backed out of the room holding the bowls, still appearing reluctant to leave.

"Bye, Landon." She bit her bottom lip and shook her head with a small smile as he disappeared.

Anna listened to his gentle footfalls as he descended the stairs, and though she could hear him speaking to Aunt Heidi, she couldn't make out what he was saying. They spoke for at least five minutes before she heard the door open and close, followed shortly by the starting of his car below her window.

Anna called down to Aunt Heidi, who appeared in her doorway seconds later.

"So?" she asked when Heidi entered the room.

Her aunt knew exactly what she was asking. "I like him," she answered, "and you know me. I don't like just anyone."

"I told you, you would."

"He offered to put your dishes in the dishwasher. And did you know he's thinking he might want to be a doctor?"

"Yeah, he told me he wants to work with cancer patients."

Aunt Heidi whistled. "Oncology is hard. Lots of burnout in that specialty, but we need good oncologists, that's for sure. He strikes me as smart and compassionate, and from what you've told me, he's tough. I bet he'd be a great fit."

"You work with cancer patients too, don't you?" Anna asked. She wiggled around under the covers and tried to get comfortable. Her aunt was a well-respected radiologist back in the Twin Cities.

"I read all kinds of scans, including the ones done on cancer patients, but I'm behind the scenes, so I'm able to detach from it all in a way that an oncologist can't. And you wouldn't want them to. They're the ones doing all the communicating with patients and their families. They have to connect on an emotional level, since cancer is a highly emotional thing. It's a little easier for me than for the other providers who work with those patients daily, not that I don't care about my patients."

"I know you do," Anna said. Her aunt had her scars. They made her come across as hard and closed off sometimes, especially to someone who didn't know her well, but Anna knew she was a big softy at heart.

"But like I said, I can see Landon being a good fit for oncology, and I only just met him. Am I right, do you think?"

"Definitely," Anna said without hesitation. "He's an amazing guy. The sweetest, kindest one I've ever met."

"Doesn't hurt that he's so cute," Aunt Heidi said with a knowing smile.

Anna nodded as enthusiastically as a girl with a fever could. "I told you a little about his life, but I found out more today. He hasn't had it easy." She filled her aunt in on the other things she'd learned about Landon.

When she finished, Heidi shook her head and said, "You know, I wouldn't wish a tough life on anyone, but isn't that how it goes sometimes? A person suffers some type of tragedy and then has to fight tooth and nail to overcome it. It builds character. You have to learn how to cope, how to do for yourself. It drives you, it motivates you." It was obvious Aunt Heidi spoke from experience.

Chapter 21

The two weeks Anna was out of school felt like an eternity. She completely missed Halloween, which was fine by her. Even as a kid, she'd never enjoyed dressing up in costumes. Last year, she'd only narrowly avoided a costume party. Alex had worked hard to coax her into going with him as Angela and Dwight from *The Office*, but she'd gotten the flu just in the nick of time. This year, she was so bored that she almost would have welcomed one of those dreaded parties. Almost.

Having Aunt Heidi there for some of her recovery time helped, as did the frequent visits from Jess, Olivia, and Landon. The day Landon had walked her to the mailbox and back again was the day Anna could finally see the light at the end of the tunnel. That had been a week ago. After that small success, she began the overwhelming task of getting herself caught up with her schoolwork.

All she could say was thank God for her dad. He was only back to work part time and was working almost exclusively from home, going in for only a few hours in the early mornings. As a result, he had the time to help her sort through all of her assignments. His engineering background came in handy, and he could fill in the gaps for her in both physics and calculus. At the beginning, Anna thought it would be impossible to get caught up, but by the time she was ready to head back, she was nearly there.

It was true, there had been a lot of boredom, and Anna was eager to get back to her normal life, but the silver lining to being basically homebound for such a long stretch of time was that she'd had loads of opportunities to spend time with her dad. Once Aunt Heidi left, they ate all their meals together, and thanks to Olivia and Heidi, they had amazing dinners to look forward to each night. Occasionally, Landon or Jess joined them, but most often, it was just the two of them. Usually they talked well after the meal was over, and it thrilled Anna to find that the changes in her father were sticking.

He seemed animated and approachable in a way he hadn't been before. They talked a lot about her mom, and he shared stories with her she'd never heard before. Some made her laugh, and some made her cry, but what they all had in common was that they seemed to fill up an empty place inside of herself she hadn't even known existed.

After the hike she'd taken with Anna's dad, Aunt Heidi also began opening up to Anna more and more about her twin. She shared stories about their childhood, and Anna loved hearing her talk about the experiences the two of them had growing up in this little town.

In the days following the hike—before she had to head back to Minnesota—Aunt Heidi told Anna all kinds of things she hadn't known. For instance, her aunt and her mother were *mirror twins*, which was the first time Anna had ever heard that term. Basically, it meant the two sisters were mirror images of each other. Shelly had a dimple on her left cheek; Heidi had one on her right. Heidi was right-handed, while Shelly had been left-handed. They were even opposites when it came to their personalities. Aunt Heidi claimed she was the boring one while Shelly had been the fun one. Anna, thunderstruck that her aunt could see herself that way, strove to reassure her that she was plenty of fun.

"When I visit you, I'm *never* bored. You always have such amazing things planned for us," Anna had insisted. "You're always coming up with some kind of adventure for us."

In response, Aunt Heidi had looked pensive before shrugging her shoulders and saying something about how maybe a little bit of Shelly's personality had rubbed off on her. She'd looked pleased at the thought. "Your mother was always scheming up some type of adventure or another for us, and she wouldn't take no for an answer. She must have gotten more of the Finnish blood in her than I did," Heidi joked. "She was more like our dad, and I was more like our mom, but wherever Shelly went, I *had* to go too. That was just the way it was with us."

Aunt Heidi told Anna about a trip they'd taken together after graduating high school. Not only had Shelly convinced Heidi to travel across Europe with her through an operation that catered to young adults called Tiki Tours, she'd even persuaded her to go on a canyoning day trip with her and a few of the others from their group while they visited Switzerland.

Initially, Heidi had signed up for the castle tour option, but at the last minute, Shelly convinced her to switch her itinerary. Canyoning, Aunt Heidi explained, was like white water rafting without the boat. A person's body was their vessel. At the top of the gorge, Shelly had been the first one to jump, while Heidi had chickened out at the last minute.

Wearing her helmet and padded wetsuit, Aunt Heidi had done the walk of shame back to the outfit's headquarters and sat at a picnic table for hours as she waited for the group to get back. Shelly, disappointed with her sister, told her she'd missed the rush of a lifetime. The very next year, Aunt Heidi told Anna, the same canyoning operation had to close its doors when a group of twenty tourists were swallowed up and killed in a flash flood in the very same gorge Shelly had ridden.

That story, as well as countless others, painted a picture for Anna. Her mother had been fun-loving and fearless. She'd been a risk-taker even before her mental illness had arrived on the scene.

Knowing this made Anna feel better about the way her mother had died. She had never mentioned this to a soul, but a niggling doubt had always existed inside of her that maybe her mom had gone out on the breakwall that stormy day with a death wish—that she'd done it deliberately. But for a woman who was a natural-born adventurer, it had probably looked like just another opportunity for a rush. Tragically, her mother's illness had simply dulled the warning bells that would have gone off in a healthy brain, and as a result, she'd miscalculated the danger.

Although Anna couldn't get enough of Heidi's stories, and she definitely had lingering questions about the ones that involved her dad—she got the sense that Aunt Heidi may have had a thing for him at one point—she was reluctant to ask questions, choosing instead to let Aunt Heidi set the pace of when and how to share that history.

Anna *had* asked both Aunt Heidi and her father about their hike up Mt. Joliet, though. Obviously, something good had brought about the change in her aunt, and although they'd both smiled and said it had been nice, they were tight-lipped about the particulars.

All Anna knew for certain was that they were gone for over four hours, and when they returned, Aunt Heidi had checked out of her hotel and moved into their guest room for the rest of her visit. And while the interactions between the two of them were still a little stiff on the whole, it was obvious they were both trying. On her aunt's last full day in Nicolet, Anna had even heard them laughing together from upstairs in her bedroom.

As for Mitch, well, honestly, Anna didn't know what to make of him. When she asked her dad how the lunch had gone, he'd smiled blandly and told her it had gone "well enough." Aunt Heidi claimed not to know anything about it, and Landon had given the careful answer that he thought it was a "good first step."

Anna could have screamed.

Nobody was saying much of anything, and she was afraid to push further for fear of putting her nose where it didn't belong. Mitch and her dad were entitled to their privacy, but she wished she knew what was going on. Whatever had happened at that lunch, it hadn't moved the needle much, if at all. At least not from her perspective.

Anna would never have characterized her relationship with Mitch as close before her hospitalization, but this recent and prolonged absence from her life was something else entirely. Before the "incident," they'd at least texted pretty regularly, but since she'd been home he hadn't called, he hadn't come by, and he'd only texted the one time. She was worried about him.

Talking to Jess about it on the way to school her first day back, Anna expressed just how concerned she was about her brother. Jess listened sympathetically, and when Anna finished speaking, Jess was silent and contemplative. Anna had the sense that she'd been about to say something about Mitch, but when she spoke, she subtly shifted the conversation away from him instead. "It's been a rough few weeks for your whole family, especially you, Anna. Are you excited to get back to it?"

"Definitely. Although, I wouldn't exactly call this *back*." Anna was attending for two periods today. She'd stay for physics and calculus and head home for the rest of the day. Landon had some free time between classes, so he was going to pick her up. Depending on how she felt after today and tomorrow, she could start adding classes into her schedule until she was in school full time again. Anna's hope was that by the end of the following week, she would well and truly be back. If not by then, definitely by the week after—the week of Thanksgiving.

Jess helped her get settled in the physics classroom before heading off to her own class. They'd gotten there early so that Anna wouldn't feel rushed, and she was alone in the room for several minutes before she heard someone shuffle through the door. She turned in her seat and was surprised to see Alex there.

He had continued to send her messages, so she eventually replied, although she'd been short and to the point in her responses. He'd known she would be back today.

"Hi," he said tentatively, stopping just inside the doorway.

"Hey." She smiled at him to ease his obvious discomfort.

His body relaxed, and he moved the rest of the way into the classroom, coming to rest against the desk across the aisle from hers. She noticed his hair was a little longer than he usually wore it, and it surprised her to see a little curl at the nape of his neck and over the tops of his ears. He looked good dressed in the powder blue Henley that had always been her favorite, and a pair of ripped jeans.

The heightened color in his cheeks revealed that he was as uncertain of himself right then as she was herself. It was weird to feel this awkward with someone she'd been super close to only a month before. How could things change so drastically, so quickly?

Unsure of what to say, she stated the obvious. "You're here early."

"Well, I wanted to catch you before classes started."

"Oh."

"Look, I . . . I just wanted to tell you, I'm really sorry. About everything. I didn't handle things well at all."

Anna gave him a tight smile. "It's okay," she said. What else could she say?

"No, it's really not. I'm not sure what got into me."

Anna knew, and her name started with a capital *B*, but she didn't say this out loud.

"I was just hoping that, you know, maybe we could be friends."

What was Alex's definition of *friends*? If it meant that they'd smile and say hello when they saw each other, she could do that. If it meant anything more than that, she was pretty sure she wasn't interested. Anna decided to believe he meant the former. "Sure," she replied. "We can be friends, Alex."

Alex let out a heavy breath and beamed. "Really? Oh, Anna, that's . . . that's really great. Thank you." He swooped down to wrap her in a tight hug before pulling back, appalled with himself. "Oh no! Did I hurt you?"

She smiled at him reassuringly. "No, I'm okay. I'm not even really sore from the surgery anymore."

He looked doubtful.

"Honest, I'm okay," she repeated. Anna glanced at the clock at the front of the room. Class wouldn't start for another ten minutes. How long did he plan to stick around?

"I couldn't believe it when I heard what happened," Alex said. "I wanted to come and see you in the hospital, but . . ."

Whoa. She was *so* glad he hadn't. He'd cast her off like an old, scuzzy t-shirt that no longer fit, and now he seemed to want her back, at least in some form. "I wouldn't have known if you had. I was pretty out of it," she said instead.

"That sucks. So, did you really need a blood transfusion?"

Anna pursed her lips before answering, "Yeah, I really did." The annoyance she felt must have expressed itself in her voice, because he cringed.

"Sorry. Do you not want to talk about this?"

Anna sighed and leveled with him. "No, I'm sorry, Alex. It's not that I can't talk about it. It's just that this seems . . . Isn't this a little weird?"

"What, us talking?"

She nodded.

"It is," he admitted slowly. "But I'm trying really hard to make it feel normal again."

Anna immediately felt bad. He was trying. "I guess maybe it'll just take some time," she said to be polite.

Alex brightened visibly. "Yes," he agreed. "We just need a little time."

Wait. Were they talking about the same thing here? "For friendship," she clarified.

"Yes, absolutely. For friendship," he agreed, nodding for emphasis.

Relieved, Anna smiled. For a second there she'd wondered where he thought this might be going. She definitely didn't want him back as a boyfriend. That ship had sailed. She was on a different ship now, or on a different sea, or some other sailing metaphor that meant she had moved on and was happy exactly where the wind had carried her.

Landon was waiting for her at the canopy entrance when Anna left the building two hours later. He must have been watching for her because he hopped out of the car and was by her side before she'd taken a handful of steps. He tucked her arm in his and walked her out to his silver Altima. Anna didn't need the support. She wasn't nearly so weak anymore, but any excuse to touch Landon worked for her. She was still waiting impatiently for that kiss. She'd been ready the day the doctor deemed her "no longer contagious," but she felt too shy about it to initiate it herself.

As soon as he was buckled, Landon turned to her. "How're you feeling? Are you anxious to get home?"

She *was* fading a little, but Anna wouldn't say no to an outing, if that's what he was getting at. "Not really. Why?"

"I thought we could grab some coffee and scones from Uptown Bakery and head over to Sable Rocks. We don't have to get out of the car if you're tired. We can just park over at the point and look out at the lake."

The excitement Anna felt might have been a little over the top, but she couldn't help it. As much as she loved her house, she hated the feeling of confinement she'd experienced these last few weeks. And Sable Rocks was one of the best spots in town. Cliff-jumping season was well over by now, which meant they might just have the entire rocky expanse all to themselves.

It was only in the fifties today. Anna had worn a wool sweater, so she should be warm enough. If she did get cold, she thought happily, she had a big, strong hockey player to warm her up. "That sounds perfect," she said with a contented smile. "Let me just text my dad so he's not wondering where I am." Anna messaged her dad to let him know of her plans, and Landon drove on to the popular bakery.

The gravel parking area at Sable Rocks was empty when they pulled in twenty minutes later with their coffees and blueberry scones. “Are you sure you’re up for this?” Landon looked closely at her, and his brows lowered in concern. “I don’t mind parking back at the point. It’s nice there too.”

Anna shook her head. “No, this is good.”

“You’re sure?”

She opened her door and swung her legs out before turning back and beaming at him. She loved it that he worried about her. “I’m sure.”

After a few minutes of walking, they found a spot on a flat slab of rock. Anna’s stomach, which had been softly rumbling since the end of second period, let out a loud growl. Landon raised his eyebrows. “Sorry,” she said with a giggle. “I just ate a few hours ago. I haven’t had much of an appetite lately, so I guess it’s a good sign.”

“You’re doing really well,” Landon agreed. He set the drink carrier and bag down between them and got to work sliding the Java Jackets over their paper coffee cups. “You’ll be back to feeling normal again in no time.”

Anna watched him work. His thick, dark lashes rested high on his cheek bones, and his hair, nearly as black as the rocks, looked especially shiny in the sunlight. Anna wondered if men ever got jealous of each other the way women did. If she were a guy, she’d be jealous of Landon. He would always be the hottest guy in the room. And the sweetest.

Anna touched his wrist with her fingertips, and he looked up. The longing she felt must have shown in her eyes because he went absolutely still for several seconds before putting the cups back in the carrier and moving them to his other side, out of the way. He took her by the hand and frowned before reaching for her other one. “Your hands are freezing.”

Anna shrugged. “I don’t feel cold.” She doubted she could ever feel cold with Landon touching her. He had the rare talent of elevating her body temperature just by looking at her.

Lifting his hand up to her temple, he ran his fingers through her hair. “I can warm you up,” he said huskily.

Anna’s eyes dropped to his mouth. Finally. He was going to kiss her; she could feel it. The air between them nearly crackled with pent-up energy.

Leaning forward, he placed his fingers beneath her chin and brought her gaze back up to his. “Have I ever told you how much I love your eyes?”

Anna held her breath. Another inch, and they’d be kissing. “No,” she said on a shallow exhale.

“I’d never seen eyes this color until I met you.” He resumed the gentle combing of his fingers through her hair, and her scalp tingled from his touch. The warm, male scent of him filled her nostrils, and she breathed him in. “You’re so soft,” he murmured. “Your skin, your hair . . . I wonder, are your lips soft too?”

Nervous laughter stuck in her throat, and she placed a hand over her stomach as if she could calm the butterflies. Anna was very still as he placed warm, gentle kisses on her lips. He was unspeakably tender with her.

"You're nervous," Landon whispered against her mouth.

"I can't help it," she whispered back. Anna could feel her face catch fire as she explained, "I know it might seem crazy—I'm eighteen—but I haven't really . . ."

She tried again. "I almost feel like I'm being kissed for the first time."

Landon rested his forehead against hers, and she could just barely make out the smile that tugged at the corners of his mouth. "Works for me. Let's go with that."

She smiled in spite of her nervousness.

Pulling back in order to look her fully in the eyes, Landon grew serious. "Listen, we can take this slow, Anna, because the way I figure, we have all the time in the world. I'm not going anywhere. All I want is to be where you are, and that's enough for me."

His words settled her like nothing else could, and she leaned in towards him with an unspoken invitation. That was all the prompting he needed. His eyes burned a brand into her eyes as he slid his hand to the back of her neck and brought his mouth down on hers.

Anna wasn't passive. Her mouth fed him deep kisses until he moved his lips lower. His warm breath on the side of her throat sent shivers up her spine while he pressed his lips to her pulse points. When he sought her mouth again, she raised both hands up to cradle his head, playing with the locks of his hair with her fingertips and wishing that this moment, this first kiss with Landon, would never, ever have to end.

But a second later, it did. "Mommy!" a young boy yelled as he bounded around the tag alders and out onto the rocks. Anna broke away from Landon in a flash. She felt like a kid who'd just gotten caught with her hand in the cookie jar, and she couldn't help the second blush that stained her cheeks. By the time the boy's mother came into view, Anna was busying herself with the unwrapping of a scone while Landon observed her with a small, amused smile.

Chapter 22

Time with girlfriends really was marvelous medicine. Olivia couldn't remember the last time she'd had a girls' night. It had probably been over a year and a half ago when she and Suze had gone to dinner and a movie while the boys were out of town for games.

Tonight she was over at Erin's house with both Erin and Sarah, and she was clutching her side as she shook with laughter. Erin was telling them about her latest interaction with Brian Benninger, and she had the other two women in stitches over how she'd handled him.

"I can't believe you said that!" Sarah exclaimed. "Who even speaks that way anymore? 'Take a long walk off a short dock?'" She burst into laughter all over again. When she'd calmed enough to speak she said, "On second thought, it sounds just like somethin' my granny would've said." She made her voice go up an octave and exaggerated her accent. "Y'all just go awn an' take a long walk off that short dock over yonder."

Olivia wiped at her eyes. She couldn't remember the last time she'd laughed like this. She was actually crying and had a horrible stitch in her side.

"Well, I figured I'd try something with a little more class since telling him to eat shit didn't work. I mean, c'mon. Technically, I'm the guy's boss, and still he has absolutely no shame. This was, like, the sixth time now that he's asked me out. I don't know how much clearer I can be."

"Yes, I'd say tellin' him to eat, uh, *excrement* is very clear," Sarah agreed. The corners of her lips twitched as she took a sip of her wine. They were drinking a robust cabernet that Erin had picked up out in Napa with her now ex-husband a few years back. Sarah closed her eyes. "This is the best wine I've had in a long while."

Olivia had to agree. It was full-bodied, and it warmed her from the inside out, easing the chill she'd felt earlier out in the wintry cold. Nicolet had been hit with a big snowstorm last week on Thanksgiving day, but

Olivia hadn't minded. She and Nora and Sean were snowed in together with all the yummy smells of their feast to make the house feel truly cozy.

Tonight, all was well in the world, and her limbs felt loose and relaxed. She could attribute some of what she felt to the wine, but not all. She was simply happy.

Erin nodded. "I know. I just ordered another case of it. I'm down to just one more bottle after this one."

"It really is good," Olivia agreed.

"I tell myself I require a glass a night for good health," Erin said with a wide grin. "You know, those all-important flavonoids."

"Hmm," Olivia agreed. "Now all we need is some dark chocolate."

"And blueberries," Sarah added.

The other two women looked at her quizzically.

"What do you mean, *blueberries*?" Erin asked.

"Well, yes. Don't blueberries have flavonoids too?"

"I'm sure they do, but it's not really about the health benefits, Sarah. It's about the guilty pleasure, and there's absolutely no guilty pleasure when it comes to splurging on blueberries, I'm sorry to say," Erin lectured brazenly before hopping off the couch to grab some cheese and crackers from the table behind her.

"There is when you coat them in sugar and stick them between two pastry crusts, right, Sarah?" Olivia asked with a wink. She could tell Sarah hadn't known how to take Erin's comment. They really hadn't been acquainted all that long, and Erin could sometimes be a bit . . . brash. She came with a few splashes of vinegar mixed in with her honey, unlike Sarah, who was all sweetness. Sarah smiled at Olivia.

"Oh, blueberry pie does sound really good," Erin said before popping a slice of cheese into her mouth.

"But back to Brian. What are you going to do if he comes sniffing around again?" Olivia asked.

"I'm sure I'll think of something."

"Well, I feel sorry for him," Sarah said. "I think he's nice. He's helped me out a few times now at school."

"Well, then *you* can date him," Erin said flippantly.

"I don't want to date him, but that doesn't mean he's not nice."

Sarah was digging in her heals, and Olivia respected her for it, even though she completely disagreed with her. Erin just rolled her eyes.

"Brian's always given me the heebie-jeebies," Olivia said.

Erin paused mid sip. "Why do you say that?" she asked, setting down her glass and crossing her arms.

Olivia darted a glance at Sarah before answering. "Um . . . well, he's just a little too *much*. Of everything. Like he tries too hard."

"Huh," Erin said with a frown. "You're saying he's pathetic?"

The challenge in Erin's voice was unmistakable, and Olivia decided she'd best keep her opinions of Brian Benninger to herself from now on. All must not be as it seemed if Erin could bash him all day long, and did, but nobody else could. "I don't know what I'm saying. Just ignore me," Olivia said.

"I still say he's a sweetheart," Sarah insisted. "You're both wrong about him. Maybe you should give him a chance, Erin, and go out with him sometime."

"You're crazy, girl," Erin replied, but she delivered the line with a smile, which Sarah returned, but when Erin looked away, Sarah shot a quick look at Olivia and shrugged as if to say, *Who knows what she's thinking*?

"Anyway, enough about Brian. Let's talk about Sean," Erin prompted. Both Erin and Sarah looked at Olivia expectantly.

"What do you want to know?" Olivia asked through a mouthful of cracker and cheese.

"Feel free to swallow that bite down first," Erin said, wrinkling her nose in distaste.

Olivia washed it down with a sip of wine and laughed. "Better?"

"Much. For starters, tell us how the hell it can be that the two of you weren't even talking two months ago, and now that you are talking, *marriage* is the topic of conversation. What happened to just casually dating? Finding out if you're even compatible." Erin leaned forward. "I mean, do you even know if he's consistently good between the sheets yet, or if he leaves wads of toothpaste in the bathroom sink?"

"Goodness, Erin," Sarah said with wide eyes.

"What?" Erin asked with an impish grin. "Isn't that what you're wondering about too?"

"Maybe just a little," Sarah reluctantly admitted. She shot Olivia a sheepish glance.

Olivia fought down a blush. She liked Erin a lot, but she doubted they'd ever completely get one another. They were totally different people. There probably wasn't any good way to make Erin understand, but she tried anyway. "Let me just say first, *again*"—she shot Erin a look—"that we aren't engaged. Not technically, anyway, so let's just get that straight. But we do love each other, and we are talking about it, and I know it must seem completely crazy.

"Don't forget, though. Sean and I have known each other a long time. It's not like we were two strangers who started dating and decided to get married a week later. It's not even like we were just mere acquaintances either. We were really, really close before, and we just took that to the next level. I guess I can't really explain it better than that." She shrugged. "We just know how we feel."

Sweet Sarah nodded supportively, while Erin took a few seconds to mull it over. She wasn't quiet long. "Here's my next question, then, but you don't have to answer it if you don't want—"

Olivia scoffed good-naturedly.

"What?" Erin asked innocently. "You know me. I am pretty direct, but that doesn't mean *you* have to be if you don't want to. I know how to respect people's privacy."

Sarah hid a smile, but Olivia didn't bother concealing her amusement. "Okay, Miss Sensitivity, shoot."

Erin had the grace to look slightly chastised, but she continued ahead with her question anyway. "Did you ever feel anything for Sean before . . . ? When Nate was alive?"

Olivia immediately shook her head. "No. I really didn't," she said definitively. "I noticed he was good looking, obviously, but I didn't look at him or anyone else *that* way." She made a lame attempt at a joke, "I wish I could say the same for my husband."

Both women looked at her pityingly.

"Sorry, I guess that's never going to be funny, is it?" She shook her head as she continued, "But no, I can say with all honesty that I never felt that way about Sean, although I did love him. I loved him as a person, and I've always respected him. He's a good man."

Erin didn't look quite convinced, but she nodded anyway. Olivia didn't take offense. After all, she *had* left something out, and Erin could sniff out a secret like a hound on the hunt. Why not be completely honest? These were her friends, Olivia reminded herself, and so she added, "But I do have something to admit."

Erin leaned forward again. "What's that?"

Olivia took a deep breath. "That night, after the funeral, I was lying in bed. My thoughts were traveling in a hundred different directions like they do sometimes at night when you're stressed out, you know?"

Sarah nodded.

"And even though I was so mad at Sean at that time . . . I mean, everything was so fresh and so unbelievably painful. But I was lying there, and—" Olivia fanned her face. "I still feel so guilty about this. The timing of it all. I had just buried my husband, and . . ."

Erin perched herself on the edge of the sofa like a leopard ready to pounce. "Go on," she encouraged.

"Well, I wondered if I would ever remarry again, and Sean's face just popped into my head. I didn't try to put it there, but . . ." Olivia put her face in her hands and held it there for a few seconds before looking up and saying, "That was the first time I realized I might be attracted to Sean. I pictured us together, and I still feel awful about it."

Erin relaxed back against the sofa cushions and took a leisurely sip of wine. "You have absolutely nothing to feel guilty about," she declared.

Olivia's jaw dropped. "Erin, I had just buried my husband *that day*."

"I know, but I don't think it's at all unusual that you were already considering what your future might look like. You had to. It was coming whether you wanted it to or not. Time marches on, right?"

Olivia looked to Sarah for some sanity, but she was nodding along in agreement.

Olivia spoke slowly. "So what you're both telling me is that what I did that night was *normal*?"

"Totally," Erin said with complete conviction. "I used to do that all the time when I was married to Seth. He was military—I'm pretty sure I told you that—and deployed a lot. Sometimes, when I'd be brushing my teeth or something, I would let the worst-case scenario play out in my head like a movie. And I'd think, what would I do if he didn't come home? Would I date again? *Who* would I date? That kind of stuff."

Olivia's mouth still hung open, and she shook her head. "I have beaten myself up over that for more than a year. And honestly, I think it made me even more angry at Sean, even though it wasn't his fault. It's not like he was responsible for my thoughts or the guilt I felt over them."

"You were just protectin' yourself, Olivia," Sarah said wisely.

Erin looked at Sarah with a small gleam in her eye, and Olivia could almost see the gears turning in her friend's head. Erin wanted to know if Sarah was speaking from experience. Thankfully, she had enough sense to leave it for now. Olivia knew intuitively that Sarah wasn't ready to open up yet.

"I can't believe it," Olivia said to no one in particular. "I guess I can let this go, then. I don't have to feel guilty about it anymore." She looked at Sarah. "That's what you're saying, right?"

"Absolutely."

"One hundred percent," Erin added.

"Okay. Well, since I'm on a roll here, can I just confess one more thing? It's something else I've never even whispered to another soul."

"Do tell," Erin said, leaning forward again.

"Okay, here goes. I used to sometimes feel jealous of Sean's girlfriend, Susan, when we'd all hang out together. Not because I wanted Sean for myself or anything," she was quick to add, "but I could see how they were together. Always teasing each other and touching. Nate didn't do public displays of affection—like, at all—and I always wished we could just take a stroll down the sidewalk holding hands and laugh together, like they did."

Olivia paused a second and added, “There, now that’s out in the open too.”

A corner of Erin’s mouth pulled up in disbelief, and she looked at Sarah before turning to Olivia. “Olivia, if these are your deepest, darkest secrets, then all I can say is—I’m in real trouble.”

Sarah found that hysterical, and she laughed and laughed before settling down and giving Olivia her two cents. “Olivia, honey, you weren’t jealous of Susan. You just envied the way Susan and Sean operated as a couple. You wanted that kind of relationship for yourself and your husband. I really don’t think that’s anythin’ to be ashamed of.”

“Oh,” Olivia said lamely. Put like that, there really wasn’t any issue. Wasn’t she supposed to be the one trained in counseling here? Yet there she sat, getting great insights from these two women who she suddenly felt extremely close to and grateful to have in her life.

“She’s right,” Erin agreed. “You can relax now in the knowledge of your perfection as a human being.”

“Stop,” Olivia said with a chuckle. But she did relax, kicking her stockinged feet up onto the coffee table. “You guys don’t know how much you’ve helped me tonight. I feel so. . . I feel almost lighter.” She put her hand over her heart. “Thank you.”

They both smiled back at her, and Sarah said, “You deserve happiness, Olivia. I’m glad you’ve found it.”

“Okay,” Erin said clapping her hands and rubbing them together, “So when’s the big day?”

Olivia groaned. “You just won’t quit, will you?”

Erin shook her head and grinned.

“I have *no* idea. When we do decide to get married, I’m sure we’ll just do it quietly. Neither one of us has any family left, so—”

“What?” Erin sputtered. “Are you kidding me? You have to have a wedding.”

“Why?” Olivia asked in amusement.

“Because I want to be there!”

“Oh, okay. We’ll have a ceremony just for you, then.”

Sarah laughed.

“Think about it, though. Seriously. You’ve had the experience before, but Sean hasn’t. Don’t you think he would want to show you off, celebrate with his friends, make an occasion out of it?”

“Well, maybe. If he wants to, I’m not opposed to it or anything. But honestly, it’s too early to be planning stuff. We only just started talking about it, and I really want us to take our time.”

“You keep downplaying this. Slow-walking it. Why is that?”

Olivia bit down on her lip. Erin wasn't going to let this go. How she was so perceptive, Olivia had no clue. It was uncanny, really. She had barely allowed herself to think about the potential complication of a happily ever after with Sean, choosing instead to stuff it away whenever it entered her thoughts, yet somehow Erin had picked up on it. Olivia had underestimated her. Erin's nose was even better than a hound's. But it seemed it was the night for sharing her secrets, so Olivia turned to Sarah and addressed her first.

"Erin knows about this already, but I had to have an emergency c-section with Nora. It's a little complicated, but basically she was in distress and they had to get her out quickly. As a result, I had a vertical incision, which is . . . problematic for any future pregnancies."

Sarah looked back, wide-eyed with concern. "That must have been so traumatic for you! I'm so sorry. Does that mean you can't . . . ?" She left the question hanging there.

Erin piped in, "It means she can, but she probably shouldn't." She faced Olivia. "Sean doesn't know?"

Olivia shook her head.

The three women were quiet for a minute, each thinking through the implications of what Olivia had just revealed. Sarah was the first to speak again. "Does he want kids?"

"He's talked about it."

"Oh, Olivia." Sarah looked grave. "What will you do?"

"Well, she has to tell him," Erin said, stating the obvious.

"I know, I know. And I'm planning to. I just have to figure out how. It was really painful when they first broke the news to me, but over time, I thought I'd sort of come to terms with it. But now . . . I don't know."

Erin and Sarah glanced at each other.

"Anyway, I don't want him to have to choose between having me or having a child. He deserves to have it all, and he could with someone else. But then there's this small part of me that thinks—Well, why not with me? Maybe it would be worth the risk. They'd just have to closely monitor me and deliver the baby early before I got too big."

Erin shook her head vehemently. "That would be a mistake."

"You don't know that," Olivia shot back.

Erin sighed heavily. "No, I don't know it. I just know I don't want anything to happen to you. Just promise to be careful. Don't rush into anything."

"I won't." Olivia looked at the somber expressions on the faces of her friends and forced herself to lighten up. "Okay, enough of that. Let's put on some music and dance." She got up with her phone and brought it over to the Bluetooth speaker in the corner of the room. “What do you want to hear?” she asked the other two.

Although they were reluctant to move on from such an important topic, her friends eventually got into the spirit of things, and the three women spent the rest of the evening laughing and dancing.

Chapter 23

"When did Olivia say she'd be home again?"

Even though Jess had asked this question already, just after they'd put Nora down for bed, Anna told her again. "I'm pretty sure she said around eleven o'clock."

Jess looked at her phone. "Another hour."

She sounded so dejected that Anna grinned. "What, you're not loving this movie?" she teased.

"No, it's cute," Jess insisted, but Anna knew she'd hardly been paying attention to it. Jess had been restless since they'd started watching *Fried Green Tomatoes*, which she'd never seen before, and Anna had been so sure she would love. They watched a little further, and when Jess didn't react during the scene where Kathy Bates rammed her ginormous boat of a car—six times—into the cute little car that had stolen her parking space, Anna picked up the remote and shut off the TV.

She turned to face Jess, drawing her legs up underneath her on the sofa. "Okay, that's it. What's going on?"

"What? Why'd you stop the movie?"

"Because you're not even watching it! You've been staring off into space all night."

"No, I haven't."

With eyebrows raised, Anna stared at her.

Jess sighed. "Okay, fine."

"Something's on your mind."

"I know," Jess admitted.

"Do you want to tell me?"

Jess toyed with the throw pillow in her lap before answering. "I want to, but I don't know if I should."

Immediately, Anna made silent, rapid-fire guesses about what might be bothering her friend. Jess told Anna everything about herself, so it must have to do with someone else. Someone Anna knew.

Jess narrowed it down for her when she added, "I don't want him to think he can't trust me."

Anna mentally flipped through the men in her life like a Rolodex and settled on Mitch. He was the only one who occasionally confided in Jess. At least, he used to.

"Is it Mitch?"

Jess nodded.

They were making progress. "Is he okay?"

"I don't know. I hope so."

Anna ran a hand through her hair. "Jessica, are you gonna tell me or not?"

For a split second, Anna thought maybe Jess had decided against it, but then she began talking, and as Anna listened, a sense of unease grew in the pit of her stomach.

"Last week, that awful night you forced me to play Scrabble with you, I saw Mitch on my way home. It was late, and I was stopped at the light on Lake Street when I saw a group of drunk idiots walking down the hill ahead of me. One of them stumbled and fell down on the sidewalk right outside the Blue Moon, and the friends he was with just laughed and went inside without him. He was laying there on the concrete, and I was thinking that the poor guy should get better friends when I recognized his jacket."

Jess, who had been staring at the pillow, looked at Anna. "It was Mitch's blue Patagonia. As soon as the light changed, I pulled up next to him and got him into my car. He helped a little, but not much. And let me tell you, your brother is *heavy*. I'm not sure he was with it enough to even know who I was or what was going on. He sat in the passenger seat with his head in his hands and his feet on the curb and threw up all over the sidewalk. I was so glad I had him sit there with the door open first." Jess wrinkled her nose. "Anyway, he kept muttering the same thing over and over."

Anna hesitated. She needed to ask, but she wasn't sure she wanted to know the answer. "What was he saying?"

"I'm not sure. All I caught was *I can't, I can't*. Anyway, I called home and asked my mom what to do. She said to take him home, to your house, but I didn't want to get him in trouble, so I asked if I could bring him to our house. My dad was working night shift, so she said yes. She just made me promise not to tell him." She finished and shrugged.

"So that's what you did?"

"Uh-huh. He stayed in the guest room with the popcorn-slash-puke bowl on the floor by the bed, and in the morning, he was so embarrassed he could hardly look at us. Although he did say thanks. I gave him a ride back to the dorms first thing, but he wouldn't talk about it. He wouldn't tell me much of anything. Normally, Mitch tells me stuff, Anna, but he wouldn't say *boo* this time."

"You get more out of him than I ever do."

"I know, and I'm sorry. Only Mitch knows why, but he doesn't confide in anyone else, and I don't mind being his person. I just hope you don't mind it too much either."

Anna treated Jess to a small smile. "No, I'm glad he has you. But I'd be lying if I said I wasn't jealous."

"I get it. I'd feel the same way."

Anna moved on. This couldn't be about her. "Did he ever explain why he tried to drink himself into a coma?"

Jess shook her head. "We haven't talked. I've called a few times. He's ignoring me right now."

"We're in the same boat, then."

Anna sat back against the pillows and reached for the soft blanket that was folded up and thrown over the back of the couch. She tucked it around herself as she gave a little shiver.

"You're cold," Jess remarked unnecessarily. "It's no wonder. You must have lost at least ten pounds. You've got nothing extra to keep you warm."

"I'm putting weight back on again, slow but sure. You know, it's been almost eight weeks, and I guess I thought I'd be a little further along with my recovery by now." Anna scowled.

"Well, you might not see it, but you've come a long way. You don't look sick anymore, and those weird come-and-go fevers are totally gone now, right?"

"Yes, thankfully."

Jess tucked her feet under the blanket, wiggling her warm toes against Anna's knees. "Anyway. Sorry about the movie. I was distracted and feeling guilty for not telling you about Mitch."

"That's okay." Anna peered closely at her friend's face. The worried notch between her eyebrows was still there. "Is there something else?"

Jess bit down on her lower lip before answering. "Actually, yes. I've been debating if I should tell you some of what he's told me over the years. I don't know how to help him, but maybe if you knew some things, we might be able to figure it out together."

"What things?"

Jess fidgeted with the pillow some more. Anna waited quietly. She didn't want to pressure her, but she was dying to know.

After another moment, Jess blurted, "Did you know he has regular nightmares about your mom's accident?"

Anna's eyes widened. "No."

"He has to relive it over and over again in his sleep. Not every night, but a lot. Too much. He said it's like torture."

A chill ran through Anna, and it had nothing to do with being cold. "He's never said anything."

"He's never told anyone," Jess replied. "I feel like a blabbermouth right now, but you should know that, for Mitch, your mom may as well have died last week. That's how fresh it is to him."

Jess paused. "It's with him almost all the time, like his shadow. The only place he can escape it is on the ice. He told me when he plays, it all fades away. He loves the game for itself, but the escape, it's the real reason he became so obsessed with hockey."

Anna slowly nodded. "He's always had such a single-minded focus on it."

"Well, that's why. And it's probably the reason he's so good too, but even that has been hard for him."

Anna frowned. "What do you mean?"

"Just that certain people root for him to fail. You know how jealous people can be, especially hockey parents whose own kids aren't as good. That bothered him a lot growing up. People hoping for his failure."

This was a lot for Anna to take in. She was beginning to realize she really didn't know much about her brother at all. "What else has he said?"

"Let's see. He's talked about how disappointed he is with your dad. How he's felt invisible over the years. He's told me he wants to be a better brother, but he doesn't know how. You know, he was worried about moving into the dorms and leaving you all alone in that big house."

Jess paused and seemed to consider her words. "He's talked about that day at the breakwall, Anna. In detail. He describes it so clearly, sometimes I feel like I was there too. And he . . . he's cried. Not the way we cry—you know, all *boo-hoo*—but still, he's cried."

Anna's eyes grew wide. "So, has he talked to you about what's going on lately? Why he's pulled even further away from us?"

"No. He's not talking right now. But I can guess."

"And?"

"Think about it. Here's Mitch. He loses your mom, and then he nearly loses you. It's a double whammy, and he blames himself for both. He blames your dad too. He tries for years to get your dad's attention, with almost no success, and now that he has it, he's not sure he wants it."

"I don't know how to help him."

Jess shook her head. "Me neither. For now, I guess we just show up for him whenever we can."

"I've been doing that my whole life." At Jess's expression, Anna held up her hands. "Not that I'm complaining. I've loved it. I can't wait for tomorrow. I don't know who's more excited, me or my dad. You're still coming, right?"

"Of course. Box seats."

Nicolet State was playing Michigan State at home tomorrow, and Sean had given Olivia box seats to share with anyone she wanted. When Aunt Heidi heard about it, she'd surprised them by booking a flight to Nicolet for the weekend. She'd been reaching out more, and not just to Anna. She was calling Steven too. Anna wished she knew what they talked about, but her dad always took the calls in his room with the door closed. She still didn't know what had happened on that hike, but she was grateful for whatever it was because Aunt Heidi was going to stay with them again this visit.

With the exception of Mitch, family relations were looking up. It appeared the changes in her father were permanent. Anna was cautiously optimistic that her new-and-improved dad was here to stay. Things between the two of them were so good that sometimes Anna felt the need to pinch herself to make sure it was real.

He had taken a new position as the head of project development for Chester Biotechnologies. He would miss the teaching aspect of his old role, but there were new challenges to look forward to in his new one, and the best part was that there was no travel involved. As a result, Anna had seen more of her dad these last few months than she had in the last few years, and she loved it.

Her father, previously a total and complete disaster in the kitchen, was even learning how to cook, and he'd only had to use the kitchen fire extinguisher once. He counted it a success, but Anna had teased him that he shouldn't quit his day job. She wished Mitch could experience their dad in this new way. Somehow, she needed to get him to come around.

Later that night, long after returning from Olivia's, Anna was still thinking about Mitch. She wanted her brother back. But even more than that, she wanted him to be whole in a way she wasn't sure he'd ever been. Maybe now that he was cleared to play again, he'd start to come around.

Chapter 24

Olivia's voice was hoarse, but that didn't stop her from yelling. Nicolet was tied with Michigan State with a little over a minute left in the third period. Any second, she'd expect Sean to pull their goalie in order to put another player on the ice. Olivia couldn't believe how much fun she was having, which immediately made her feel guilty. She'd never left Nora two nights in a row, and she wondered again if she should have stayed home tonight. Meredith was babysitting for the second time now, and Olivia hoped she'd gotten Nora to go down without too much trouble. Glancing quickly at her phone, Olivia figured no news was good news.

"Yes!" Anna shrieked, and Olivia looked up in time to see Landon gain control of the puck. He'd stopped the opposing player in his tracks with a well-timed poke check and had dished off the puck to one of the wings with a crisp pass.

"Here we go," Olivia yelled, as the boys skated back towards their offensive zone. Sean pulled the goalie, and Mitch hopped out onto the ice to join his team as the sixth player.

MSU struggled to attack the puck, but the other Nicolet winger, number thirty-four, pulled out some amazing stick-handling and footwork moves. "Look at him go," Heidi marveled.

"See Mitch, see Mitch," Steven yelled to the wing. Mitch was moving into perfect position for the pass, and Olivia clutched her phone with both hands.

Thirty-four passed off to Mitch a half-second before taking an enormous hit. It all happened so fast, but Mitch, with an effortless-looking wrist shot, scored in the upper left corner of the net with three seconds left on the clock, and the crowd went absolutely wild. All five of them in the box cheered and jumped and hugged each other as they celebrated the imminent win. They didn't even bother watching the last seconds play out. Olivia noticed the heightened color in Steven's cheeks and the brightness of his eyes, and felt her heart squeeze. He was so proud of his boy.

Steven wasn't the only one. They all chatted excitedly as they walked out to Olivia's van. Olivia was the designated driver for their group because she had the largest vehicle. While Steven cleared off her snow-covered windshield, Heidi asked where they were headed for dinner.

"We have reservations at 906 Pizza with the whole team," Olivia answered.

"You'll love it, Aunt Heidi," Anna assured her. "It's got the best pizza in town."

"Oh, I remember well," Heidi said. "906 Pizza was one of our favorite hangouts growing up."

Jess piped up. "Wow! I had no idea it's been open for so long. It's like a historic landmark."

Olivia could almost hear the rolling of Heidi's eyes as she gave a wry laugh and informed Jess she wasn't *that* old.

"Sean takes the guys there a few times a year. Since it's the start of Christmas break, he thought it would be nice to go there tonight before everyone heads off." Olivia blew on her hands and rubbed them together. She hadn't brought mittens along tonight, and she was wishing now she had. The steering wheel was freezing. At least she didn't have to be the one to clear off the van. She thanked Steven when he'd completed the task and gotten back in.

"No problem," he said, rubbing his own hands together.

Heidi revisited the topic of the game. Still marveling over her nephew's athleticism, she said again, "I didn't realize Mitch was so good. And to think he's only a freshman. That was such a thrill, wasn't it?"

The question wasn't directed at anyone in particular, but Steven answered as he reached for his seat belt. "A huge thrill." He looked back as he fastened the buckle. "I think we've got a new hockey fan here, ladies. She's drunk the Kool-Aid. No going back now, Heidi."

"Aunt Heidi, you'll have to come to some more games," Anna insisted from the back row.

"Now that I have the schedule, I'll have to plan another trip."

Olivia saw Steven's smile as she backed out of her narrow parking space and joined the line of cars waiting to exit the lot. "It's going to be a while before we get out of this parking lot, guys," Olivia warned them. Game nights always required multiple traffic cops to help fans leave safely.

"That's okay," Anna responded happily. "The reservations aren't for another half hour anyway. We've got time."

Cheerful chatter filled the car as Olivia inched forward little by little. The light snow that had been falling all day was getting steadily heavier, but nobody seemed to mind. Groups of college students trudged past them, already kicking off their celebration of the win. Shouts and laughter echoed all around the outside of their vehicle, and Olivia smiled.

She listened as Steven explained "cross-checking" to Heidi. Then she wanted to know more about Mitch's position, which Steven was more than happy to discuss. If Steven were any prouder of his son's playing, the buttons on his parka would pop off as a result of his puffed-out chest. He began replaying all the key moments of the game, taking special care to leave no detail out when it came to the plays Mitch had been a part of.

It sure had taken him long enough, but Olivia found nothing at all to criticize about the man now. She'd observed him enough times over the last few months to see he was genuinely trying. In fact, she'd go so far as to say he'd been transformed. Gone was the withdrawn, laconic man, and in his place was this affable and engaged one. She'd observed something else tonight as well. There had been some subtle sidelong glances exchanged between Heidi and Steven, and Olivia got the sense that something might be happening between them. She hoped she was right.

Something about being happy and in love herself made her want that for everyone around her. She thought of herself and Sean and how easy it had been for them to take that step. It had been the most thrilling and natural thing in the world. The only thing keeping it from being perfect was the knowledge that Sean had hopes for children, and Olivia just wasn't sure she could give him any. Maybe they'd be able to adopt a child together. She knew there were plenty of kids out there in need of a good home and loving family.

The more she'd thought about it as she'd lain awake last night after Erin's, the more she warmed up to the idea. She could picture their family —herself, Sean, Nora, and a son or daughter they would adopt together. Olivia knew she could love an adopted child just as much as she loved Nora; she just wished she knew what Sean would think.

Would he feel cheated? Adoption wasn't for everyone; she knew that. She also knew that she could never stand in the way of Sean experiencing what she had with Nora if that was what he wanted. Having given birth to a child of her own, Olivia knew about that special moment when a parent gazes upon their baby for the first time—the awe and wonder that they, with all their imperfections, could have made something so perfect. How could she rob him of that?

Olivia's own special moment, although still incredibly powerful when it had finally happened, had been delayed after Nora's birth. The chatter in the car faded into the background as Olivia remembered that day. It had been the most terrifying experience of her life. Even now, she had a hard time thinking about it. Thank God she'd listened to her gut.

After noticing the baby wasn't moving as much as usual, Olivia had called the doctor's office, and even though the nurse reassured her it was natural for movements to diminish closer to the delivery date, Olivia couldn't shake the sense that something was wrong. That evening, she went to the ER, and Nora had been delivered via emergency c-section not long after.

The chaos began almost as soon as they had hooked her up to the fetal monitor, and Olivia recalled being confused about what was happening, even as they whisked her to the operating room. Her baby was in distress, she knew that much, and she learned the rest as she listened to all the nurses and doctors scrambling around and directing one another as they prepped the OR. Nora's heart rate had dropped dangerously low. That was the bottom line, and the intense fear and awful tugging sensation Olivia experienced when the doctor had performed the emergency caesarean, well, she could almost feel it again now.

Olivia had been all alone and unsure if her baby would live, and it was the thing of nightmares. She wouldn't wish that kind of trauma on anyone. And those weeks with Nora in the NIC unit? She wasn't sure she could do that again. If something went wrong, she wouldn't be able to forgive herself. And this time, her own life could potentially be at risk. She'd been warned.

Nora had already lost one parent. Olivia was all she had. Putting herself at risk wouldn't be fair to her daughter. But then again, wasn't every day a risk? Every single time she got behind the wheel, there weren't any guarantees she'd make it to her destination in one piece. Look at what had happened to Nate.

Olivia hated feeling this confused. She took a deep breath and—realizing all her muscles were tense—willed herself to relax. She was going to make herself crazy with worry over this. It was time to talk to Sean. He deserved to know the truth before any more time went by, and Olivia was embarrassed she'd lacked the courage until now.

She made the decision. They'd talk tonight after pizza, back at her place, and she could finally get this off her chest and be at peace. For now, she needed to get back into the spirit of things. They had a fun night ahead of them, and she wanted to enjoy it.

Surprisingly, it didn't take long before they were out of the parking lot and on their way. The topic had switched to what pizza they should order, and it looked like Olivia just might get her Margherita pizza again tonight. It was Heidi's favorite too. Regardless of how things went with Sean later, at least Olivia would get her fill of garlic.

When Sean entered the restaurant, he stopped in the doorway and performed a visual sweep over the dining area. His eyes locking on hers, he gave Olivia a slow, flirtatious smile, which she returned with one of her own. Would her heart always go slightly haywire when she looked at him? He headed towards their reserved section, followed by his boys.

Olivia had chosen the same booth they'd occupied the last time they were here with the team, and Anna and Jess had reserved the booth across the partition from them. Heidi, who sat inside the booth next to Olivia, talked across the table with Steven, but their conversation stopped abruptly as Sean arrived at their table and reached down to haul Olivia into his arms. He moved with startling quickness and held her a little longer than was probably appropriate, but Olivia didn't mind. She loved when he held her and she could breathe in the scent of him and feel his warm body against hers. Kissing her lightly on the lips, Sean finally released her and took his seat across from her on the end. No words had been spoken yet, but Olivia saw Heidi and Steven exchange knowing smiles.

Steven was the first to speak, congratulating Sean on the win as he gave him a solid pat on the back. "Let me pour you a beer."

"I won't say no to that," Sean replied with a grin. Steven lifted the pitcher and tilted the cup for a good pour.

Sean glanced around their section as the players all took seats.

"Do you still need to order the pizza?" Olivia asked. "I wasn't sure. We ordered ours already, but we asked them to wait and bring it all out at the same time."

"I put ours in before the game. They'll start making them now that we're all here."

"Perfect."

"They played so well tonight," Heidi interjected.

Sean nodded. "They did. And your son." He looked at Steven and whistled. "What a game."

"He looked good, didn't he?" Steven said, appearing careful not to boast too much but unable to be completely humble.

"To think I get three more years with that kid."

Steven beamed.

"Speaking of Mitch, where is he?" Heidi asked. She looked around the restaurant. "I want to congratulate him."

Olivia peered over at the booth attached to theirs. She'd assumed Mitch would sit there, but another boy had joined Landon and the girls. Olivia recognized him as one of the boys who'd teased Sean about feeding Nora the last time they were here. Were all hockey players good looking? It sure seemed that way, at least with this bunch.

"I don't see him." Turning to Sean, she asked, "Who's that with the girls?"

"Who? Oh, that's Drew Lancour. Number thirty-four."

"Ah." Steven looked impressed. "That kid had a great assist there at the end."

"Oh, him," Heidi said, making the connection. "I'm glad he's okay. He took a really bad hit."

"Drew's tough," Sean said dismissively.

Heidi pursed her lips. "Well, tough or not, hits like that can end the careers of boys like him. I'm the one who reads their X-rays."

Olivia had noticed this about Heidi. She spoke her mind, and Olivia admired that about her. Apparently, that hadn't always been the case. In one of her more recent conversations with her father, Steven had told Anna about the early days when he first met the twin sisters. Shelly had been the outspoken, spirited one, while Heidi had the more quiet demeanor. Olivia wondered what had changed.

Sean inclined his head to concede the point. "Hits are part of the game. There's no getting around it. But don't worry. Drew's smart. He knows how to take a hit, and he checks smart too. He'll be alright."

Heidi looked ready with a reply, but Steven put a staying hand out and rested it on top of hers. Heidi met his gaze, and Olivia watched her turn a pretty shade of pink. Oh, yes. There was definitely something happening there.

Sean noticed too, because he grinned and gave her foot two quick jabs with his own under the table before turning the subject back to Mitch. "I don't think Mitch is here yet, but the rest of the team is, so he's probably not too far behind."

"I'll just give him a quick call." Steven pulled his cell phone out of his back pocket. The three of them were quiet while they waited for him to connect.

Olivia sneaked a glance across the booth at Sean. She felt an unspeakable tenderness towards him. She loved him and he loved her, and she wrapped that knowledge around herself. It was all she needed. But what did he need? She wanted to give him everything.

Chapter 25

Anna and Jess had excused themselves to the restroom to talk about Drew Lancour, who'd spent the last ten minutes hitting on Jess.

"I'm sure he's a player," Jess said, but she still asked to borrow some of Anna's lip gloss, and she gave her cheeks a quick pinch before leaving the bathroom. Anna trailed behind her with a smile.

No sooner had they sat back down than Drew started in again. He scooted closer to Jess under the guise of looking at the dessert menu in front of her, and the amused look Landon shot Anna told her he knew what Drew was up to.

The bell on the front door opened with a jingle, and Mitch entered the restaurant. He shook off the snow from his collar, while Anna did a double take. He wasn't alone. Standing there with her brother was a stunning brunette wearing a ridiculous fur coat and far too much lipstick. Mitch sure did know how to pick 'em.

"Mitch is here," Anna announced, and the four of them turned to wave. Mitch returned a wave while the girl stared vacantly back at them.

Jess turned around again and rolled her eyes. "Can't your brother date somebody normal for a change?"

Drew waggled his brows. "I don't think you can call what Mitch does *dating*."

Anna wrinkled her nose, and Landon shook his head at him.

"Gross," Jess said.

"What'd I say?" Drew asked with a puzzled laugh.

"Dude. She's his sister." Landon tipped his head toward Anna.

"And I've known him long enough to have played naked with him in a wading pool," Jess chimed in.

Drew's lips curled into a grin, and he gave a slow nod of his head. "Nice."

Jess swatted at him.

Anna shot Landon an apologetic look. "Can I get out again real quick?" Landon nodded and pressed a small kiss to her temple before sliding out of the booth. She beamed at him as she stood. He was always doing things like that. Little displays of affection that weren't gross or over the top, just . . . sweet.

"Hey, big brother," she said when she reached Mitch at the front of the restaurant. He'd just finished hanging their coats, and Anna gave him a hug before congratulating him on his goal and on the team's win.

He grinned. "Thanks. It feels good."

"I'm glad we were all there to see it. And Dad's *so* proud. We all are."

"Thanks," he said again, looking over her shoulder distractedly. He cleared his throat. "Um, so this is Cassie. Cassie, this is my sister, Anna." He made the introductions in a perfunctory manner and not with any real enthusiasm. That pretty much told the whole story. Cassie wasn't important to him.

Anna reached out and shook Cassie's hand, which was cold and limp and reminded her of a dead fish. She hated when people shook hands like that. She felt like it said something about their personality, and she had to fight off a feeling of immediate dislike for Mitch's flavor of the week.

Anna had been in the middle of asking Cassie if she'd been at the game when Mitch interrupted her, looking over her shoulder again. "Who's that sitting with you guys? Lancour?"

Anna turned to look back at her booth and at the backs of Jess's and Drew's heads.

"Yep. We just met him, but I think he's got a thing for Jess."

Mitch frowned. "She should stay far away from that guy."

"You don't like him?" Anna asked in surprise.

"I like him fine, but he's not good enough for Jess."

Anna shrugged. "Well, tell her that."

"I will," he said darkly, still looking at their booth. He directed a quick nod of his head at Landon in greeting, and then Cassie tugged on his sleeve. "I'd better go say hi to Dad and everyone before we sit. See ya, Anna."

"Oh, okay. See you."

He walked around her.

"Hey, listen," Anna called after him. "Maybe you could come by tomorrow. I know Aunt Heidi wants to spend some time with you. We've all really missed you." She held her breath.

After hesitating briefly, Mitch answered, "Yeah, sure."

He made his way to their dad's booth, and Anna watched Cassie follow him like a little puppy. He might not have been all that warm, but he hadn't been cold either, and at least he'd said he'd come by. That was good, but

Anna worried about what Mitch would be doing in the meantime. Was he going to go out again tonight and completely wreck himself? What if he got hurt or did something stupid?

Anna locked eyes with Landon as she returned to their booth. The worry must have shown on her face, because he smiled sympathetically. He stood up for her to slide by again, but before she slipped in, he wrapped her in a hug and whispered in her ear, “It’ll all work out, you’ll see.”

“Alright, you two. Let’s see if you can last a full minute without touching each other,” Jess teased.

Drew put his arm around Jess and joked, “Aww, are you feeling a little jealous over here, honey? ’Cause I can give you some attention. How ‘bout a little sugar.” He pointed to his cheek, inviting Jess to plant one on it. It was all said in jest, and Jess responded good-naturedly as she pushed him away, but a quick glance at Mitch left Anna puzzled. He was shooting a murderous look across the divider at Drew, completely oblivious to what their father was saying to him. He was being awfully protective of Jess. Odd.

Their two meat-lovers pizzas came out a few minutes later, piping hot and smelling delicious. All four of them dug in, the boys especially. While Anna and Jess stopped at two pieces each, both Landon and Drew, already on their fourth slices, were still going strong. Where they put it, Anna didn’t know.

The conversation flowed seamlessly among the four of them, although they periodically broke off into little side discussions as well, and it was during one of these that Landon leaned in closer and whispered, “You look really pretty tonight.”

Anna couldn’t help the bright smile that broke out on her face. “I do?”

Landon nodded and regarded her intently before speaking again. “Anna . . .”

Anna felt a little shiver run through her. He seemed too serious all of a sudden. “What is it?”

“Listen, this isn’t really the time or place, but I just have to tell you. These last few months have been so—”

But Landon was cut off by a commotion to their right. Sean was standing up at the edge of the booth and was working to get everyone’s attention. Slowly, their section, which was the only part of the restaurant that still had patrons at the tables, quieted down.

“Guys,” he began. “I know we already had our pep talk back at the rink. But I just have to say again how proud I was of you tonight. Coach Jackson had to run after the game, so he couldn’t be here with us tonight, but I know he feels the same. You played well. You hustled. You fought hard for the win. Everything I asked you to do, you did, and then some. You communicated well out there. You anticipated each other, and you worked together—like a family. It's not our first win, but tonight was different. Tonight was magic."

There were murmurs of agreement.

Sean continued, "This was our last game before Christmas break, and I know many of you will be going home to your real families, but I don't want you to forget this night. Remember this feeling. Remember this game. This is the night you became brothers, and I want to see you play like this —like a team, like a family—when we come back in January. Now that I know you can, I'm gonna expect it. Nothing less."

A couple of guys groaned good-naturedly.

"Now, bear with me, 'cause a few shout-outs are in order. Shannahan and Maki, you two are a force on those power plays, I gotta say. And Shaeffer, you defended the net like your life depended on it. Well done, buddy. Stevenson and LaFleur, your defense was outstanding tonight. Just outstanding. You shut 'em down time and time again."

Landon gave a small, humble smile beside her, and Anna squeezed his knee.

Sean paused and everyone waited expectantly for what he'd say next. The boys were loving this praise, Anna could tell. It was obvious they respected their coach and cared about what he thought of them. "And last but definitely not least, that last goal . . ." He whistled, and the boys cheered.

"LaFleur," Sean said, looking directly over the divider at Landon, "without you recovering the puck, it wouldn't have even happened. Drew, your quick moves, sharp eyes, and willingness to get leveled like that, just waiting for the right moment to pass off . . . Wouldn't have happened without you either." More cheers erupted. "And you, Mitch, with those soft hands. You made it look easy. That great, big sieve didn't have a chance."

Sean paused and shook his head with a small smile. "That was some beautiful skating, boys. Just beautiful. To every single one of you," he scanned the room, "you made me proud tonight. And listen, we're a family on the ice, but we're a family off the ice too. We go through the good, the bad, and the ugly together. Well, tonight, for me, there's something really good happening . . . and I want you to share it with me." He looked down at Olivia and placed a hand on her shoulder. "You see this beautiful woman here? This is Olivia, the love of my life."

Anna glanced at Olivia. She glowed.

After waiting for the catcalls to fade, Sean continued, "Tonight, with all of you here, I want to make it official."

Understanding came slowly for Anna, but Sean confirmed her suspicion when he got down on one knee. Anna saw the moment Olivia understood too. Her hands flew to her mouth as Sean produced a black velvet box from his pocket.

The place grew silent and still as a picture. Even the clanging in the kitchen stopped. The moment was suspended in time as everyone froze—eyes glued on Olivia and the coach. "I know a pizza parlor doesn't exactly scream romance, but then I've never really been a smooth kind of guy. And I've been carrying this ring around with me for weeks. I thought I should maybe wait until Christmas, but Olivia, I just can't wait another second. Please say you'll be my wife."

The hush inside the pizza parlor stretched on as everyone held their breath and waited. It went a little too long, which—along with Olivia's ghost-white face—clued Anna in to the fact that something wasn't quite right. Olivia should have been jumping up and down and crying tears of joy, but she just sat there with her hands over her mouth, looking stunned.

Sean's eyebrows squinched together as he remained kneeling in front of Olivia with the velvet ring box in hand, waiting for her to give an answer or say anything at all, really. For Anna, it was just like when she watched something embarrassing happen to someone in a movie. She always felt mortified herself and sometimes even had to fast-forward through the scene. But she couldn't fast-forward through this, and it was agonizingly awkward. She could feel her face flush.

Looking around, Anna could see everyone else was experiencing similar discomfort. Mitch was even covering his eyes, although he was peaking through his fingers. Landon rested his hand on her thigh and squeezed, and Jess gave her a wide-eyed stare. Everyone in their section began to fidget and squirm and clear their throats.

Sean must have decided he'd given Olivia enough time, because he leaned forward and whispered something in her ear. Olivia leaned in and whispered back. This went on, back and forth, for what felt like a solid minute before Sean took the ring and put it on the finger of Olivia's outstretched hand. After another moment of awkward and confused silence, someone clapped, and then the rest of them slowly joined in. When Olivia and Sean both stood and hugged one another, the place erupted.

Anna turned to Landon, laughing with relief, and hugged him. Then she reached across the table and squeezed Jess's hands as they both shook their heads and grinned at one another. Jess pulled two tissues out of her purse and handed one to Anna. Only then did Anna realize her eyes were wet.

The joy of the occasion caused everyone to forget the awkwardness and uncertainty of mere moments before. It had also effectively distracted Anna from what Landon had been about to tell her. Later, lying awake that night, she would remember and wonder.

Chapter 26

Olivia was grateful to Heidi, Anna, and the others for arranging their own rides home. Heidi and Steven had begged a ride off Mitch and his fur-cloaked friend, and Jess and Anna had ridden home with Landon. They must have known Olivia needed time to collect her thoughts, which would have been impossible with a van full of people.

Sean was following behind her in his truck; Olivia could see the outline of his shadow in her rearview mirror. What was she going to say to him? They'd be home in a matter of minutes and, unfortunately, Olivia still hadn't found the perfect words to explain to him what had happened back at the restaurant.

She knew he'd been embarrassed. He must have been. What kind of woman was she to have just left him hanging there like that, in front of everyone? She wasn't even sure she understood what had happened to her, except that she'd simply frozen. Of course she wanted to marry Sean! She would have liked to have given him an immediate, exuberant, and unequivocal *yes*, but she needed to give him the out first. She didn't think he'd take it, but she couldn't be completely certain. Sean deserved to have all the facts before making such an enormous, life-changing commitment

Added to that, Olivia simply hadn't expected a formal proposal from him, certainly not at a pizza parlor in front of his entire hockey team, for Pete's sake! To say that she had been blindsided was an understatement. She just hoped she hadn't hurt Sean with her hesitancy. She recalled their whispered words:

Do you love me?

Yes.

Do you want to be my wife?

You know I do.

Then give me your hand, Olivia.

And she had. Put like that, it was so simple. She loved Sean and wanted to spend the rest of forever with him. Taking her left hand off the wheel, Olivia fingered the ring gently. *Please let this conversation go well,* she prayed.

Meredith, although she was great with Nora, wasn't nearly the full-service babysitter Anna was. With Anna, Olivia knew Nora would be safe and happy, *and* her house would be tidy when she got home. Not so with Meredith, who had left Nora's dirty bottles out on the counter and both their dishes in the sink. She must have made herself a quesadilla because the skillet was out and a few pieces of shredded cheese remained on the counter. Toys littered the floor of the living room, and the throw blanket was in a heap on the table. Sean picked up the blanket and folded it as he waited for Olivia to take care of business.

Meredith seemed oblivious to the mess as Olivia wrote out the check, which the young teen must have considered generous because her eyes lit up, and she was still smiling when she said goodbye and closed the door behind her.

It wasn't all bad, Olivia thought as she surveyed the damage. Cleaning up would give her something to do to keep her hands busy while she and Sean got settled in.

But no sooner had she gotten the bottle brush out of the cabinet under the sink, than Sean had appeared behind her, putting his arms around her. He spoke into her neck, "I'll help you with these in a minute, but let's sit and talk for now, okay?"

Olivia nodded. "Okay."

He led her to the couch, holding her hand, and when they sat down, he touched the ring. "Do you like it, Livvy?"

She looked down at the brilliant, solitaire, high-set in the gold filigree band. It was just her style—simple, yet elegant. Somehow Sean had known she wouldn't want anything too flashy, although this diamond must be a full carat, at least.

"It's beautiful, Sean. I love it."

He nodded with a small smile that didn't show his teeth. "Are you okay? I put you on the spot back there. I'm sorry."

How like Sean to put her first—to apologize to her when she'd been the cause of his own embarrassment. "Please, don't apologize. You didn't do anything wrong."

He blew out his cheeks and released a breath as he sat back into the cushions. "Livvy, then what happened back there? I don't understand. I thought we were on the same page. I saw this as more of a fun way to seal the deal, you know? I mean, I shouldn't have assumed, and I know it put some pressure on you. I just—"

"I can't have kids, Sean," Olivia blurted out, before putting her head in her hands and groaning. That was *not* the way she had planned to introduce this topic. After almost fifteen minutes in the car, practicing, this was the best she'd been able to come up with?

Sean leaned forward and reached over to move her hands away from her face. "What?" He looked at her blankly. "What do you mean? You have Nora."

Olivia wet her lips. "Sean, I should have told you this sooner. I should have told you right away, as soon as things got serious. I knew that day—when you fed Nora and told me about Suze—I knew you wanted to be a father. I knew you wanted to have kids of your own."

Sean held his hands up in front of him like a traffic cop. "Wait a minute —"

"I'm sorry," Olivia interrupted. "Let me . . . just let me explain."

He nodded and allowed her to continue.

As she explained the circumstances of Nora's birth, she watched the emotions flash across his face. His concern for her was obvious. It made Olivia feel worse. She shouldn't have kept him in the dark these last few months. In truth, she should have called him from the hospital that very day. If she had, he would have been there for her, and she wouldn't have been so alone during one of the scariest situations of her entire life. And Olivia wished she had been there for him too—to support him after Nate's death and during his breakup with Suze. She had such regrets for how she'd treated him. He was such a good man; she didn't deserve him.

"So, I want to make sure I understand," Sean said slowly when she'd finished. "Because they had to get her out so fast, they did a different incision than they'd normally do?"

Olivia nodded. "It's a last resort because it increases the chance of uterine rupture if I were to get pregnant again."

He pressed a finger to his lips before speaking again. "And that, of course, would be life threatening. For both you and the baby."

She nodded again.

"Well, then we're not doing that, that's for sure."

Olivia openly stared at him. "That's it?"

Sean spoke with absolute conviction. "Of course that's it. We can't risk that."

"But Sean, just because maybe I can't have any more children, that doesn't mean you should settle for the same."

Now it was Sean's turn to stare at Olivia. "What does that even mean?"

"I don't want to stand in the way of you becoming a father. You could find someone else and—"

Olivia's words were cut off when her nose and mouth were crushed against his chest. He hugged her against himself tightly before he pulled back and looked her closely in the eyes. "Don't finish that thought, Olivia. Don't talk about someone else. There will never be anyone else for me. Only you. You and Nora—you're all I need. And as for being a father, I will be. I am. Nora is a daughter to me already."

A cautious hope took hold, but she needed to be certain. "Sean . . ."

"No."

"Just listen to me. I know you're sure now, but what if one day, you aren't so sure. What if you come to resent me one day when you realize that you never—"

"Olivia, please! Give me some credit. I know my own mind. I know what I want. And you're it. And listen, if we decide we want more kids one day, then there are ways to do that that don't put your life at risk."

Olivia nibbled on her bottom lip. He made it seem so simple.

"Livvy, you just don't get it. You are everything to me now. You and Nora. Understand?" Sean smiled mischievously before he amended, "Well, you two are a close second, anyway."

Olivia's mouth fell open. He couldn't possibly be referring to hockey. If he was, she'd hit him over the head with a couch pillow.

"God has to be first, right?" He winked before adding, "C'mon, I'm a preacher's kid. It's been drilled into me since before I could talk."

Olivia remained grim. "I don't know how you can joke right now. This is the night that, if we move forward, you say goodbye to a dream. Forever."

He turned serious and shook his head adamantly. "No," he corrected. Tonight's the night that, if we move forward, you make my dreams come true."

Olivia blinked rapidly, and Sean took hold of both her hands. "Livvy, will you please marry me? Please be my wife. I need you. If you say yes, I will cherish you all the days of my life. I will be faithful to you. I promise you that. And I'll dance with you and feed you cloves of garlic whenever you ask, before you even *have* to ask, and I'll do it with a smile."

Sean grinned broadly, although there were tears in his own eyes, and then he sobered. "And I'll promise right now to help you keep Nate's memory alive. I'll help you remember the good in him. I'll help you tell Nora all about her daddy up in Heaven, only the appropriate stories, of course"—he chuckled—"and I'll be the best dad on Earth that I can be to her. Be my wife, Livvy. Say yes, and make us a family."

Olivia didn't hesitate. She flung herself into his arms and kissed him senseless after saying *yes* more times than she could count. She knew now she never would have been able to let him walk away. She would have fought for Sean. Whatever it took.

Chapter 27

"You didn't have to pay," Anna told Landon as they walked away from the table just inside the high school's front entrance. "I'm just glad you could come with me."

Landon placed the ticket in her hand and gave a look of pretend annoyance. "Of course I'd pay. I'm the guy."

Anna laughed. "Don't let my aunt hear you talk like that. She's a feminist. According to her, a girl should always pay her own way."

"Alright, alright. Twist my arm. You can pay for dinner tomorrow."

Anna gave a puzzled smile. "Tomorrow?"

"Yeah. You can take me to Rebecca's."

Anna elbowed him.

"What?" Landon asked innocently.

"Rebecca's is the most expensive place in town, and you know it."

Landon grinned playfully. "Alright, I guess we can go to 906."

"We were just there three nights ago with the team. It's okay, I'll think of a place. And I *will* pay."

Landon responded by planting a quick kiss on her cheek and throwing his arm around her as they walked into the gym. "Everyone's still talking about Coach and Olivia, at least the guys who haven't left for home yet."

"You know, it might not have been the smoothest proposal, but I think the real magic happened at the house later, the way Olivia tells it."

Landon nodded. He already knew the story. "You want to sit here?" he asked, indicating the bleachers about halfway up and behind the girls' bench.

"Perfect," Anna said, and then glanced at the running clock on the scoreboard. "I guess we got here early. They aren't even warming up yet."

"It's okay. I don't mind sitting awhile. I'm still really sore. Swinging a hammer is a lot harder than playing hockey, I'll tell you that. Only two days on the job, and I'm already exhausted."

Anna reached over to rub his shoulders. "How long does it take for you to get used to it?"

"Last summer it took just a couple weeks."

"Oh, good! You'll be all set just in time to quit once the holidays are over."

A smile tugged at the corners of his mouth.

She chuckled. "It *is* nice that this construction company lets you work for them on your own terms though."

"The owner, Wade, he's great. He told me at the end of last summer that I have a job with him anytime I want."

"Is construction in the winter a lot different than it is in the summer?"

Landon smirked. "It's a lot colder, that's for sure."

"Ha! I'll bet. You know, it's crazy how you're independent like this already. Paying your own way in life."

"When it comes to money, the scholarship helps, and I'm not really a big spender." He shrugged. "As for the rest, you know how it is. Mitch says you've been more or less on your own and running things at your house for years. I guess we both just do what we have to do. What other choice is there?"

"True." Except her situation had improved drastically. She wished things could change for Landon too.

"Do you think you'll ever go home while you're here in school—for breaks and stuff?"

"No." Landon pinched his lips together.

"And you're okay with that?"

"I kind of have to be. I'm on my own now. And if I did go home, it would just make trouble for my mom. She doesn't need that. I'll just keep writing my letters, and that will have to be enough for now. Maybe after this next summer, I'll have enough money to fly her here for a weekend of home games."

"That would be so great. Then I could meet her." Realizing she'd made the assumption they'd still be together in a year, Anna blushed, and to cover it, she quickly asked, "Do you think she'd come?"

"I don't know." Landon looked thoughtful. "I'd like to think she would."

"You said the team flies to Anchorage to play once a year. Do you think she could watch you play there?"

"Uh . . . no."

"Why not?" Anna demanded.

Landon chuckled. "Because Juneau is, like, nine hundred miles from Anchorage."

"Oh."

Landon gave her a playful nudge with his shoulder.

"I guess I should brush up on my geography, hey?"

They were momentarily distracted by the girls varsity basketball team running out for their opening warmup. "Get Ready for This" blasted through the PA system.

"Here we go," Anna said close to Landon's ear so he could hear her over the music. She squeezed his arm. "You're gonna love watching Jess play. She's *so* good."

"It's been a long time since I've been to a basketball game. I used to go all the time back home. I'd always get popcorn and skittles."

"Hmm, yummy." Anna waited a beat before saying, "You know, I should probably run to the bathroom quick. I'll be right back." She stood and turned to look at him.

His eyes crinkled at the corners. "I'll be right here waiting."

Could he be any cuter? Anna thought to herself as she headed towards the concession stand. She had popcorn and skittles to buy. It took her longer than it should have because the gym was filling with people, and she stopped and talked to several friends on her way out to the lobby. David spotted her and dove in for a hug.

"Lookin' good, Anna Bear," he said and let her go. "I sure am glad that awful plague didn't do you in. I'd be a king without a queen."

Anna rolled her eyes. "Thanks, David. You always know just what to say."

David grinned. "You just let me know when it's safe to kiss you. I think it's time we took that next step in our relationship."

Anna shook her head and laughed. "Bye, David."

He winked. "Bye, girl."

The line to concessions stretched all the way around the corner and into the main hallway that led to the high school office. Anna groaned inwardly and got in line at the very end. At least they'd gotten there early. She figured she'd be able to get back to Landon well before the buzzer.

The doors at the end of the empty hallway opened with an echoed bang, and Anna turned, looking behind her to see Alex walk in with Blythe and a few of her ever-present friends. Anna hadn't seen much of Blythe over the last several weeks. She must have decided harassing Anna was pointless now that Anna and Alex had split.

As for Alex, Anna wished she saw a little less of him. He popped up everywhere, and it was getting harder and harder to ignore the sneaking suspicion that the frequent run-ins and increasing texts weren't an attempt on his part to get close again, and not in a "just friends" kind of way.

A few months ago, she would have jumped at the chance to get back together with Alex. But now, things were different, and not just because of Landon, although that was certainly a big part of it. Anna was pretty sure even if she hadn't found someone new, she wouldn't take Alex back. She deserved better.

Anna registered the moment Alex noticed her, even with the distance and dim lighting between them. He stood that much straighter and walked that much faster. She could see the moment Blythe noticed her too. The younger girl's stride faltered slightly, but she quickly recovered, and her smile pinched itself into an unattractive smirk.

Uncertain of how this would play out, Anna braced herself. She hadn't seen Alex and Blythe together since the homecoming football game. Schooling her features into what she hoped was a type of friendly indifference, Anna greeted them with a nod when they drew close enough. Blythe pressed her lips together into a hyphen, but Alex said hello and asked her if she was there to watch Jess play.

Anna shrugged. "You know me, I try not to miss a game."

Blythe gave Anna the old once-over, the one that used to leave her feeling so small and insecure. This time, Anna had to choke back a laugh. Blythe looked ridiculous—like a bad actress in a low-budget, mean-girl movie. It had seemed like such a big deal before, but now Anna almost felt sorry for the girl. Almost.

Sensing that her super powers no longer worked on Anna, Blythe took a different tack. She looked at Alex from under her clumpy, overly mascaraed lashes and reached for his hand. "Come on, Alex. Let's go find seats." She returned her gaze to Anna, and her eyes narrowed in a way that said, *You're not invited*, which was fine by her.

Anna smiled. "Okay, then. See ya later." Those cheerfully spoken words produced an eye roll from Blythe, and Anna's smile widened. She was having fun with this. But her humor faded when Alex spoke again.

"You go ahead, Blythe. I'll catch you later."

Blythe looked murderous. "Alex!"

His long-suffering sigh betrayed his annoyance, and he cocked his head towards her with a warning glance.

Through gritted teeth, she tried again. "Alex, come with us. Right now."

"No," he said slowly, as if he were explaining something to a small child, "I'm going to stay with Anna."

He turned to her. "That's okay, right?"

"Well, actually—"

"I knew it. I just knew this would happen," Blythe spat, but Anna could see the tears in her eyes. "I knew you wanted to go back to her."

"Whoa!" Anna backed up a step and put up both hands defensively. "I'm here with my boyfriend, so . . ."

Alex's jaw dropped. "Your *what*?"

Blythe beamed in triumph. “Her *boyfriend*,” she repeated slowly. This time she was the one lecturing the small child. Alex was still shaking his head in disbelief when Blythe tossed her hair over her shoulder with renewed confidence and attitude and said, “We’ll be across from the home side, Alex. Maybe I’ll let you sit with me . . . if you’re lucky.”

Alex’s only response was a slight flaring of his nostrils as Blythe walked away.

The elderly couple in line in front of Anna had already advanced ahead several feet, and she had taken a step to do the same when Alex stopped her with his arm. He pulled her aside, effectively pinning her against the wall. It wasn’t a threatening stance, but it was designed to keep her from leaving, and Anna didn’t like it.

“Look,” he said, cutting to the chase. “I made a mistake, Anna, a huge mistake. I’m so sorry. I’ve tried to make that clear to you. I really miss you. I miss you so much, and I think you miss me too.”

Anna put a hand on Alex’s arm and applied slight pressure to make him drop it. He didn’t take the hint. “I don’t know why you would think that, Alex. It’s over.”

“It’s not,” he insisted. “You must know it. You’re even wearing my sweatshirt.”

Anna looked down at her powder blue and very well-worn sweatshirt. “No, I’m wearing *my* sweatshirt.”

“The one I bought for you.”

Anna squeezed her eyes closed for a quick moment before explaining with forced patience, “Alex, this is my favorite sweatshirt. I wore it because it’s my favorite. It has nothing at all to do with you.”

Alex shook his head. “I don’t believe you. What we had was so good. You wouldn’t just throw it away.”

“*You* did.”

Alex took a deep breath. “I know, Anna, and I’m sorry. I was crazy. Actually”—he jerked his head toward the gym where Blythe had just gone—“she’s the crazy one. I didn’t know how good I had it. You’re so . . . *normal* and easygoing and sweet. She’s not. Like, at all.”

Anna couldn’t help but feel gratified. “I’m sorry, but Alex, that’s not my problem.”

He tugged at his shirt collar and looked away from her, but when he fixed his eyes on hers again a moment later, Anna could see the pleading in them.

“Just listen a minute,” he said. “You have every right to be mad. I messed up big time. But there’s a reason I did what I did. It’s hard to explain, and it’s gonna sound stupid, but . . .” He ran his other hand, the one not bracing the wall behind her, through his hair in a single, agitated stroke. “Look, my parents are getting a divorce. They separated over the summer and filed the beginning of October, and I—I didn’t handle it well.”

Anna gasped. She loved Alex’s parents. How sad for them! How sad for the whole family! She put her hand on his arm again, this time in a soothing gesture. “Oh, Alex, I’m so sorry. Why didn’t you tell me?” It began to make sense. She knew he hadn’t been himself.

“It’s okay. Things are a little better now. And I’m sorry, I should have told you. I just—I didn’t tell anyone, well, except for Mrs. Reeves. I didn’t even tell her at first because I wondered if she might tell you. You guys are so close. Anyway, I’m better now, Anna, and I want us to be together again. I still love you, and Christmas is coming. We need to be together for Christmas and bake cookies and watch *It’s a Wonderful Life*, like you always make us do.”

Anna felt a momentary nostalgia for what used to be. They’d had some very special times together. He’d been the man in her life when she really hadn’t had one. Mitch and her dad had been unreliable, at best, but even at *his* best, Alex had been selfish, taking more from her than he gave.

“Alex,” Anna said gently. “You need to let me go.” She pushed down on his arm again, this time with a little more force. He didn’t budge, and he didn’t back up. He was still very much in her personal space, and she knew they must look . . . intimate. Like they were having a cozy little moment together. Anybody walking by might get the wrong idea. She needed to find the words to get through to him. It was over.

“I’m not saying this to hurt you, Alex. You’re an amazing person, and you’re right, we did have a good thing, at least up until the end there. But I’ve found someone new, and I—I love him, Alex. I’m sorry, but that’s the truth.”

She may as well have slapped him. Alex flinched and all the color drained from his face. “Y-you can’t! Already? It’s been, like, a week!”

They both knew it had been a lot longer than that, but she didn’t argue with him. “I’m sorry,” she repeated.

“Who is it?” He stared at her with an intensity that made her want to squirm.

She fought the urge to drop her gaze and forced herself to be still. “His name’s Landon.” She continued to look him in the eye and added, “He’s Mitch’s roommate.”

Alex stared at the wall behind them, and Anna watched his jaw muscles flex repeatedly. He was thinking hard about something, maybe trying to figure out what to say next. Anna really hoped he wouldn’t lash out and try to hurt her. She wanted to leave things on good terms. It was important to her somehow. But it wasn’t to be.

Alex's lips curved into a sneer. "Well, I think you really had best get your head checked, Anna. Because something's not right there. College guys only date high school girls like you for one reason. They only want one thing."

Anna shook her head. "It's not like that. Not that I owe you any explanations, but we care about each other."

"You care about each other, huh? You think you *love* him." Alex spoke with unveiled contempt. "Come on, Anna. You were just saying that to *me* a few months ago. Emotions aren't that cheap. People don't just flit in and out of love like that. It's crazy and—unfortunately—we both know *crazy* runs in your family. So yeah, better get that head looked at."

Anna sucked in a breath and wrapped her arms around herself as Alex pushed off the wall and turned to leave. Something caught his attention though, and he stopped short. There, some thirty feet away, stood the large and imposing form of Landon, leaning against the opposite wall. His features were hard and his arms were crossed over his chest. Landon followed Alex with his eyes. As he passed, Alex tipped his head down to look at the floor, a submissive gesture, but Anna noticed his fists clenched at his sides, even as he disappeared around the corner. Only then did Landon look at her.

She felt herself pale. What had he seen? What had he heard? Did he think she'd come out here to meet up with Alex? Anna thought frantically about what to say to him as Landon made his way over to her.

"That might have looked like something it wasn't," Anna began and stopped when Landon shook his head.

"I don't want to talk about that," he said simply.

"Oh." What did that mean? "Um, are you mad?"

Landon smiled and reached out to tuck a lock of hair behind her ear. "No, not at all. Not at *you*, anyway."

"Oh. Good, because what you saw—" She stopped short as he shook his head again.

"I don't want to talk about what I saw. I want to talk about what I heard."

"What you heard?" Anna echoed weakly. He must have heard everything, then. He'd heard her say she loved him. They hadn't even said that to each other yet, but here she was telling her ex-boyfriend. She felt like a total idiot. What if Landon thought she was nuts, like Alex did?

"Don't do that," he admonished gently.

"Don't do what?"

"Don't feel embarrassed. Don't second guess. Anna, let me just put you out of your misery." He smiled. "I love you too."

Her entire body suffused with heat from the inside out. "You do?"

His grin grew even wider. “I really do. I wanted to tell you the other night, but then Coach interrupted with his proposal and stole all my thunder.”

Anna laughed.

“It’s not too soon,” he reassured her. “And you’re definitely not crazy. Or if you are, then so am I.” He looked around. “I know this might not be a good time or place, but I really need to kiss you.”

He took her hands and pulled her close, never taking his eyes from hers as he ran his hands up her arms and over her shoulders in a slow caress.

“Well, I guess if you have to,” she said, her heart rate picking up in anticipation. A small smile played on her lips as she tipped her head back and closed her eyes. His lips, when they pressed down against hers, were soft and warm and deliciously wet, and when he nibbled on her lower lip, it sent out a little *zing* to all of her nerve endings. He splayed his hands out under her hair, cradling the back of her head in a touch that was at once strong and tender.

Landon moved to deepen the kiss, and Anna brought her hands up to cup his face, feeling the rough stubble of whiskers against the smooth pads of her fingers, and when she moved her hands into his hair, she marveled again at how soft and silky it was. She didn’t think she could ever get enough of this. She wanted to kiss Landon and play with his hair all night long, but the sound of the buzzer brought her back to the reality of where she was and why she was there.

Jess’s game was about to start, and Anna probably shouldn’t be seen like this with Landon in the office hallway of her school. Reluctantly, she pulled away, feeling breathless and off-center, but she could see with satisfaction that Landon wasn’t much better.

“*Ah*, Anna,” he whispered hoarsely. His cheeks were flushed, and he looked dazed.

“*Ah*, Landon,” Anna echoed, and then she giggled, drawing a slow smile from him. She reached for his hand. “Come on. We have a game to watch.”

The skittles and popcorn would have to wait until halftime. There was no way either of them was going to miss any part of the game. Jess played almost every second of the first half as Nicolet struggled to maintain the lead. No sooner would they advance the score by two or three, than the Nimrods would answer with a bucket of their own.

“Who names their team the *Nimrods* anyway?” Landon asked back at the concession stand during halftime.

Anna laughed. “I know. But I think I remember someone explaining that the Nimrods were, like, hunters or something like that. Babylonian hunters.”

“Huh. Well, that’s weird.”

Anna agreed with a small snicker, but what she thought was really weird were all the looks she was getting from the surrounding students. At the beginning of the game, Alex had stared daggers at them from where he sat —directly across the court. But after several minutes, he said something to Blythe, and they'd both gotten up and left.

That had been an enormous relief. Anna hadn't wanted to feel on display like that for the entire game, but it appeared half the school was watching her anyway. They were curious about Landon, it seemed, and even the guys who were usually so easygoing with her were keeping a respectful distance. Anna supposed she couldn't blame them. Landon probably was a little intimidating. Most of these guys still looked and acted like boys, and Landon was no boy.

She felt a surge of pride. Landon was the complete package, not just an empty shell of good looks and athleticism. Just the other night, he told her, somewhat self-consciously, that he'd gotten together with Sean a couple of times to talk about spiritual things. Sean had grown up in a Christian home and still had a strong faith. It was something Landon wanted to explore for himself, and he wondered what Anna might think about that. It was almost as if he thought she might consider him weak or less of a man, but the opposite was true. It made Landon even more attractive to her.

Landon had been storing up questions for a long, long time. Deep questions about things like the purpose of life, why bad things happened to good people—questions Anna had definitely thought about but never tried to get answers to. She definitely believed in God, but beyond that, she really hadn't given much thought to what it might mean for her personally. That was changing the more she talked about it with Landon, and it felt . . . exciting.

Exciting. It was a perfect description of how Anna viewed her life right now, but unfortunately, it didn't apply to the second half of the basketball game. While she and Landon shared their bag of popcorn and box of skittles, the Nicolet girls fell apart, and nothing Jess did could pull them back together again. She was playing as well as ever, but the rest of her teammates were off their game. The Nimrods were up by eleven points when Landon leaned over and asked her, "Who's that guy across the court from us? The purple-faced one standing up and yelling."

Anna didn't even have to look. "That's Jess's dad. Sorry, just ignore him. That's what the rest of us do. Any other time, I might go up to him to say hi, but I avoid him like the plague at games. See that lady on the other side of the bleachers from him, the one in the red jacket with the blond hair?"

Landon nodded.

"That's Jess's mom. She can't even sit with him."

Landon whistled. "Poor lady."

"Sports bring out the absolute worst in him." Anna watched as Jess's dad whipped his hat off and threw it down in disgust.

"First string's coming out," Landon observed.

With a little over two minutes left on the clock, the Nimrods were up by thirteen. Anna clapped for Jess as she jogged back to the bench. She'd played well and done her best, although Anna doubted Jess's dad would see it that way. He'd focus on the one free-throw she'd missed or a "lazy" foul or some other mistake.

Now that Jess was out, Anna let her mind roam, and she thought back to Sunday evening two nights ago. Mitch came over, as he'd said he would, but he'd surprised them all by hanging out for hours, even staying for the amazing chicken and dumplings that Aunt Heidi and their dad had made together.

Clearly, the two of them had basked in the experience, and a near-constant stream of laughter poured out of the kitchen as they'd prepared the meal together. At one point, Mitch had looked away from the TV and the game they'd been watching to share a smile with her, and Anna had thought: *This is what's been missing in this house our whole lives.*

She experienced a small stab of longing in that moment. Being that Aunt Heidi was her mother's identical twin, Anna supposed that's what her mom and dad would have looked and sounded like in the kitchen together. What kind of couple would they have been today if her mother were still alive? Would they laugh and flirt in the kitchen while they made dinner?

The question had entered her mind, unbidden, and as soon as it registered with her, Anna froze. She even stopped chewing her gum. Was that what was going on right then in the kitchen? Flirtation? On the one hand, that would be really, really weird, but on the other, weird didn't always mean bad. Sometimes it just meant . . . different. This blossoming friendship between Aunt Heidi and her dad was a stark contrast to the way they'd always been towards each other, and it was as refreshing as a spring thaw after a long winter. Who knew what would happen in the future?

The delicious dinner that followed had not only fed their bellies, but Anna was pretty sure it had fed their hearts too. They'd talked and laughed easily around the table, and even Mitch had been mellow and friendly as Bing Crosby's holiday album played in the background. The house, decorated with the newly purchased Christmas decorations, courtesy of Aunt Heidi, felt warm and homey, and the tree, trimmed to the point of garishness the way all Christmas trees should be, filled the house with the fresh piney scent of the holidays. Everything had worked together to make for a perfect night with the cozy, warm atmosphere of one of those cheesy Hallmark films she and Aunt Heidi loved so much. The evening had left Anna feeling grateful for the small pleasures in life.

Sitting here next to Landon in her school's gym, she felt that same way now. Sure, the atmosphere here was different, but somehow the moment spoke to Anna in the same way. It was a sort of simplistic *completeness*—if that was even a word—and she reached over and took hold of Landon's hand. He treated her to his warm, sexy smile and gave her hand a little squeeze. They watched the last minute of the game like that, and even though their team lost, she was still smiling when Landon drove her home.

Chapter 28

Just when Anna didn't think her life could get any better, Aunt Heidi announced on Friday after school that she would be staying with them through Christmas. Anna, who had already been ecstatic that her aunt had stayed through the week, literally jumped up and down like a preschooler who'd discovered candy on her breakfast plate. To conclude her exuberant antics, she threw her arms around her aunt and rocked with her happily while Heidi laughed and protested half-heartedly.

Still hugging her tightly, Anna asked, "Aunt Heidi, how did you get so much time off from work?"

"Okay, okay. That's good." Heidi pulled away, but her smile was bright as she brushed herself off. Her aunt had never been completely comfortable with lots of affection, but Anna never let that stop her.

"How, though?" Anna repeated. "Christmas is still a week away."

"I don't have to take any additional time off. I read scans remotely a lot of the time anyway, so all I need is my computer, which I have with me, and my phone. I'll just work from here until after Christmas."

Anna hugged her arms around herself. "This is just the best news."

"It'll be nice," Heidi agreed. "We can watch a Hallmark movie every night until Christmas, if you want to. It'll be cozy."

"It'll be *super* cozy! Let's watch one tonight."

"You're on. Maybe I'll make us some puppy chow to munch on. It might even entice your dad to watch with us."

"Ooh, he hates Hallmark movies, but he loves that stuff. But then, who doesn't?" Anna asked rhetorically. That reminded her of something. "You'll think this is funny. My English teacher, Miss Josten, had us doing demonstration speeches a few weeks ago. We all had to let her know in advance what we were going to demonstrate. One girl told her she was going to show us how to make puppy chow."

"A good choice."

Anna nodded. "Miss Josten told her that sounded really interesting and asked her how you made it. The girl started listing off ingredients, and when she mentioned chocolate"—Anna giggled—"you should have seen the look on Miss Josten's face. It was so funny. She looked at us with these wide eyes and said, 'But y'all, dogs can't eat chocolate!'"

Heidi looked confused. "Wait, she thought her student was making actual dog food?"

"Yes!" Anna laughed again. "Can you believe that? She'd never heard of puppy chow before."

"And this woman is an *educator*?"

"Oh, come on! It's funny!"

Heidi's lips twitched. "It's a tragedy, that's what it is. That woman is missing out! Okay, that's it, I'm making puppy chow tonight, and you're going to bring a bag of it to school on Monday for your teacher."

"Oh, she's already had some. She asked to try it on speech day. I'm pretty sure it was a hit."

"I'll make her some anyway. Then she can snack on it while she watches Christmas movies too, like us."

They had almost everything they needed—minus a few ingredients—so Anna ran out to the store to grab the rest, as well as some Mexican takeout for dinner. Neither she nor Aunt Heidi felt like cooking up a big meal.

Mitch was planning to come home later this evening to stay in his old room for the rest of Christmas break. It was welcome news to the rest of them. At this rate, things would be back to normal with Mitch in no time at all, and maybe they could even help him move past some of his lingering issues.

He'd let them know earlier that day, saying the dorms were almost empty and there wasn't much going on, so he might as well. Steven was over the moon about it, and Anna would have been too, if she hadn't felt so sorry that Landon would now be at the dorms all alone at Christmas. She wanted to ask her dad and Heidi if he could stay with them.

Over their burritos, she broached the subject. It looked like her dad might say yes, but it was Aunt Heidi who spoke up first with a definitive *no*. "Teenage girls do not have their boyfriends over for sleepovers," she said.

Anna tried to argue her point, saying that Landon wouldn't have to be anywhere near her bedroom. They had a pull-out couch on the lowest level of the house. Why couldn't he stay down there? But Aunt Heidi was adamant. "He can stay here all day long, but at night, he needs to go back to his dorm."

Anna blew out a frustrated breath. She really didn't understand what the big deal was, but this was the closest thing to a fight she and Aunt Heidi had ever had, so she wouldn't push it much further. In one final attempt she looked to her dad for his input, but instead of weighing in one way or the other, he quickly averted his eyes and looked down at his plate. Anna couldn't be sure, but she thought she saw him fighting an amused smile.

Later that night, once Anna had talked to Landon and been reassured that he would be just fine at the dorms—he was dead on his feet at night anyway—she came back down in a t-shirt, sweats, and fuzzy Christmas socks. She was ready to make puppy chow. Aunt Heidi was already in the kitchen, pouring the melted chocolate and peanut butter into a mixing bowl. Anna grabbed the rubber spatula and helped her by scraping the pan. Once that was done, she wordlessly grabbed the cereal for her aunt to pour while Anna stirred.

They worked together this way for another minute before Heidi spoke. "You're mad at me."

"No. I'm not mad."

Heidi gave her a *yeah right* look.

"Okay, well, maybe a little. I don't like how that felt." At Heidi's raised eyebrows Anna clarified, "You telling me what to do and, you know . . . us sort of . . . fighting."

"Well, that's the tamest fight I ever had," Heidi said with an amused snort. "But listen. I love you. I just want what's best for you, but I spoke out of turn tonight. I don't get to just show up here and start parenting you. You've been on your own—more or less—a long time, and you've always had a good head on your shoulders. Plus, you already have a parent. I was wrong to take over like that. I'm sorry. I've apologized to your father too."

Anna put down the spatula and feigned shock. "Aunt Heidi, are you feeling alright?" She placed the back of her hand on her aunt's forehead. "Did you just admit to being wrong *and* apologize too? Twice?"

"Knock it off," Heidi said with a sardonic smile. She nudged Anna before grabbing the bag of powdered sugar and measuring cup.

"Shoot! I knew it couldn't last," Anna joked. She picked up the spatula and got back to work.

Anna headed up to bed that night feeling sick to her stomach. It turned out there really *could* be too much of a good thing. She must have eaten a pound of puppy chow. If she never saw it again, that would be okay with her.

The movie had been entirely predictable, but Anna and Heidi still loved every minute. Surprising them both, Steven had grabbed himself a small bowl of puppy chow from the kitchen and plopped down between them on the sofa. He'd only criticized the film a handful of times.

He and Heidi remained there on the sofa when Anna headed off to bed. She thought maybe they'd continue watching TV, but after she finished showering and brushing her hair, she headed back downstairs for a glass of ginger ale. The TV was no longer on. Instead, Steven and Heidi were poring over old photo albums, their heads so close together they were almost touching.

Anna froze on the steps, listening a moment before creeping back up and sitting on the top landing.

"She was so beautiful, Steven. Look how young she is here. Mitch must be, what, one year old in this picture?"

"Yes. I remember this day. Shelly had just taken him to the beach for the first time. She put his feet in the sand, and then in the lake. She said he howled." He chuckled. "She was sick about it. Couldn't believe a child of hers wouldn't love the beach as much as she did. She brought him there at least twice a week for the rest of that summer, determined to make him like it. It worked too."

"Hmm. She *was* stubborn."

Steven chuckled. "Yeah, and you're her identical twin."

Heidi corrected him. "I'm her *mirror* twin, so technically, I should be the exact opposite of stubborn. I'm just a chill, go-with-the-flow type."

"I'm not going to argue," Steven replied with laughter in his voice.

Anna heard a page turning. "Look at this one. This was when you guys were in Arizona. I came and stayed with Mitch. That was really fun for me."

"It was fun for us too. A nice little getaway before Anna came along. Before Shelly got, you know . . . sick."

They grew quiet for a minute, and Anna wondered if they'd decided to stop their little walk down memory lane. She was about to lean forward and peek through the railing when her father spoke again.

"Heidi, I know we've covered most of this already, but I'm sorry I didn't take better care of her. I wish I could go back and do it all differently."

Heidi didn't answer right away. When she did, her voice was gentle. "Nobody could make my sister do anything she didn't want to do. You knew it then, and I admit it now. It was just so much easier to be angry with you than to be angry with her. She was gone, and you . . . well, you were an easy target. It wasn't fair to you."

Steven sighed. "It *was* partly my fault. I never said it out loud, but I'm pretty sure she knew it anyway. The medicine changed that part of her personality I'd always loved . . . that free-spirited part of herself. I should have done more to reassure her that I loved her no matter what. What if she kept going off of it because of me? For my sake?"

Steven was quiet a moment before he continued. "That whole month, Heidi, she was doing so well. I really thought we had a handle on it. You told me it was too soon for me to get back on the road, but work was pressing in on me, and she seemed ready. But you were right. It was too soon to leave her, and a week was too long to be away. Looking back, I just can't believe I did that. And I left my kids—"

"Steven," Heidi interrupted gently. "Shelly knew she needed to take that medication, but for some reason, she chose not to that week. I don't think we'll ever know for sure why she did what she did, but we can't keep guessing and blaming ourselves. You and I could go on doing this for the rest of our lives. There are countless things we could have done or should have done or said that *might* have made a difference. We'll never know."

"It's so hard." Steven cleared his throat. "Can I ask you something?"

"Of course."

"I've never asked, but I've always wondered. Did you know, Heidi? Did you know that something was wrong that day? You left so many messages on our answering machine. I listened to them late that night, but you were already here, and there was so much going on, and it was all just so terrible . . ."

Anna waited, hardly breathing, her stomach ache long forgotten.

"It wasn't until later that I wondered if you'd sensed it. Like that day she broke her arm in the second grade, or the day that creeper attacked her at the golf course. Both times you knew she was hurt. You girls always explained that you had a sixth sense with each other."

Heidi waited a beat before responding. "Do you know I haven't talked about this to a single, solitary soul? I suppose . . . who would I have told? You and I weren't exactly speaking, and Mom and Dad, God rest their souls, were the only ones besides you and Shelly who could have understood. Nobody else knows we could communicate like that. But to answer your question, yes, I knew. I was in the middle of a department meeting, and one of the docs was reviewing an MRI with us when I jumped up. My chair fell over behind me, and I just stood there in this panic. I felt it deep inside. It was Shelly's soul calling out to mine."

Heidi went silent, and all Anna could hear was the ticking of the clock on the mantle until she spoke again.

"That's the best way I can describe it anyway, and then all of a sudden I couldn't breathe. Steven, it felt like I was suffocating—or I suppose now I would have to say it felt like I was drowning."

She paused.

"A few of my colleagues got me down onto the floor—helped me catch my breath—and a few minutes later it was all over. To say I felt ridiculous is an understatement, but I still excused myself and called the house. I think I left you eight or nine messages. I just needed to hear that everything was okay.

"But when my phone finally did ring, that wasn't the call I got. How much I wish it had been Shelly's voice on the other end telling me to stop being such a worry wart. And that's something else I've never told anyone. I didn't know she was gone, Steven . . . I was with her when she came into this world, and long before that, even. Shouldn't I have known the moment she left it? She was a part of me, and I was a part of her. How could I not have known that? I can't—" Heidi's voice broke. "I've never been the same since."

She got the words out, but just barely, and Anna brought her knuckles to her own mouth, biting down to keep from crying herself. Ducking down to peer under the railing once more, she was touched to see her dad holding her aunt in a tender embrace. Steven was stroking Heidi's back and shushing her while she cried silently. Her body was shaking, and Anna thought she saw a tremor run through his own body as he gently rocked them both side to side.

Anna knew she really should go back to her room. This was a private moment, but her feet might as well have been made of lead. She couldn't leave yet. She sat up straight so they would at least have privacy from her prying eyes.

After another minute, Heidi spoke again in a still-shaky voice. "Sometimes I wonder what kind of role I played in your backing off from the kids and shuttering yourself away from them for so long."

"No. That wasn't your fault."

"I don't know about that. I blamed you when you were already heaping blame on yourself. I piled on."

Steven didn't speak right away, but when he did, Anna heard the regret in his voice. "There's just so much I wish I could change."

"I think it's time to let all of it go, Steven," Heidi whispered. "Otherwise, it'll just keep tearing us apart. There's so much we both could have done differently. I swooped in once or twice to help out and get Shelly's appointments and pills sorted out, and then I left you to manage work, Shelly's needs, and the kids. You needed me. You all did. But it's done now, and we need to forgive ourselves and move on. It's time. She wouldn't have wanted us to torture ourselves like this. You remember what she always said, right? *There's only the joy of today and the hope for tomorrow.*"

"Of course. I remember. Your mother coined that, I believe."

"Actually, it was my dad's mom who did. But Dad and Shelly said it all the time."

"She doesn't want us living in the past, Steven. She wants us to enjoy the moment and look forward to the future."

"I know you're right, and I am trying. I knew from the beginning it wouldn't happen overnight, but I never expected it to take fifteen years. Although, I have to say, I've noticed—it's getting easier now. These last few months have brought a sort of breakthrough for me. Anna and I are getting closer every day. Do you think Mitch is coming around?" Steven asked.

"I get the feeling. But Steven, that boy is still grieving. You know that, right?"

"I do now. I didn't before. I was so blind, just running on autopilot. I think it would help him to talk about it, but so far, he won't. I've tried."

"Keep trying."

"I won't stop, Heidi. I won't ever quit on him, even if he does hate me."

"He doesn't hate you. He loves you. He just needs to reconcile his past to move on with his future. He was getting by, more or less, but that was never going to work long-term. Oh, Steven! I should have helped you with him."

She scoffed. "There I go with the *should've*s again. But even if you and I had been on speaking terms, I knew he couldn't look at me back then. It crushed him to see me. Remember? That was so painful."

"I remember."

"It took him a long while."

"There was a time I wondered if he'd ever be able to," Steven admitted.

"Was it hard for you too? To look at me?"

Steven sighed. "I'm sorry, Heidi." The admission was in his voice.

"It's okay. I could tell when you'd drop Anna off for her visits those first few years. I really do get it. Remember, I'm the one who had to look at myself in the mirror every day and see Shelly there looking back at me. It wasn't until I started aging that I stopped seeing her in my reflection—thanks to all the wrinkles and sagging skin," Heidi joked.

Steven's voice brooked no argument when he responded, "You are beautiful. You have always been, and you will always be, and that's the truth."

"Thanks." Heidi paused. "I wasn't a help before, Steven, but I'll help you now, however I can."

"Thank you for that. It means a lot."

Anna waited for several minutes while the clock ticked on, and she was about to get up when her father spoke again.

"Heidi?"

"Hmm?"

"We've never talked about that day at the rocks."

Heidi took a second before responding, and when she did, her voice sounded funny. Too high. "Oh goodness, that was so long ago. At least twenty years." She laughed nervously before quickly dismissing the subject. "We don't need to talk about that."

"It *was* a long time ago," Steven agreed. "But lately I've felt the need to explain."

"You don't have to. You made the right choice."

"That may be, but—"

Heidi cut him off. "Not tonight, Steven. Tonight, let's just sip our wine and look at the Christmas tree."

"Okay," he said slowly, "if that's what you want."

Let him explain! Anna shouted in her head, wishing telepathy worked for her too, and that her aunt would somehow get the message. What had happened at the rocks? Were they talking about Sable Rocks? And what choice? It sounded like something big had happened between them, and Anna wanted to know what it was.

After waiting a few more minutes and hearing nothing else, Anna grew more and more sheepish. She'd never snooped like this before on anyone. She quietly got up and headed back to her room, forgetting about the ginger ale. But while she was still tiptoeing down the hallway, she heard her dad speak one more time.

"I'm glad you're staying for Christmas."

"Me too."

Chapter 29

Olivia doubted Erin and Sarah would have bonded without her, not because there was anything necessarily special about herself, but because the two of them were on completely opposite ends of the personality spectrum. While Sarah was soft-spoken and reserved, the perfect southern belle, Erin was loud and outgoing and slightly obnoxious. Olivia figured she herself was somewhere between those two extremes, or maybe, more accurately, she had elements of both inside of her. A person could have several personas, or at least that's what Olivia had always believed.

Once, Olivia's mother had referred to her as a chameleon because of her ability to befriend wildly different people. Though her mom hadn't intended to be critical, the implication was that Olivia changed herself to match the personalities of whomever she happened to be with at the moment. But now that Olivia was older, she respectfully disagreed.

To Olivia, being a chameleon meant being fake, which she could confidently say she was not. She had never pretended to be anyone other than who she was. Instead, she was of the opinion that different people brought out different aspects of her personality, and she knew that was why she'd been able to connect so meaningfully with both Erin and Sarah. Her red-headed feistiness was every bit as much a part of Olivia as her quiet, introspective nature. And that was at least one reason her friendship with the two women worked.

Today, the three of them were having lunch at Olivia's. It was Saturday, and there were only three days of school next week before the holiday break began. Knowing that time off was close at hand seemed to energize them in a way that would have been obvious to anyone observing, although the only one to witness their giddiness was the disinterested, recently turned nine-month-old who only occasionally looked up from the toys in her playpen.

It was because of this carefree atmosphere that Olivia shared the news she'd promised herself she wouldn't mention just yet. There were still details that needed to be ironed out before any announcements were made, but on a whim she blurted, "Sean and I applied for a marriage license yesterday."

Abruptly, the laughter and conversation in the kitchen ceased. Sarah's hands remained suspended over the salad she'd been tossing, and Erin, who had been about to take a sip of pop, paused mid-action. Nora, noticing the silence, pulled herself up in the playpen and openly stared at them. Olivia laughed.

Erin was the first to speak. "Does that mean it's happening soon?"

"We're planning for Christmas Eve Eve at five o'clock, and I cannot wait!"

"Olivia, how perfect!" Sarah exclaimed.

"We've secured Grace Church. It's such a pretty church; you know the one, right? It's got that gorgeous limestone exterior?"

Both women nodded.

"And the sanctuary's already decorated for Christmas. We really wouldn't have to do much of anything to it. And Sean's pastor is free to do the ceremony. So, that's everything. We just have to make sure the license comes through in time, which it should. It's only supposed to take three business days."

"What about the reception?" Erin asked.

"And your dress?" Sarah added.

Olivia responded to them both. "I already ordered one. It's on its way. And as for the reception, we'll hold off on that for now and have a little something this summer."

Erin raised one eyebrow. "It's awfully fast, Olivia. I know you're both more than ready, but don't you want time to plan something really special?"

Olivia cocked her head. "It *will* be special, Erin. I mean, come on, a Christmas wedding? Isn't that so romantic?"

Erin looked doubtful, but Sarah nodded vigorously.

"We're already doing more than I'd originally intended. Honestly, we just want to be married. That's the most important thing to us, and the sooner the better."

Those last few words had a barely concealed hidden meaning behind them, and Erin latched on to them like a barnacle on an ocean liner.

She narrowed her eyes and brought a hand up to her chin, studying Olivia, who saw the exact moment she put it all together. "No way," Erin said, breaking into a wide grin. Olivia quickly averted her eyes and busied herself with counting out napkins for them. *One. Two. Three.* Too bad she didn't have more guests.

"What?" Sarah asked. "Did I miss somethin'?"

Olivia shouldn't have alluded to this at all. Too late now. Erin would badger her all afternoon if she didn't dish. "We're, um . . . waiting," Olivia demurred.

It didn't take long for Sarah's face to light up in understanding. "Oh, I see! Well . . . I think that's sweet!" To clarify, she asked, "You do mean y'all are waitin' until your weddin' night?"

Olivia laughed. "That's what I mean."

"You're crazy," Erin said, a look of genuine puzzlement on her pretty face. "Why in hell's bells would you want to do that?" She smirked and added, "Or *not* do that?"

"We want it to be special, for one thing, and Sean's making me see this kind of stuff differently than I used to. We both see this as a fresh start for us, and we want to do it right."

"Huh," Erin grunted and bit her lower lip, thinking. "But what if you're not, you know, *compatible* that way?" She raised her eyebrows suggestively. "By the time you're married, it's too late to go back if things don't quite work out under the sheets. Like, what if there's no wowzer in his trousers?"

"Oh, for the love—Erin!" Sarah touched her temples with her fingertips.

The small grin Olivia directed at Erin betrayed secret knowledge. "Don't you worry your pretty little mind about his *wowzer*."

Erin shrugged and grinned back. "Okay, then. If you say so."

It seemed that particular conversation was done—thank goodness, and Olivia moved to finish the vinaigrette she was making. Stealing a glance at Sarah, Olivia could see she was still shaking her head over Erin's lack of filter, and Olivia marveled again that the friendship could work at all. She glanced at the bowl of vinaigrette—it was evidence, wasn't it? Oil and water weren't supposed to mix.

The questions continued during their lunch as they sat around Olivia's small kitchen table. Were they going to be inviting people to the ceremony? Erin wanted to know. Olivia assured them both that they would receive electronic invitations once the license came through, and reminded them of the time so they could plan ahead. When Sarah seemed a little too pensive, Olivia asked her if everything was alright.

"Just fine," Sarah reassured her. Noticing Nora's tray was empty, she shook out a few more puffs for her, making Olivia smile. Sarah had taken the seat next to Nora's high chair deliberately, and Olivia could tell she was enjoying her time with the baby. "I was just tryin' to work out how I can make it to the ceremony."

"Oh?" Erin asked, her interest piqued. "Do you have other plans?"

Sarah hesitated only briefly before explaining, "I'm supposed to spend Christmas back home with my mama and sister in Alabama."

"Please don't change your plans—" Olivia began, before Erin interrupted.

"Is that where you're from?" Erin clamped her lips together, catching herself. "Sorry. Go ahead, Olivia." She sighed. "I was just being nosy, as usual. I promise to work on it."

"I won't hold my breath," Sarah retorted in a rare showing of sassiness.

Erin dropped her mouth in feigned surprise.

Sarah got up and walked toward the fridge. "I think I'll have a soda after all, if that's alright, Olivia."

"Of course."

Erin turned in her chair. "It's called *pop* here in the Midwest, honey." She turned back and winked at Olivia.

Sarah held the refrigerator door open and turned around to address them. "I will never, ever call it that. *Pop*," she said derisively. "Who in the world came up with such a stupid name for soda?"

Olivia grinned. There was hope for Sarah yet. Maybe not so much for Erin and her plans to fundamentally change her personality, but she'd give her points for trying. Not wanting to lose the thread of their conversation, Olivia said, "I was just going to say, don't change your plans on my account, Sarah. I know it's really last minute, and it's the holidays. We knew odds were good that a lot of people wouldn't be able to make it."

Sarah gave Nora's thin hair a small tousle before sitting down again. "If I can, I'll be there. I'll call the airlines today and see if I can't change my flight. I know there was another one out of Nicolet later that night, and if your weddin' is at five, that might work."

"Only do that if you want to. You know I'd love for you to be there, but I understand that family always comes first."

Erin had formed her hands into a steeple, and was bouncing her knee so rapidly that Olivia could feel the vibration on her side of the table. To keep from laughing at Erin's obvious distress, she focused on stabbing her next bite of salad. The cherry tomato sprayed a little juice, and Olivia was wiping it off the table with her napkin when Sarah sighed in resignation.

"Alright, Erin. I know you're dyin' to know more about my past, but I'm afraid you'll be disappointed. It's really not that interestin'."

Erin leaned forward in her chair. "I doubt it. Anybody who avoids a topic so carefully all these months definitely has a reason. Heck, you even avoided it in your interview. Well done, by the way. You kept all of us guessing. Other than your education and related work, we left the conference room still knowing next to nothing about you."

Sarah smiled sheepishly. "Then I guess I'm lucky I got hired."

Erin shook her head vehemently. "Let's not get off topic too much here, but you should know there was no luck involved. You were by far the best candidate, and that's the truth."

Blushing with pleasure, Sarah thanked her.

"Now, let's get back to the Heart of Dixie. You were saying?"

Sarah looked impressed. "How do you know our nickname?"

"Oh, I'm all-knowing."

Olivia snorted. "That's scary."

The corners of Erin's mouth twitched. "Go on, Sarah."

Sarah took a deep breath and let it out. "Okay, I'll say this fast. My daddy is a total shit. He left us when we were little and started a whole new family just an hour's drive away, not that he ever made the trip."

Erin drew back in surprise. Olivia understood why. She hadn't been expecting that either. Somehow, she'd imagined Sarah coming from a home where the family gathered on the front porch every evening for a cup of tea and a poetry reading.

Sarah looked at each of them in turn. "My mama didn't . . . *handle* it well, and she never got over it. I left as soon as I could and came almost as far north as possible without endin' up in Canada." Looking pained, she added, "But I had to leave my baby sister behind in that mess, and—" She shook her head. "Well, anyway, that's basically it."

There was a long, pregnant pause. "That wasn't even slightly boring!" Erin blurted after digesting Sarah's short, rapid-fire explanation of her past.

"Erin," Olivia chided.

"What? She said her story wasn't interesting, and it is. And I'll bet there's a lot more to unpack."

"Which you don't have to do if you don't want," Olivia quickly reassured, placing a hand on Sarah's arm.

"You're right. There is more, and I can and I will share it, okay? But another time. Right now I'm just fixin' to have a nice lunch with my friends and this gorgeous child over here. If that's okay with y'all?"

With that, the conversation turned to other topics until it was Nora's nap time. Olivia dismissed their offers to help clean up, telling them she'd get to it later, and helped them into their winter coats. With Anna coming over for a cup of coffee in a few hours and Sean coming for dinner and a movie later that night, Olivia thought she just might indulge herself with a rare nap too.

Chapter 30

Anna was really going to have to start watching her sugar intake. This was getting out of hand. Aunt Heidi loved to bake, especially around the holidays, but somehow she never felt tempted to sample her dough or batter, and often she wouldn't even eat the finished product.

For her, it was more about the love of the process—a creative outlet of sorts. For Anna, it was more about the love of eating, which worked fine when she baked only every now and again, but this constant stuffing of her face with baked goods had caused her stomach to revolt in protest. It was now demanding fruit and vegetables instead. Even her skin was making its displeasure known. She touched the large pimple on her chin.

Bummer.

Already today, Heidi and Anna had made gingerbread cookies and chocolate cupcakes, and Anna had two Tupperware containers of each in hand as she climbed the stairs to Olivia's porch. When she'd left the house, Aunt Heidi was still going strong, gathering together all the ingredients necessary to make cinnamon rolls.

Even Anna's dad, who had a huge sweet tooth, wondered how long this sugar high could last in their household. He'd raised his eyebrows as he watched Heidi walk to and from the pantry, and he and Anna had shared amused, slightly desperate smiles before she left the house for Olivia's. And while Anna knew Olivia couldn't possibly eat everything she'd brought with her, what else could she do? She had to get it out of the house! Maybe Olivia could give some to their neighbor, that nice old man, Harry. She used her elbow to ring the doorbell and waited.

It was a chilly day, and snow fell languidly in fat, fluffy flakes. Anna looked around at the trees, which were coated in pure white frosting, and breathed in deeply. As she exhaled, she could see her breath condense in a small, misty cloud that floated away on the light breeze.

One thing that always struck Anna about the winter was how quiet it was. How could snow fall without making a sound? She knew the answer was rooted in physics, but she preferred to see it as a magical mystery instead. Right now, the only sound Anna could hear were the noises coming from the inside of Olivia's house. She could hear muffled cries and approaching footsteps.

The door opened, and there stood Olivia, dressed in an Icelandic sweater, leggings, and shin-high wool socks. She looked frazzled as she greeted Anna and ushered her inside.

"Sorry to make you wait," she said, taking the Tupperware containers and raising her eyebrows in silent question before going on. "Nora woke up from her nap all stuffed up and crabby. I wondered when she'd get her first cold of the winter, and here it is." She frowned. "I hate using that syringe thingy in her nose. It's so gross."

"I'll bet."

"So, what's all this?" Olivia lifted the containers slightly.

"The baking efforts of Aunt Heidi from just this morning alone. There's more to come, if you want it."

Olivia laughed. "Uh, no, but thanks. This should be plenty. Hey—why don't you send some to the dorms with Mitch and Landon?"

Why hadn't Anna thought of that? "Good idea. Mitch is staying with us over Christmas, but Landon's at the dorms. He mentioned there are still some people there who aren't going home for Christmas. He can share with them."

"There you go," Olivia said, looking satisfied she wouldn't have to stuff loads of pastries into her freezer. "I'll give some of these to Sean and Harry. You can take the rest back with you."

"Sure," Anna agreed. She followed Olivia into the kitchen, stopping to scoop Nora up off the floor where she sat with a board book. She planted a kiss on the little girl's cheek and was rewarded with a wet smile. It seemed her entire face was wet, but whether with drool or snot, Anna wasn't sure. She took a tissue from the box on the counter and wiped it all away.

Olivia spoke from across the kitchen. "I have your usual, of course, but I've also got this new holiday blend, if you want to try it." Olivia took out a basket of single-serve coffee cups. "I've even got some decaf, if you want that, since it's a little late in the day for coffee."

"I should probably choose the decaf, but Jess is coming for a sleepover tonight, so I'm sure I'll be up late. I'll try the holiday blend."

"You won't be sorry. It's my new favorite." Olivia worked on the coffees as they talked. She told Anna about her afternoon with her friends.

"I just love Miss Josten," Anna gushed. "She's one of the best teachers I've ever had, which is crazy because this is her first year. She's so young too."

"Did you know one of her students asked her out?"

"What? No way!" Anna laughed. "That's so creepy!"

"He figured since he's eighteen and an adult, and she's just four years older than him, it shouldn't be a big deal." Olivia shuddered. "She handled it fine, though."

"I'm sure it was awkward for her. You know, it's funny. I've had teachers on power trips who won't let you say *boo* in their classes, but they never had control of their classrooms the way she does. She's just so darn sweet! I think everyone behaves just so they don't disappoint her."

Olivia finished stirring in the creamer and gave her coffee a small sip test. "*Mm-hmm*. I think you're right."

Anna added, "As for Mrs. Hennings, she scares everybody into submission. She's never mean or anything, but you can just tell she's not one to cross. You know, I feel like you can hear her heels clicking down the hallway from a mile away. She has a distinct walk. We always know when she's coming. It reminds me of that two-note warning in the *Jaws* movies."

Olivia laughed. "She'll love that."

"You can't *tell* her!"

"She'll think it's hysterical, but I won't if you don't want me to."

"Well, just don't tell her *I* said it." Anna set Nora down at her feet to doctor her own coffee. As she stirred, she looked around the kitchen and noticed two little black velvet boxes. "Are those rings?"

Olivia nodded. "One is Sean's. Let me show you." She set down her coffee and moved to the rings. Anna followed. Opening the one on the left, she turned to Anna, revealing a thick, black wedding band with diagonal groove detailing.

"This is nice," Anna said, admiring the band. "What is it? I mean, what's it made of?"

"It's black tungsten carbide," Olivia replied, and at Anna's blank look added, "Don't ask me. I hadn't heard of it before, but Sean really liked the look of it."

"It's great. Very manly," she said with an amused gleam in her eye. She turned her attention to the second box. "Is that one yours?"

"No. Well, yes and no, I suppose. My ring is at the store getting sized down. This one," she said as she opened the box, "is my ring from Nate."

"Oh, yeah," Anna said breathlessly. "I remember this one. You used to still wear it a few months ago. I always thought it was beautiful and super unique."

"It's an heirloom," Olivia said. "The only one of it's kind." She looked at it lovingly for a moment before closing the box gently. "I had it cleaned last week. I'm going to give it back to Nate's mom. She asked for it a few months ago. I got angry and said no, but now . . . it just seems like the right thing to do."

Anna drew her eyebrows together. "But Olivia, won't you be sad to let go of this?"

"Yes. And a big part of me wants to keep it. A *really* big part. It's a piece of Nate. A piece of the past. But then I think, it's just going to sit in my jewelry box. And I do have a piece of Nate," she said, looking down at Nora, who was playing with the red, balled nose of Rudolph on Anna's Christmas sock.

"But," Olivia continued after taking a deep breath, "I can't shake this feeling that giving it back to Nate's mom is the right thing to do. It belonged to Nate's grandmother, so it has meaning to Janet too. I'm going to ask her if she would consider leaving it to Nora in her will, so it stays in the family. I would hate for Nora to lose this piece of her history, but I guess I'll risk it to settle my conscience."

Anna hugged her. "You're such a good person, Olivia.

Olivia laughed and hugged her back. "I've sure fooled you! Now, let's sit." She set down the ring box and retrieved her coffee, and the two of them moved to the couch. "Nora can crawl around for a while and tire herself out. She's been pretty good about not getting into trouble when she's out of her playpen. I just shut all the doors to keep her out of the bedrooms and bathroom. It's been working out."

Anna sipped her coffee. If Christmas had a taste, this was it. "When are you going to give the ring back?"

"Tomorrow."

"Are you nervous?"

"Oh, yeah. Janet is not an easy person to be around, in general. And the woman hates me. I'd rather not have to deal with her at all, to be honest. But . . . I have to do this."

"Is Sean going with you?"

"No. I thought it might be best to go alone. He's told them about the wedding. We wanted to be fair to them. It wouldn't have been right for them to hear about it from someone else. But I don't want to throw it in their face by showing up together."

Anna nodded. That made sense, even though a part of Anna wanted this mean lady to see how happy Olivia was. It would be the best kind of revenge.

Olivia ran her finger around the rim of her mug. "I have something else to tell you," she said casually, but Anna could see the sparkle in her eyes, and once she'd finished filling Anna in about the wedding plans, Anna could hardly contain her excitement.

"A Christmas wedding is so cool. And just think, you'll always celebrate your anniversary at the coziest and sweetest time of the year. It's just perfect."

Olivia beamed at her. "I'd like you to stand for me, Anna, if you're willing."

Anna gasped. "If I'm willing? Are you crazy? Of course I'll stand for you!" Anna threw her arms around Olivia again, almost spilling her coffee, and Olivia laughed happily as Anna squeezed her like a vise.

"I've never been in a wedding before. I'm so stoked and so . . . *honored*, Olivia."

"Honey, apart from Sean, you're my very best friend. I have to have you by my side up there. Plus, Nora loves you, and I'll need help with her during the vows. She'll probably end up being a handful, but we want her up there with us."

"No problem." She looked down at Nora, who had just found Rudolph's nose again, and chuckled. "Maybe I should just wear these socks."

For the next hour, Anna and Olivia discussed the details of the wedding. Then, huddled over Olivia's laptop, they searched Pinterest to get ideas for bridesmaid dresses and floral arrangements. Anna even showed Olivia her own wedding board she'd put together with Jess one night when they were bored. They both wanted beach weddings. Sure, it was a long way off for both of them, but it was fun to dream. Anna couldn't wait to tell Jess about Olivia and Sean's plans. Olivia was going to invite her, as well as Landon and Anna's whole family.

By the time their coffee date ended, a gold matte sequined dress with a cowl back had been rush ordered for Anna. Olivia had let her pick it out, telling her to choose something she could wear to the holiday dance in January. They'd even found a sweet, gold dress with long sleeves for little Nora.

Anna was still talking about the wedding hours later. She and Jess were downstairs on the sofa wearing Christmas pajamas and chatting excitedly with Aunt Heidi, who promptly got on the internet to order dresses for herself and Jess that she'd have shipped overnight.

"Are you sure?" Jess asked again. "It's so generous of you."

"Of course I'm sure! You're the one doing *me* the favor. Just ask Anna, shopping is my favorite hobby."

"Aunt Heidi missed her true calling," Anna joked. "She should have been a buyer for Macy's."

Heidi laughed and finished entering her credit card number. "In my next life. Now"—she looked up at them—"we need to get our accessories. Purses, shoes, and . . . let's see, what else? Oh, jewelry! And do you girls have dress coats?"

They both shook their heads.

"We can't have you covering these beautiful dresses with ski jackets. We'll need some dress coats or shawls or something."

Heidi was in her element, and the two friends had to admit internet shopping was fun, especially when money was no object. But it was exhausting too, and both Anna and Jess were asleep in Anna's room before midnight.

It was still dark when Anna woke up to Jess's nudges early the next morning. Jess was standing over her.

Anna groaned. "What time is it?"

"It's almost five," Jess whispered. "Something's going on."

Anna sat up. "What do you mean?"

"Your dad's car just pulled back into the garage."

"Pulled *back* into the garage?"

"Yeah, and now I hear Heidi talking downstairs."

Both girls got up and went to investigate. Heidi was on the phone in the brightly lit kitchen, and she had her computer opened in front of her on the counter. There was an X-ray on the screen, and even with Anna's untrained eye, she could see bones were broken.

"Just sit tight," Aunt Heidi was saying. "I'll be back by eight o'clock. That's when the nurse said the doctor would be in."

She listened for a moment and answered, "No. No, Steven. He'll be okay. Try not to worry." She was quiet again. "I know, but he's tough, so —"

Something alerted her to their presence, and she turned around. "Listen, Steven, the girls are awake, so I'd better fill them in. We'll talk soon. I'll have my phone on me." She nodded at Anna as if to say, *Everything's okay. Don't worry,* which was easier said than done. Anna's heart rate had picked up, and she felt a rising panic.

Heidi signed off and put the phone down next to the computer. She took a deep breath before she spoke. "Well, girls, Mitch is in the hospital with a broken ankle."

Anna reached for Jess's hand and held it. Heidi continued, "He thought it would be a good idea to get drunk and jump off the roof of an ATM vestibule downtown." The sarcasm in Aunt Heidi's voice was thick, but Anna could hear a thread of worry there too. Her aunt pulled an agitated hand through her curly hair, leaving a few ends sticking up.

Jess found her voice first. "Is it bad?"

Heidi nodded. “It’s a pretty nasty fracture. It’ll need surgery.”

“That’s it?” Anna pointed to the X-ray.

“Yes. This is Mitch’s right ankle. He has what’s called a *pilon* fracture.” Heidi touched the screen. “You can see here, this is the tibia, or the shin bone, which is broken in pieces here at the bottom.” She clicked the track pad and changed the view. “This right here, this is the fibula, and you can see it’s broken as well, which isn’t all that unusual in this type of injury. And right here, this is the talus. It sort of works like a hinge between the tibia and fibula. Together, these three bones make up the ankle joint.”

Anna felt Jess sway, and she looked at her with concern. Jess returned her glance and smiled weakly before turning her attention back to Heidi.

“This fracture gets its name because *pilon* is the French word for *pestle,* as in mortar and pestle, and you know what a pestle is used for—to pound and grind things down into small pieces.”

Mitch’s bones were in pieces, all right, and Anna was having a hard time looking at the computer screen. How could something that looked like that be fixed? It wasn’t as if they could go in there and glue it all back together again.

“Anyway, like I said, it’s a mess. To incur an injury like this requires tremendous force. We typically see pilon fractures when someone falls from a great height or gets in a high-speed car accident. The brake pedal will drive the talus up into the tibia and break it into little fragments, like you see here. They can be tricky to put back together again.”

“But you said Mitch is going to be fine,” Anna insisted.

Heidi nodded. “Looking at this X-ray, I think he will be. Believe it or not, I’ve seen these look a lot worse. His fractures aren’t displaced all that much, but yes, he’s going to need plates and screws to put this all together again. I imagine the doctor will repair the fracture of the fibula first and then use an external fixator to hold things in place until the swelling goes down. The second surgery will take care of the rest. That’s my guess, anyway.”

“What’s an external fixator?” Anna asked. This did not sound good for Mitch.

“It’s a metal device with connected pins that travel through the skin, and into the bone to hold it in place.”

Heidi had barely finished speaking when Jess pitched forward. Anna moved quickly to grab her before she fell. Heidi was there in an instant, and together they brought Jess carefully down to the floor. She was out cold, and Anna cried out in alarm.

“Well,” Aunt Heidi said, out of breath as she moved from taking Jess’s pulse to lifting her feet and raising them up off the floor, “I think it’s safe to say Jess won’t have a career in medicine.”

Her aunt's cavalier attitude surprised Anna, but also calmed her down. She'd never seen anybody faint before, but if Aunt Heidi wasn't worried, it must not be too big a deal. She must have still looked worried because Heidi reassured, "She'll come to in a minute, and she'll be just fine."

Suddenly overwhelmed, Anna burst into tears. Jess chose that moment to open her eyes with a flutter, and taking in Anna's disposition, began to cry too. She was still on her back, and she brought her forearm up to cover her face as her chest heaved out great sobs.

"Okay now, girls. It's all going to be alright. Jess, you just had a little vasovagal syncope. It's no big deal. It just happens sometimes in response to an emotional trigger. I'm sorry to be so . . . unfiltered about Mitch's injuries. I'm so used to it, that I don't even think twice about it anymore." She patted Jess on one of her feet after she set them both back down on the floor. "As for Mitch, this won't be an easy recovery for him, but he *will* be okay in the end. Alright?"

On a hiccup, Jess asked, "What about hockey?"

Heidi was pensive. "Well, he won't finish this season, certainly. I'm no orthopedic surgeon, but based on what I see and what I know about this type of injury, he'll play again. His fractures look bad, but like I said, they're not too badly displaced, and he's young. He'll need a lot of rehab first, though."

"Is he in pain?" Anna asked, blinking away fresh tears.

"He's seen better days, I'll say that much, but he has fairly good pain control right now." Heidi addressed Anna. "When I left, he and your dad were talking. Having a very good conversation, in fact."

Anna touched her cheeks and shook her head. "Oh my gosh, I just—I can't believe this is happening. My poor dad! He's had two kids in the hospital in that many months. Is *he* okay?"

Heidi shot her a rueful smile. "He's worried, of course. But, yes, he's okay. In a strange way, this may actually help things between him and your brother. Like I said, they were talking when I left. I don't want to say too much, but there were some tears for both of them. Sad tears, but healing tears too. It was . . . touching."

Heidi, her eyes shining, reached out and ran a hand over Anna's hair in a caress. "You know, your dad is stronger than he thinks he is. You all are." Blinking rapidly, Heidi hopped up off the floor. "Okay, girls," she said authoritatively, "let's get ourselves some coffee and breakfast." Anna helped Jess off the kitchen floor and made sure she was steady before letting go. "We'll wait on that phone call together."

It didn't take long.

After choking down a small breakfast of buttered toast and raspberry jam, the three women sat together in the living room with their second cups of coffee. Anna stared at the lit Christmas tree while Aunt Heidi chattered on and on. She was doing her best to distract them from Mitch's situation by discussing Olivia's upcoming wedding, which she insisted they could still attend. It seemed wrong to be planning something so festive, though, and Anna had a hard time showing much enthusiasm. Determined that they shouldn't alter their plans, Aunt Heidi suggested they make reservations for after the ceremony at Rebecca's since they'd all be dressed to the nines anyway. She was just pulling up the menu on her phone when it rang. Anna and Jess leaned forward, elbows on knees, and listened.

"Steven," Heidi said in greeting. She listened for several minutes, and the silence nearly drove Anna crazy. "Shoot! Sorry I wasn't there. I didn't expect him until eight, but no, I'm not at all surprised by that. I think it's a good plan." She listened a few more seconds and responded, "I know it's frustrating to think about two separate surgeries, but it really is best considering the swelling. You don't want to risk infection."

Anna looked at Jess with wide eyes. A broken ankle had never seemed so serious to her before.

"Do you have the surgery time?"

Silence.

"Good."

More silence.

"Sure. Okay, I'll see you soon." Heidi put her phone down on the marble-topped end table next to the couch and massaged her temples. As she relayed the plan, Anna noticed the dark circles under her aunt's eyes and wondered how long she'd been awake. The doctor had come through early, and Mitch was scheduled for surgery at eleven.

Anna regretted that second cup of coffee. It had gone sour in her stomach at the thought of what Mitch was about to go through. At least she'd get to see him before he went into the operating room. He'd asked to see her before the surgery, and Jess insisted on going too, so they all showered and drove in together.

Anna wasn't sure what she'd been expecting exactly, but it surprised her to see a rosy-cheeked Mitch sitting up in bed and talking to their dad when they arrived. He was in the ortho unit up on the eighth floor, and his window looked out over the lake. Jess hugged him first, making him laugh with the joke that he should throw out the pixie dust since it obviously hadn't made him fly.

Wishing she could have been the one to make her brother laugh, Anna stood at the foot of the bed and looked out the window, fighting back a jealousy she really didn't want to feel. The wind had stirred up white caps on the lake, and while she watched the moving waves, she realized it might be time to come to terms with the fact that she would never be as close to her brother as Jess was. But then, in the next instant, Mitch called her to his bedside and asked everyone else to leave so the two of them could have a moment alone. Anna passed Heidi as she moved to the head of the bed, and her aunt gave her a small pat as she left the room with Jess and Steven.

Once the door closed, Mitch blurted, “I messed up, Anna. I keep messing up.”

She sat down in the chair that was pulled up close to his bed and shushed him before saying, “It’s okay. Don’t worry about that now.”

His green eyes were glassy, probably from the medication, and his sandy blond hair stuck up in tufts. Anna felt a surge of protectiveness toward her brother. He looked so fragile.

“I’m so sorry you’re hurt.” She reached for his hand before pulling it quickly back again. She didn’t want to make him uncomfortable. Growing up, she’d always had the sense that she forced her little touches and hugs on him.

This time, he surprised her. After looking her square in the eye, he reached for her hand and held it, resting them both on the edge of his bed. It didn’t appear he was going to let go.

Mitch stared at their intertwined hands. “I haven’t been a good brother to you.”

“You’ve been fine!”

He smiled sadly. “Liar. I always knew you wanted to be closer, and I never let you.”

“Mitch, it’s okay.” Anna didn’t want him to worry about this right now. He had enough going on.

He shook his head. “It’s not okay.” Pausing, he gathered his thoughts. “Anna . . . don’t think I haven’t seen you.”

Her mind froze. “What?”

But he didn’t clarify. He continued speaking as if he hadn’t heard her. “Don’t think I didn’t notice you sitting there in the stands all those years in all those rinks next to whatever family we could bum a ride from. I can still picture it. You sitting there on the bleachers, shivering in your purple coat and that pink unicorn hat.”

He stared at the far wall as if he could really see her younger self there, and a small smile played on his lips.

“I’ve never told you this, but I’ve always seen you as my good luck charm. Even now, I play my best when you’re there watching. As much as I always want Dad at my home games, I need *you* to be there.”

Anna would replay and savor his words later. For now, she tried to downplay the pleasure they brought. “Well, it’s not like I’ve hated it. I always love watching you play.”

He pressed his lips together, and it was only then that Anna noticed the tiny quiver there.

"Thank you, Anna. For being there for me when nobody else was. I tried to push you away a thousand different times in a thousand different ways over the years, but you wouldn't budge. You stayed. You cheered me on, you made me meals, you worried about me. Until Dad took me to lunch that day a few months back, you were the only person since Mom to say 'I love you' to me—" His voice broke and his throat worked in overdrive as he swallowed repeatedly. Anna's own throat began to ache.

"And I never said it back. I don't know why. But I *do*, Anna. Even though I suck at showing it."

A single tear slid down her cheek, and she squeezed his hand. He squeezed back, looking off over her shoulder while he gathered his emotions.

His voice shook when he spoke again. "Thinking I could have lost you a few months ago . . . I've been trying so hard *not* to think about it, *not* to feel. But nothing I do can block it out. Not even a sixer and a short flight off the top of an ATM vestibule." He chuckled before visibly shuddering and scrubbing his face with his free hand.

Anna wasn't sure what to say. It touched her that he cared so much, but at the same time, she didn't want to be the reason he was struggling. "Mitch . . ."

"I want to be for you what you've always been for me. I want you to be able to depend on me. I'm just so messed up, Anna. I need to figure myself out. I don't know why I can't move past what happened to Mom."

She took a deep breath. "I wish I could help."

He treated her to a sad smile. "I know you do, and sometimes I wish you could remember with me, but you were so little." He chuckled ruefully. "Do you know what dad used to say to me every day before leaving for work? I remember it like it was yesterday. He'd say, 'Mitch, you're the man of the house while I'm away. Take care of your mother and your sister.' He'd tousle my hair, and I'd promise I would. I really thought I *was* the man. But I wasn't, and I didn't take care of her. I knew she wasn't right that day. I was scared, and I should've done something. I should have told someone. We dropped you off at the Diedrich's house before going to look at the waves. I could have said something then."

Anna shook her head vehemently. "Mitch, you were five. You would never put that kind of responsibility on a five-year-old today, would you?" He didn't answer, so Anna answered for him. "You wouldn't, so why would you expect that of yourself?"

He bit down on his lip and thought for a moment before answering, "I don't know. But I've held on to it for so long, I don't know how to . . . let it go."

Anna understood. Sometimes emotions were more powerful than logic.

Mitch blew out a long breath. "Anyway, Anna, I want you to know that I'm gonna start working through all of this stuff with someone, a therapist or something, and not just for myself, but for you and Dad too. I want things to be different. I'm ready for things to be different."

Anna clutched her chest with her free hand and gave him a squeeze with her other one. "I'll help however I can."

He smiled. "Dad said that too."

They were both quiet.

"Listen," Mitch began before clearing his throat. "Dad asked me to forgive him that day we met for lunch. For everything. I couldn't then, or I wouldn't. Today I have, and it feels . . . awesome to finally let it go. And now I need to ask you, before I have this surgery, if *you'll* forgive *me*."

She didn't hesitate. "There's nothing to forgive, Mitch." She stood up to hug him. He didn't rush her. He didn't push her away or squirm, and when she finally let go and pulled back from him, he smiled and spoke the words she'd thought he'd never say to her. And while *Love ya* might not have packed the same punch as the real, three-worded deal, it was more than enough. In fact, to borrow one of Mitch's words, it felt absolutely *awesome*.

Chapter 31

Olivia waited for Sean to return from the hospital. Anna had unwittingly started a phone chain early that morning. She'd called Landon with the news of Mitch's injury, and he, in turn, called Sean, who had then called Olivia. While Sean and Landon headed to the hospital, Olivia waited at home with Nora, texting with Anna and Sean periodically to keep updated.

Olivia looked at her watch. It was just after one o'clock, and she expected Sean any moment. She'd just put Nora down for her nap, but Sean would stay here at the house with her while Olivia attended to the returning of the ring. Janet and Karl were expecting her at half past one, although she hadn't given them the reason for her visit.

Opening the velvet box, Olivia studied the ring. Instead of a diamond, it featured a clear, blue sapphire, but there were four round brilliant-cut side diamonds, two on each side, to offset the round stone, which was slightly under a carat. It was an exquisite ring, and she'd loved wearing it. She remembered the day Nate had given it to her.

They had driven over to the Shaker Mountains for a day-long hiking trip, and they'd taken their time climbing to the top of the highest peak. It had been a cool summer day, not warmer than sixty-five degrees, and the breeze kept the bugs away. From the top, they could see a bank of dark clouds approaching from the west, so Olivia had reluctantly suggested they head back down quickly to beat the rain.

Nate asked for a little more time. Olivia smiled as she recalled how annoyed she'd become as he stood there, staring off at Lake Superior, and rehashing for her every moment of their relationship while an enormous storm blew in. The poor guy had just been trying to set the stage and work up the courage for his proposal. It had taken fifteen minutes before he finally dropped to one knee and asked her to marry him. Almost as soon as Olivia said yes, the rain hit, and it fell in sheets. Kissing Nate on that mountaintop in the rain, with his ring on her finger, had been one of the most romantic and exhilarating moments of her life.

Olivia had to acknowledge that there had been many good times in her marriage to Nate, especially early on. Maybe because she'd been angry about the affairs, or maybe to help with the grief, or perhaps for both of those reasons, she tended to only remember the bad parts.

She didn't want to do that anymore. She was letting it go. Sean said he would help her keep Nate's memory alive, and Olivia felt profoundly grateful that the man in her life had also known and loved Nate.

Nate had given her Nora, and in many ways, he'd given her Sean as well. She'd always love him for those two reasons alone, and so today she would honor his memory by giving this ring back to his mother. Maybe it would help Janet heal. Maybe she'd be able to let go of the bitterness before it ate away at her completely. Olivia could only hope.

Five days later, Olivia stood at the front of Grace Church, wearing a simple white gown, surrounded by those she loved most, and held out her left hand so Sean could slide a new ring on her finger as he spoke his vows. She looked up at him with shining eyes and smiled so widely her face hurt. The joy she felt in that moment had her wanting to kiss him before she was supposed to. She spoke her own vows in a strong, clear voice and placed Sean's ring on his finger. Nora, held by Anna, watched the exchanging of the rings in rapt attention. Just before the pastor declared them man and wife, Anna transferred Nora into Sean's arms, as they had planned, and with a squirming child held between them, Sean kissed his bride.

Epilogue

"Great running, honey." Steven wrapped Anna in a tight hug.

"Thanks, Dad." She cast a smile at Aunt Heidi, who was standing just beside him.

"I know you already have that NSU scholarship," Heidi said, "but it must still be gratifying to go out on a high note like this, especially knowing the cross country coach was here watching."

Anna looked around. "He was? I didn't even see him." She shrugged happily. "At least now he won't have any doubts about bringing me on."

"As if he would," Steven scoffed. "They're lucky to have our girl, aren't they, Heidi?"

Heidi laughed and nodded. "What were your times?"

Anna thought for a quick second. "I ran a 4:45.20 in the 1600-meter run and a 10:25.76 in the 3200-meter run."

"My girl's a winner, alright," Steven said, smiling with pride.

"Oh, here we go!" Heidi teased. "You'd think it was *you* who'd won those races, Steven."

"Hey, my progeny, did, and that's close enough."

Heidi's amber eyes sparkled.

"Speaking of which, where's your brother?" her father asked.

"Um," Anna looked behind her. "I saw him on the field a minute ago. He was helping Jess carry her starting blocks."

"It's such a nice afternoon. So warm for early June. Heidi and I were thinking we could all go get some ice cream over at that new ice cream shop by the water to celebrate. Jess and Landon can come too."

Anna's face lit up. "Ice cream sounds amazing. Landon just went to go get his car, so I'll ride with him and meet you there. You'll let Mitch and Jess know?"

"Will do. We'll see you in just a few."

"Okay. Bye guys. And thanks for coming. I know these meets get long."

Her dad reached for her a second time, squeezing her gently. “I wouldn’t have missed it. I can’t believe your high school career is officially over now. You grew up too quick, kiddo.”

“You know, I can stay a kid a little longer, Dad. I’ll even let you keep paying for my car if you want,” Anna said. She patted him on the shoulder several times and stepped back with a sassy grin.

Heidi laughed. “Nice one.” She pulled Steven away towards the field where Mitch and Jess were and turned to Anna. “We’ll see you there, honey.”

Twenty minutes later, the six of them licked their cones at a picnic table overlooking the water and chatted about different things. Heidi was finishing the renovations on her new house. She’d surprised them all back in March by announcing she’d given her notice and was moving back to Nicolet to be closer to them. In no time at all, Aunt Heidi had fallen right into step with them, and it felt as natural as if she’d always been a part of their daily lives.

Landon gave them the specs of a new house he was helping to build. Between his work and studying for the MCAT, he had a busy schedule for the summer, but somehow, he still had time for Anna and his friends. Soon he’d be adding a few practices a week back into the mix, but Anna knew he’d make it work.

Mitch was pretty tight-lipped about the grief counseling he was getting twice a week, but it was obviously helping him. Anna knew it wouldn’t be a quick fix, and while he seemed happier and more engaged with them overall, he still had a quiet sadness about him sometimes.

He’d moved home for the summer, and Anna was already enjoying all the extra time she got to spend with him. It was like finally being given permission to open a book whose cover had intrigued her for years, but that she hadn’t been allowed to read. She was learning so much.

While Mitch didn’t openly speak about his emotional therapy, he did love to share his progress with physical therapy, as he was doing now. He told them all, with obvious relief, that his physical therapist planned to turn him loose after next week.

“Does that mean you’ll be able to start dryland with us next month?” Landon asked.

“That’s what they say, although with a few modifications at the beginning.”

“Hmm, I’m thinking you should sit out the bleacher runs,” Landon said with a wink.

Mitch laughed. “Oh, man. Those really suck, don’t they?”

“So, Jess,” Steven broke in. “You finished strong today too. What’d you get, two firsts and a second place?”

"Yep," Jess said, catching a dribble of vanilla ice cream on her chin with her napkin.

"Are you still planning to go to NSU in the fall?" Heidi asked.

Jess lifted her chin slightly. "I am."

It had been a tough pill for Mr. Swanson to swallow, but Jess had passed up two partial scholarships in lower Michigan, both for basketball. Since the partial tuition at those private schools would still have been more expensive than NSU, he didn't have much of an argument to make, not that he didn't try. But Jess had stuck to her guns, and with the support of her mom, she'd be enrolling at NSU for the fall.

"Good for you, Jess," Steven said. He knew enough about Jess's dad to know this was a fairly big victory. Anna was thrilled Jess had finally spoken up for herself. She was following her own dreams now. Not her dad's.

"Thanks. It feels good knowing I can do athletics on my own terms. There are tons of opportunities at NSU for pick-up games and intramural stuff." She looked at Heidi. "I was even thinking I might run that 5K with you and Anna in July."

"The more the merrier. Steven's going to start training for it too."

This was news to Anna. "Wow, Dad!"

Steven nodded. "That's right, and I'll start my diet just as soon as I finish this ice cream cone."

Heidi laughed. "You've been about to *start your diet* for the last two weeks."

"Yeah, well. This time I mean it." He winked.

The conversation continued, bouncing around as conversations within larger groups tended to do, but Anna noticed Mitch glancing frequently at something just behind her. Aunt Heidi had just turned the topic to Olivia and Sean's wedding reception, which was happening tomorrow evening in the green space at Nicolet Harbor, when Mitch peered behind her yet again. This time, Anna turned to look—and immediately, she understood.

It used to be that Anna couldn't look at it without thinking of their mother, but today, it hadn't even registered. She didn't know how she could have missed it. The breakwall stretched out behind them, with the lighthouse standing proudly at the end about three hundred yards from the shore. Although they'd parked right near the gate that led to the structure, Anna hadn't given her mother a thought.

But Mitch had, and when she turned back around, he was looking at her, and she knew he knew she'd just realized where they were. "I didn't think," she said softly.

"It's okay."

Heidi stopped talking and looked to Steven, who wore an expression of regret. "I wasn't thinking, either, when I suggested this place," he told Mitch. "Heidi reminded me when we parked, but then you pulled in next to us, and I wasn't sure if—" He shook his head. "I'm sorry, Mitch."

Everyone was quiet for a moment before Mitch spoke. He took a deep breath and slowly let it out. "You know, I'm not. I've wanted to come here again, especially these last few months, but I've been a little . . . scared, I guess." He looked sheepish. "Mostly, I've avoided it growing up. It's out of the way enough where it wasn't too hard, and if I had to drive past, I just didn't look. But today I don't want to ignore it. My therapist"—he blushed at the words—"he told me I should come here, maybe even walk out there."

"I'll go with you. Right now, if you want," Steven offered.

Anna hesitated before asking, "Do you think I could go too?"

Steven looked at Mitch questioningly.

"Let's go as a family," Mitch suggested quietly, and then he turned to Landon and Jess, who were both quiet and still as statues as their ice cream cones melted onto the picnic table. "Would you guys mind if we left you here for a few minutes?" He looked worried, as if he might hurt their feelings by leaving them out.

Landon shook his head. "Go, man. We're fine here."

Jess gave Mitch a reassuring smile. "It's okay."

Landon nodded encouragingly at Anna, and Mitch got up and walked around the table. He pitched his cone into the trash and held his hand out to Heidi. "You too, Aunt Heidi. If you want," he qualified.

"I've wanted to for a long time."

The three of them joined Mitch in standing, and Landon and Jess watched them silently as they turned to cross the parking lot. Steven put one arm around Mitch's shoulders as they headed down the embankment, and Heidi reached for Anna's hand.

To the strangers they passed on their way out, Anna knew her family would look like any other group out for a stroll along the boulder-lined breakwall. The view was postcard perfect, with the water a deep, rich blue that matched the cloudless sky. Though no longer directly overhead, the sun blazed hot and bright, creating thousands of dazzling sparkles in the ripples of the water. The red and white lighthouse at the end of the breakwall added a touch of whimsy to the scene, and while those strangers seemed to feel inspired to take a picture to remember the day, Anna and her family didn't need a picture to help them remember.

They would never forget this day. It was the first of many times they would come here to remember her together. The woman who had made an indelible impact on each of them, who had loved them fiercely, and whom they all had loved in return. There were no tears, only gratitude for her and for one another, and as they walked back towards the shore, Anna noticed her father reach for Aunt Heidi's hand. Anna and Mitch met eyes and smiled.

As a reminder to keep from dwelling on things of the past, Aunt Heidi liked to say there was only the joy of today and the hope for tomorrow. Anna had always considered those wise words to live by, and today she knew without a doubt they were true.

Next in Series

Stay connected with your Nicolet friends, and get more closely acquainted with Sarah Josten, English teacher at Nicolet High. Erin was right. Sarah has a story to tell, and you won't want to miss it! Available for preorder at your favorite retailer. Release date: October 28, 2022

Acknowledgments

This book may never have come to be without the help and support of my amazing beta readers, Shirley and Laura. Thank you both for the thoughtful and enormously helpful feedback. Additional thanks to Emily Poole at Midnight Owl Editors for great insights and advice and to my medical consultants, Jeff and Laura, as well.

About Author

For Charlotte, few things are more relaxing than an escape into a cozy, little story, and that's what she hopes you'll experience within the pages of her books. An author of contemporary women's fiction, Charlotte writes about small-town women and their families, sprinkling in just the right amount of romance for all the feels. She lives on the Lake Superior shore with her husband and three children, and like most of her characters, she can't imagine ever living anywhere else. Visit her website to learn more, and join her monthly newsletter to receive bonus material and other news.

Website: www.charlotteeverhartbooks.com

Facebook: @CharlotteEverhart.Author

Made in the USA
Monee, IL
24 November 2022

18378792R00152